Escape from Jonestown

By Billy Rivers

Dedication

I dedicate this story to Jeff, my son and a United States Marine. When Jeff was twelve, he harvested his first buck. Its wide, sturdy rack was large enough to make a grown man proud. The next day, Jeff was running through the snow, armed only with a handgun, trying to head off a black bear that was running through the ravine below our hunting camp.

My boy grew to be the kind of man a father can be proud of and has brought great joy to his mother and me. By the way, if he had actually caught up with that black bear, the previous sentence might never have been written.

Foreword

E *scape from Jonestown* is not like any other adventure novel you've ever read. After telling the real life story of the tragedy at Jonestown, Guyana where 914 men, women, and children drank the kool-aid and died, Billy Rivers takes us deep into the jungles of South America where survival means not losing your life to pythons, anacondas, crocs, and jaguars. Pitted against the forces of nature, Terrance Clark and young Timmy see their courage and faith tested to the limit. As if the jungle itself was not enough, there's a rogue outfit of murderous, corrupt army personnel out to kill anyone and everyone who gets in their way.

I love this book and encourage everyone who reads it to keep their eyes peeled for the secret treasure that is hidden somewhere in the story. So buckle yourself in and enjoy the ride. And thanks Billy Rivers for a great adventure!

Todd Hoffman
Gold miner

Chapter One

*T*o a casual observer, the tall figure standing at the back of the hut was merely leaning against the rear wall and staring out of the room's one tiny window. The man's broad shoulders were accented by the tightness of his khaki tee shirt while his baggy camo pants partially concealed the fitness of his lean form.

Most days, there wasn't much to see out back except a tangled mass of lush foliage which ended a scant ten feet from the back of the hut, a hut that had served as the man's prison for the past month. Still, hour after hour, the prisoner stood there, arms extended, leaning hard against the back wall and staring out of that same little window.

A more observant watcher, however, might have noticed that there was a faint but constant movement in the man's upper body, as if the muscles in his shoulders were constantly exercising, though ever so slightly.

An hour earlier, a dark cloud had passed directly overhead and dumped torrents of warm rain down on the compound – and then moved on. The sun was out again and the steaming forest seemed to be reaching out to the man, beckoning him to break free, to come and disappear into its cool darkness.

Actually, Terrance Clark could think of nothing he would rather do. For four weeks now, this little window had been his only connection to the outside world. Well, that and the little blond haired boy who visited three times a day, bringing the prisoner cornbread every morning and steamed rice and terribly bland beans for lunch and dinner.

The meals were always the same, day after boring day, except some days the beans were a little soupier than others and the cornbread a little harder.

A month ago, the foliage out back had ended a good thirty feet from the back of the shack, but the living thing that it is, the jungle had crept slowly forward, day by day, until some of the new growth reached almost to the wall of the hut. One day, the relentless jungle would swallow up the entire compound where the man was imprisoned, but today he didn't know that.

Terrance was staring down at the ground outside when suddenly and without warning the guard appeared, rounding a back corner of the building. The split second the prisoner caught sight of the guard, he loosened his grip on the metal window frame, stepped back towards the middle of the tiny room, and held his breath. He could see the side of the guard's face as he passed by the window and was thankful that the man didn't glance up at the window or down at the ground beneath it. The consequences could have been disastrous had he done either.

This same scene had played out several times a day with great regularity. A couple of times every hour, at no specific time, the guard would leave his post at the front door and walk briskly around the shack. The entire trip would consume less than fifteen seconds, but the prisoner knew that if the guard came at exactly the wrong time, all would be lost.

As soon as the guard passed the window, Terrance stepped quickly forward to catch a glimpse of the man's backside to see what kind of weapon he was carrying today. The guard's body blocked most of his view, but

Terrance knew weapons and could tell by the length and size of the barrel that the guard was carrying a shotgun, likely a twelve-gauge. The weapon looked to be a single shot, probably loaded with buckshot.

Some shifts, this guard and the one who came on duty after dinner carried an older model, lever action thirty-thirty rifle, the weapon cowboys call a *saddle gun.* Either gun could be deadly at close range, but it might prove important to know which weapon they were carrying on any given day – especially this day.

The window in the back of the hut was one of those aluminum models, the kind that is typically nailed into place from the outside with scores of little nails hammered into a one-inch strip of metal bordering the entire perimeter. This model was a slider, about two-foot square. It opened only a few inches on the right side for ventilation. The window had been modified so the opening was too small for a man to stick his head through. Still, it was big enough for Terrance to get his fingers through and grip the frame with both hands.

Day after day, Terrance had shaken and wiggled the window frame, hoping to feel just a little give. He would stand there at full alert, and then apply pressure anytime there was enough noise in the compound out front to mask the noise he might perchance make at the window.

For the first ten days or so, the little frame had held tight with no sign of give. But just about the time Terrance had begun to conclude that his efforts were in vain, there was a tiny bit of give on the right side of the frame. From that moment on, hour by hour, the plywood siding gradually gave way and the nails became increasingly loose in their settings. It was slow, tedious work, but a resourceful man, one not accustomed to imprisonment, will eventually explore every possibility that could lead to his escape. He will pursue a plan, even if it serves no purpose but to give him a reason to hope.

The floor of the hut was a solid concrete slab and the only door was guarded day and night. The rear window was Terrance's only hope, the only way out. One thought, however, haunted the prisoner. Terrance was not entirely sure he could get his broad shoulders through the tiny two-foot opening, if he succeeded in getting the window out.

The last couple of days, he felt like he had made serious progress, more so than in the previous two weeks combined. Two sides of the window were noticeably loose now. Terrance was pretty sure that very soon now he would be able to use the two loose sides as leverage to bend the window back and out of the way with one good push. He was almost certain that in another hour or two and he would be able to remove the frame completely. If some overly conscientious guard didn't notice all of those loose nails lying on the ground outside or notice that the window was not quite as tight as it was supposed to be, come nightfall, he would make a run for it.

Terrance was not exactly looking forward to trekking unarmed into a tropical jungle in pitch darkness. He knew from his own research that there were likely several species of pythons, thirty foot anacondas, and all kinds of poisonous snakes in the tangled forest that began right behind this little shack and stretched on and on for hundreds of untracked miles.

Snakes were Terrance's biggest concern, especially at night. Just two evenings ago, just before dark, out of this very window he had seen a nine-foot bushmaster, one of the deadliest and most feared snakes in all of South America. The giant viper was working its way along the edge of the forest, rearing up and greedily snatching giant fireflies out of the air.

And of course Guyana is famous worldwide for being home to one of the largest concentrations of jaguars in all of South and Central America. Be that as it may, even the possibility of encountering a carnivore of that magnitude would be worth the risk if he could just get out of this cage. At least it seemed so at the time.

It was upwards of ten in the morning when breakfast finally arrived. Instead of little Timmy delivering the plate, like he had every day for several weeks, an older black man brought it. Terrance had never seen the fellow before, but he seemed more than a little irritated about something. Maybe he was just grumpy by nature, but Terrance got the feeling that there was more to it than that.

He had tried to engage the man in a conversation and hopefully glean some news about the goings on in the compound outside, but all the man would say was that the womenfolk were acting *kinda peculiar*, and the *higher ups* seemed a bit uneasy today, '*specially Dad Jones*. The old man said he thought it all had something to do with some *big-shot dignitary* who had visited the compound and got everybody all riled up.

A dignitary? Hmmm, who could that be?

Terrance had heard talk about a congressman from the United States who was going to visit the compound sometime in the near future, but he had doubted the story. Whatever was causing the fuss, though, judging by the old man's demeanor it was a big deal and it was making a lot of folks in Jonestown more than a little nervous.

According to Terrance's stomach, that conversation with the old man had taken place several hours ago. It had to be way past two by now and Timmy was late with lunch. Lunch had never been this late and that got Terrance to thinking.

Maybe the boy won't come anymore. Maybe it will just be the grouchy old man from now on. Too bad. I liked that kid. He's smart for his age and smiles easily. It probably won't matter whether he comes anymore or not. There's a decent chance this will be my last day in this God-forsaken place.

Terrance Clark had been in Jonestown long enough to recognize that this was one messed up bunch of people. And whatever was wrong with them likely had trickled down from the top. He had spent enough time around *Dad Jones,* as his followers called the man, to be leery of him. There was clearly something not right about the man. The group had called itself a church back in the States, but Terrance's experience in Jonestown had persuaded him otherwise. The folks here rarely if ever talked about God or Jesus. Jones never preached from a Bible. He mostly talked about the "glories of communism" and the "wonders of socialism" and how much better communist Russia is than capitalist America. Terrance had concluded that Jim Jones was not a spiritual leader at all, but more of a wannabe political revolutionary who had surrounded himself with people foolish enough to follow him down the failed and discredited road to socialist collectivism.

Terrance had left his place at the window and was pacing the floor of his cell. His hunger was quickly overcoming his patience. Finally, he went to the door and yelled out at the guard. "Hey, what time is it? Isn't it about time to feed the prisoner?"

An unusually harsh voice responded from the outside. "Shut up in there. You'll get fed when you get fed. Bug me again and you won't get fed at all the rest of the day. It makes no difference to me."

The guards were never friendly, but they had not been particularly mean either. Today was different. Something was up and it was affecting everyone's attitude. It occurred to the prisoner that all of this uneasiness could work to his advantage.

"Hey fellow, could you answer something that's been bugging me? What kind of snake is about ten feet long and eats fireflies?" There was no reply from the other side of the door, so Terrance continued.

"It was really ugly with a heart-shaped head. Anyway, I saw one right behind the hut last night. It was crawling all around back there, snapping at the air. I was surprised by how far up it could strike. Any idea what it was?"

Terrance had spoken calmly, as if his question was merely a matter of curiosity. There was no response for a couple of minutes.

"How big did you say?" The guard's tone sounded tentative and there was a barely discernible tremor in his voice.

"I would say it was a ten-footer," the prisoner said, talking to the inside of the door.

"Ugliest snake I ever saw. Mean looking too. I'm sure glad there's no holes in these walls."

Terrance waited but there was no further response. Still, it seemed unlikely that this guard would make any unnecessary trips to the back side of the hut for a while. Bushmasters are nocturnal. Everyone in Jonestown was aware of that, so it was reasonable to assume that the same ploy would work even better on the night guard.

Another two hours passed with no food. Terrance was considering yelling at the guard again. What could it hurt if they weren't going to feed him anyway?

Before he had a chance to express his displeasure, there was a clattering of keys at the door. A moment later in walked little Timmy. The boy was carrying a plate with a washcloth covering the contents. As was his custom, the guard stood back from the door with his weapon pointed at the opening while Timmy entered the shack. When the door closed behind the boy, Terrance heard the sound of the padlock being slipped back into the clasp on the outside of the door.

"Timmy, my man. Good to see you, even if you are half-a-day late. I requested the Beef Wellington with extra gravy and the baked potato. I hope the chef got my order right this time."

Timmy giggled. Terrance's "order" was always some new and exotic dish the boy had never heard of.

"It's rice and beans," Timmy said innocently.

"Oh, dang," Terrance said, feigning disappointment.

"I brought you this too," Timmy whispered low, pulling an overly ripe banana out of his shirt. A banana was a real treat. Terrance accepted the gift with his left hand and gently rubbed the top of the boy's head with his right, messing up Timmy's straight blonde hair.

"Oh, and this too," Timmy continued, reaching into the pocket of his baggy shorts and pulling out a half empty shaker that had salt on one side and pepper on the other. Seasoning of any kind was a real prize for the prisoner. The rice was never seasoned at all and the beans were in sore need of a little pepper.

"I don't want you to get in trouble, Timmy, but I appreciate this. Salt and pepper are a real treat. Seriously.

"So tell me, what's going on out there? I missed you at breakfast. Some grouchy old man brought me my ham and cheese omelet. He seemed upset about something. Do you know what it is?"

Timmy chuckled. He wasn't quite sure what a ham and cheese omelet was, but he was pretty sure Terrance hadn't received one.

"Well," the boy began, "the ladies in the kitchen said some political man from the United States was visiting today, but he left. They said he was going to report back to the government about what's going on here in our town. They said Dad Jones was pretty nervous about it all. You know how he don't trust government people from the United States."

Terrance understood exactly what was behind all that. The Peoples Temple had moved en masse from California to Guyana a year or so earlier. The plan had been to start the perfect socialist utopia. They had named the place the *"Peoples Temple Agricultural Project."* Most of the members of the Peoples Temple were outright communists and everything about Jonestown shouted collectivism. Jones even maintained ongoing communications with Soviet Russia and with the Castro regime in Cuba.

Somewhere in the middle of the transition from the Bay area, his client's thirty-two year old daughter had gone missing.

Actually, the young lady had disappeared from her parents' lives a decade before Jonestown. Sometime in 1968 she had dropped out of college and submersed herself in the drug culture that permeated the San Francisco college scene at the time. The last time her folks had spoken to her, she was living with a bunch of "free love" hippies in an apartment near the now infamous Haight and Ashbury district of San Francisco.

All the girl's wealthy parents had learned after that was that Sarah had somehow got hooked up with the Peoples Temple. That was sometime around the Spring of 1977. The girl had disappeared from California about the time the group had migrated *en masse* to Guyana. Sarah Stanford's parents had done their best to keep track of their only child, but in spite of all their efforts they had not had a single conversation with her for several years. They kept hoping that eventually she would grow up and come home or at least check in, but of late that hope had faded to nothing.

Then, two people working at the Freedom House in Berkeley reported that they had seen Sarah Stanford in Jonestown and that she was doing some kind of nursing work there. They also said that she had given them the impression that she wanted to leave, but was not being allowed to. They described *Freedom House* as a recovery organization run by ex-Peoples Temple members and family members of people who had been caught up in Jones's web.

Out of all the private investigators in the Bay area, Terrance had been chosen to track the woman down because of his religious and mixed racial background. Terrance's dad was a Caucasian and a Baptist preacher. His mom was part "old country" Basque and part Navajo Indian. Her hair and eyes were as black as the night and her skin a deep brown.

Terrance's color and facial features were neither dark nor white nor Indian, but a pleasant mixture of the three. His wavy hair was dark brown and his eyes were a slightly lighter shade of the same color. Terrance Clark was a handsome man and at a full six foot three inches, he stood out in most crowds.

When he first arrived at Jonestown, he was accepted right away by the Peoples Temple crowd and blended in easily. The first thing he had said upon arrival was how disillusioned he had become with all of the corporate greed in the United States, and with that he was in.

That was two and a half months ago. He had kept his eyes open and had been careful about asking too many questions. The people in Jonestown were suspicious of all strangers and rather than draw attention to himself, he had hoped to eventually meet Sarah Stanford just by running into her. He had studied an old photo of the girl. It wasn't much to go on, but in a community of only nine hundred people and a good share of them black, it shouldn't take much to spot a blonde, white girl in her early thirties. At least that was what he had hoped.

Truth be told, Terrance had taken the Guyana assignment as much for the adventure as for the money. The monthly stipend the clients offered was generous and there was a fifty thousand dollar bonus if he found out for sure what happened to his clients' daughter. Plus there was another fifty thousand if he was able to bring the woman back to the United States willingly.

Of course, all that sounded a lot rosier back before he was taken prisoner and locked in a tiny shack with a six inch hole in the floor for a toilet. A month in a wooden cage had somewhat changed his perspective, definitely knocking the stuffing out of that whole *adventure* angle. The only adventures he was enjoying now were three boring meals and chats with a ten-year old boy.

But who is that politician and why was he here?

"Did they say who the political guy was, Timmy? Did they mention a name?"

"No sir, they didn't. Well, they might've, but I didn't pay much attention."

Chapter Two

Terrance was sitting on the floor in the corner and eating his beans one at a time, one bean and a little rice with each bite. Mealtimes were the highlight of his day and he made them last as long as possible. Truth be told, he was never anxious for the boy to leave anyway. Over the weeks, he had grown fond of young Timmy. The lad had a sunny disposition and honest blue eyes that betrayed a natural intelligence. Terrance and Timmy had become surprisingly good friends considering their age differences.

"Did the cooks say anything else about the man, maybe why he was coming or how long he would stay?"

"I don't remember anything about him, 'cept one of the women said her husband had the 'pression that the guy was going to give a bad report about us when he got back to America.

"Oh yeah, and she said that her sister works in the main office and she said she saw Dad Jones fill some suitcases with money this afternoon. She said he gave the suitcases to some older guys and told them that the money was to go to the Communist Party, I think like in Russia or someplace like that. Then he told them to take the money and leave right away. She said she heard Dad Jones say something to the men that sounded like 'a half a million dollars.' At least that's what I think she said."

Alarms were going off in Terrance's head. His somewhat casual interest in Timmy's news suddenly heightened in intensity.

Half a million in cash? That's a lot of money. Why would they give it all away? People are not exactly living high on the hog here.

Terrance kept most of his thoughts to himself. He trusted Timmy, but the lad was, after all, just a boy. No one knew why Terrance had come to Jonestown, but there had to have been suspicions. Why else would they have locked him in this shack and kept him under armed guard round the clock for the past month? Possibly, the group suspected that he was a covert government agent or something of that nature. The leaders in Jonestown were a suspicious lot and saw CIA and capitalist conspiracies everywhere they looked. They always suspected they were being infiltrated by CIA operatives from the U.S.

Whatever the reason, Terrance's arrest had come seemingly out of nowhere. One evening after work hours, the residents were all practicing one of the group's bizarre loyalty tests, where everyone in Jonestown gathered at the Pavilion and drank Kool-Aid or some kind of flavored drink after being told that it contained poison and that they were killing themselves as an act of "revolutionary dignity." It was the strangest thing. Even after being told that the stuff contained deadly poison, everyone drank it down while the leaders looked on to make sure everyone participated.

Well, Terrance didn't "drink the Kool-Aid" and half-an-hour or so later, after no one had died and Jones had informed the crowd that the drink wasn't really poisoned, Terrance suddenly found himself being led at gunpoint to this shack and locked up without explanation.

At the faux suicide ceremony, Jones had told his followers that the American capitalists hated them far more than they realized and could come to Jonestown and destroy them at any time. Jones had said that it would be better for them, and more dignified, if they were to control their own fates and end their lives on their own terms. In a soothing voice, he had told the group that they would all go to a better place if the time came, a place where there was no more greed, just sharing and selflessness. There had been a lot of hushed "amens" from the crowd and a few comments about reincarnation and a better life after they all "crossed over."

As the group was gathering that evening, one of the older men had told Terrance not to worry, that they had done these drills several times before and it was always the same and no one ever died. Still, there was no way Terrance Clark was going to drink anything that might be laced with cyanide. After all, there was really no way of knowing whether this time was a trial run or the real thing. It bothered Terrance that the people of Jonestown trusted Jim Jones so completely that it never seemed to occur to any of them that he might be wrong about anything. Some called him *the only one*. Some said he was their *savior*. Others said crazy things like, "There's nothing I'd rather do than give my life for socialism and communism."

Replaying the bizarre scene in his mind, Terrance remembered the sick feeling he had felt in the pit of his stomach as all of the mothers had slavishly given what they were told was real poison to their children before taking it themselves.

Like a thousand lemmings rushing headlong off a cliff, he had thought.

The prisoner's thoughts about that day were interrupted by unfamiliar noises coming from behind the hut. With a quickness that belied his size, Terrance was on his feet. Peering out the window, he saw two middle-aged black women and a white teenage boy with wavy blonde hair hacking at the jungle with machetes. It was late in the afternoon and an unusual time to start a new project.

Not good, he thought. *The shorter the space I have to cross to reach the jungle, the less chance of my being seen. I reckon the guards are smarter than I thought. They are doing a little maintenance work on the perimeter on the very day I plan to make a break for it. I bet no one told them about the bushmaster.*

"What is it?" Timmy asked. "What's going on?" The boy was too short to see out the window, the bottom of which was a good five feet from the floor of the hut.

Before Terrance could answer, a voice came over the compound's loudspeaker. The voice told everyone, men, women and children, to drop what they were doing and gather immediately at the Pavilion. Terrance knew the voice. He had heard it rant on and on *ad nauseum* over the public address system every day since he had arrived in Jonestown; always praising the beauty of communism and decrying the "greedy capitalists" of corporate America.

There was something different in the tone of Jones's voice today, a blend of nervousness and urgency. Without a moment's hesitation, the three working at the back of the hut dropped their machetes at the edge of the jungle and turned and walked quickly in the direction of the Pavilion, which was located roughly in the center of the compound.

Timmy turned toward the door. He knew that *everyone* meant him. Like everyone in Jonestown, Timmy knew that he was expected to obey when Dad Jones spoke.

Terrance reached out and put his hand on the boy's shoulder and put his finger to his lips, motioning him to be quiet. Through the door, he heard the guard rise from his chair and walk away from the building at a brisk pace.

"I have to go, sir," Timmy whispered. "Mr. Jones said *everyone.*"

"Do you trust me, Timmy?" The boy nodded.

"I think the guard has forgotten that you are in here. Don't go just yet, okay? Can you keep a secret, Timmy? Do you promise?" The boy nodded again.

Thoughts were racing through Terrance's head. *Trial suicide runs. A United States Congressman visits the compound and the rumor has it that he will take back a bad report to the United States. The same day, Jim Jones gives a suitcase full of the group's money to the Communist Party in Russia, then calls everyone in the compound together for a meeting. This could be the real thing! The unthinkable may be about to happen. Nine hundred members of the Peoples Temple may be about to knowingly and willingly drink poison and commit mass suicide, killing their own children in the process.*

The thought of 900 people committing suicide was too crazy for Terrance to wrap his mind around, but the signs were all there. That part was undeniable.

"Timmy, I am going to be leaving Jonestown today. I am going to go into the jungle and escape. I want you to come with me. It's not safe for you here."

"I don't understand. That's what the Evans family told me last night. I spent the night with them and then they left early this morning with the Wilson family. They snuck out while people were still sleeping. They said it wasn't safe for me to stay either and asked me to go with them, but I said I wanted to stay with my friends.

"Why is it not safe for me, Terrance? I don't feel scared here."

How much can I tell this boy? What are my chances in the jungle with a ten-year old boy in tow? What if I'm wrong? Even if I am wrong, if not today, then another day. These people are living their entire lives in a state of perpetual deception. It is just a matter of time before they do something crazy. I can't take the chance and wait this one out.

The voice speaking over the loudspeaker seemed calmer now, more relaxed. Almost tired, in fact.

"How very much I've loved you. How very much I've tried to give you a good life. But we are sitting here waiting on a powder keg. If we can't live in peace, then let's die in peace." (*Editor's note: Quotations by Jones and others are taken directly from the 44 minute "Jonestown death tape."*)

Sitting on a powder keg? What did Jones mean by that? The voice continued.

"What's going to happen here in a matter of a few minutes is one of the few on that plane is going to shoot the pilot. I know that. I didn't plan it, but I know it's going to happen. They're going to shoot that pilot and down comes that plane into the jungle and we had better not have any of our children left when it's over, 'cause they'll parachute in here on us."

This sounds real. These people are crazier than I thought. They are going to kill a United States Congressman and then kill themselves. Well, if they kill a congressman, the government will indeed come calling. They've got that part right.

Terrance dropped to one knee and looked the boy in the eyes. "Look, Timmy," he said quietly. "This is going to sound crazy, but I believe everyone in Jonestown will be dead by nightfall. You know those Kool-Aid drills we have been having, where we all drink the poisoned Kool-Aid so we can all go to a better place? I believe today is going to be the real thing. Today, drinking the Kool-Aid will mean you will really die. This is not a test."

Timmy's eyes grew wide, but it was clear that he could not quite comprehend the scope of what the prisoner was telling him.

Over the loudspeaker, Jim Jones rambled on with his final sermon.

"So my opinion is, we be kind to children and we be kind to seniors and take the potion like they used to do in ancient Greece and step over quietly because we are not committing suicide. It's a revolutionary act. We can't go back; they won't leave us alone. There's no way we can survive. If any of our children are left, we are going to have them butchered. I'm not speaking as an administrator today. I'm speaking as a prophet. You'll regret it if you don't die."

Yeah, you're a prophet alright, a false one. A prophet of death!

Timmy was listening to the voice. His eyes were welling up. A new voice came over the speaker. It was a woman.

"If you tell us to give our lives now, we're ready. When all of those white people left us today it broke my heart because all of those years they were with us they were not a part of us. We might as well end it now because I don't see. . ."

Jones interrupted the woman, cutting her off mid-sentence. He sounded like he had just received a report from someone. There was a sense of finality in his voice when he spoke again.

"The congressman has been murdered. It's all over. . .all over. What a legacy. What a legacy. They invaded our privacy. They came into our home. They followed us here 6,000 miles away. The Red Brigade shows them justice. The congressman is dead. Please, get us some medication. It's simple; there's no convulsion with it. Please get it before it's too late, the GDF (*Guyana Defense Force*) will be here, I tell you. Get moving. Get moving. Get moving. Don't be afraid to die. They'll torture our people. They'll torture our children. They'll torture our seniors. We cannot have this."

They've actually done it. That's it. These crazy fools have killed a United States congressman! There's no going back now.

Terrance knew this moment was likely the only chance he and the boy would have. They would either get out now or die here.

"Timmy, I am going to leave now. You have to decide whether to come with me or stay. The guard could remember at any moment that you and I are here and come back for us. When they give out the Kool-Aid, they are going to make sure everyone drinks it. That's why I am locked in this shack, you know. I wouldn't drink the Kool-Aid when they did the drill last month, so they made me their prisoner. I failed the loyalty test. So, do you want to stay here and die or come with me?"

Terrance knew he was laying something inconceivably heavy in the boy's lap, but the truth was what it was. Timmy gravely shook his head "no," then nodded "yes." He looked stunned and confused, but he had made a decision. He would leave with this man he barely knew.

"When they come for me, they will shoot me if I don't drink the poison and I don't plan on hanging around and waiting for that. So we are going to leave now."

With that, Terrance strode to the window and pushed the two loose sides out and with one powerful effort, bent back the other two sides until the nails popped and the frame hung loose in his hands. He tossed it away from the building. The die was cast!

Turning to the boy, he whispered, "If you're coming with me, let's go!"

Timmy joined him by the opening and held up his arms. With no other words Terrance lifted the boy up and slid him feet first through the window and with one arm lowered him gently down as far as he could and then let him drop. Now it was time to see if Terrance could fit through the opening. The entire plan hinged on that.

Terrance was an athletic man. His six foot three inch body was slender and hard, but his shoulders were broad. That would be the challenge. His thin tee shirt did not add much to his dimension, so he left it on.

Other voices were speaking over the public address system. One rational sounding woman said she was concerned about the children and urgently implored the group to consider airlifting to Russia, rather than killing themselves. Jones shot the woman down. With a note of finality, he dismissed the woman's suggestion and said it was too late for that. Another voice, a younger man told everyone how much "Dad" meant to him and how much he had changed his life.

In the hut, Terrance decided to exit headfirst. If his shoulders made it, the rest of his body would follow easily enough. The bottom of the window was about chest high. He put his arms through first and stood on his tip toes and took a tiny leap upward. The rough edges of the plywood siding around the window scraped the tender areas under his arms. He wiggled his way further into the opening and in a moment was wedged in tightly. He couldn't budge. At first, it appeared that it would be impossible for him to squeeze through the opening.

Timmy stood outside looking up at the odd sight of his friend wedged in the window above him. There was nothing he could do to help. Terrance's wide frame was jammed tightly into the opening, but with each painful, snakelike motion, he seemed to be moving forward ever so slightly. His face was red from the strain and he was quite sure that he looked more than a little silly, judging by the look on the face of the boy gazing up at him.

Terrance ignored the sharp pain under his arms and continued to writhe and wiggle his body. Finally, the widest part of his chest cleared the opening and the rest of his slender body followed quickly after, scraping against the rough cut edge of the plywood all the way down. Hands first, he hit the soft ground and rolled over. He sprang to his feet and looked sheepishly down at the boy.

"Whew!" Timmy said, swiping his right hand across his forehead. "That was close."

Timmy's quick smile eased the older man's embarrassment. Terrance responded merely by rolling his eyes and looking away.

Nearby lay the three machetes the workers had dropped when they responded to the call over the loudspeakers. Quickly, Terrance picked up the best two and handed one to Timmy. The boy's eyes lit up.

Chapter Three

Jones's voice over the public address system sounded increasingly urgent.

"Please, can we hasten with that medication. You don't know what you've done! Maximum, we've got forty minutes."

A new woman's voice came on. The loud sound of babies and young children crying could be heard in the background. The new voice was trying to calm the mothers.

"There's nothing to worry about. Everybody keep calm and keep your children calm. Older children help the little children and reassure them. They're not crying out of pain. It's just a little bitter. They're not crying out of pain."

Timmy seemed visibly affected by the sounds he was hearing. Terrance took him by the hand and led him into the foliage. Terrance was a California boy. He had never been in a jungle and was surprised by the gloominess. The dense canopy of interlocking branches high overhead made for an eerie darkness below. In spite of the lack of light, the undergrowth at the jungle floor was surprisingly thick and tangled. In places, it was almost impenetrable. With machetes in hand, they weaved their way through the branches and vines.

Even the gloomy darkness of the jungle could not dampen Terrance's enthusiasm. He was free and it felt good. He wanted to shout. After a month of imprisonment in a tiny hut, which was no more than an oversized tool shed, this was heaven. He headed straight away from the compound with Timmy right behind him. After just a few minutes of hacking at branches and making slow progress, he stopped to listen. He half expected to hear a shout of alarm or the sound of pursuit, but the only sound other than the fading voice of Jim Jones over the sound system was the humming of the insects, the chattering of the monkeys, and the calls of the birds.

Jones's voice was more distant now, but the two escapees were able to make out what sounded like a desperate last plea.

"Lay down your life with dignity," Jones was saying. "Don't lay down your life with tears and agony. Don't be this way. Stop these hysterics. This is not the way for people who are socialists and communist to die. We must die with some dignity.

Mothers, mothers, mothers, please. Don't do this. Put down your life with your child, but don't do this. Free at last. Keep your emotions down. It will not hurt, if you'll be quiet. I don't care how many screams you hear, how many anguished cries. Death is a million times preferable to ten more days of this life. . .Let's be dignified. Are we black, proud and socialists or what are we?"

Terrance hardly knew what to think or feel. It was all so surreal. He tried to push the scenes he was imagining from his mind. It was all too awful.

After an hour or so of winding their way through the muddy jungle floor and up and over small, heavily forested hills, Terrance was reasonably confident they had escaped undetected and he could give Timmy a break. He had pushed the boy pretty hard up til now and the going had indeed been rough. This was the kind of jungle that could swallow a man up in a matter of seconds. Terrance had counted on that as he plotted his escape. But now, surrounded by all of this wildness and armed with nothing but a machete, he felt suddenly responsible for the kid he had brought along. And he was all of a sudden acutely aware that he was not entirely sure that he knew what he was doing.

Better here than dead, he told himself. *Both of us. Just keep moving, Clark. Put as much distance between us and Jonestown as possible. It's not over!*

About an hour after they had made good on their escape, Terrance heard two or three gunshots somewhere back toward Jonestown. They sounded like pistol shots. Except for the humming of the insects, the shots were followed by silence. He and Timmy stopped and listened for a few minutes, making use of the opportunity to rest, but there were no other sounds coming from the direction of Jonestown. Whatever was going on back there was probably over, but there was no way of knowing that for sure or whether a party had been sent out after them. Maybe the shots signaled the execution of residents who didn't drink the poison or were caught trying to escape.

Unsure of what else to do, they pressed on.

The farther they got from Jonestown, the more wildlife they encountered. There had been snakes almost from the beginning, mostly small ones that slithered out of the way. Twice, Terrance had changed directions when he had spotted pythons stretched out or curled over branches right in front of them. One was brown with diamond shapes on its back. It looked to be more than fifteen feet long. That one was lying on a branch about chest high and easy to spot.

The other snake was smaller, maybe seven or eight feet long and a greenish yellow color. Had it not moved, he would never have spotted it.

As the afternoon wore on, the sounds of other animals increased. They routinely heard the noise of heavy animals crashing through the jungle. Sometimes they heard the squealing of wild pigs, though they never saw one. Sometimes they heard the thumping sound of larger animals bouncing away through the brush.

Before leaving the United States, Terrance had read up on the wildlife of Guyana. One thing had stood out in all of the literature he had poured over – the abundance of snakes, especially the poisonous kind. Never the kind to venture into a strange place unprepared, Terrance had invested in a pair of snake boots and loose fitting snake pants. The pants were a green and tan camo design and were snake proof clear to the waist. The idea of wearing snake gear had seemed silly once he had settled into the semi-civilized ways of Jonestown, but he had been wearing those pants and boots the night he was locked up. Today, they were going to save his life.

Quite by chance, their path led them into a patch of small boulders. The rocks were covered with green moss and what looked to be some kind of tropical ivy. Nestled between two of the larger boulders lay a ten-foot bushmaster. Bushmasters are not only highly venomous. They have a nasty reputation for being fearless and aggressive when trapped or startled.

Terrance was leading the way and didn't see the snake until it was too late. His foot came down not more than two feet from its heart-shaped head. With a blurring quickness, the snake curled back and struck at the intruder's leg. The attack came with a suddenness that stunned Terrance for one dangerous moment.

The bushmaster's first strike hit the man just above the right knee. Its two-inch fangs dug in hard, but failed to penetrate the densely woven material. Terrance could feel the pinch of the fangs squeezing his skin and was surprised at the sheer force of the bite. Acting purely by instinct, he launched himself backward, knocking Timmy to the ground. As Timmy tried to right himself, the beast struck a second time. This time the viper's fangs bit at Terrance's left boot. It shook its head and upper body viciously, trying to penetrate the snake-proof surface.

With all the power he could muster under the circumstance, Terrance swung the machete at the snake's body a foot and a half below its head. The blade caught the snake straight across the scaly skin and penetrated a good inch. Stunned, the bushmaster let go of Terrance's boot and began thrashing about like a high voltage wire. It was a sobering sight. Terrance backed away, picking up Timmy and pushing the boy along behind him. They left the snake there, thrashing about among the boulders, its long body flailing sometimes on top of the rocks and at times down between them.

They were a good thirty feet away before Terrance finally felt it was safe to take his eyes off the snake. Looking down, he was surprised to see the sheer amount of venom that coated the knee of his pants and the top of his boot where the bushmaster's fangs had attempted to clamp down. There was probably enough venom there to kill several men his size. Had he not been wearing snake gear or if the viper had hit him above his waist, certain death would have followed.

Timmy had not said a thing the entire time. When Terrance turned and looked down at him, the boy's face was white.

"Did it bite you, Terrance?" he whispered. "It looked like it did."

"It tried. But I am wearing snake proof pants and boots and it couldn't penetrate. I thought these duds were a stupid waste of money after I got all settled in at Jonestown, but I guess they just saved my life."

"What was that thing?" Timmy asked, still whispering. "I have never seen a snake attack like that. Usually they try to get away."

"I think that was what they call a bushmaster. Very poisonous. That was a big one. From now on, remember to stay behind me. That was a close call."

Timmy didn't answer. He just nodded his head.

For some time after that, the going was slower as Terrance watched the ground for snakes. They made a wide circle around the patch of boulders where they had left the wounded bushmaster and then continued hacking their way through the brush. A few minutes later, they came upon a game trail that led roughly in the direction they were going. The ground sloped gently away from them now and for the next while the going was easier.

Eventually the ground underfoot became muddy and then soggy. Before long they were sloshing through water four or five inches deep right at the edge of what appeared to be a large swamp. Out in front of them were patches of open water, which was a blackish color and smelled foul. Patches of tangled vegetation floating or suspended in the water like seaweed and here and there large patches of lily pads with bright yellow flowers floated on the surface.

From where they stood, there was no telling how wide the swamp was or how deep the water, but twenty or thirty feet out from the edge, two bulging round eyes surfaced and then sank back into the blackness. Timmy had not seen the eyes, but Terrance had. Terrance had read that anacondas and eighteen foot crocs inhabited the swamps of the Guyana rain forests, so wisdom and a little God-instilled caution dictated that they look for a way around rather than through what lay before them.

Gripping Timmy's shoulder, Terrance quickly shoved the boy back away from the water. Something in his head told him not to stand too near the open water and he quickly heeded the voice. Terrance may have been raised in the city, but once in the wild his instincts were good.

Deciding which way to proceed from there, however, was a coin toss. For no particular reason, they turned to the right. They had traveled about a mile along the edge of the swamp, avoiding the open water, when they came to a place where a wide, shallow stream emptied into the swamp. The water in the stream was clear and flowing. Above was blue sky. Terrance had only been able to see a tiny bit of the sky from the hut back in Jonestown and was surprised by how much it lifted his spirit to see blue overhead.

The streambed was covered with football sized rocks. Large boulders lined the banks on both sides. This appeared to be an excellent place to cross over and get around the swamp. Before wading into the water, the two exhausted escapees sat down at the edge of the stream to rest.

Terrance was looking at the water flowing slowly past and debating whether it was safe to drink, when thirty feet away from where they sat a shiny head about the size of a cocker spaniel broke the surface of the water. As he and Timmy watched, the animal climbed up onto a flat rock. It was a good ten feet from the far side of the stream.

"River otter," Terrance whispered. "By far the largest I've ever seen."

Terrance glanced down at Timmy and saw that the boy was watching it too.

"Cool!" Timmy whispered without looking up.

The otter shook its sleek, glistening body and then stretched out full length on the rock to sun itself. It was a beautiful animal and graceful.

No sooner had the otter stretched out to full length, when without warning a large, silent form flew out of the jungle at the far edge of the stream, aimed directly at the boulder where the otter was peacefully sunning itself. There was no time for the basking animal to react.

In motion, the thing flying through the air was a tawny colored blur. It landed fully on top of the hundred pound otter and in an instant long fangs and powerful jaws were crushing the animal's head like pulp. The sound of the skull crushing made a sickening noise easily heard over the soft, melodic noise of the stream. The forward momentum of the predator carried both animals off of the rock and into the water. Not once did the black and yellow animal loosen its grip on its prey.

The killer, its body mostly submerged for the moment, turned and waded back towards the far shore. The body of the otter was hanging limp in its jaws. As it crawled out onto the rocky bank, the two spellbound watchers could see that it was a large spotted cat.

"Jaguar!" Terrance whispered. "Did you see that?" Terrance spoke without taking his eyes off the cat.

There was no response from the boy. Terrance shot a quick glance his way and saw that Timmy's eyes were wide, as was his mouth.

The jaguar dropped its prey on the rocks at the edge of the stream and shook itself violently from stem to stern. Shiny droplets of water sprayed in every direction, shimmering in the fading sunlight. For a moment, the cat stood there, casually looking around in every direction. Then its eyes came to bear on the man and boy sitting motionless on the rocks at the opposite side of the stream. The jaguar craned its neck forward and sniffed the air and then it stood motionless and stared.

The two humans held their breath. As if by agreement, neither of them breathed or blinked for what seemed an interminable period of time. Finally, the jaguar seemed satisfied that whatever was on the other side was of no consequence to it and turned back towards its meal.

Terrance was awed by the fluidity and grace of the jaguar's motions as it picked up its heavy prize in its mouth, as if its weight was nothing, and silently faded into the jungle on the far side of the stream.

Neither Terrance nor Timmy said a word for another minute.

Finally, Timmy whispered without looking up. "We can't go over there, Terrance." There was fear in his voice. "We can't go over there."

The man reached over and put his arm around the boy's shoulder. He was a grown man, but the raw savagery of the scene they had just witnessed had left him emotionally numb. It was more than understandable that the boy would be afraid.

"We have to," he whispered gently. "We have to get to get to the other side of the swamp. We'll be alright. But before we go any further, let's make us a couple of stout spears. If we run into one of those guys and he is in a bad mood, I would prefer a sharp spear to this lousy machete."

Timmy nodded, but this time he didn't look up. He continued to watch the place where the jaguar had disappeared into the jungle.

There was no shortage of spear material and in a matter of minutes they were both armed with long spears, sharpened to a fine point at one end. Timmy held this spear with both hands and jabbed forward as if attacking a foe. The feel of the weapon in his little hands seemed to bring back some of the courage the brief ordeal they had just witnessed had drained from him.

The two travelers rested for a few minutes longer beside the stream and then slowly waded out into the shallow water. The stream was never more than two feet deep all the way across, and though the rocks on the bottom were smooth from thousands of years of tumbling over and over, they were able to maintain their footing.

There was an abundance of cool, clear water right there at their feet to quench their mounting thirst, but Terrance decided against drinking any of it. One thing he knew about the water in South American streams was the revenge it often exacts against visitors from the north. The microscopic bugs in one river system might be entirely different from the bugs in the next one over, and dysentery was nothing to mess with down here.

They waded past the rock where the otter had been taken. Bright drops of blood dotted the surface of the stone, the only evidence of the brief struggle that had occurred there minutes earlier. Finally it was with some trepidation that Terrance and Timmy approached the jungle on the far side, near the place where the jaguar had disappeared behind the foliage a few minutes carlier. With the points of their spears at the ready, they carefully made their way up over the rocks and into the dense vegetation beyond. There was always the possibility that the big cat was feeding somewhere close by and they did not want to come upon it by surprise.

Once they had moved away from the stream, the terrain on this side of the river was markedly different. It sloped gradually upward and was rockier than in the dense jungle on the other side. The higher they went, the sparser the undergrowth became. This made for faster and easier travel and also made it easier to spot any predators that might be lurking about. Timmy turned often and nervously watched their back trail. He was now acutely aware that they were in big cat territory, and that was a fact he would not quickly forget.

Chapter Four

With a thinner canopy overhead, the two weary travelers could see blue sky much of the time now. The gloominess of the dark jungle they had passed through had worn on their minds more than either of them had realized.

The late afternoon sun was suspended just above the western horizon when the two weary humans reached the top of the ridge they had been scaling. Directly before them was a rock cliff that dropped off about a hundred feet or so. At its base, the terrain sloped away gradually into what appeared to be a vast wilderness of primitive forest. Terrance and the boy stood gazing out over the scene, overwhelmed by the sheer immensity of it all. Like a giant green carpet with flowing wrinkles and bumps, the forest went on for mile after mile until eventually it faded into the slopes of grayish blue mountains far off in the distance.

They had escaped Jonestown. They were safe from pursuit, or at least so it seemed. But in Terrance's mind, that thought was replaced by another less comforting one. With all of the twists and turns they had taken, usually choosing the path of least resistance through the tangled underbrush, they now were completely and totally lost. In the dark shadows of the jungle, they had lost sight of the sun for long stretches. Where they stood at this moment, all Terrance knew for sure was which direction was west. The sun was setting directly in front of them, so they were looking outward toward the Pacific Ocean – several hundred miles away.

No need for Timmy to know that I have no idea where we are. It's bad enough that he knows there are jaguars and angry snakes about. For the boy's sake, I must exude some level of confidence.

Timmy interrupted the man's thoughts. "We're lost, aren't we Terrance?"

The honesty of the boy's question caught the man off guard. Terrance swallowed hard.

"Well, that's a matter of perspective," he replied. His voice was calm and he continued to look out over the landscape.

"The mountain men who explored the American frontier and the Rocky Mountain wilderness of the Old West used to have a saying. People would ask them when they would return after six months of exploring uncharted territory, if they ever got lost."

"Did they get lost sometimes?" Timmy asked innocently.

"Well, when people would ask *them* that question, they would generally reply, 'Nope, never been lost. Been a might *confused* for a week or two at a time, but never lost.'"

Timmy smiled. "Well, I think we're lost."

"Not to worry, lad," Terrance replied with his most confident voice. "We are armed with sharp spears and machetes in a land full of wild game. We will be fine. We'll just camp out for a while."

Terrance hoped he sounded more confident than he felt. He noticed that Timmy was standing a little straighter, and that was encouraging.

Terrance stepped closer to the edge of the cliff and scanned the terrain just below for any sign of movement there. Satisfied with what his keen eyes saw, or to be more precise, what they didn't see, he let his eyes wander slowly out towards the horizon, looking for signs of human activity. From what he remembered about Guyana, almost the entire population lives near the coastline and not many in the inland. The longer he stood staring out across the distance, the more he realized that they really were in the middle of nowhere and were entirely on their own. And really were lost.

The sun was beginning to set now. Before their eyes, the jungle was transitioning from daylight to darkness, but still there were signs of life everywhere. Bright colored tropical birds flitted about among the high branches of the trees just below the cliff. In the middle of a rockslide off to their right, a band of Red Howler monkeys was carrying on a minor skirmish over some especially succulent morsel of food one of them had found. Ultimately, the fight would be as brief as it was loud, but not before keen monkey teeth had drawn more blood than the prize could warrant.

For as far as they could see, nothing suggested that men were anywhere in the vicinity or that men had *ever* been here. Terrance recalled from the research he had done before arriving in the country that Guyana contains one of the largest and least molested rain forests in the world. A man could get lost in the jungles here and never be seen or heard from again. It had happened many times.

The air here at the top of the ridge was noticeably dryer than the moist jungle down lower. There was sunlight and fewer insects. A sudden updraft brought cooler air up from below the cliff. Terrance's dark hair was drenched with sweat. His clothes were soaked as well, so the cool air felt good. At twenty-five, the man was physically fit, in the middle of his prime actually. Yet even for him the long trek through the jungle had been taxing.

If I'm worn out, how exhausted little Timmy must be, he thought.

Hiking through dense jungles and up and over hill after hill had been physically taxing on the both of them, but the greatest toll had been on Terrance's hands. Using the machete to hack their way through the brush had left several painful blisters on both hands. The blisters had popped hours earlier and now both hands burned. He would worry about that later. At the moment, he knew he had to focus on a place to spend the night.

Having the boy along forced the private investigator from California to stop and assess the situation they were in and to be realistic about it.

Okay Clark, you did your homework before you came. What do you remember about Guyana? Let's see. The jungles are as unspoiled as any in the world. The country is called the "land of the giants," because there are so many critters here which are the largest of their type anywhere on the planet. The rivers contain the biggest otters, one of which we just saw. The rivers also have the biggest snakes and the biggest fresh water fish known to man. In the swamps and slower moving rivers, there are also Black Cayman, which is some kind of alligator or crocodile that commonly grows to fourteen feet long and sometimes nineteen or twenty. That's great! There are also giant eagles, and of course the jaguar.

What do I remember about jaguars? Let's see, pound for pound, the jaguar is among the strongest mammals on the planet with a bite more powerful than the lion and the tiger. That's comforting! What else? Most big cats bite their prey on the back of the neck or choke them out at the throat. The jaguar's jaws are so powerful that it bites right into the top of the skull of its prey until the bone crushes under the pressure.

Are they man eaters? Well, leopards are, at least some of them are. And jaguars look a lot like leopards. But if I remember correctly, jaguars are not prone to attacking men. It happens, they say, but it is not common like with lions and some of the other big cats.

As a boy, Terrance had read all of Jim Corbett stories about his hunts for man-eating tigers and leopards in India back in the 1920's. The leopard was much smaller than the tiger, but Corbett believed that the leopard's cunning and the fact that they climbed trees made them more dangerous to hunt than the tiger.

Jaguars sure look a lot like leopards! They climb trees like leopards. And from what we saw this afternoon, they have no fear of the water. What am I supposed to do if I encounter one and it's aggressive? My private investigator training never mentioned anything about fending off a hungry jaguar.

Don't work yourself into a frenzy, Clark. A jaguar is not a notorious man eater. If Jim Corbett were here, he would say that with any of the big predators, the difference between being ignored and being eaten is sometimes just a matter of luck. If the animal has not fared well at hunting for a couple of days, its dietary flexibility comes into play quickly enough. Or if it's injured or too old to hunt, it goes after any prey it can find. A healthy animal will usually seek other prey over humans. Well, I hope we only meet healthy jaguars!

And God, if you're up there and if you're listening, I have to look out for this boy and I'm not sure I am up to it. I've had my doubts about you, but if you're there, help us.

Terrance felt Timmy's hand rest lightly to his right forearm, as if the boy was hesitant to break the prolong silence. Terrance shook off the thoughts he'd been pondering. He sensed that it was time to stop thinking and act, whatever that meant. By now, the sun was only half visible above the horizon. It would be dark soon and the thing they needed most was a safe place to spend the night. It probably wouldn't get too cold where they were, but they needed to be safe, if that was possible.

Terrance looked down at the scrawny, blond haired kid standing there beside him. The lad was only ten, but had not complained once during the hours of tough hiking they had put behind them. In the back of Terrance's mind, he knew it had been nuts to bring Timmy along. It had made everything riskier. But another part of his mind told him that if he had left Timmy behind, the boy likely would be dead by now.

After he had survived the encounter with the bushmaster earlier in the day, the first thought that had come to Terrance's mind was what if the snake *had* bitten him. The boy would have been stranded and all alone in the middle of the jungle. That hadn't happened. They were alive and not in Jonestown. But the stakes were still very high for the both of them.

Terrance tried to imagine the scene that must have unfolded back at the Pavilion after they left, but he couldn't. It was too awful. All he could think of was bodies in bright colored clothing lying everywhere, mothers with their babies. Elderly couples lying together with blank looks on their faces. Hundreds and hundreds of dead people who had followed some fool, some false prophet over the edge and into the darkness.

No time to ponder that now, Clark. It is what it is and it's behind us. Your job now is to keep this boy safe.

"Timmy, my man," he said, looking down at the boy. "We need to find a safe place to spend the night. What say we look for a place with air conditioning, room service, and two queen size beds?"

The youngster looked up at the six foot three inch man towering over him. Then, through the sweat and streaks of dirt that lined the smooth skin of his young face, he smiled. It was a tired smile, but it was a smile.

Terrance reached down and rubbed his hand roughly over the top of the boy's head. Tired or not, this kid was a gamer. Terrance knew a lot of men who would not have done what Timmy had done that day, or if they had, would have whined the entire way.

Just as they turned away from the cliff and started back toward the jungle there came a deep-throated coughing sound from somewhere near the foot of the cliff. Both of them stopped in their tracks. A few seconds later, the sound was repeated. For a moment, everything around them became strangely still and quiet. The birds were silent and the monkeys stopped their chattering.

So, that's what they sound like. I remember reading about that cough. It sounds a lot scarier when you are standing in the middle of nowhere armed with nothing but a sharp stick and a machete.

A moment or two later, the forest came back to life. Living one step from death is a way of life for every denizen of the jungle. Every trip to a watering hole, every step out into the open was tempting death one more time, yet prey animals do it every day. They live their entire lives with death close at their heels.

In a matter of seconds, the birds and the monkeys had forgotten the terror they had felt a moment earlier and were back to living their lives.

"What was that coughing sound?" Timmy asked. There was a hint of fear in his voice.

"I'm not sure," Terrance lied. "But let's find us a place to sleep. Some place dry. It will probably rain again tonight."

Chapter Five

*T*heir first night in the jungle was spent in cramped quarters, perched a dozen feet off the ground in the crotch of a giant tree. It didn't rain that night, but the constant noises of the jungle night stretched their frayed nerves to the limit. The brief moments of sleep they caught were fitful.

The sounds of a tropical rain forest at night can at times defy description. There were growls and screeches and occasional screams of terror or pain, as some hapless creature was caught and devoured by something bigger or stronger. Terrance and Timmy would just begin to drift off to sleep again when some new scream or screech would jar them back to full alert.

The sounds grew quieter just before dawn and with the first hints of sunlight, the birds began their morning songs. Only then, did the two weary humans drift off to a merciful sleep. The sun was half way to its midpoint in the morning sky when they were awakened by the fluttering of wings as the most brilliant colored bird either of them had ever seen landed on a branch just above Timmy's head. The bird's feathers were a fiery orange, the brightest orange imaginable.

At the first sign of movement below it, the bird launched itself upwards and outwards with a screech of alarm.

"What was that? That was the prettiest bird I have ever seen," Timmy whispered.

"Got me, little man, but I think it was as surprised to see us as we were it. We're probably the first humans it has ever seen. What a bird that was, though."

Terrance stood up in the crotch of the tree and stretched his long limbs. He was sore from head to toe. Truth be told, there wasn't a part of him that didn't ache and the long night had brought little relief to the blisters on his hands. Terrance's dirty tee shirt was torn in places. He ripped a piece from the bottom and wrapped it around his right hand to allow him to use at least one hand with less pain.

Sore hands or not, there was no more ignoring their hunger and thirst. Terrance was thirsty and starving and knew the boy must be feeling the same. He was surprised that the Timmy had not once complained.

Once they were back on the ground, with spears and machetes in hand, they began in earnest their search for food and water. They had gone less than a dozen steps from their tree, when Terrance stopped and looked down at the boy.

"Timmy, we need food and we need water, water that is safe to drink. And we need to figure out what we are going to do next, where we will go and where we will spend tonight. We need to find something better than last night. Last night was a nightmare.

"So, I was thinking maybe we should pray or something. Maybe we don't have to do this all on our own. I didn't tell you this before, but when I was locked up I prayed many times for a way out of Jonestown. I didn't think God was listening, not really, but I said some prayers anyway. I don't know if He had anything to do with it, but we made it out and probably just in time."

Timmy smiled. "Praying sounds like a good idea to me. I've been saying some already, especially yesterday after we saw that jaguar kill that thing in the water. I prayed a bunch of times after that."

Terrance chuckled. He leaned his spear against a tree trunk and put his bandaged hand on the boy's shoulder. "Let's get to it then," he whispered.

"Dear God," Terrance began, "thank you that we are alive. Thank you that we made it this far. If you're listening, we need your help, God. We are in the middle of some of your most beautiful creation, but it is not exactly friendly here. We're not sure where we are and we're hungry and thirsty. It would be good if you would protect us from the dangers that are all around us and from sickness, especially regarding the water. And help us find food and a safe place to spend the night. Oh, and we ask that you lead us back to civilization when it's safe. Amen."

Terrance looked down at Timmy. His eyes were closed and he had an earnest look on his face.

"Lord Jesus," Timmy began. "I remember my mom reading stories to me about angels protecting people and fighting their enemies for them. Please send a couple of your angels to hike through these woods with us, Jesus. Big, strong ones. Strong enough to handle a jaguar or a anaconda. Don't get me wrong, God. Terrance is strong and brave and I trust him, but angels would be kinda nice, too. Amen."

Terrance smiled at that last part. He reached down and rubbed the top of the boy's head again. He did that when he was impressed with Timmy or wanted to give him confidence. Then he leaned over and retrieved his spear.

"That was a good prayer, Timmy. My mom and dad read me lots of Bible stories when I was a kid, probably the same ones. I still remember them, but I guess I kind of stopped believing they were true. You may have to believe enough for the both of us – at least for a while. But I'm trying."

Terrance was feeling some discomfort with the little chat he had started. He had been raised in a home where faith was taken for granted. He knew the words. He had listened to hundreds of sermons growing up. As many do, however, he had more or less walked away from the whole religion thing and had decided to make his own way in the world. It was time to change the subject.

"So where are your mom and dad, Tim? I was kind of under the impression you were more or less on your own back in Jonestown."

"My mom died last year and I never knew my dad," Timmy replied thoughtfully. "I sort of had a lot of moms and dads back in Jonestown. Lots of people were nice to me. Mrs. Evans was real nice to me and I thought about leaving with them yesterday morning. I guess I should've. The Evans were white, but I stayed with black families, too. It didn't matter."

Timmy paused for a moment. "Do you think all of the people back there are really all dead or something? I've been thinking about that a lot, especially the little kids and my friends."

This was a tough question. The meaning of it all, if there was any meaning, might be beyond a ten-year old's understanding, but standing here in the light of day, miles away from the compound, it did seem kind of nuts to imagine all of those people actually going through with it and committing suicide, even if they *had* heard them going about it over the loudspeakers.

Maybe I am the one who is losing it? Everything is probably fine back in Jonestown. It was probably just another trial run and like a mad man, I dragged this innocent kid out into the jungle where we could both die.

Deep down inside, though, Terrance knew that such thoughts were just his emotions talking. Emotions can sound perfectly logical at times. But as he played back the entire scenario in his mind, the decision he had made at the time had been perfectly rational. Taken as a whole, all the things that had gone on leading up to his and Timmy's escape only made sense if the residents of Jonestown were really going to go through with their plan this time.

But how should he answer the boy's question? He was only ten.

"I don't know, Timmy. I hope I was wrong, but something tells me I wasn't. Maybe they are all alive and well after all. If they are, I'm sorry I brought you out here. I was going to escape yesterday one way or the other, with or without you, because I was not going to stay locked up in that hut any longer."

The look on the boy's face said he appreciated the frankness.

"Well, I think I understand what you're saying," he replied. "And I hope my friends are all alive and happy, but I'm glad I came with you anyway. I'm glad you didn't leave me there when you escaped. I don't think the Evans's and the Wilsons woulda left yesterday morning if they weren't really scared of something. They seemed pretty upset and in a hurry to leave. They said it had to be right now.

"To tell you the truth," the boy continued, "I was kinda scared last night with all of those loud noises and stuff. It's daytime now and I feel safe with you. But I hope we don't have to fight a jaguar with these," Timmy said, holding up his spear. He was smiling.

Terrance smiled back and nodded his head in agreement. He looked deeply into the boy's bright blue eyes. There was intensity there and it stirred something deep within the man. Suddenly the most important thing in the world to Terrance Clark was not to disappoint this kid or let him down.

"Thanks for saying that, Timmy," was all he could bring himself to say. He felt an urgent need to change the subject.

"By the way, my fine friend, I gave the chef the day off so I'm afraid we're going to have to make our own breakfast."

Timmy giggled. Terrance could always make him laugh, even when he was afraid or tired or hungry.

So the man and the boy, each with a machete in one hand and a sharp stick in the other, set off in roughly the same direction they had been heading the night before, a direction they thought was directly away from Jonestown. Terrance's hands were too sore to swing the machete, so he went to some length to take the path of least resistance through the forest, even if that was a winding path and meant a further loss of bearings.

An hour or so after they left the tree, they stumbled upon a place where a tiny rivulet of crystal clear water bubbled up out of the ground and formed a small pool of water on the hillside to their left. The water came to the surface at the base of a small boulder. From that little pool, the water cascaded down three or four feet into a second, slightly larger pool. From this lower pool, the rivulet flowed down the hillside a few more feet before disappearing back into the soft, muddy ground. They had discovered a natural spring.

The water in the two pools was clear and inviting. The bottoms of both were covered with small round gravel about the size of peas. Most of the stones were a dull grey, but scattered here and there were dozens of shiny stones that were a shiny translucent green. The green pieces were odd shaped and looked like little chunks of glass.

Terrance knelt down beside the upper pool and smelled the water. There was no discernible odor.

"I think we can drink this water, Timmy. It comes up out of the ground right here. It should be well filtered and is probably as safe to drink as anything we will find. If it rains again, we can drink the water that gathers in the bowls of some of the larger leaves in the jungle below us, but for now I think we should drink this."

The two took turns lying on their bellies and drinking from the cool, clear water in the upper pool. The cold water seemed to ease their hunger for the moment.

Suddenly Timmy whispered, though not all that quietly, "Look, Terrance! Fruit!"

Sure enough, in the direction Timmy was pointing was a tree with wide spread branches, some of them reaching almost to the ground. The branches were heavily laden with a yellowish green colored fruit about the size and shape of an apple. As they approached the tree, half a dozen Common Squirrel Monkeys screamed out, protesting their intrusion. As the monkeys abandoned the tree, some of them carried fruit in their hands.

Terrance reached up and plucked one of the low hanging pieces. Rust colored speckles dotted the yellow surface.

"I don't know what this fruit is, but the monkeys eat it, so it is probably safe enough for us," he said. "I will take the first bite. If I keel over dead, don't try any," he said laughing.

The fruit was not very juicy and not all that tasty, but it was food.

"As hungry as I am, this tastes pretty good," he said approvingly. Reaching up, he picked another of the low hanging pieces and handed it to Timmy.

"You know what, Terrance," Timmy said, after swallowing his first bite. "It sure didn't take long for God to answer our prayer this morning. And I'm glad, too. I was getting kinda ready to eat something."

Terrance laughed and reached for another piece. It would take a fair amount of fruit to satisfy the cravings of a man his size. They had prayed and they had food and water. He would give the boy that.

After they had both eaten their fill, they returned to the spring for more water. Terrance removed his sweaty and somewhat shredded tee shirt and washed it in the lower pool. Satisfied that it was as clean as he was going to get it without soap, he stretched it out flat on the boulder to dry. Following Terrance's lead, Timmy did the same.

Again using the lower pool, Terrance carefully washed his blistered hands and exposed the raw places to the fresh air. His right hand was noticeably worse than the left. When he was finished, he looked down at his ten-year old traveling companion. It was clear to the boy that Terrance had something to say, but for some reason was hesitant to speak.

Timmy wrinkled his forehead as if to say, "Well, what is it?"

"I'm thinking, we could stay here for a while and give my hands time to heal a bit. We should be alright while there is fruit on this tree. There is plenty of fresh water. We could figure out how to build a fire and maybe cook us some meat, if we can lay our hands on some. I still have that salt and pepper shaker you brought me yesterday. If we're good hunters, we might have us some fine dining."

"Maybe some of that Beef Wellington you keep talking about," Timmy said laughing. "I wonder if there is such a thing as Monkey Wellington."

"Sounds good to me." Terrance exclaimed. "Any kind of Wellington sounds good after a month of rice and beans. But I think I would prefer deer or maybe even wild pig. I haven't seen a single pig, but I've heard quite a few."

The hillside above the spring was steeper and much rockier. Many of the boulders farther up were the size of cars and some bigger. Terrance pointed up the hill at the rocky outcroppings.

"Let's climb up there among the rocks and see if we can find a place we could use as a shelter. It's early in the day and we would have time to gather some heavy branches from some of the windfall trees down the hill. Maybe we could erect us some kind of barrier and sleep all night long tonight."

It only took three or four minutes to climb up to where the heavy boulders began to dominate the hillside. They scrambled atop the first big one they came to. From where they stood, they could look down on the two pools below them and see the boulder where their shirts were drying. They could see beyond that, down into the valley where the sparser vegetation of the hillside ended and the dense jungle stood almost like a green, tangled wall. This was like a perfect lookout to sit and watch their back trail. It was doubtful that anyone was following them now, or even could if they tried. They had not used their machetes for the last couple of miles and thus had left little sign of their passing.

Timmy liked climbing. While Terrance was still surveying the landscape below, he went a little farther up the hillside on his own. Circling one especially large rock, he came out on a grassy ledge from which he could look down on Terrance one level below him. Timmy turned and looked around him. Suddenly, he stopped and stood motionless, as if staring at something behind him.

"What is it?" Terrance whispered up at him. "Do you see something? Is there a snake?"

Terrance kicked himself for letting the boy get that far from him. Thoughts of the bushmaster from the day before flashed through his mind.

"No, no snake, but you gotta come up here and see this."

Terrance breathed a sigh of relief. Then with spear in hand, he scurried up to where Timmy was. Following the boy's eyes, he looked in the direction Timmy was staring. There, visible only from the small, grassy ledge where they were standing, was the mouth of a cave! The dark opening was maybe five feet across and almost as high.

How far back it went was anybody's guess, but it definitely had possibilities. It was also entirely possible that the cave was currently occupied.

"Whoa, what have you found here?" he whispered. "It might be empty. There might be a jaguar in there or a bushmaster den or even a python. We better check it out before getting too close."

Chapter Six

*K*eeping one eye on the opening, Terrance knelt down and carefully examined the ground at the entrance to the cave. The grass was maybe six inches tall and stood erect, showing no sign of having been walked on recently. There was no visible path leading to or from the cave's mouth. Possibly, the cave had been the lair of a jaguar or some other large predator at some time in the past. Maybe it still was and there was another entrance. But unless there *was* another entrance, the cave Timmy had found had every appearance of being uninhabited.

"I think it's empty," Terrance said in a low voice. "There's no sign that it has been used recently. You stay out here and keep watch for a minute while I try to see how far back it goes. This could be a great place for us to hole up for a while. If we built a fire right in the entrance, I doubt if any animal would try to enter."

Ducking down, Terrance stepped into the cave. He kept the sharp end of his spear at the ready, probing the darkness with it and brushing it across the floor of the cave, sweeping for snakes or debris that might trip him in the darkness. The light from the outside illuminated the first few feet, but there was nothing but pitch darkness further in.

After yesterday's run in with the bushmaster, Terrance's biggest fear was snakes. He knew the anacondas stayed near the water and the boas tended to stay in the forests and tall grasses, but there were lots of species of poisonous snakes and they could be found anywhere, especially in dark places.

Slowly, the young man's eyes adjusted to the darkness and inside a minute he could see further back. He stepped to the side to let more of the outside light in. The cave seemed to go back several feet, but exactly how far he couldn't tell.

"We need light, Timmy. A torch or a fire."

"What do you see? Can I come in?"

"Yeah, come on in. I don't want to go looking around 'til we can see what's back there. Stay behind me."

"Don't worry about that," Timmy whispered. His voice betrayed both excitement and caution.

In a moment, Timmy was standing just behind Terrance and slightly to his right side. His left hand was gripping Terrance's right bicep. Timmy's grip was a bit tight and his fingernails were digging into Terrance's arm. Terrance smiled in the darkness, but said nothing.

"It sure is dark in here," the boy whispered. "But it smells fresh. I think there's light coming from somewhere further back. See, it looks lighter back there."

Terrance strained his eyes, but could not perceive any change in the darkness.

"Do you see it?" Timmy whispered.

"No, it all looks the same to me."

"Move over here where I am, just a little bit this way."

Terrance stepped directly in front of Timmy and stared into the darkness. Sure enough, it *was* lighter farther back. Something must have been blocking the view from where he had been standing.

"I am going to go farther back and check it out. Maybe there's another entrance. Stay right behind me, okay? There still could be snakes."

Timmy reached up and took a hold on the back of Terrance's belt as the older man slowly inched his way forward towards the lighter area, leaning down and constantly probing in front of him with the sharp point of his spear. In a dozen feet, they entered a narrow passageway that turned to the left and then in a few more feet turned back to the right again. As they inched their way along, it got lighter the further they went.

Terrance could see the ceiling of the cave now. It was two or three feet above his head. He straightened up and walked erectly.

Up ahead, the light was brighter and there was the sound of water dripping. It was more than a drip though, more like a steady trickle. Terrance could see more clearly now. The passage way was opening up. In a few more steps, they found themselves in a large open area, a natural cavern with light coming in through a hole in the ceiling.

As they looked up at the opening, they could see the bright sun directly overhead. It was disappearing from sight even as they watched. It was apparently the brightness of the sun directly over the opening that had created the light Timmy had seen back in the first cave. As soon as the sun was no longer directly over the opening in the ceiling the lighting in the cavern became more subdued. Still it was sufficient to explore their surroundings.

Men had been here. Charred remnants of blackened wood marked the place where a campfire had once been. There was no way of telling how long ago that had been.

Against the back wall of the cavern was a pool of water, fed by a heavy trickle of water that came down from the ceiling and ran down the rough surface of the back wall. The pool was maybe ten feet across and a foot or so deep. The water looked pure and clear. The bottom of the pool was covered with the same grey and green pea gravel as the smaller pools they had discovered just down the hillside.

"I think this is the rivulet that feeds the spring where we drank this morning," Terrance said. "This is quite a find, Timmy. It's a miracle to find this place and you did it. Good job, Davy Crockett!"

Timmy beamed at the accolades.

"Look, Terrance. It looks like people have been here," he replied, pointing at the charred pieces of wood. "I wonder how old that campfire is."

"Hard to tell, but we need to figure out how to start our own. It doesn't look like anyone has been here for a long time, so I think we can make this our home for a little while; least 'til we figure out what to do next. It's dry. The entrance would be easy to block or guard. We just need fire and some meat to go with that salt and pepper. I think the smoke would go out that hole up there. It's directly above the old campfire. Let's find some dry branches and see if we can start a fire. I don't care if its monkey or deer. I'm hungry for some meat."

Timmy walked over to the charred wood and kicked one of the larger pieces with his foot. To his surprise, the entire piece turned to dust. It didn't just break apart or crumble. It disintegrated.

"I think that was pretty old," he said, looking up at Terrance with wide eyes.

"I've never seen burnt firewood do that before," Terrance replied. "You didn't even kick it that hard. Probably, no one has been here for a very long time."

Timmy followed Terrance back through the passageway to the outside entrance to the cave. Judging by the sun, it was early afternoon. The monkeys were back at work on the fruit tree on the hillside below them. Lest they eat every bit, the two humans scurried back down and filled their arms with prime specimens and took them back up to the cavern for safe keeping.

On the way back up the hill, they spotted a deadfall about a hundred feet from the entrance to the cave. The branches that were in contact with the ground were soft and rotten, but the trunk and the branches up off the ground were dry and appeared to be perfect fire-wood. The surface of the wood was almost a silver color, bleached out by the sun. From a distance, the fallen tree looked like the white skeleton of a dinosaur or of a beached whale lying against the rocky hillside.

With one blow they discovered that the dry wood was much too hard for their machetes to cut. The blades never even penetrated the surface. Most of the branches broke easily, however, when Terrance stomped on them or kicked at them with the soles of his sturdy boots.

In no time, they had accumulated a hefty pile of broken limbs, several of them small enough for kindling. Lest it rain and dampen their store of firewood, they decided to carry it all to the cave before attempting to build a fire.

Leaves had blown up against the side of the boulders near the mouth of the cave and were sheltered enough there that they had dried out. Terrance instructed Timmy to pick up a couple of handfuls of the driest ones, but not to crush them too much.

Finally, with the last load of firewood piled against a side wall in the back cavern, Terrance set about starting the fire. He had grown up in Oakland, but his dad had been an avid bow hunter and had taken Terrance along on several hunts into some seriously remote wilderness areas. They had always taken along matches or lighters, but his dad had made sure that young Terrance learned how to start a fire with whatever tools were at hand.

It had been a while since he had started a fire by striking stones against one another, but the conditions were right and the dry leaves were perfect tinder. After several violent strikes of the stones and a little soft blowing the leaves ignited into the most beautiful little flame either of them had ever seen.

Timmy knelt down next to Terrance and watched the entire maneuver with great interest. When the first tiny flame erupted, he jumped to his feet in a shout of exaltation.

"Fire! We have fire," Timmy cried out, literally dancing around the tiny flame as if their little fire was the first any man had ever seen.

Terrance carefully fed the fire little twigs until those were going strong and then added the kindling and later the larger branches. Within a matter of minutes, they had a full-fledged fire going. Neither knew whether it had been ten years or a thousand years since there had last been a campfire in their new home, but there was something almost mystical about the moment. Nothing transforms a wilderness camp like the crackling of a fire and the life of the dancing, darting flames. The sight invigorated them both.

Terrance watched with satisfaction as the pale smoke made its way up and out of the small round hole in the cavern's ceiling. Leaving Timmy there by the fire, he went back outside to see if the smoke was visible to anyone who might be out and about. They had not explored the forest around the cave and had no idea whether they were alone in this faraway jungle or just across the hill from some native village. Until they knew, it seemed wise not to broadcast their presence.

Terrance was pleased with what he saw outside. There was a slight updraft coming up from the valley below and the soft current was pushing the faint smoke up the hill and into the trees above the cave. As the light smoke filtered through the leaves of the trees higher up, it was so dissipated as to be all but invisible.

Back in the cave, he suggested to Timmy that there was still time to make a stab at hunting down some dinner. Timmy had never hunted before, but he leaped to his feet with the exuberance of a ten year old on Christmas morning and grabbed his spear and machete.

"I don't suspect you'll be needing the machete, killer," Terrance said teasingly. "One weapon should be enough."

Timmy looked sheepish for a quick second, but a moment later that now familiar smile returned to his face. "Yeah, I don't know what I would do with a machete anyway. Probably couldn't get close enough to anything to use it."

The boy caught on quickly.

It was now the middle of the afternoon. It would be nice to return from the evening hunt to a fire rather than a dark cave, so Terrance laid a couple of the larger pieces of wood on the fire to keep it going while he and the boy scouted around for food.

Once outside, they dropped down to the two small pools below the cave to pick up the shirts they had left drying on the boulder. The shirts were completely dry, but more than a little stiff.

"I'm afraid I will have to speak to the butler about the laundry," Terrance whispered. "Too much starch in my shirt again."

Timmy giggled quietly. He was not quite sure what starch was, but he assumed it was one of those Beef Wellington kind of things, something rich people know about. He saw Terrance wad his stiff shirt up into a ball to loosen it up before putting it on and followed suit.

"You know, Timmy, I'm not sure how good these spears are going to be for hunting. We would have to be pretty close to something to use them effectively. What say we carry a couple of nice sized rocks for good measure? We might do just as well with them. We're probably more likely to see a rabbit or something small than a deer anyway. My hand's going to kill me if I have to grip this spear hard enough to throw it. I will if I have to, but I could throw a rock easier."

Terrance found a couple of rocks about the size of tennis balls and Timmy a couple about half that size. They each carried one in their left hand and put one in a pocket. That left their right hands free to carry and hopefully chuck their spears, if the opportunity presented itself.

They checked the fruit tree, but at the moment there were no monkeys. They dropped down into the valley below the cave. The day before, they had seen more wildlife in the jungle than in the open areas, and they thought they could get closer to potential victims where there was more cover to conceal their approach. As fate would have it, however, the only thing they saw was a green python that was almost exactly the color of the leaves. It was about six feet long and was curled around a tree branch about four or five feet off the ground.

"Maybe tomorrow or the next day if we don't find anything else we could try one of those, but I am not quite sure I am hungry enough yet to eat a snake," Terrance whispered.

"Yuk," Timmy said, scrunching up his face in disgust.

Still exhausted from barely sleeping the night before, the two hiked around the valley floor for several hours, but their efforts were in vain. They had seen plenty of game while they were traveling cross country earlier in the day, but now that they were actually hunting, there was not an edible creature in sight. There was no shortage of tracks in the soft earth, but no actual game.

Just as dusk was setting in, they abandoned their search and started making their way back toward the cave. Terrance had been careful to keep his bearings, so he could find his way back. He knew it would be heartbreaking for the boy if they to spend another night in the crotch of a tree.

As they approached the fruit tree below the cave, they came from the direction of the valley floor. Suddenly, Terrance stopped and knelt down. Doing precisely as he had been instructed earlier, Timmy did the same. Up ahead, three deer were feeding beneath a fruit tree, their tree. Apparently, some fruit was scattered about on the ground, probably where the monkeys had dropped them or shaken them loose as they scampered about the branches. Two deer were feeding on those while one was standing on its hind legs nibbling at the tender leaves.

There was no cover between the two hunters and the tree, so there was no way to approach close enough to get within spear range without being seen. It was a frustrating moment. Right there in front of them was enough meat to last them for several days and they had no chance of harvesting it.

"What shall we do," Timmy whispered. "It's getting dark."

"Nothing," Terrance replied. "There's nothing we can do. Let's not frighten them and maybe they will come back tomorrow."

Suddenly, out of the jungle behind and below them came that same coughing sound they had heard on the high ridge the night before. It sounded close. The deer heard it, too, and with the silence of shadows faded into the increasing darkness farther up the hillside.

"Let's get back to our cave before it gets completely dark," Terrance whispered.

"What was it that makes that coughing sound," Timmy asked, keeping his voice low.

The boy and I are in this together. I don't want to scare him, but he probably should know. . .

"That's the sound the jaguar makes," Terrance whispered. "I read somewhere that they hunt mostly at dusk and dawn, so it might be wise to have fruit for dinner tonight."

Timmy nodded in whole-hearted agreement.

Chapter Seven

*T*he light outside had all but disappeared by the time they made it back to their little ledge. It was pitch dark inside the front cave. If there was still any flame alive on their fire, it was clearly not enough to light the passageway back to the cavern. They were going to have to navigate their way back by feel and memory. Even Terrance found it a bit nerving to step out of the twilight outside and into the inky darkness of the cave. He groped with his hands along the wall of the cave, looking for the passageway back to their cavern home, such as it was.

In the darkness, he stumbled over something and fell to his knees. There was a cracking sound, as if he had stepped on something fragile, like an empty soup can. Timmy had been following closely, clinging to Terrance's belt, and came crashing down on top of the larger man.

More quickly than it takes to describe it, Terrance was back on his feet, lifting Timmy with him. Finding his footing again, he continued on towards the back wall of the cave until he found the passageway. In a few more seconds, they were back in the main cavern.

Tiny flames were still flickering on what was left of their fire. It was a welcome sight. Quickly, Terrance placed some small branches on the fire. There were enough glowing coals left to set the fresh fuel ablaze and in a few seconds they had their fire going again. The bright flames flickering in the darkness was a beautiful and welcome sight.

That night, they made a supper of the fruit they had wisely picked earlier in the day. Then they fell asleep with the pool of water at their back and the fire between them and the passageway back to the outside. Twice during the night, Terrance got up and placed more wood on the fire. Timmy never stirred. The boy was sleeping the sleep of exhaustion. Terrance watched the lad sleeping for a minute or two and again his heart was stirred. There was something about this whole situation that was changing him.

"Lord," he whispered in the flickering light of their little fire, "this little man has just lived through two of the most exciting and frightening days of his life. If it was you who led us to the fruit tree and the water and this cave, well thanks. Maybe you could give us some meat tomorrow. I'm trying to believe. I just don't know."

Terrance Clark had prayed more in the last month than in the last five years. He was a strong man, both physically and mentally and he tended to be the self-sufficient type. But the last couple of days had shaken him. Those people back in Jonestown might have had some kind of religious experience, but whatever it was, if it had been truly based on faith in God, he was pretty sure they would have turned to God and not mass sui cide when push came to shove. Whatever religion they had, he was sure he didn't want it.

Lying there by the fire, he recalled something one of the women of the town had said at the "White Night" trial run he had attended, the one that had ended with him locked in a shed. What the woman said had troubled him at the time.

The woman, who looked to be in her thirties, had stepped up to the microphone, looked over at Jim Jones and said to him, "I thank Dad very much. Dad's love and goodness and mercy and kindness in bringing us to this land of freedom. His love and mercy will go on forever. Thank you, Dad."

Jones had not turned the woman's love and adoration back to God or Christ, but had accepted it as if it was his natural right or just due. There was something about that moment that had troubled Terrance and stuck with him. Fire alarms had gone off in his head and he had never shaken the sense of foreboding that had come over him. Terrance had been more than a little slack with his church attendance for the past few years, but he remembered clearly something his father had told him and had said more than once from the pulpit: God shares His glory with no man. Never forget that.

And Terrance hadn't. He fell asleep that night thinking of his dad and mom and home. He remembered his dad up there on the platform preaching and sharing his *rock solid* faith with the members of his flock. Those were simpler days and Terrance realized that he missed them. After high school, he had at times forgotten that his dad was a dad to be proud of, a man's man, a preacher of great faith, a spiritual warrior of sorts, and yet at the same time tender with his wife and son. His dad was also the one who had shown a younger Terrance Clark how to gut and quarter a bull elk and preserve the hide. He was the one who had shown him how to move though the woods like a shadow when on a stalk and how to start a fire with two pieces of rock. If his dad could just see him now.

What would pops think if he heard me pray? He would probably be disappointed that this little boy has more faith than his son, who was raised in church. But he would be glad I was trying.

With thoughts of his mom and dad and home drifting lazily through his mind, Terrance Clark drifted off to sleep.

The dark sky above the opening in the ceiling was just beginning to give way to the morning light when he awakened. He rose to his feet, stretched his long frame and quietly placed several pieces of wood on the smoldering coals. Clearly, he and Timmy were going to have to gather more wood as soon as it was fully light. The wood was dry and burned quickly and already their supply was all but depleted. As Terrance knelt there on his haunches tending the fire, Timmy stirred in his sleep and mumbled something unintelligible, then became quiet again. The boy's eyes remained closed and Terrance let him rest.

Running over yesterday's events in his mind, a thought leapt to the forefront. Taking a flaming brand in his hand and using it as a torch, he strode back through the passageway to the place where he had tripped the night before. What he saw there was the most puzzling sight his twenty-five year old eyes had ever seen.

Lying on the floor against the side wall of the cave was a curved piece of rusty metal. It was shaped like a breastplate, the kind soldiers or warriors wore centuries earlier. It was large and must have been worn by a good sized man. There were no remnants of clothing, but there was what was left of a large metal belt buckle on the ground near the bottom of the breast plate. There was no sign of the belt.

Below the buckle and off to the side near the cave wall was a large sword with a heavy blade. The blade was covered with a crusty coat of rust, except for the handle which appeared to have been wrapped with strands of a less corruptible metal.

The flame was beginning to go out on his makeshift torch, so Terrance retraced his steps back to the cavern. Timmy was still sleeping, but awoke as the older man knelt and laid the smoldering branch back on the fire.

"Is it morning?" he asked in a sleepy voice. "I think I slept good."

"It's barely morning. Why don't you lie there for a minute or two, okay? I want to look at something in the front cave. I will be right back. I won't leave you." Timmy smiled meekly and nodded. A moment later his eyes were closed again.

Terrance took another branch from the fire, a larger one, and returned to the front cave. This torch was brighter and lit up the entire front cave for a minute or so. With the increased light, the mystery only deepened. There, against the opposite wall was what looked to be a metal helmet, the kind Spanish conquistadors wore toward the end of the Middle Ages, maybe the 1500s or so. A dozen questions crossed Terrance's mind as he knelt and examined the armor.

What have we stumbled on here? Are these the remains of a man who lived and died centuries ago? It sure looks like it. The buckle is there beneath the breastplate, right where the belt would have been when the man was alive. Moths and mice would have eaten away the man's clothes and the leather of the belt long ago, and the bones would not have lasted very long in such a humid climate. But why would the remains of a Spanish or Portuguese soldier be lying here in this remote cave, deep in the jungles of Guyana?

Terrance knelt and examined the ground around the breastplate and buckle more carefully. Running his free hand through the dusty earth of the cave floor, he uncovered a handful of round, flat objects lying just below and to the side of the buckle. The pieces felt heavy, like coins. He applied a little saliva to one of them and rubbed it between his fingers and thumb. After some effort, a telltale yellow color began to appear.

These are gold coins. Very old gold coins, I bet. A man died in this cave, apparently hundreds of years ago. He was miles from the coast, deep in the jungle, and armed for battle. What could his story be? Was he a good man?

How did he die? Was he alone? What was he doing here?
So many questions. . .

Terrance returned to the cavern and knelt by the fire. As soon as Timmy's eyes opened, he told him what he had discovered, the thing he had tripped over the night before. The boy was anxious to see for himself, so once again Terrance took a burning brand from the fire and led Timmy back to the front cave. Timmy reached down and reverently ran his hand over the breastplate. He tried to pick up the sword with his right hand, but it took both of his arms to lift it.

"I think whoever this belonged to must've been strong," Timmy said, laying the weapon back down precisely where it had been. Its former resting place was clearly outlined in the dust of the cave floor.

The flame was dying on the branch, so Terrance tossed it on the floor towards the back of the front cave. They were only a few steps from the entrance, so they stepped outside into the fresh morning air.

It had rained during the night before and the ground was wet and soft. Timmy started to step forward, towards the edge from which they could see down into the valley, but Terrance put his hand on the boy's shoulder and held him back. Timmy looked up and saw that Terrance was not looking down at him, but instead casting quick glances above them and off to the sides. Finally, he turned to Timmy and pointed down at the ground where he would have stepped. There in the damp earth was a track. It was a pug mark, the kind a cat makes. It was a large one, and it was obviously fresh.

Terrance stared at the track for a couple of seconds and then pulled Timmy back into the cave. Quickly, they made their way through the dark passage and back to the cavern where Terrance quickly retrieved his spear and handed Timmy his.

"We must not be caught off guard. Two wooden spears might not be much, but they are better than nothing. From now on, we go nowhere without them."

A thought crossed Terrance's mind. Retrieving another branch from the fire, he returned with Timmy to the front cave. He handed the branch to Timmy and then knelt on both knees and with his fingers began sifting through the dry dirt of the cave floor. Four or five feet down from the breast plate, he found smaller bits of rusty metal, maybe boot buckles. Farther down, he found the thing he was looking for. Out of the dust he lifted a chunk of rusty metal, roughly resembling a spearhead, the kind a soldier might have carried into battle in days long past.

With the heavy chunk of rusty metal in hand, he and Timmy returned to the larger cavern where the light was better. The spearhead was covered with a thick coat of rust, more so than the breastplate and helmet. Judging by its weight, Terrance surmised that the spearhead was probably solid at its core and possibly salvageable.

"If I can get this rust off and sharpen this thing up a bit, an iron tipped spear would provide a much better defense against predators than these sharp sticks we're carrying now. And with the heavier weight at the forward end, I should be able to throw my spear more effectively and possibly bag us a deer."

Timmy nodded his head approvingly.

There were plenty of rock chips, large and small, strewn about the cavern floor. Terrance selected a good sized one and went to work on the spearhead, chipping away at the rust and scraping the edges. The surface rust came off with ease, but the next layer did not give way so easily. The rock broke faster than the rust on the spearhead gave way. The longer Terrance worked at it, the more obvious it became that sharpening the sides and the tip would be all but impossible with stone tools.

"Here, try my machete," Timmy suggested, peering over the older man's shoulders. Terrance looked up at the boy and chuckled.

"Good idea, Timmy! I should have thought of that. Steel is a lot harder than these stupid rocks."

Utilizing the heavier back side of Timmy's machete blade, Terrance began to scrape and grind the edges of the spearhead. Progress was slow, but eventually the rust was scraped away and the edges grew sharper and the end more pointed. When he was satisfied, Terrance held the spearhead up and smiled broadly.

"That's probably about as good as I am going to get it without a file, but I think it's good enough. Now let's figure out how we are going to attach it to my spear."

With his machete, he hacked off the sharp point of the wooden shaft and made the end dull and flat. Then, he carefully cut a notch large enough to slide the spearhead into place. Holding the head into place with his hand, he turned to Timmy.

"All we need now is something to secure this thing and we'll have a real weapon."

Back outside the cave, Terrance carefully surveyed their surroundings, taking special notice of any place from which a predator might ambush them. All the big cats like to ambush their prey whenever possible. There was no way of knowing whether the jaguar had followed them back to the cave during the night merely out of a sense of curiosity or if it had other designs. Terrance knew that mountain lions back in the states were known to follow hikers and even hunters simply because they were curious. But there was always the possibility that this jaguar had a more sinister motivation. Again, Terrance didn't share his every thought with the boy.

If the jaguar had really wanted to, it could have followed us into the cave. It sees much better than we do in the dark. Either way, it's better to err on the side of caution. I don't think the cat was really after us or he would have followed us inside, but I would hate to be wrong about that.

"Here, trade me, Timmy. You carry my spear, which is not of much use until we get the head attached, and I will carry yours in case we run into trouble before we get the spearhead attached."

With that, they began making their way down into the valley below the cave. Terrance was certain he could find the materials he needed there. The fruit tree was only slightly out of the way, so they stopped by for a quick breakfast. There were no monkeys in sight and no sign that the deer had returned during the night.

The man and the boy approached the jungle with some caution. Once they entered the mass of growth, visibility would be very limited. Among the thick vegetation would be an abundance of creeping vines, perfect for binding the iron spearhead to the shaft of Terrance's spear. All they had to do was pick some good ones and not run into trouble before the spearhead was firmly attached.

Thirty or forty feet back into the foliage Terrance found what he was looking for. He selected a stringy looking vine and cut off several two-foot long pieces. Then he carefully separated out individual strands of the stringy fiber and braided them together into little pieces of cord.

After the first strand was completed, he pulled tightly on the two ends to test its strength. It held. Satisfied that the vines would do the job, Terrance made three more lengths and used them to tie the spearhead to the shaft of his spear. The spearhead was snug, but Terrance was not entirely satisfied that it would withstand heavy stress. This time, he repeated the braiding process using much longer strands of fiber. With these he circled the end of the shaft over and over until the entire upper end of the spear, where the spearhead had been inserted, was wrapped tightly with the braided cord.

After tying off the end of the cord, he tested the tightness of the spearhead. Satisfied that it would hold, he turned to Timmy and smiled.

"I like it," Timmy said, nodding his head approvingly.

"I feel armed now, Timmy. I say we go hunting"

Terrance's spear felt for the first time like a real weapon. Standing there, armed with an iron tipped spear, twenty-five year old Terrance Clark, handsome young private investigator from Oakland, California, felt for the first time since they had left Jonestown a real sense of confidence. This new weapon seemed to transform the man. It turned him into a hunter, not just some puny human slinking through the jungle from one hiding place to another.

Terrance was relishing his new sense of strength and confidence when he heard Timmy whispering something low and quiet.

"Turn around very slowly," Timmy whispered to him. The boy's voice was low and there was fear in it. Terrance looked down and saw that Timmy's eyes were wide. He was staring at something a little to the side and behind Terrance's back.

Chapter Eight

S lowly, Terrance turned around, raising the tip of his spear as he did. At first, he saw nothing behind him but foliage. Then, his eyes caught sight of the cat. It was sitting on its haunches not more than a dozen feet away, staring directly into Terrance's eyes. The yellow hide and large black spots were barely visible behind the foliage that separated them. Timmy had done well to spot it.

"Stay behind me, Timmy. I am going to slowly back away. If it charges and I have to fight it, don't stay and await the outcome. Head back to the cave and wait for me. Put more wood on the fire and stay there. For as long as you can."

"Okay," Timmy whispered.

As Terrance and Timmy began to back away, the jaguar rose to its feet and stepped out into the open. It was a large animal, larger than the one they had seen at the river that first day. And it was a lot closer. The jaguar's head was large, larger than Terrance remembered leopards having, and this animal seemed to have no fear of man. Terrance spoke to the cat, his voice low and steady.

"You've probably never seen a man before, have you, big fella? Are you going to attack, or are you going to just stand there and stare me down? We're willing to walk away if you are. Okay, we're walking away now."

As Terrance spoke, the cat stretched its neck forward as if to listen better. It had likely never heard a human voice before. Powerful shoulder muscles rippled beneath its spotted hide as it took one small step forward. Slowly, Terrance and Timmy inched their way backward. The cat took another step toward them and then stopped. Terrance and Timmy continued to back slowly towards the clearing behind them. The cat was still standing where it had stopped when the foliage eventually blocked it from their view. The sense of fear was keenest at that moment. Terrance knew an attack could come from anywhere now and there would be little time to react, if the cat came for them. He slowed down a bit and walked with his knees bent and his upper body forward, prepared to meet the weight of an attack.

They had not had to go far into the jungle to find the vines Terrance wanted, but now it seemed to take forever to retrace their steps. Terrance kept the tip of the spear pointed toward the place where they had last seen the cat, scanning the foliage for the slightest hint of movement. It occurred to him that if the jaguar came from another direction, there might not be time to turn and take the charge head on. There was nothing he could do about that now.

Finally, there was not jungle beside him, only in front. They were back out into the open. Quickly, but without running, they made their way back up the hillside to the mouth of the cave. From there, they could peer back down into the valley. There was no sign of the cat. Timmy was the first to speak and he did so with the honesty of a child.

"I thought it was going to kill us and eat us like it did that big thing back at the river."

Timmy's voice sounded relieved but still a little scared. Terrance managed a strained but low laugh.

"It was a little scary," he replied. "This wasn't the same jaguar we saw before, you know. I don't know what was going through this one's mind, but it just seemed to be watching us like it was curious or something. Maybe it has never seen humans before. Maybe it just ate and wasn't hungry. It's a good thing you spotted it, though." Terrance said, reaching down and putting his hand on Timmy's head.

"I don't know how I saw it. I don't know how long it was there before I did. It was like all of a sudden it was just there and I felt it staring at us. I think I felt it staring at us before I saw it."

"Well, I think we will stay out of the jungle for the rest of the day. We still need to hunt though. Let's go up to the top of the hill above us and see what's up there. That's where those three deer went when they left the tree last night."

With Timmy casting regular glances back down into the valley behind them, they headed up the hillside. The terrain at the top was rocky and sparsely covered with small scrub bushes. There were a few taller trees scattered here and there, but the average height of the lower brush was about up to a man's eyes. There was plenty of open space between the bushes. The two hunters moved slowly and quietly among the shrubbery, wisely doing more looking and listening than walking. Timmy stayed in the rear, ever watching their back trail. Terrance was surprised and pleased with how silently the boy moved. There was an abundance of dry leaves and twigs about, but somehow young Timmy carefully avoided stepping on them.

The boy's a natural hunter. . .quiet as a mouse.

As they were rounding a low boulder, Terrance stopped, then took a slow step backward. He turned to motion to Timmy, but the lad had already frozen in his tracks. Terrance knelt and placed his spear on the ground and picked up a couple of baseball size rocks. He motioned for Timmy to do the same.

"Some kind of grouse or rock hen," he whispered low. "There's a bunch of them just on the other side of this rock. We can step out together and throw at the same time, but we will have to be quick. They'll scatter the second they see us."

Timmy nodded and reached down and found a couple of nice throwing rocks near where he stood.

"Ready?"

Timmy nodded.

Armed with the most primitive weapons known to man, the two hunters stepped abruptly into the open. Instantly, the covey made a break for safety. Some took to flight and some ran. Both hunters threw their first rock immediately, and then with rapid fire motion shifted their second into their throwing hand and released it no more than a second after the first.

Terrance's first rock landed short of the bird he was aiming at, but it bounced off of the hard ground and hit the bird a glancing blow. His second rock was a clean miss. Timmy's first rock went right through the covey, hitting nothing. His second was aimed at a bird already in flight and landed square in mid body. The bird fell to the ground and lay there quivering.

Terrance's bird was flopping about. Leaping forward, he caught the hen and dispatched it before it could escape. Timmy was on his just as quickly.

With birds in hand, they looked at one other and grinned widely, both equally pleased with the outcome. There they were, seconds after spotting the flock of hens, each with a bird in his hand and a smile on his face. They were hunters now. Real hunters.

"Today, we eat good," Terrance said, still smiling broadly. "I hit mine on the bounce, which was sheer luck. You hit yours in the air didn't you? That was a great shot."

Timmy beamed. "I couldn't believe I hit it. Mostly luck, I think."

"No, it was a good shot. Nothing lucky about that one."

Terrance showed Timmy how to clean and pluck his bird and less than an hour later they were sitting by their fire, tasting their first hot food in three days.

"Mountain hen roasted on a stick and lightly seasoned with salt and pepper. That is the best meal I have ever tasted," Terrance confessed after finishing off his entire bird.

"Yeah, me too," Timmy replied. "I never knew chicken could taste this good."

In reality, there was more to the experience than just the meal. There was a growing sense in both of them that they really could survive out here. They could eat, drink, and stay dry and warm. They could live off the land. They had just stared down the fiercest and most powerful animal in all of South America, armed with only spears, and they had come away unscathed. Terrance knew, of course, that the encounter with the jaguar could have ended quite differently, but it hadn't and they were all the stronger and more confident for it.

"You know what, Terrance? We forgot to pray over our birds. Remember what happened when we prayed on that first morning? We said a prayer and then we walked for a little while and found the spring and then the fruit tree and then this cave. Today, we escaped from a big jaguar and now we are eating chicken. I think God heard our prayers and answered us."

Terrance wiped his greasy fingers on his pants. The greasy stains he left were barely visible on the camo design. He hesitated a bit before answering.

"Well, I guess you're right about all that, Tim. I have a tendency to think that because I use my mind and my body to cope and survive that I don't need God. It is only when I look back that I can see that my every success could have gone quite differently.

"And maybe you're right about those prayers we prayed. What were the chances of us finding a cave with an old Spanish spearhead in it, all situated close to food and water? Maybe God heard us.

"My dad used to say that one of the things God dislikes most in people is ungratefulness. He said God gives us good things and we murmur and complain because we don't have more and forget to thank Him for what we have. It's easy to do that, but my dad and mom taught me better."

Timmy nodded in agreement. "I was thinking that too. That was one of the things my mom didn't like about Jonestown. She came there to do nursing work and to help the people and stuff, but most of the time they never appreciated what she did and didn't say 'thanks' very much."

Terrance looked thoughtfully at the boy. "Until yesterday, I didn't know you knew your mom. I thought you were an orphan and just stayed with different people in the town. I guess I never thought to ask. I assume she was a member of the Peoples Temple?"

"No, not really. We just came down here with them so she could do nursing stuff. She was paid at first, but after a while, her nursing work was just kind of expected. She talked about us leaving some day and going back to California, but for some reason, she couldn't get permission from the government people to leave and then she got really sick. That's when she died."

A single tear had formed in Timmy's right eye.

"How long ago was that, Timmy? I mean, when she died. Were you little?"

"No, it was about a year ago, but I still remember her just the same. She was a good mom. She used to read me stories at night before we went to bed, mostly Bible ones, but other ones too. And we always said prayers before we went to sleep. I miss her a lot. I always do. There was no one like her in Jonestown. The people there were nice to me and let me stay at their houses after my mom died, but they were not like my mom. No one was. If my mom was still there, I would not have come with you unless she came, too."

"Why *did* you come, Timmy? It had to be a scary thing, leaving everyone you knew and running off into the jungle."

"Well, first of all, I was scared about dying. The things you said sounded kinda true. The people back there talked a lot about dying. They said they weren't going to let anyone come and take them away. They said they would kill themselves first. So when you said you thought they were serious this time, I believed you. Especially after my favorite families, the Evans and Wilsons left.

"And the other thing is, I trust you. You are like my mom was. You were the only person I met in Jonestown who was like her and it gave me a good feeling to be around you."

Terrance was not sure what to say. He was not even sure what he felt. The words Timmy had spoken were pure and honest and they touched the man in ways he was not used to feeling. Terrance had enjoyed strong relationships with both of his parents, but he was an only child and had never married or had children of his own. It took him very much by surprise to feel such a strong desire to reach out and hug this little boy and to protect him, even at the cost of his own life if necessary.

"Thanks for saying that." That was all the man knew to say. Even at that, he felt the skin on his face tighten and he had to look away. Time to change the subject again.

"I think we should do what you suggested and say thanks, even if we already ate our birds."

Timmy laughed. "Do you want to pray or should I?"

Terrance nodded at Timmy and without hesitation the boy said a short, innocent prayer, the kind children do best. He named off the "good stuff" God had given them and thanked the Lord that the jaguar had not eaten them. Then he ended with a prayer for all of those people back at Jonestown.

"One more thing, God," he said in a most sincere voice. "I pray for all those people we left back there. I hope they're not all dead, 'specially the little kids and the babies. If they are, I am sorry for what they did. I hope you might forgive them, but maybe not Dad Jones. He might be too bad. Anyway, amen."

Just then, the sun broke over the hole in the ceiling of the cavern. The brilliance only lasted for a few minutes each day, but it filled the cave with light. Terrance saw something on the wall behind Timmy and leaped to his feet.

"Look at those drawings. There on the wall. They look like people and animals."

On the wall on the right side of the cavern, drawn with a rusty red colored paint of some kind, were pictures of men and what looked like dinosaurs. There was a triceratops looking creature with the boney hood behind its head and there were two men wearing loin cloths. The men held spears aimed at a mean looking creature standing in front of them with its mouth open wide and big teeth showing.

The drawings were not all that detailed, but they were remarkably clear.

"I recognize those dinosaurs," Timmy said excitedly. "I have a book about them. Well, I used to. That's a triceratops over there and the one in front of the two men I think is a T-rex. I wonder who could of drew these pictures? My book says the dinosaurs all died lots of millions of years before there were people. My mom said that what it said in the dinosaur books was probably not true."

The images left little doubt as to what they were depicting, men and dinosaurs in the same scene as if they were facing off.

"Maybe the Spaniard drew them," Terrance suggested. "He might have been here for a while before he died."

"Maybe," Timmy said, "but you said the soldier guy was here four or five hundred years ago. The book said they only discovered dinosaur bones two hundred years ago. If that's true, it's probably not possible that the soldier drew them."

"Yes, it's very odd," Terrance remarked. "This little cave has been hiding two mysteries, maybe for a long, long time. The drawings and the armor may have nothing to do with each other, but they are both quite remarkable. I would have guessed that no human would ever have found this cave before us, but we're definitely not the first ones to ever come here."

The last of the direct rays of the sun were fading quickly. At its zenith, the sunlight only touched a small area of the floor in the middle of the cavern and only partially lit the rest of the room. But compared to the rest of the day, it was quite bright. In a few moments, however, the wall with the red colored drawings was again shrouded in shadow.

Returning to his spot by the fire, Terrance crouched there for a couple of minutes before speaking, clearly lost in his thoughts. It had been his study of evolution in high school and college that had done more to undermine his faith in God than anything else. He had fed unbelief and it had grown. If these drawings were older than two hundred years, and they almost for sure were, then there had been a time when men and dinosaurs were alive at the same time – just like his father had always said. Terrance Clark found himself in a dilemma that was at once intellectual and spiritual and it was going to take time to sort through it all.

Chapter Nine

With the sun just past midday, there was an entire afternoon of daylight left to burn. The best hunting would be in the late afternoon and evening hours, but there was work that had to be done before they went out. It was Terrance's job to think ahead. The biggest threat to their sense of security was their lack of firewood. Coming back to the cave after dark with no light whatsoever would be more than a little spooky – for him and the boy.

After a few trips to restock their supply of burnable wood, the two hunters started out again, armed with their spears and at least one good throwing rock in their pockets. They were after bigger game, something that would last for a while, but every man who lives off the land knows he has to be flexible. A rabbit on a stick is better than a nice fat deer disappearing out of sight.

"While we're out, let's keep our eyes peeled for a sharp piece of rock that we could fashion into a spear-head for you. That's the way the Indians used to do it and it worked well enough for them to survive. We might as well have two good spears."

Timmy liked that idea. He liked it a lot. From then on he kept one eye peeled for a long slender piece of sharp stone. It was their agreed upon strategy that while Terrance scanned in front of them and off to the side for possible prey, Timmy would monitor their back trail to make sure that nothing was hunting the hunters.

They made their way back to the top of the hill behind the cave. There were no mountain hens about, so they moved on. They wouldn't turn down another tasty bird, if the opportunity availed itself, but they were looking for something quite a bit bigger.

They still-hunted for the next couple of hours, again doing more stopping and looking than walking. Maybe it was still too early in the afternoon, but nothing stirred. As always, there were plenty of splendidly colored birds in the trees. Channel-billed Toucans and red and green Macaws flitting from limb to limb. And they saw another one of those fiery orange birds. At sight of the humans, the birds would often shatter the silence with shrieks of warning to the other denizens of the forest, letting them know that intruders were in their midst. There was nothing to do about that. They kept moving, quietly making their way through the lesser cover of the sparsely treed terrain at the top of the hill, their eyes ever peeled for game worthy of their attention.

It was an hour or so before dark when they had their first opportunity. They came up over a small rise and were just about to drop down on the other side when two deer passed in front of them about fifty yards out. They were both standing still when they spotted the two does. Both Terrance and Timmy stayed perfectly still and the animals never knew that two hunters were watching them. The distance was too far to throw a spear with any degree of accuracy, so they waited while the animals strolled casually out of their view.

When there was no chance the deer could spot them, they crept silently down to where they had been. On the side of the hill they came upon a heavily used game trail. There was almost no vegetation on the path, just muddy earth covered with countless hoof prints. Terrance stared at the ground for a moment and then looked both ways up and down the trail.

"I have an idea," he said. "This trail looks like it gets used a lot. Let's find a tree that overlooks it and set up an ambush. If we wait long enough, something will come."

It sounded like a good plan and before long they found a tree that was sturdy enough to climb and close enough to the game trail to afford Terrance a decent opportunity for a throw. There was another suitable tree about fifty feet away and close enough for Terrance to see it. Terrance positioned Timmy in that tree and then he climbed the one he had selected for himself.

"Animals like deer rarely look up," he told the boy. "So unless you move, a deer will never see you up there. Just be ready. If one comes from your direction and it's on the trail, let it go past and come to me. My spear will be much more effective. If it comes past me first and I miss, then give it your best shot. But if it's running, lead it a foot or two to allow for its speed."

The boy nodded knowingly, but in truth he never quite understood what Terrance meant by *lead it*.

The two hunters stood in the forks of their trees without moving for the next half hour. Other than birds, the only thing they saw was a long-nosed armadillo slowly making its way past them a few feet below the trail. They could hear the faint rustling sound the creature made as it nosed its way through the damp leaves.

Finally, with darkness approaching, Terrance signaled to Timmy and they both dropped back to the ground to begin their trek back to the cave.

The game trail led in the general direction they needed to go, so they followed it for a while. It was fully dusk when they spotted their fruit tree up ahead. They had hunted in a wide circle that had led them back to the place where they had started. Beneath the fruit tree were two deer. Timmy spotted them first and pointed silently.

Once again, they were too far away for a toss and there was no cover to speak of. While they were kneeling and watching, there came that now familiar sound from the direction of the jungle below them and up ahead. It was the coughing sound of a jaguar. They had heard that sound twice before. It was safe to assume that the cat had a lair in the jungle somewhere below their cave. It was dusk now, hunting time for the big cat, and he was starting to stir.

The two deer heard the same sound they did. Their heads came up immediately. Nervously, they moved away from the tree. As fate would have it, the deer started moving in the direction of the two hunters and the trail they were on.

Quietly, Terrance motioned Timmy off to the side. They concealed themselves behind a large, leafy bush. They could see the trail right in front them, but could not see enough of it to tell if the deer were still on it. They waited, both of them afraid to breathe. A few moments seemed like an hour. Still there was no sound. If the deer were coming, they were being quiet about it and were not in much of a hurry.

Long, painful moments passed before suddenly, moving with the silence of a shadow, a nose came into view, followed by a head and a shoulder. Terrance was already standing with his throwing arm poised to cast his spear with all of the muscle he could put behind it. Having thrown javelin in track back in Oakland, he knew the basics. He knew that merely hitting the deer would not guarantee penetration. There had to be muscle and weight and follow through, even at close range.

Just as the animal's front quarter and midsection were becoming fully visible, it turned and looked back over its right shoulder. Terrance saw his opportunity and at that instant threw the spear with everything in him. He aimed for the vital section right behind the front left shoulder. The deer was less than ten feet away and started to react the split second it caught the sight of motion out of the corner of its eye. It was too late. The heavy shaft was well on its way.

The impact of the iron spearhead was devastating. The tip penetrated a foot into the animal's vital area. The deer took one faltering step forward and then sank down dead.

Not knowing from which direction the danger had come, the second deer in a state of panic leaped off the trail and ran directly behind Timmy. The boy wheeled and tossed his spear, but he didn't lead the animal and lacked the strength to penetrate its body with just a sharpened wooden stick. His spear bounced harmlessly off the rear haunch of the deer. With blinding speed the terrified animal disappeared over the rise above them.

"Grab your spear, Timmy," Terrance whispered. "Let's carry this one back to the cave before it gets dark. We will try and leave as little of a blood trail as possible. Oh, and I guess I should say, 'Thank you, Lord, for the provision. Something brought this hapless creature right to us and we appreciate it."

Timmy smiled broadly. "Amen to that," he said.

Terrance pulled the bloody spear out of the deer's body and handed it to Timmy. Then, ignoring the blood that was spilling out, he threw the hundred and twenty pound animal over his shoulder and set off at a brisk pace for the cave.

Chapter Ten

*O*ver the next couple of days, Terrance cut generous pieces from the deer carcass and roasted them over their campfire. He and Timmy ate as much venison as they could hold and then continued to cook and dry as much of the meat as possible – before it could spoil. To their dismay, even though they had used it sparingly, the little salt and pepper shaker ran out two days before the venison did.

Terrance and Timmy had lived in the cave for almost a week now. They were rested and their strength had returned. Terrance's hands had healed completely and he was beginning to feel restless. The boy was surprisingly good company and they were comfortable enough, but it was getting to be time to head back toward the coast.

A couple of days earlier, Timmy had found a long, sliver of stone. With several hours of careful chipping he had succeeded in shaping the piece into a spearhead. Terrance had offered to help, but Timmy had insisted that he do it himself. The new spearhead wasn't iron, but it would work. The first day out with it, Timmy managed to bring down a rabbit. That accomplishment seemed to instill a different kind of strength in the boy. He cleaned the animal and cooked it on his own, happily sharing the meat with Terrance. Afterward he scraped the hide clean and made himself a pouch with a tie at the top.

From then on, the leather pouch always hung from the boy's belt.

Several days had passed with no sight or sound of the jaguar. This didn't mean the big cat was not around, but with each passing day thoughts of it were less and less at the forefront of their minds.

One day, Timmy was kneeling by the upper pool of the spring staring at the pebbles at the bottom, when out of the ground with the gurgling water popped one of those little green rocks. It was as if the ground had belched it out. The little stone dropped down into the pool and nestled in among the other pea sized pieces.

Having seen this particular piece come to the surface, Timmy was intrigued by it. Almost without thinking, he reached down into the shallow pool and retrieved the stone. Turning it over in his hand, he saw that it was a bit larger and shinier than the others. He opened his rabbit skin pouch and dropped it in. Seized by an impulse, he made his way around the pool and picked up several more of the green stones and added them to his bag. As he was picking out the stones he liked, he found one that was much bigger than the others. It was buried deeper in the gravel with only a small portion of it showing. This particular stone was almost as big as a golf ball and would be perfect for throwing. He tossed that one into the bag along with the others.

That night Terrance and Timmy finished off what was left of the venison. They had eaten deer meat and fruit from their tree every day, but the end of both was upon them. Between the two of them and the deer and the monkeys, the fruit tree had been all but picked clean. After dinner, with the fire crackling and a wisp of faint grey smoke curling upward toward the ceiling, Terrance stood to his feet and began to share with the boy what he had been thinking.

"It is time for us to either kill another deer or move on" Terrance said simply. "The dry wood from the deadfall is all but gone and we will have to travel a lot far-ther to get more. The fruit is gone, too. I was thinking, maybe we should think about heading back toward the coast. We can't stay here forever, you know."

Timmy never said anything for a while. Terrance could tell he was thinking. Timmy typically did more thinking than talking, which was one of the things he liked about the boy.

"We can talk about it in the morning, if you like," Terrance said, breaking the silence.

"No, that's okay," Timmy began, "I feel like this cave is our home now and I like it here, but I think it's prob-ably time to leave pretty soon. I think maybe we could stay here forever, but I would kinda like to know what happened to all the people I knew."

Terrance was watching the boy's face. He had obvi-ously been thinking about the subject and was ready to talk.

"Yeah, it would be good to find that out for sure what happened without actually going back there," Terrance replied. "I have to tell you though that I am not entirely sure where we are. I know the coast is back to the east of us, and I remember from the map the way the coast-line curves kind of inward up north, where we are. That means the shortest distance to the ocean is more to the northeast. If we head away from the setting sun and keep slightly to our left, we should miss Jonestown and come out somewhere on the western shores of the Gulf of Mexico. All we have to do is head south from there to find towns.

"And we both have spears now and machetes, so we can live off the land as we go. I think we should say goodbye to the cave in the morning and head out. If we build ourselves fires at night, we should be able to sleep on the ground safely enough. Are you up for that?"

Timmy nodded and held up his stone-tipped spear. Nothing else needed to be said.

Chapter Eleven

*T*he next morning, Terrance and Timmy started out shortly after sunrise. To ensure that they missed Jonestown, they traveled due north for the first half a day before veering back to the east.

As much as possible, they stayed in the higher country where there was less mud, less underbrush, and fewer trees. In this manner they made better time. Eventually, however, the high country played out and they found themselves with no way to go but down into the heavy foliage of the jungle. From then on, the going was slow and tedious. In every direction, there were gullies to cross and streams to ford. Shortly before sunset a dark cloud poured buckets of rain down on them, so they spent their first night away from the cave with their backs against the trunk of a huge uprooted tree with no fire. Try as he might, Terrance was unable to get one lit.

The imagination can go wild in the dark and the sounds of the jungle night provide plenty of fodder for a weary mind, but these were stronger men than had escaped from Jonestown several days earlier, and they were armed. Both of them slept reasonably well that night.

The next day was more of the same unforgiving terrain. Trekking up and down muddy slopes, wading through tangled brush and marshy lowlands, then up and over hill after endless hill. Maybe it was coincidence and maybe this part of the forest was infested with them, but they encountered more snakes than they had seen yet. One rattler coiled up as they approached and let them know he was there. The little red and black banded snakes were everywhere. They had no idea whether these little guys were poisonous or not, but Terrance always stayed in front in hopes that his somewhat worn boots and pants, both snake proof, would provide adequate protection.

Toward midday they were making their way through fairly flat ground and hacking their way through tangled vines and branches when they came upon a decent sized pool of muddy water. The pool was perhaps fifty feet across and was surrounded by twenty feet or so of mud leading up to it, giving the impression that the pond was sometimes a fair amount larger.

Lying in the mud with half of a wild pig still protruding from its mouth was a giant snake. Neither of them knew whether the beast was a python or an anaconda, but it was easily twenty-five feet long and a good eight to ten inches thick. It was in the process of swallowing its prey head first. A large bulge had formed just below the snake's head as the constrictor worked its unhinged jaw to somehow get the pig down its throat.

Terrance and the boy stood and watched the grotesque sight until the pig had magically disappeared out of sight. Then the snake writhed its way into the jungle and disappeared from sight. Apparently it had lay in wait in the muddy water until the pig had come in for a drink and then seized it and squeezed it until it stopped breathing.

The two sojourners circled around the mud hole and continued on their way.

Finally they came upon a stream that was wide enough and shallow enough that they could walk down the middle of it with relative ease. The stones on the creek bed were about the size of softballs and were very slippery, but even at that, the going was easier in the streambed than hacking their way through the dense jungle.

Being out in the open in the middle of a stream reminded Timmy of the attack the jaguar had launched against the giant otter back on the first day of their escape. He told Terrance so. With that thought in mind, they kept their spears ever at the ready and their eyes on the jungle on both sides of the stream. Terrance knew that they were probably no less susceptible to an ambush on dry land, but the memory of that first day was indelibly imprinted on their memories.

They had been following the stream in a winding, northeasterly direction for a good half hour when up in the distance they began to discern the sound of rushing water. After two more turns, the stream widened out at a place where another stream, at least as large as the one they were in, joined with theirs. From that point on, the stream was three times as wide as before. An hour or so later, the stream they were wading dumped into an even larger stream and from there on they had to keep close to the left shoreline to avoid the deeper, faster moving current.

On and on they waded. More and more small streams joined the one they were in. Eventually the wide stream became a full-fledged river. Terrance thought he could hear off in the distance a muffled, roaring sound. As they continued on, the dull roar gradually increased, becoming ever louder and more ominous.

In front of them, the river curved sharply back to the right. On the left shore stood a huge boulder, a large grey rock easily the size of a two-story house. At the base of the rock where the river turned was a small sand bar, shaped like a crescent moon. Over the roar of the rushing water up ahead, Terrance pointed at the beach and he and Timmy headed for it.

Safely ashore, the two weary travelers collapsed on the soft sand and lay there for a few minutes, their faces turned upward toward the early afternoon sun. After a few minutes rest, Terrance took off his boots to let them dry. Timmy sat up and looked out across the river.

"I don't know, Terrance, if that was easier or harder than cutting our way through the jungle. I am tired of walking in the water."

"Yeah, me too, but the good news is, the stream has become a river and that means it goes somewhere and wherever it goes, eventually there will be people."

"Yeah, but it sounds pretty loud up ahead, like one of those waterfalls you see in the movies," Timmy replied.

"It sure does. When we have rested a bit, I will make my way along this side of the shore and see what lies ahead. Whether its rapids or a waterfall, it can't be very far ahead. I can't see the river up ahead, so maybe it drops off right up there."

Terrance hadn't sat still for very long before curiosity got the best of him. He told Timmy to stay put. Leaving his boots and spear there in the sand, he waded back into the water. Keeping close to the edge, he made his way downstream through waist deep water to the place where the water disappeared from sight. How far the river dropped, he couldn't tell. Standing this close, the sound was a deafening roar. Glancing back, he could see Timmy sitting in the sand watching him intently.

Off to his left, the jungle stood back from the river bank a good twenty feet or so and there appeared to be a well worn path that came out of the jungle and down to the edge of the river. The path and the clearing looked to be manmade. This was the first sign of humans they had encountered since they had left Jonestown. Turning, Terrance motioned for Timmy to follow him. At the top of his lungs, he yelled for the boy to stay near the shore and to bring his boots and spear. Not going back for the boy was a mistake.

Timmy waved as if he had heard and understood and then waded out into the water, leaving the boots there in the sand. For the first few yards, all was well. Then Timmy ventured a little too far from the shore. Suddenly, the water was up to the boy's chest and Timmy was having a hard time keeping his footing. Terrance yelled for him to move back closer to the shore. He motioned with his arms, but the boy was struggling to keep his balance and didn't look up.

Twice, Timmy stumbled on the slippery stones and almost fell. But each time, he regained his footing and took a few more steps, moving more cautiously than before. His arms were out to his side as he made every effort to keep his balance. Just as it appeared that he was going to make it, his feet slipped out from under him. His legs did the splits and the swift current caught him. Instantly, his entire body slipped beneath the surface. Terrance's stomach leaped to his throat as he watched the boy tumbling head over heels through the water. There was no chance Timmy would regain his feet on his own and neither of them knew how far the water behind Terrance dropped or what lay at the bottom. Judging by the roar, it could be a monstrous fall.

The swift current was carrying Timmy at an angle away from the shore, leaving little time for Terrance to wade further out in the stream where he could try to cut the boy off before he was swept past him. He knew if he failed to reach Timmy in time, there was nothing between the boy and the place where the torrent of water disappeared over the edge.

Then, just for a moment, Timmy's head was above water. Terrance saw him gasp for breath and then a half second later he was tumbling through the water again, hopelessly out of control. Then he disappeared completely. Terrance waded deeper into the current in a desperate attempt to cut Timmy off, but there was no sign of him.

Desperately the man scanned the water, searching for anything, a flash of clothing under the water, a flailing arm. The next two seconds lasted forever. Then suddenly there he was. Terrance saw the flash of Timmy's shirt beneath the water a couple of yards farther out, but he was already past the place where Terrance was standing. There was no saving him. There was no way to reach the boy except a desperate plunge that would certainly send them both over the edge and likely to their deaths.

Terrance's heart sunk. He felt a cold wave of fear such as he had never felt before. In his mind he could see Timmy's young body hurdle out over the edge and fall downward through the rushing water, only to dash upon cruel boulders at the base of the falls. Never before had he felt so helpless. The boy had entrusted his life to him and now he would be just as dead as if he had stayed back in Jonestown.

All this went through Terrance's young mind in a split second. Then, without another thought, the twenty-five year old preacher's kid from California threw himself into the deep current and with powerful strokes swam outward and downstream toward the top of the falls. It was a desperate act.

Terrance's long strokes moved him faster through the water than the speed of the current. He could not see Timmy, but he swam in the direction the boy was being carried. He was less than twenty feet from the edge when his right hand hit something in the water. His hand slid along it, unable to find a grip, when as fate would have it, his fingers snagged the place where the rabbit skin pouch was tied to Timmy's belt. He pulled the boy to him. There was no response from Timmy. No grasping. No flailing, just a limp, lifeless body. Terrance pulled the boy close to his chest and the act of doing so turned the man over onto his back. Terrance knew that the end was near and they would both plunge over the edge at any moment. Then there was a heavy thud and everything went black.

Chapter Twelve

When Terrance awoke, he could feel the cool water rushing past him. He could hear the deafening roar of the falls behind him. He had no idea how long he had been out, but he knew it could not have been more than a second or two, because he had not yet plunged over the falls.

As his foggy mind tried to wrap itself around what had happened, he reached out for Timmy. He must have lost his grip and lost the boy. Wherever poor Timmy had gone, he would join him in a moment. Yet he had the strange sense that he wasn't moving, but rather lying on his back on something hard. As his eyes slowly came into focus, he could see blue sky overhead and slowly realized that the river was moving, but he wasn't.

Carefully, he slipped his hands beneath him to see what was holding him up. It felt like a rock. It felt flat and was pitted with tiny holes. The top of the rock was just beneath the surface of the water maybe two or three inches. As he tried to sit up, he felt a weight holding his legs down. Reaching down, his hands came in contact with wet hair and beneath that a wet shirt. Glancing down, he saw the body of little Timmy sprawled across his left thigh, his face just above the water.

Terrance reached for the boy and with even that slight motion he felt his own body slide backward on the slippery surface of the rock. Turning slightly, he saw that his body was lodged, but barely, right at the edge of a monstrous waterfall. Behind him, the river plummeted downward a good two hundred feet, maybe more. Through the mist and spray, it did not appear that there was a deep pool at the bottom of the falls, just huge boulders. Beyond the boulders a good hundred feet or more was a deep pool of pale green water, glistening in the bright sunlight.

It only took Terrance a couple of seconds to take all that in. Then as carefully as he could, he slowly pulled Timmy's limp body further up onto his lap. As he pulled on the boy, he felt his own body slip a little closer to the edge. His heart leaped to his throat. After that he moved with even greater caution. He *had* to see if the boy was still alive. He was afraid to hope, but still he had to know.

To say that Terrance had awakened in a strange and precarious predicament would be the height of understatement. To all appearances, someone standing on the shore would have thought there was a man sitting on the top of the water in the middle of the river at the edge of a two hundred foot waterfall. The submerged rock was not visible from the shoreline. It had only been by the greatest of good fortune or divine providence that he had somehow lodged on the rock, face-up and unconscious, instead of going over the falls.

Terrance pulled Timmy a little closer to him and as he tugged on the boy's belt, he saw Timmy's eyes suddenly pop open. Instantly, the boy began to cough and sputter and then instinctively, as if he was still drowning, he began to crawl farther up onto Terrance and away from the water. With that sudden motion, Terrance felt his own body slide a little more forward on the rock.

"You're alright, Timmy," he yelled over the roar of the falls. "You're alright. Stop moving or we're going to go over the edge."

Timmy could barely hear Terrance's words, but the look in the older man's eyes seemed to penetrate through the boy's fears and a moment later he stopped moving. He clung tightly to Terrance's left arm with both hands and just lay where he was.

"Where are we, Terrance? I'm afraid. I was under the water and I couldn't breathe and now I am here. You look scared, too. Where are we?"

Terrance wracked his brain for a way to explain their predicament without scaring the boy to death. The rock they were on was maybe five feet across and six feet long. It was entirely underwater, but only by a couple of inches. It was flat, but a thin coat of green algae made it slippery. If either of them slipped sideways off the rock, the rushing water on either side would carry them to a certain death two hundred feet below. They were somehow alive, but they were hopelessly marooned.

The current was too swift for them to swim back. The water was too deep for them to wade. Behind them was certain death. The deep pool at the bottom was farther out than a man could leap and they were too high to jump anyway. Landing in water, even deep water, from this height would be fatal. Terrance had lived in the vicinity of the Golden Gate Bridge long enough to know the truth of that.

Terrance swallowed the lump in his own throat and then told his little friend the truth.

"Well, Timmy. I'm afraid we are sitting on a rock in the middle of the river. Behind us is a very large waterfall. I was knocked unconscious when I hit my head on this rock, but it kept us both from going over the falls. Think of it this way: We are alive and we have plenty to drink."

Terrance tried to manage a little laugh, but the effort made the back of his head hurt.

"What are we going to do, Terrance? Are we going to die?"

101

"Well, we should already be dead, but we aren't. We are miraculously stranded at the top of these falls instead of dead at the bottom. But, if we ever needed help, it's now. I don't know what we are going to do to get out of this mess. Why don't you say some of your best prayers, while I try to think?"

Timmy closed his eyes and Terrance saw that the boy's lips began to move.

For half an hour, Terrance sat there in the middle of the river racking his brain. Eventually, he noticed that as he moved his hand along the rock at his side, the green algae wiped away, leaving a less slippery surface. That gave him something to do and gave him a little hope. Gradually, he cleaned the surface on both sides the best he could. After a few minutes he felt he could move his body around without slipping quite as much.

Each motion Terrance made caused Timmy to tighten his grip on his arm, but eventually he was able to sit Timmy up between his legs, facing back upstream. This new position was more comfortable for both of them. With Timmy up higher, Terrance found that he could rotate his own body just a little from right to left without slipping. This allowed him to lean back and look behind him, though he dared not turn much. Behind him was a dizzying sight.

From this new vantage, he could see that below the wide, deep pool at the bottom of the falls were some shallow rapids that went on for maybe two hundred yards or so. From there the river flowed peacefully on its way. Off in the distance a mile or so, it turned to the right and disappeared out of sight only to reappear father out. For as far as he could see, the jungle grew right to the edge of the river on both sides and even overhung it. There was no sign of a town or village.

As Terrance watched, two dark forms moved up through the shallower rapids between the peaceful river and the deep pool near the bottom of the falls. As the creatures headed for the deep water below the falls, Terrance saw that they had long slender bodies. It was hard to judge their length from so high up, but he guessed they were maybe ten to twelve feet long.

Great! Crocodiles or gators or whatever they call them down here. From here on down, the river will probably be full of them. If we get out of this predicament alive, there will be no more wading in the river; that's for sure.

Terrance watched the long, dark forms disappear into the depths of the green pool. He noticed that neither moved exactly like the alligators and crocodiles he had seen on television or in the movies, but he was certain they were too big to be anything else.

Chapter Thirteen

*I*t was still dark when businessman Ryan Ashcroft met his guide at the small wooden dock at the edge of the river. There was no electricity and thus no streetlights in the Annari village. The American had to find his way to the dock with his flashlight, a device he had found indispensible everywhere upriver in Guyana. Below him, the river was dark and the current barely discernible. The guide was already sitting in the boat. He stood up when Ryan approached.

Without speaking, the man motioned Ryan to the seat in the middle. The boat was just larger than a row boat and had a small outboard motor at the back. After sliding his tackle box under the wooden seat and gently laying his $1,200 rod and reel across two of the seats, Ryan settled into his appointed place and folded his arms across his chest.

Even at this early hour, the temperature was in the low seventies. Ryan was wearing a tie dyed tee shirt with all of the colors of the rainbow all jumbled together into some indescribable, psychedelic pattern. Below his waist, his blue and yellow "Tommy Bahama" swim trunks clashed horribly with the shirt, a fact evident even in the predawn darkness. Ever one to keep the customers happy, the guide pointed at the shirt and with a toothy smile gave Ryan a "thumbs up."

"Not much chance this Northerner get lost in jungle," the guide said to himself. *"Not with that shirt."*

In broken but understandable English, the guide introduced himself to his client. "My name is Jonny. Much good fishin' today, Misser Asscraft. Big fish where we go."

Ryan smiled and returned the thumbs up. The guide service had informed him that the boat ride was only about half an hour long and ended at a place where really large Arapaimo were known to lurk. He had paid a sizeable sum to make this trip and his hopes were high. Guyana had a reputation for being home to the largest freshwater fish in the world and he had oft fantasized about landing a world record.

Jonny started the ten-horse Mercury on the first pull and flashed Ryan another one of those toothy smiles. "Jonny be right back."

While the engine sputtered on in the darkness, sounding like it was going to die at any moment, Jonny Tolen stepped back up onto the dock and jogged up the ramp. There was a small hut sitting as close to the bank's edge as a building could sit without falling off. Jonny opened a padlock on the door and entered. A few seconds later, he was back at the boat, carrying a bright red ice cooler.

"Jonny bring lunch and beer for Misser Asscraf," he whispered as he slid the cooler under the seat in the middle of the boat. That was all part of the package Ryan had purchased. An experienced guide, bait, a sack lunch, and a cooler full of beer. The service also included a fishing pole and reel, but the American was an experienced fisherman and preferred his own equipment. He had caught several large marlin off of Cabo San Lucas with this very rod and reel. He had replaced the line just for this trip and had brought along two extra spools just in case. There was no way he was going to entrust his prize catch to untested gear provided by some local guide service.

"Jonny, I thought there would be another person on the boat with us this morning. Has that changed?"

"Misser Tomson no come this day. He come tomorrow. Maybe next day. Just you this day."

With that, Jonny untied the boat from the dock and pushed off. There was enough current for the boat to start drifting slowly downstream, but once Jonny revved the engine a little the boat turned and headed upstream at a slow but steady pace. The smoke from the engine hung just above the surface of the water like a cloud of blue fog. The smoke gradually thinned as the engine warmed, but never disappeared entirely. In three or four minutes, the village disappeared from view behind them and they were alone on the river. Dark foliage overhung the water on both shorelines, but Jonny was careful to navigate the craft near the middle at all times.

"Any crocodiles around here, Jonny?" Ryan whispered just loudly enough to be heard above the putter of the engine.

"Not too many, Misser Asscraf," Jonny lied. "Sometimes though. Not safe swim in some places. My papa killed nineteen foot Black Caiman one time, but that long time ago. Most only twelve or fourteen foot now."

"How about anacondas? I read that they live in these parts."

Jonny smiled. The sun had turned the eastern sky a lighter shade of grey and it was becoming easier to make out shapes. Jonny's toothy grin was easy to see even in the dim light. Every tourist asked about anacondas, so the guide was fully prepared for Ryan's question.

"Anacondas in water. Boas in trees. Bushmaster on ground. Many snakes in Guyana. Anacondas afraid of boat with motor. We probably not see one. Sometime though."

"Do they ever attack boats? I mean little boats like this one."

Ryan was not really afraid of that happening, but he thought it was an interesting question to pose, just for conversation sake.

"Not so many times. Some stories about men alone in canoe in swamp or far away part of river, but not too much. Sometime maybe though. Snakes and crocs not like motor so much. No worry. Keep motor running."

Ryan nodded and smiled a small smile. He had learned enough from marketing his own business to know that customers were only told what they needed to know. No one advertises shark attacks in tourist areas or talks about the number of swimmers taken by salt water crocs. Jonny's remarks about the motor keeping bad boys away made sense though.

As the boat came around a wide curve in the river, Ryan heard a heavy splash near the shore off to the right side of the boat. The splash was followed by another and then another. He glanced up at Jonny, but the guide was staring ahead, watching the water. Whatever the source of the splashes, the guide was ignoring them, at least it appeared that he was.

As the sun turned the morning sky a deep orange and lavender color, Ryan became aware of the roar of rushing water up ahead. The farther upriver they traveled, the more powerful and ominous the sound became. In a couple of minutes more, he could see the white of the falls in the pale morning light. A cloud of mist shrouded the base of the falls, but the fisherman was impressed with the height from which the water dropped.

Jonny turned the bow of the boat towards the right hand shore and when the boat was close enough, he raised the outboard and let the momentum of the boat drive the bow up onto the soft sand. Jonny leaped over the side and into water up to his waist. He retrieved a long rope from under the front seat and proceeded to tie the boat to a sturdy tree farther up on the bank.

"This is as far as boat will go, Misser Asscraf," he shouted upon returning to the boat. "Fast water up ahead and not too much deep for boat. Short walk to big, deep pool. Big Arapaimo there lots of times."

Ryan handed his tackle box to Jonny, but elected to carry his own pole. The guide reached under one of the seats and pulled out a small canvas folding chair and tucked it under his free arm. With the cooler in one hand and the tackle box in the other, Jonny led the way to a path that bypassed the rapids and led to the deep pool beneath the falls. The path led through a short stretch of jungle and it was still almost completely dark there. Fortunately for Jonny's client, the path was wide and well worn.

Five minutes later, they were at the edge of a deep pool just out from the base of the falls. In less than a minute, Ryan Ashcroft's hook was baited and he was making his first cast out into the clear, green water. The fisherman settled back in the folding chair and awaited that much anticipated, powerful tug on his line. Ryan could imagine a twelve foot Arapaima eyeing his bait even now.

Truth be told, the entire setting was almost too sur-real for the man to take in. Here he was, the owner of a moderately successful plumbing company in Gresham, Oregon, sitting at the base of a two hundred foot water-fall in the middle of a tropical rain forest in South America, fishing for the largest fresh water fish in the world. The roar of the water, the beauty of the falls, the clear green water; it was almost too good to be true. Life was good.

Several hours passed and the morning wore on. Twice, the tip of his pole had jerked lightly, but nothing he would call a bite. He had changed from bait to lures and had brought in two bass, maybe a couple of pounds each, but he was not fishing for bass. Two pound fish would barely serve as bait for the prize he was after.

With each fish Ryan would pull in, Jonny would appear, dislodge the hook from the fish's mouth, put the catch in a mesh basket in the shallow water near the shore, and then rebait the hook or change lures as the client requested.

"Maybe Jonny fix Misser Asscraf fishes for dinner or take home to village."

The businessman all but ignored his guide's comments. He had no interest in the little bass he was catching. They were nothing more than a nuisance to him. He waved dismissively and mumbled something about not caring what someone did with the stupid little fish he was catching.

The sun was hot overhead when the American finally decided to take a break. He had fished all day for Marlin in the Gulf of Mexico without a bite. He could be patient, if he had to. Eating might make the wait easier, though.

The cooler contained two ham and goat cheese sandwiches, two oranges, a Snickers Bar and twelve cans of cheap Tecate beer. The beer was surprisingly cold and Ryan downed two with his lunch. Twelve cans were more than he would need, unless of course he didn't land anything worth catching.

"I am not having much luck, Jonny," Ryan told his guide, crumpling the second can with one hand and tossing it back into the cooler. "Have you got any suggestions? Am I doing something wrong?"

"No sir, everything just right. Big fish hard to catch. Jonny's customers catch lots of big fish here. Sometimes though."

"Well, it's a beautiful place to be. If I am not going to catch anything, this is a great place to do it."

Jonny wrinkled his forehead, not sure he understood what his customer was saying.

Overhead, a pair of harpy eagles floated lazily above the river at the top of the falls. They circled out over the pool and then back over the top of the falls again. Suddenly they screamed their piercing scream at something above the falls, then turned sharply and flew out over the jungle and out of sight.

After finishing off the Snickers Bar, Ryan casually took rod and reel in hand and waded out into the shallow water a good twenty feet and cast his line farther out. The heavy lure made a large splash as it hit the water and two seconds later the end of his rod bent downward with a power jerk and he felt the weight of something substantial on the other end. With the instinct of a natural catcher of fish, the man arched his body back and set the heavy hook.

The reel screamed as the line played out at an alarming pace. This was it! He had traveled thousands of miles and spent a small fortune for this moment and the feeling was exhilarating. The fish, which was breaking directly away from him, came to the surface and rolled over. The back third of the fish's body gleamed a bright red in the early afternoon sun. It was an Arapaima alright, and a really big one. The fish appeared to be at least ten or eleven feet long and maybe more.

Subconsciously, Ryan could hear Jonny shouting advice in his ear, but he wasn't listening. His attention was focused entirely on the task at hand. Almost without thinking, he reached down and loosened the drag on the reel some more.

"This could be a long fight, Ashcroft," he whispered to himself out loud. "Let the fish run. Don't let him break the line. Keep it tight. No slack. You've got him!"

The fish was on for a good fifteen or twenty minutes. Ryan felt his quarry swimming away from him at times and then from side to side. It was a powerful creature. Ryan knew the game. He knew how to fight a large fish. He had caught a few pretty impressive sharks that had fought less than the fish he had on the end of his line was fighting right now. He was confident that he was in control and would eventually wear the fish down and drag it up into the shallow water at his feet.

Then suddenly, the tip of the rod relaxed. Ryan assumed the fish was coming back toward him and reeled as fast as he could to take up the slack. Ten seconds later, he saw his lure coming through the water right at him. The fish was gone.

He turned to Jonny, who looked as sad as a hundred dollar a day guide could look.

"Not yer fault, Misser," he said matter of factly. "Big fish get away. Sometime."

In utter disgust, the plumber from Oregon lifted his $1,200 rod and reel above his head and then threw it a good ten feet out into the clear, shallow water. He turned back for the shore, sloshing through the shallow water with no further attempt at stealth.

Jonny started forward to retrieve the gear, but Ryan motioned him away.

"Leave it," was all he said.

Chapter Fourteen

At the top of the falls, Terrance Clark continued to twist his body and arch his back to look around him. He had wracked his brain for every idea possible, but no matter what plan he contrived, he kept coming back to the conclusion that their predicament was entirely hopeless. There was no way off of this rock.

If it rained and the river rose even a little, it was entirely possible that they could be swept over the falls. In the meanwhile, the sun was hot and Timmy's pale skin was beginning to show signs of sunburn.

Looking back over his left shoulder, Terrance could peer down into the deep pool below the falls. It was simply too far out to even consider jumping. While he watched, a long, dark form rose to the surface of the water and rolled over and sank back into the depths. The roll was violent, almost like the creature was in some kind of death throe. As the sunlight hit it, he saw that the back third of the thing's body was a bright red. And then it was gone.

That was a fish! That was one unbelievably huge fish, and in a river no less.

Terrance scanned the wide pool for another sight of the monster. Turning and looking over his right shoulder, he saw two men. They were standing in the water, far below him. He blinked his eyes a couple of times, but they were still there.

"Men! Timmy, there are two men down there at the bottom. They're fishing."

"I can't see them, Terrance. I want to see them. Can they see us?"

"I don't think so. We're too small from this distance," Terrance replied with a hint of desperation in his voice. "I need to stand up, little man. I need to wave my arms."

Terrance tried to move, but with each motion he felt his body slip closer to the edge.

"I can't move. The rock is still too slippery. There's just not enough room for me to turn around. I need to get onto my knees. Then I can stand up."

Below him, he saw one man lift something above his head and throw it out into the water. Then they both turned and walked back towards the shore. Terrance watched until they disappeared beneath the trees. Several times, he turned and looked, hoping the men would reappear. Finally his heart sunk. Below the shallow rapids a small boat came into view. It moved away from the riverbank and then slowly made its way down the peaceful river.

Terrance almost didn't have the heart to tell Timmy that the men were leaving. After a few minutes of silence, the boy finally broached the question.

"Do they see us yet? Are they coming?"

"They left, Timmy. They got in a boat and left."

"They left? I didn't even get to see them." Timmy was silent for a while, and then he said quietly, "Maybe they went for help. I prayed that they would see us."

Terrance sat there in silence. He had never felt so utterly helpless in his life. The sun was hot out here in the open, but nightfall would come soon enough. He could not dare fall asleep. The slightest motion, even turning in his sleep, could cause them to slide off the flat rock and over the falls to their death. His desperate act of launching himself into the swift current had saved Timmy from going over the falls, but it occurred to him that perhaps he had he only prolonged the inevitable.

Chapter Fifteen

*T*here were other boats at the dock when Jonny and Ryan Ashcroft arrived back at the village. Ryan had not spoken the entire way. As soon as the boat was secured, he retrieved his tackle box from under the seat and stepped up onto the dock.

"You did what I paid you to do, Jonny. You guided me to a large fish, the kind I wanted. Here, consider this a tip." With that, Ryan handed Jonny a hundred dollar bill and turned and walked up the ramp without looking back. Ryan Ashcroft was a self-made man. At least that's how he saw himself. He cut himself very little slack in life. He cut his employees none. He had one teenage son still living at home and one who had moved out as soon as he had turned eighteen. The older boy had lived with his dad for eighteen years and yet barely knew him. And what little he knew, he didn't like. The kind of success Ryan Ashcroft had enjoyed was hardly enviable.

Nonetheless, the day had been a highly successful one for one man. A hundred American dollars was a very big tip for a local guide and Jonny couldn't wait to share his good fortune with his wife. There would be a big celebration at his home tonight. But there would be time for that later. It was early afternoon still and there was time to buy a gift for Marietta and each of their five children before returning home. Siesta was probably over by now and business was about to pick up again. He would see to that. A local guide with a hundred U.S. dollars to spend would be a popular man in Annari.

Quite by coincidence, Jonny's good friend, Thomas Kerel, was the first soul he met as he made his way up the dusty street toward the market. His hundred dollar bill was clasped tightly in his right hand. Thomas waved at his friend.

"You back early, Jonny. Catch a big one?"

"Client had big one on and lost it. He give me one hundred dollars for extra."

"One hundred American? You rich man, Jonny Tolen. Today, you rich man," Thomas said, slapping his friend on the shoulder. "Where you fish?"

"Big pool below falls. Fish no break line. Just let go and go away. Then client toss pole in water and walk away."

Thomas's forehead wrinkled and his lips tightened. He knew American fisherman. They did not tend to use cheap equipment. They didn't fly all the way to South America to fish for monster fish with junky rods and reels.

"Did client throw pole in deep water?"

"No, Thomas. Not deep water. Easy to get. Jonny plan to go back later, if still there. Want make sure client not change mind first."

"I think we better go now. I know place to sell. Maybe we split money?"

Jonny thought for a moment. Everyone in Annari knew there was no one better than Thomas Kerel when it came to selling things for top dollar.

Hmmm. . .if Misser Ashcraf come back, I give him rod and reel. Maybe get another tip. If he no come back, we sell.

"Okay, Thomas, we go now. But wait 'til client leave for sure. Then sell."

116

It was mid afternoon when Jonny and Thomas arrived back at the falls. Jonny ran the boat ashore in the same place and the two men raced each other up the trail to the deep pool. Jonny knew exactly where the rod and reel had landed and he ran out into the water with Thomas close behind.

The water was cool and clear and the shiny reel was easy to spot. Jonny retrieved their prize and held it out to his friend. Thomas turned the rod and reel over and looked at it from every angle, like a jeweler would a fine gemstone.

"Very expensive. Worth one year's pay. More even. Maybe not too easy to sell."

Jonny smiled. He knew Thomas well. His friend would find a buyer.

Chapter Sixteen

A nother hour passed at the top of the falls. The sun was a little more than half way between midday and dusk. Terrance had twisted his back around and looked behind him several times, but had seen nothing. As fate would have it, he had missed the arrival of Jonny's boat the second time. He had not seen the two men wade out into the shallows and retrieve the rod and reel.

For no particular reason other than the sudden onset of a cramp in his right shoulder, Terrance lifted his right arm far above his head and stretched it as high as he could. He held it there for a good thirty seconds, stretching his stiff muscles all the way from his shoulder to the tips of his fingers. Then he switched arms and stretched the other one.

We could be here for a long time. Who knows when someone will come back or if they would ever spot us if they did?

Terrance settled down and waited. He could think of absolutely nothing he could do. In his mind, he knew he was as trapped here, even more trapped than he had been when he was locked in that hut back in Jonestown.

Several minutes passed and suddenly Timmy moved. Terrance held the submerged rock with both palms to keep from sliding. The places where he had rubbed off the algae gave him just enough of a rough place to hold on to, but his grip was hardly secure.

"Don't move, Timmy. You can't move," Terrance said in a voice more stern than he intended.

"But I heard something. I heard a voice."

From his sitting position, Terrance was able to see quite a bit more than the boy lying across his lap could see. He turned and looked back down towards the base of the falls. Nothing. He looked back upriver. Nothing.

"I don't hear anything, Timmy. Be still and don't move around so much."

Then Terrance heard a voice. It sounded like a shout, though barely discernible over the roar of the falls behind him. He glanced upriver and then off to the shore. Then he saw them. Two men were standing in the small clearing on the bank at the top of the falls. They were yelling and waving their arms. Their voices were barely audible over the roar of the rushing water.

"There are two men over there on the bank! See them?" he shouted at Timmy. There was no hiding the excitement in his voice.

"I can't see them, Terrance. Do they see us? I want to see them!"

"They see us. They're waving at us."

Jonny stepped into the water and began to wade out. He got almost as far out as Terrance had been standing when he made his wild plunge out into the river to save Timmy. That was as far as the shorter man dared go. The water got deep quickly from that point on and the current much swifter and the little Amerindian dared not take another step. How the man and boy had got to where they were and not gone over the falls was beyond him. From where he stood, it looked like they were sitting in the middle of the river and not sinking. It was the strangest thing he had ever seen.

Jonny waded back to shore. After a quick discussion, the two of them decided that Thomas would stay there and Jonny would take the boat and go for help. They might need a couple of more men and some long rope, more than Jonny had on board his little boat.

Jonny waved at the two men sitting in the middle of the river and tried to signal to them that he was leaving but would come back. Then with break neck speed, he all but ran down the steep winding trail that ran along-side the falls and back to his boat. In less than half and hour he was back at the village gathering several long pieces of strong rope and recruiting the help they would need to execute their plan.

Jonny's story spread quickly through the little town and when he headed back up river ten minutes later, he was followed by two other boats and four strong men.

It seemed like forever before Jonny and the men he had recruited appeared on the riverbank at the top of the falls. In the interim, Terrance had often splashed cool water on Timmy's sunburned face and shielded him the best he could with his hands. Timmy's face was clearly showing the effects of prolonged exposure to the equatorial sun.

Terrance could see the men on the shore. They were talking excitedly and pointing at Terrance and Timmy and then pointing back upstream. After what appeared to be a heated discussion they began whatever it was they had planned.

Three of the men waded out into the shallower water upstream a good two hundred feet from where the river cascaded over the edge. They carried a long piece of rope with a loop tied in the end. They had tied another smaller loop in the same rope but about fifty feet up from the end of the rope. A second rope was tied to the smaller loop. That rope led back to the shore closer to the falls, where three other men held the end of it.

Upstream, where the river was shallower, the three men waded as far out into the stream as they dared. One of them carried a long tree branch. When they were roughly aligned with the rock where Terrance and Timmy were sitting, they began to let out the coils. The looped end of the rope was carried along by the swift water and headed in the direction of Terrance's outstretched hand. In less than half a minute, Terrance watched the end of the rope glide past him and out over the edge of the falls just beyond his reach. The looped end of the rope danced up and down at the top of the falls.

He dared not reach for it. If it was going to float to a place where he could get a hold of it, the men upriver had to get farther out toward the middle, if they dared. They would have to maneuver the rope right into his lap or any effort to grab for it could send them both over the edge. With one hand, Terrance pointed at the end of the rope off to his right and motioned to the men upriver to maneuver the rope more toward the middle of the flow.

The men on the shore closer to the falls let out more slack on their piece of rope to let the longer rope floating down to Terrance from upstream move more freely. It was this second rope that was sinking and pulling the longer rope back toward the shore. Seeing that, one of the men upstream used the long branch he was holding to push the rope farther out toward the middle of the river. It was a simple but ingenious plan.

From where they stood, the man standing up to his chest in the river could not see the far end of the rope, but by following Terrance's gestures he somehow guided the looped end to precisely the right spot.

Terrance could hardly contain his excitement when the small loop, floating like a snake through the water, crossed his right leg. He reached down with his right hand and grabbed it. He held it up near his chest so the men could see that he had it. Carefully, he pulled the slack in the rope through the loop to make a lasso and slid it around Timmy's shoulders. Then he pulled it tight.

"Okay, Timmy. These men are going to pull you to shore and then send the rope back for me."

"No, Terrance. You come, too. Don't stay here. We can go at the same time."

"It's safer if we go separately. Don't worry, little man. I will be right behind you."

Timmy continued to protest, but Terrance motioned for the men to tighten the rope and pull the boy to shore. All six men acting in concert began to pull the two ropes tight. Terrance felt Timmy's weight begin to lift off his left leg. His hand was still on the section of the rope in front of the boy and he gently began to release his grip. In a moment, Timmy would be on his way to safety.

Instinctively, Terrance held on to the rope for as long as possible. Just as he was letting go and Timmy's weight began to shift off of his leg and into the water, Terrance felt his entire body begin to slide sideways off the rock. There was nothing he could do. His legs were caught by the swift current on the right side of the rock. He spun sideways and off into the water. At that moment, three fingers on his left hand caught in the loop where the rope circled Timmy's chest.

Instantly, both he and Timmy were adrift in the swift water. Terrance could feel his feet dangling out into space. The rope seemed to give for a quick moment, as if the men upstream could not hold the weight of both of them. At that moment, Terrance realized he would either have to let go of the rope or both him and the boy would be lost. In his mind, he pictured his body plummeting through space and crashing onto the boulders below. He wondered if it would hurt. He wondered if the boy would be okay and live a good life.

And then, just as he began to let go, the rope tightened and he felt his body being pulled strongly at an angle back through the swift current and toward the riverbank. His head was entirely submerged, but his fingers held tightly to the rope. He held his breath as the powerful current rushed by. A long ten or fifteen seconds later, strong hands were grabbing at him and pulling him and the boy out of the water.

Terrance did not see what happened on the bank when he was spun sideways off of the rock into the water, but the second rope, the one tied to the loop in the long rope, was what saved them. The men upriver were too deep in the water to hold the weight of both Terrance and Timmy. But as soon as they had begun to be dragged downriver, the men on the bank had pulled tight on their end. They were much closer to Terrance and Timmy and had the advantage of standing on dry land. Though it had been a struggle, they had been able to pull their human cargo to the shore and safety.

Timmy and Terrance lay there on the bare earth at the top of the falls. It was strange for dirt to feel so good, so solid, and so safe. They were aware that hands were slapping them about the arms and shoulders. Voices were talking excitedly. It took a moment for it to all come into focus.

The men wanted to know how in the world the two of them had got into such a predicament. They wanted to know how they were able to sit in the middle of the river. The questions overlapped and stumbled over each other and the English of two of the men was entirely too broken to follow.

Terrance found himself hugging total strangers with reckless abandon and saying thank you over and over, meaning every word. A few moments later, the three men who had waded out into the water upriver appeared out of the jungle and the hugs and questions started all over again.

Soon enough, however, the eight of them were making their way down the steep trail and back toward the boats, Terrance in his bare feet. Two of the men had Timmy by the shoulders and were all but carrying him.

Terrance's legs were severely cramped, but he somehow managed to stumble his way down the trail on his own.

At the bottom, down by the deep pool, Jonny explained how he and Thomas Kevel had just been getting ready to leave and head back to the village when he had looked up and seen what looked like a man's arm waving in the air at the top of the falls. The arm had disappeared as quickly as it had appeared. He and Thomas had argued over what he had seen or thought he had seen. Thomas had insisted that there could not be a man's arm in the middle of the river at the top of the falls and that what Jonny had seen was likely a bird or maybe a tree limb going over the falls.

The argument between the two friends had become so heated that eventually they had placed a small wager. Then, as men intent on winning a bet are prone to do, the two of them had hiked all the way up the steep trail to the top of the falls to settle their wager. It had been Jonny's stubbornness, or something, that had led them to find the two strangers stranded in the middle of the river two hundred feet above them.

"I prayed that someone would see us," Timmy kept saying on the way down. "I prayed lots of times."

"The boy prays a lot," Terrance said, looking back at the top of the falls. "Good thing, I guess. We would not have lasted the night up there. You guys saved our lives."

The men laughed and then playfully slapped each other on the back in self congratulations. "This time we catch two fish at one time," one of them said. "One big fish and one little fish."

Timmy insisted on riding in the same boat as Terrance and in no time the three boats were back at the village. One of the boats was swifter and had gone on ahead to announce the news to the village. It made a man important to be the one to deliver big news to the town, so by the time Terrance and Timmy arrived in

Jonny's boat a hundred people were gathered on the shore just above the dock.

As Terrance climbed out of the boat, he looked up into a sea of smiling faces. He politely scanned the crowd, nodding and waving from right to left. Everyone's hair was black. Everyone's eyes were brown. All but one. One face was unlike all the others. The skin was paler with just a hint of freckles about the cheekbones. The hair was a reddish brown color and though he was twenty feet away and couldn't tell for sure, Terrance thought the woman's eyes looked to be a pale green.

For a moment, the hundred smiling waving people didn't exist. The lady with the reddish brown hair and light case of freckles smiled the most perfect, the most radiant smile Terrance had ever seen. He smiled back and then, with a sudden onset of embarrassment, remembered the hundred other people. He turned his attention toward them and smiled and waved dutifully. When he finally looked back to where the beautiful woman with the radiant smile had stood, she was gone. She was gone, and like that, so was the young man's heart.

Chapter Seventeen

*T*errance and Timmy spent the night in the home of the village chief, Leroy Harkin. Actually, the man served as chief, local judge, and mayor of Annari. In any event, he had the biggest house in the village and insisted that the two celebrities spend the night with him and his wife. The accommodations were not up to par with American standards, but they seemed first class to Terrance and Timmy. That night they ate at a real table and sat in real chairs. There was butter and spices on the baked fish and homemade bread with more butter. And at the end of the meal, the chief's wife brought out a tray holding four glass bottles of Coca Cola. The soda was not exactly cold, but it tasted like heaven to the two guests.

"So," the mayor began. "How did you two end up stranded at the top of the falls?" The man's English was excellent. "I usually know when foreigners pass through my village and I don't recall seeing or hearing of you two before. You can't get to the falls without going past my town. Did you go past before daylight?"

Not entirely sure what had transpired since he had last been in civilized company and not entirely sure if taking Timmy with him when he left Jonestown con-stituted some form of kidnapping, Terrance chose his words carefully.

"Well, Timmy and I went on a hike in the forest about ten days ago and got lost. We have been wandering about the jungles ever since. "

The chief's forehead furrowed as he raised his eyebrows. Terrance knew instantly that he had only made the man more curious.

"But where did you start out from? There's nothing out that way that a man could hike from except Jonestown, and that's a long ways from the falls and across some pretty rough country. You know, swamps, snakes, Caimans, and jaguars."

"Well," Terrance began. "We did start out at Jonestown."

Chief Harkin's eyes bore down on Terrance. He waited a bit before speaking, the sign of an experienced politician.

"So you know about Jonestown; you know what happened there?"

"No, can't say that I do. Everything was fine when we left," Terrance hedged a little.

"So you don't know about them killing a United States Congressman and then the whole town committing suicide? Heard all about it on the short wave. Then soldiers came through here four or five days ago with four teenage girls and a boy who had escaped and got lost in the jungle. They barely survived. You boys made it ten days. That's quite a feat, but I suspect you may not be telling me the whole story."

The chief was direct. Terrance glanced over at Timmy. The boy was staring down at his plate. There were tears slowly rolling down his cheek. Due to Harkin's indelicate way of delivering it, the somewhat shocking news about Jonestown had become all too real to the ten-year old in a matter of seconds.

"Well, we left the day the congressman died," Terrance replied. "We heard Jim Jones talking about it over the loudspeaker and decided to take our chances in the jungle. When we left, he was telling all the people that they had the opportunity to control their own destinies and decide how they would go out. I thought I knew what that meant, so I took the boy and made a break for it."

"Ginna, get me the newspaper about the Jonestown massacre," the chief ordered. "I suspect this fellow will want to read the story."

The chief's wife left the table and disappeared into another part of the house.

Terrance reached over and laid his hand on Timmy's arm. Timmy looked up and both eyes were red and bloodshot. Terrance slid his arm around the boy's shoulders and pulled him closer. Timmy's voice was quiet and shaky when he spoke.

"They all killed themselves? They really did it? The little kids, too?" Timmy looked up at the chief. "The babies and little kids too?"

"I'm sorry, son, but yes," Harkin replied, apparently realizing that he may have been a little insensitive with the way he had first spoken of the massacre.

"I have been told that the story has been running nonstop all over the world with wide television coverage. The newspapers have front page, full-color pictures of all of the bodies. It was a mess. We don't get television out here, just short wave radio. But one of the visiting fishermen had a newspaper and he left it with me."

"Ginna, where's that newspaper, woman?" The chief's voice was stern and demanding.

Ginna returned shortly with a copy of a Los Angeles newspaper. She meekly handed it to Terrance. Across the front page was a color photo of the scene around the pavilion back at Jonestown. There were bodies lying everywhere, some in contorted positions. The bright, cheerful colors of the people's clothing belied the deadliness of the awful scene. It was unreal.

The story told how the Peoples Temple, before the migration to Guyana, had played a substantive role in the election of Mayor Moscone back in San Francisco. It told how Jim Jones had been publicly honored by California Governor Jerry Brown and Assemblyman Willie Brown. There was a smaller headline about Senator Walter Mondale and President Jimmy Carter's wife, Rosalynn, being somehow connected to Jones.

A second article told how one of the members of the Peoples Temple, a woman, had been stationed in Guyana's capital city of Georgetown. Apparently, on the same day the people at Jonestown had committed suicide, she had used a knife to kill her three daughters and herself, apparently on instructions received from Jim Jones.

The article went into great detail about the killings at the airstrip where Congressman Ryan and several others, including members of the media, were murdered by Jones's Red Brigade. A short time later, the nine hundred residents of Jonestown had taken their own lives. The story said Congressman Ryan had been shot and killed with a .308 caliber hunting rifle.

According to news reports, a handful of other Jonestown residents had saved themselves by feigning death or escaping into the jungle on the day of the massacre. Terrance and Timmy had not been the only ones to get out alive.

I guess I wasn't crazy to take the boy and leave. Timmy would have been one of those bodies lying there by the Pavilion if he had not come with me that day. . .

Terrance reverently laid the newspaper on the table. It had been several minutes since anyone had spoken.

"We found a cave on our second day," he said. His voice was low. "We made spears and killed a deer. We ate fruit and drank from a spring. We did okay until we tried to hike out and got ourselves stranded at the top of the falls. I don't know how we kept from going over. Your men saved us. We would not have lasted the night."

"Yes, Jonny told me about spotting your arm at the top of the falls and how he and Thomas Kerel made a three chicken bet, a serious wager down here, and Thomas lost. Apparently the two of them got a nice rod and reel out of the deal though."

"Well," the mayor continued, "maybe you can tell us more about your ordeal tomorrow over breakfast. You must both be exhausted and in need of rest."

Without waiting for an answer, the chief pushed himself back from the table. At his signal, Ginna rose and motioned the two guests to follow her. The chief's wife was Creole. She was taller than most of the women in town and not altogether unpleasant to look at. Ginna was not quite as proficient in English as her husband, or at least that's what she wanted people to think. She showed the two guests to their rooms, where she lit kerosene lamps for them and turned back the blankets on their beds.

That night a tropical storm broke. In some places not too far from Annari the powerful storm was a *category three* hurricane with a few spin-off tornadoes. But not at Annari. Still, lightning flashed and thunder shook the house for much of the night. The rain pounded the tin roof above Terrance's bed as if it was trying to break through. The big man tossed and turned throughout the night. His body was longer than the bed and the cramped position made it hard to sleep. Eventually though, he drifted off to the steady rhythm of the rain pounding on the roof.

When Terrance awoke the next morning, he saw old fashioned flowery wallpaper surrounding him and it took a moment to realize where he was. When he rolled over and started to climb out of bed, he found Timmy sound asleep on the floor beside the bed. He hadn't heard the boy come in.

We made it, little man. I don't know how, but we made it. You're safe now.

The scent of frying bacon drifted into the room. Terrance stepped carefully over Timmy's body and tiptoed out of the room, quietly making his way to the kitchen.

"River is up two feet this morning," the chief said loudly, looking up from a cup of something hot and steaming. "Water is thick as pudding. You were right about not making it through the night up there at the top of the falls, not in the storm we had last night. So tell me, how *did* you get stranded there?"

The chief wasted no time picking up where things had left off the night before.

Ginna magically appeared with a steaming cup for Terrance. As he nursed the hot brew, he recounted how he and Timmy had waded down the river for a long time and had lost their footing and were swept toward the drop off and how he was knocked unconscious by the submerged rock right at the top of the falls. He left out the part about plunging into the water and risking his life in a hopeless attempt to save the boy.

"Pretty lucky," the chief said when Terrance was finished. "I don't think anyone knows about that rock. What are the chances of you beaching yourself on it while totally unconscious? One in a million, I'd say. And pure luck. That will be a good story when you get back home."

Terrance was increasingly uncertain about the whole *luck* thing. A lot of things had gone right for him and Timmy, things that could easily gone the other way and probably should have. Mayor Harkin kept on with questions.

"So tell me, Mr. Clark, you seem like a normal fellow. What were you doing at Jonestown? You hardly seem like the type to join a religious cult like that."

"Actually, I am a private investigator, sir. I was hired by clients back in California to find their daughter. Last known word was that she had gone to Jonestown with the Peoples Temple.

"I did some nosing around looking for her, but before I got anywhere, they caught me not drinking the Kool-Aid on one of their 'White Nights,' which were essentially trial runs for their eventual suicide. They locked me up and I was held like a prisoner for a month before escaping with Timmy."

"So what about the boy? Is he yours or just some kid you met there?"

"Timmy is just the kid who brought me my meals for a month. We got to be friends and so when I surmised that they were going to kill themselves and probably kill all the kids as well, I couldn't exactly leave him behind. I wondered for the last ten days that I had possibly made a huge mistake and had risked the boy's life for nothing, but after seeing the newspaper and the photos, I guess I did the right thing. Either way, I just couldn't leave him behind."

"No, I guess you couldn't," Harkin continued. "Still, it's a miracle that you survived for ten days out there unarmed. There are a lot of ways to die in the jungles around here. We lose village people from time to time. They go out to hunt or fish and never come back. The villagers usually mark it up to jaguars or anacondas. Personally, I suspect quicksand or crocodiles. Some of the Black Caiman get up to twenty feet around here.

"Either way, you and the boy look pretty darn good for what you just went through. That speaks well of your survival skills. I suppose you will be wanting to catch a ride back to the coast soon. Do you have money for a boat fare?"

"Well, I do have some. Plus I have a fair amount of expenses due me for my work. But do you mind answering a dumb question? It might even be an inappropriate one."

"Son, I'm the chief and mayor of this place," Harkin replied with a chuckle. "I hear more inappropriate questions than you could count. Fire away."

"Well, yesterday when we arrived at the dock and all of the folks came out to see us. . .Well, there was a lady there with reddish brown hair and freckles. I saw her for a few seconds and then she disappeared. Well, is she. . . I mean, does she live here and is she married or something?"

It was hard to read the fleeting look that crossed the politician's face. He hesitated a while before answering. At the moment Terrance hated that trait.

"I assume you are talking about Rebekah Hamilton," he said quietly. "Red-haired ladies with freckles are a bit rare around here. I didn't know she was in town yesterday, but she is the only one around here who fits your description.

"And to answer your question, which is perhaps a little presumptuous for a guest in my town, the woman's not exactly what one would call available. . ."

Just then, Timmy walked into the room, still rubbing the sleep from his eyes. Both men turned and greeted the boy with cheerful voices, Harkin's being decidedly the louder of the two.

"I guess you kinda liked sleeping in a real bed for a change," Terrance said, motioning the boy to the chair next to him. "Did the thunder and rain keep you awake?"

"I think I was pretty tired," Timmy replied, leaving out the part about sleeping on the floor in Terrance's room.

"I suppose you were," the chief chimed in. "Not many grown men could go through what you did. You'll have a remarkable story to tell when you get back to the states."

Timmy responded with a shy grin as he sat down next to Terrance. Terrance hadn't let on how disappointed he had been with the chief's remarks about the young woman at the dock being taken. After all, he had only seen her face for maybe two or three seconds and then, just like that, she was gone. Terrance knew it had been foolish of him to let his emotions get the best of him, but the smile the girl had flashed at him hadn't seemed like the smile of a *taken* woman. Maybe he had misread what he had seen.

Oh well, better to find out right away rather than get yourself all worked up for nothing, Clark. I never liked red heads anyway. She was something, though. That smile could launch a thousand ships. At least one I know of. . .

"Ginna, how about getting these boys some breakfast?" the chief yelled back toward the kitchen. There was not a shred of politeness in his tone. Before the woman could answer his first question, Harkin shot her another.

"Did you know Rebekah Hamilton was in town yesterday? I never saw her."

The voice came back from the kitchen, accompanied by the clanging of pans. "I needs to go to the marketplace, but I gots you some frying bananas and some bunches of eggs and some bacons, if you mens wants to eats now. No, never saw Miss Hamilton lady come around yesterdays, but some time she come only short while and go. Do eggs and bananas and bacons be enough?"

Eggs are eggs. But fried bananas, or plantains as some call them, may seem like strange fare to the uninitiated, but they are like potatoes in the tropics, only with a slightly sweeter taste.

After seeing everyone nod their heads approvingly, Mayor Harkin placed the order for bacon, eggs and fried bananas. At that, there was more clanging of pans in the kitchen.

"So, have you gentlemen thought more about your plans?" Harkin continued. "It's a long way to the coast from here and the only way is by boat. I could make a shortwave call out for you and let your folks know you are okay, if you have someone you need to reach."

"I haven't got no one, sir," Timmy said. "Everybody I knew was back at Jonestown and they are all dead. Well, except for the Evans and Wilsons, but I don't know where they went."

The chief looked at Terrance questioningly. The American leaned forward and explained.

"Those two families must have known something was about to break, because they packed up and left Jonestown the morning of the massacre. Timmy told me about them. At least some folks got out alive. I believe both families were white."

The mayor nodded. "I heard over the shortwave that there were a few other survivors. Some guy lay in a ditch and played dead. Another guy escaped into the jungle. Then there were those five teenagers I told you about, the ones the soldiers found in the jungle, barely alive.

"Anyway, Mr. Clark, after we eat, we can take a walk into the village. You both could use a new shirt and you look like you could use a pair of shoes, though I doubt you will find any that will fit. The streets will be pretty muddy, which is not unusual here, but the sun will dry them out soon enough. It was a pretty big storm and the town folk need to see that their mayor is looking out for things."

Ginna brought a big platter of undercooked bacon, scrambled eggs, and fried bananas, enough for twice as many people. There was lots of pepper on the eggs, but mixed in with the bananas they were surprisingly tasty.

"I's worry 'bout Miss Hamilton some time," Ginna interjected while Terrance was refilling his plate. He looked up slowly, trying to show only casual interest. "She's go way back in forest some time to place where not safe for womans to go and she too pretty too."

Mayor Harkin shot an annoyed look at his wife, who quickly glanced away.

"Maybe we will ask around when we get to the market," he replied, looking at his wife who still was not looking back. "Rebekah always buys things there for the tribes she visits. If she was going further inland, someone will know about it. Funny, I didn't see her yesterday. Must have been all the excitement. Our guest says he saw her yesterday, at least he saw some red haired lady with freckles," the chief added.

Terrance caught an indiscernible look in the man's eyes at that last remark and it made him uncomfortable.

"That be Miss Hamilton, I sure that," Ginna said matter of factly. The woman was still staring at the wall. "She only one like that. Why Mr. Terrance see her?"

The chief studied Terrance's reddening face for a while before answering his wife. Harkin was continuing his annoying habit of pausing too long before speaking, especially when addressing sensitive subjects.

"Terrance doesn't know Mrs. Hamilton, Ginna. He just saw her for a moment yesterday." There was a touch of sarcasm in the man's voice. Terrance was beginning to not like the man.

It was Ginna's turn to stare at Terrance's red face.

"Oh, I sees now," the woman said with a knowing look, the kind older women get when they think they understand perfectly what is not being said.

Poor Timmy was totally lost. "Who is Miss Hamilton?" was all he could get out before the mayor jumped to his feet and announced that it was time for them to see how the village looked after the storm. No one answered Timmy's question.

The streets of the village were indeed muddy. It was a red mud, the sticky kind. The town had been built on flat land at the edge of the river and the soil there didn't drain well. Steam was rising from the mud and already the carts had made narrow ruts. Most of those were full of standing water. There were broken off branches and heavy tree limbs lying everywhere, providing ample evidence of the fierceness of last night's storm.

"What a mess," the chief said under his breath. "I just get the roads leveled off and then another storm comes and leaves more ruts. Not good for business."

"So chief, what's your line of work? There can't be much money in being mayor of a small town," Terrance observed.

"Well, I own the land where the market sits. The vendors pay me a share of their revenue as rent. I only take a small share, so no one will start another market somewhere down the street. I mostly get paid in fruits and vegetables and some meat. Not a lot of money changes hands here, except what comes in from the fishing guides and their clients. And we get some tourist trade from folks coming to see the falls. We're the last stop on the river."

"How is it you speak such good English this far back from the coast?"

The mayor chuckled. "I speak English. I speak some Creole. Ginna made me learn some of that. I speak pretty good Spanish, too. And some of the native dialects. Enough to get by. Learned the English at a Catholic mission. Went to school there and the nuns drilled us pretty good. I mean pretty *well*," he added, correcting his own grammar.

As they approached the market area, one of the shops was just rolling up the woven grass curtain that served as the shop's front window. Inside the booth, a teenage boy was draping a large, yellow and black spotted skin across a pole for display. It was clearly a jaguar hide, a large one at that.

Terrance pointed at the skin. "That for sale?" he asked his host.

"That hide has been for sale for over a year now. No one around here has the money to buy it, except fisherman from the States, and it's illegal to bring spotted or striped cat hides into your country. The shopkeeper, Perto, doesn't really expect to sell it. He just likes to tell visitors the story of how he killed it. The story gets more grandiose with the passing of time."

"How *did* he kill it?" Timmy interjected with obvious interest. "They seem pretty scary. We saw two of them in the jungle and they were pretty close to us and I have never been so scared in my life, 'cept sitting in the middle of the river at the top of the waterfall. That was scarier than anything. Where I was, I couldn't see down, or I probably would've died of being scared. When we got down to the bottom and I could see back up there to the top, it was a good thing I never knew how high we were when I was up there."

That was the most Timmy had said since they were rescued. He had endured quite a bit and it was to be expected that he would be a bit traumatized by it all.

"Well, lad, I could tell you the story of Perto's jaguar, or at least the latest version of it, but Perto would be upset with me for stealing his glory, so let's ask him."

Harkin hailed the middle aged man who was the apparent owner of both the shop and the jaguar skin. The man was short and not too stocky. At maybe five foot four inches, the shopkeeper looked rather unassuming for a slayer of jaguars.

"Perto, the boy here was admiring your jaguar and wants to know how you killed it. He says he saw two jaguars this past week up above the falls, but didn't have time to toss his spear before they got away. He was pretty upset about missing two great opportunities. He was looking for one he could have stuffed."

Perto looked a little put off by the chief's nonchalant remarks about such a sacred subject. He bit down on his lower lip as he looked the boy up and down a couple of times. Then he laughed. He had seen the two Americans at the dock the day before and had heard bits and pieces of their story.

"No, he really did," the mayor repeated. "He saw two jags up top and all he had was a spear and a machete. He's really upset because they got away."

The chief gently held Timmy's shoulder as if to motion him to silence.

"I think maybe next time boy try gun. Only a little bit safer though," Perto replied half smiling. Terrance was watching the man closely. Immediately, he liked the little shopkeeper. The man had good eyes.

"Okay, I tell Americans jaguar story, but only real story. No added parts. Here, come sit down in shade by tree."

Perto said a few words in Creole to his son and made a few gestures, apparently instructing the lad to continue setting up the booth for the day's business. He motioned to Mayor Harkin and the two Americans to follow him to the shade of a nearby tree where several sturdy chunks of wood were standing on end to serve as seats.

When everyone was seated, Perto began. His English was broken, but better than most of the locals, as is often the case with shopkeepers.

"Downstream from village, another river joins this river. It also good for boat and go long way back. There is villages back there, but small ones. Much jungle. Much animals. Crocodiles and big snakes. Last village on river is where Perto find wife twenty years past. She expensive but worth it.

"Perto take wife back to her village one years past. See mother and father and sisters and one brother. Perto have good boat and make ride only one days. Perto take gun to be sure. Always take gun.

"Village not happy place when Perto get there. Many goats no longer there. Big jaguar tracks in mud. One boy have big scratches. He try drive off jaguar with spear when it take goat he sposed to be watching. Scratches deep and boy get sick. Boy would die but pretty mis-

139

sionary lady with red hair come with medicine and fix and boy get better. Big scar still."

At mention of the pretty red haired missionary, Terrance caught himself involuntarily leaning forward and listening more intently. A vision of a perfect face and radiant smile framed by dark reddish brown hair flashed before his mind's eye.

No one seemed to notice Terrance's increased interest in the story and Perto continued talking.

"Some peoples say jaguar not attack people. People in city say this though, not people in far village. Not easy prove this thing, but some people from village sometime disappear. Womens or childs, but sometime men too. No one know why peoples disappear but jaguar tracks found at place sometime.

"One men say jaguar jump off bank of river when he ride by in boat with paddles. He get away but stay in middle of river now.

"When Perto talk to wife's father, he show Perto boy with scars and tell where he attack by jaguar. Close to village. People there scared. Goats sometime stoled from pen by house. Wife's father and Perto go hunt for jaguar next day. Jungle real thick. Not see anything but track by water. Big track, but too olds.

"Next day, Perto take little goat and tie in clear place in jungle near village. Perto climb tree and sit. Wife's father climb tree other side clear place and sit. Close to dark, goat make much noise then lay down and sleep. Then little goat jump up and make much more noise and look ascared of something on one side. Perto look hard but not see nothing. Get gun ready in case though.

"Suddenly, Perto hear gun shoot by other tree. Big jaguar run into clear place. Cross one side clear place only. Gone before Perto shoot. Jaguar run funny. Maybe hit in leg. Perto climb down and run to other tree. Wife's father climbing down. Say he shoot dead jaguar. Perto say no, he see jaguar run away. He say no. He kill. Sure nuff, there jaguar on ground by tree. Dead. Not big like jaguar Perto see run.

"Perto look back where he see big jaguar run away. Perto see goat not there this time, but blood on ground where goat tied. Real fast, Perto and wife's father follow blood of goat to jungle but very dark soon. Go back to tree and get little jaguar and go back to village. People happy there until wife's father tell story. Big jaguar still alive and take goat. He only kills womans jaguar.

"Next morning, we go back to clear place and try follow jaguar. Some more men come too. Look hard but find feet of goat and head but no more. This night, wife's father and Perto tie up one more goat. All white goat, not too big. This goat make much noise all the time but no jaguar come. Stay 'til all the way dark. Climb down tree. Wife's father climb down tree. Untie goat and start back to village in dark. Goat follow close on short rope, maybe eight foots long.

"We walking on trail to village and then hear loud sound behind like bone break. Rope jerk in Perto's hand. Look back and jaguar bite head of goat much hard. Break everything quick. Jaguar turn to run away with goat. Perto hang on to rope and drag on ground. Jaguar turn around and growl at Perto. Jaguar drop goat and take step toward Perto laying on ground, rope in this hand and gun still in this hand."

The little shopkeeper was obviously at the most exciting part of his story. He was standing now. He held out his right hand like he had a rifle in it and his left hand with fist clenched, like he was holding on to a rope.

"Perto scared a little," he continued. "Just then, wife's father shoot at jaguar but too dark. He hit dead goat. See hole in goat later. Perto let go of rope and shoot fast very close. Bullet hit jaguar in face. When nothing moves, Perto see jaguar face this close to Perto's face."

Perto held out his hands about three to four feet apart.

"So, Perto kill jaguar and save village," he said triumphantly. On his face was a look that said he was partly jesting and partly serious.

Terrance stood up from his stump of a stool and extended his hand to the shopkeeper.

"That's quite a story, sir, and I am glad you shared it with us. But I have one question. You said when you first saw the jaguar on that first night, it was running funny, like it had been shot in one leg. But your wife's father didn't hit the jaguar you saw. His shot killed the smaller, female jaguar. Did he shoot two times?"

"No, wife's father shoots one time only this night and one times only when he shoot dead goat. When Perto skin big jaguar, he find one leg sick. Big sore and white sickness come out. Jaguar cannot use this leg much. That why jaguar running wrong."

"That makes perfect sense," Terrance replied. "A man who hunted man-eating tigers and leopards in India, often found that the cats he killed had turned man-eaters because they were injured or old and could no longer hunt their normal prey. Often it was a porcupine quill that had gotten lodged in a front paw or leg and become infected, or *sick* as you say."

"That would explain why Perto's jaguar had lost much of its fear of man," Harkin chimed in. "It was desperate to eat and the village goats were easy prey. Jaguars are usually quite reclusive. But if one were hungry enough, I would not bet on what it wouldn't kill and eat."

Finally, Timmy spoke up. He had been spellbound by the shopkeeper's story.

"That's the best story I ever heard, sir," he said, his voice just above a whisper. "Were you afraid? That jaguar could have killed you."

"Yes," Perto replied. "Perto afraid a little bit. More afraid later. It lots dark, but Perto see jaguar teeth and yellow eyes when he shoot. *El tigre* not like Perto. Perto happy he not miss this time. Goat shot 'nuff already."

The little shopkeeper laughed heartily at his own joke.

"You said one other thing that puzzled me. You said the pretty missionary lady with red hair came to the village to help the boy who was scratched by the jaguar. Is she a doctor?"

"No, she not doctor. Husband doctor, but she know how to fix too. He not come no more cause he dead now. Dead then, too."

Terrance looked over at Mayor Harkin. Something was not quite clicking. Harkin fidgeted a bit on his seat.

"Well," Harkin began lamely. "Rebekah's husband *is* deceased. He contracted malaria and was too deep in the forest where there was no medication to save him. Took a long time dying, I heard. He was always somewhere in the most remote regions, preaching religion and doctoring the native folk. Sometimes, he took Rebekah along and sometimes she stayed in one of the less remote villages. Sometimes he would be gone for weeks with no word. It was a hard life for her.

"Anyway, the poor woman was pretty broken up by the news that John had died. He had been dead for over a week before she finally got the news. She hired a boat and retrieved his body and returned to the states to bury him. Somewhere in Indiana, I think. She was gone for several months and then suddenly she returned and even though she is not a doctor, she more or less took up where John left off. But like her husband, she takes too many chances and goes places that are not safe."

"I don't mean to be rude, sir," Terrance said a bit briskly, "but you left me with the impression that she was not available. Why did you say that?"

The mayor shifted his weight, he eyes looking downward. For a moment the man had lost some of his brashness.

"Well, it's my brother. My younger brother has been in love for the woman for a long time, even back when her husband was still alive. They have even had dinner together recently, so I don't think she is really available. I think they like each other."

"But they're not married or engaged?" Terrance asked a little more sharply than he intended.

"No, not exactly. But my brother says they will be." The mayor was back on his game now. His eyes were meeting the younger man's now and not flinching.

Then just like that, Leroy Harkin stood and indicated that he needed to be about the town's business and that he would leave the Americans to explore the village at their leisure. Terrance thanked the man for his generous hospitality. As soon as the mayor had left, Terrance sat back down and let the emotions that had been coursing through him settle a bit.

He had just accepted the fact that the beautiful face that had captured his heart and imagination a day earlier was beyond him. He had done the right thing in his mind and heart. He had refused to even so much as dream about a woman who was the wife of another man. Then suddenly he had learned that the woman was by some tragic turn of fate, now alone in this remote land. And. . . she was free. Terrance's young head was spinning with thoughts he wasn't at all prepared to deal with.

Who is this brother the mayor spoke of? Did the woman love him back? Was he a welcome suitor? Was the glorious smile she had given him yesterday the smile of a woman whose heart was taken?

For the moment, Terrance had forgotten Timmy and the shopkeeper. When finally he looked up, he saw that the little man was sitting there quietly studying him.

"You have love thoughts about pretty missionary woman, no? Do you know her? No, I think you could not. You only come to Annari yesterday. Mayor hope brother get her, but chief's brother not good man and she is much good women. She in trouble now."

Chapter Eighteen

*T*errance stood up walked over and stood in front of the man.

"What do you mean, man? What kind of trouble? Do you know where she is?"

"Perto not know where Miss Hamilton is this day. But day before, she goed with chief's brother up other river very far to little villages. She take medicine and vitamin to people she preach to sometime. Chief's brother, Gorton Harkin, have only boat Miss Hamilton can pay to take her that day. They leave after when you come. Then big storm come.

"When big storm come, big tree sometime fall cross little river and hard get past. Maybe Miss Hamilton get up river long ways not get back long time. Not good she be alone with man Gorton Harkin many nights. One thing chief not say. People in village not know too. Gorton Harkin come here after he 'cused of hurting two womens in Georgetown. Maybe he did or not, but Perto think Gorton not safe man womans be with."

Terrance could feel his face flush. He didn't know this Gorton fellow, but he didn't like him. When the next words came out of his mouth, he was surprised by the emotion in his voice, emotions he was unable to disguise.

"I want to hire a boat, Perto. I must go after her. Can you help me?"

Perto was a little startled by the emotion in the American's voice. He stared at the man towering over him, deciding how to respond.

"I mean, right now," Terrance continued. "You said you had a boat. Can I rent it? I have gold."

Timmy looked at Terrance in surprise. Terrance had all but forgotten about the coins and had not even dreamed of their worth. He couldn't even guess what five hundred year old coins made of Spanish or Mayan gold might be worth. The gold in each coin should be worth maybe two hundred dollars per ounce, plus any antique or collectible value. The collectible value could be many times the market value of the gold itself.

Cost, at the moment, was the last thing on Terrance's mind. The woman he sought might not give him the time of day once he found her. He knew that. After all, all she had done was cast him one momentary smile. But her response to him was a bridge he would cross when he found her, but find her he must, especially if she was in trouble.

Terrance reached into his pant pocket and drew out one of the coins from the cave. He wiped it a little cleaner and handed it over to Perto. "This should be enough," he said.

Perto's eyes lit up at the sight of the coin. He examined the piece carefully, turning it over and over in his hand. In his heart he was an honest man. Still, the sight of a real gold coin made his heart pound just a little faster.

"I think this much more than 'nuff moneys. Need boat and supplies and ropes and saw for trees cross river. Perto take you hisself. Son run shop. Maybe this boy who hunt jaguar with spear stay at Perto's house," the shopkeeper said, nodding in Timmy's direction.

146

"No. I want to stay with you, Terrance," Timmy insisted. "I don't want to stay in this place where I don't know no one."

Timmy had a point, but the truth was, he would be a lot safer her in Annari with Perto's family than he would be traipsing back into the wilds with Terrance where who knows what could happen.

"Timmy, you have been a trooper. You have been as good a companion as any man, better than most. But you have been through quite an ordeal and I would never forgive myself if I dragged you back into the jungle again and something happened. You stay here 'til I return, and then we will go the states together and figure out where we both belong."

Timmy protested more, but an hour later, he was at the kitchen table of Perto the shopkeeper and being fed cured ham and fruit salad with sweetened goat's milk. Perto's not so slender but ever cheerful wife, Marza, was fawning over the boy like a long lost son – notwithstanding the fact that she had five of her own.

Meanwhile, Terrance and Perto were down at the dock loading the last of their supplies onto Perto's boat. They had rations for five days, two thin sleeping bags and tarps for the rain. Piled in the front of the boat were ropes, a small chain saw, and two extra cans of fuel. Laying across the center seat were two lever action rifles and two boxes of shells.

Terrance took a seat between the two rifles. Before they pushed away from the dock, Perto reached inside his shirt and brought out a bag and tossed it to his new friend. Inside was an extra large size brown tee shirt and a large pair of handmade leather moccasins.

Terrance held the mocassins up to his feet. The fit looked close enough and the soft leather felt good in his hands. He gave Perto a thumb up.

"You need shoe. These better than no shoe," the shopkeeper said smiling.

Terrance laughed at the little man's remark. A moment later though, his feet were covered and he was sporting a clean new shirt.

"I'm here one day and already you are turning me into a native," he said holding his feet up for Perto to see. The shirt and moccasins were a thoughtful gift. There was no way around that.

There was no one at the dock to see them off as Perto pointed his little boat downstream. Terrance had no idea where they were or where they were going, but he had a strong sense that he could trust the man at the helm of the craft. There was something about this *not so tall* shopkeeper, a man who had shot a jaguar in the face at a distance of one pace, that made Terrance Clark trust him. That was enough for now.

As soon as they were out of sight of the village, Terrance picked up one of the rifles and examined it.

"If you don't mind, Perto, I will load the guns, but leave the chambers empty."

Without waiting for an answer, Terrance started opening one of the boxes of shells. The rifle was a Marlin thirty-thirty saddle gun. The other was the same caliber, but a Winchester.

"I was in the jungle for ten days armed with nothing but a homemade spear and a machete. Now that there's a gun around, I would like to know that mine is loaded. Makes me feel better."

Perto nodded. The shopkeeper was standing at the rear of the boat, steering the craft by turning the small outboard motor from side to side. When the two rifles were loaded, Terrance leaned them against the pile of ropes in the front of the boat with the barrels pointed up and forward. He was tempted to fire off a couple of rounds to get a sense for how the weapons were sighted, but he decided against it for the moment. Maybe there would be time for that later.

Terrance shifted his long legs over the seat to the other side so he could face the front. He had little interest in seeing where they had been. Looking about, the first thought that crossed his mind was how wild and untamed the landscape was. They were only a few minutes from Annari, but they could just as well have been a hundred miles from civilization of any kind. The jungle was lush and stretched out over the water on both sides, as if each branch and leaf was fighting for every ray of sunlight it could steal from its neighbor. Here and there along the shore were brief patches of grass or mud. Invariably each was home to a handful of dark colored crocodiles of some kind.

"Dangerous?" Terrance asked, pointed at a half dozen Caimans sliding off the bank and into the water as the boat neared where they lay.

Perto smiled grimly and nodded in the affirmative. "You not want to fall in river here. Crocs rush to water 'cause many mens shoot guns at them other days, but they also rush to water in hope they get chance to eat you."

"Do they come upriver to where the village is?"

"Somctime they do, but village people shoot at them when they come, so they not come too much. Other time many people lose goats when they come to river to drink. This bad place here. Water is very slow this spot. Crocs like slow water.

"Where we go, water is slow but not so many crocs. Some though. Some big anacondas. Some snake very longer than boat, but afraid of motor. Not too dangerous for big man, but small womens and child not safe sometimes by water."

Terrance kept his thoughts to himself, but he had to admire this man who was his guide. Perto lived in a land full of poisonous snakes and spiders, huge crocodiles and anacondas, and jaguars, but the little man seemed to have no fear of them, only respect for what they could do to a careless or unfortunate human.

In a sense, Perto was like men everywhere. The dangers they face every day seem common to them and do not frighten them like they do visitors from other places. Surfers in Hawaii give little thought to the sharks swimming in the surf with them every day, yet tourists who visit the Islands are often afraid to wade in water up to their waist, lest they be devoured alive. People who grow up in "tornado alley" in the Midwest are nonchalant about the devastating tornadoes that come with great frequency to their world and only worry about one when it is actually on the horizon or closing in. Sometimes, however, those same people are afraid to live in Washington or Oregon because there are dormant volcanoes there, mountains there that could "blow at any minute."

Terrance remembered visiting relatives in Iowa when he was a kid. His cousins took him catfish fishing at a shallow lake that was literally teeming with water moccasins, a seriously poisonous snake. His cousins would go running through the tall grass beside the lake as if it were nothing, ignoring the snakes that were most certainly present. Terrance on the other hand, avoided the tall grass whenever possible. When he had no choice but to venture into the weeds, he moved slowly and beat the grass with a long stick before taking each step.

The American was brought back from his thoughts by the sound of the engine slowing and the sense that the boat was losing speed. He glanced up and saw that a large tree had fallen across into the river, probably during the storm. The river was narrow in this spot and the tree's trunk was long enough to reach almost to the other side.

Perto maneuvered the boat over to the far side of the river where there was room for them to bypass the tree, but only by passing under the canopy of branches that stretched out over the water a good twenty feet or more.

"Keep low," Mr. Terrance. Sometimes spiders and small snakes in branches above water. Try not to touch branches."

Terrance ducked as low as he could, but Perto could not get quite low enough and still keep a handle on the outboard and steer their way through. They had almost made their way around the far end of the tree when one large overhanging branch caught Perto by the shoulder as he brushed under it. The resistance of the branch and momentum of the boat jerked the little man's shoulder backward and caused his hand to twist downward on the throttle and rev the engine.

The boat shot forward and headed deeper into the branches overhanging the water. At that moment, Terrance caught sight of the largest bees' nest he had ever seen. Its shiny grey form, fully the size of a large beach ball, was hanging from one of the lower branches barely above the water. There was no way they would miss it. The front of the boat caught the branch the nest was hanging from, and gave it a sharp jolt. When the branch broke free of the bow, the nest snapped loose and fell onto the pile of rope in the front of the boat. From there it rolled down the pile and between the two rifles to come to rest at Terrance's feet.

It all happened so fast that there was no time to think. Instinctively, Terrance leaned to his right to roll over the edge of the boat and into the dark, crocodile infested water. He shouted for Perto to do the same. A thousand angry bees in close quarters were every bit as dangerous as a crocodile in the water, if not more so.

Terrance's hands were on the rail of the boat as his legs coiled to push off and launch his long body into the water. His eyes were fixed on the terrible shape just in front of him. Thin layers of a gray paper-like substance had broken off as the nest had rolled down the coils of rope. The pieces were settling slowly to the deck at his feet. The big man hesitated for an instant before rolling into the water, his eyes still fixed on the dark hole at the bottom of the ball. He knew what to expect. He could see it in his mind, but oddly nothing happened. Nothing came out of the nest. There was no loud buzz of angry insects. No cloud of tiny bombers rushing out to punish whatever intruder had dared disturb their home. Except for the sound of the little outboard, there was only quiet.

Terrance felt the weight of Perto leaning over his left shoulder.

"Nest empty. Good for us," was all he said.

Carefully, Terrance picked up the nest and gently laid it in the water at the side of the boat. The nest was still floating there beneath the branches as Perto maneuvered the boat back toward the center or the river.

"That was pretty scary. While I was worrying about crocodiles and jaguars, I could have been stung to death by bees. What a place!"

Perto smiled sheepishly. "Sorry. Lots of ways to die in jungle," he said simply.

They had only ridden another hour or so downriver when another large river came in from the left and joined the one they were on. Where the two rivers met, the current was rough. Perto swung his little boat in a wide arc so as to enter the new river head on, rather than at an angle. The boat bumped its way through the rough ripples for a half a minute and then the water was smooth again.

"This river go long way back. Not so big sometime. Wind around much. Split many times. Easy get lost. Perto think he know where Miss Hamilton go to help peoples. We look first at Napoteri village. We stop first though. Not safe to drive boat in dark. Bilokut village not too far up river. Good peoples there. We spends night there first."

There was still a good hour of daylight when they rounded a curve in the river and saw spread out on the right side of the river a good size village, bigger than Annari. Men were out in the river casting nets over the sides of their boats. Women were washing clothes in shallow water at the river's edge. The shallow place was blocked off from the rest of the river by a wooden fence that stretched out into the water ten or fifteen feet.

Terrance pointed at the fence.

"Croc fence. Safer this way. Let water in. Keep crocodile out."

"I thought so," Terrance replied. The he said what was more on his mind.

"Maybe it is too soon to stop, Perto. Maybe we should go farther upriver while there is still good light." Visions of the pretty red haired missionary lady off alone somewhere in this primitive land with a villain named Gorton Harkin had been haunting Terrance's thoughts all afternoon. He very much wanted to press on and use every minute of daylight.

"Perto understand. But there no good place camp for long ways now. And people in village here might have news about Miss Hamilton. Perto know good peoples here."

Perto seemed to have his mind made up, so Terrance shrugged his shoulders in acquiescence.

"I'm sure you're right. Let us stop here and see what we can learn. We can rest and start out early in the morning. Hopefully, someone here will know exactly where they went."

Perto guided the boat towards one of the smaller, but somewhat rickety docks. Near its outermost end, a young boy was kneeling on his knees holding a little homemade fishing pole in his hand. As Perto's boat approached, the boy pulled in his line and lay the pole down on the wood deck. Then, as if it was his duty, he took the rope Terrance had tossed up on the deck and tied it tight to one of the sturdier posts.

Perto greeted the boy in Creole. His Creole sounded much smoother than his English. The boy smiled a broad smile and ran up the ramp towards the village as if he were on a mission.

"They know already we was coming," Perto remarked with a shy smile. "Before we leave, Perto radio ahead. No more radio now after Bilokut. Last one."

Chapter Nineteen

*T*hat night, Terrance and Perto dined with Samuel Torsono, the mayor of the Bilokut village. Torsono was a short, stocky Amerindian with heavy thighs and powerful looking arms. He looked to be in his fifties. Mayor Torsono had news that Perto had not learned when he called ahead on the shortwave back in Annari.

The mayor informed his two guests that Miss Hamilton and Leroy Harkin's brother had indeed stopped in Bilokut the day before. They had only stayed for a short time and had left early that same afternoon – hours before the storm struck. Apparently, Gorton Harkin had wished to spend the night at Bilokut before heading upriver, but at Miss Hamilton's insistence they had continued on.

Terrance listened intently as Torsono repeated as much of their plans as Miss Hamilton had shared with the local villagers during her brief stop. She was going to Napoteri and Arakaba with antibiotics. Both villages had come down with some sickness and half the villagers were seriously ill.

"I know about this," Samuel Torsono explained. "We hear from fishermen from these two villages. They come here three days past and use radio to reach Miss Hamilton. No radio in any village upriver. No radio and no generator."

Mayor Torsono said he had no idea which of the villages the missionary would have gone to first. That was a problem because the river forked a few miles above Bilokut and Napoteri and Arakaba were on opposite forks.

That night, Terrance spent the first part of the night tossing and turning. The bed was too short and the old springs creaked loudly every time he turned over. Eventually, he retired to the wood plank floor with just his pillow. It was only then that he slept.

Terrance was awakened before daybreak to the sound of someone preparing breakfast. He dressed quickly and went to the kitchen where he found Perto and Samuel already sitting at the kitchen table sipping some sort of hot drink. Mrs. Torsono was cooking eggs on one of those old antique looking, cast iron wood stoves. She moved quickly from chore to chore and seemed every bit the master of her domain.

"Americans sleep a little late," Samuel remarked with a smile. Terrance had noticed the night before that the chief's English was a fair bit better than Perto's.

"My good friend Perto and me has been speaking more about your trip. There are some things you should know. After you go to bed last night, I talk to some men in my village that fish upriver. They say that many trees lie across river. Too many to pass. They say some trees are good logs to cut up too. And the storm hit very much harder in some places. I ask how far upriver they have went since storm hit. They say they cannot go too far because too many trees fall. They stop before first fork. Look bad upriver more.

"I think Perto's boat is not big enough to pull big trees out of way so boat can pass. Maybe you hire one man in village with bigger boat with inside engine. He can help until afternoon today. Then he must be back to coast. He will work for cost of gas, but no pay for boat. He want to help Miss Hamilton. Many people here love

Miss Hamilton and sorry about her husband's dying. Perto says you paid him enough money already to also pay this man for fuel after he sells gold coin you give him. Boat owner says then is soon enough."

Terrance glanced over at Perto, who nodded. Perto's honesty about the value of the gold coin again raised his estimation of the little shopkeeper. It was becoming apparent that the people in these villages placed a lot of stock in a man's word and character and if he was trusted, his word was all they needed.

"That would be very helpful, sir. How soon will this man be able to start?"

The mayor laughed, and when he did there was a twinkle in his eye.

"You are very excited to help Miss Hamilton, Mr. Terrance Clark. She is beautiful woman and good one. Her guide though is not as good as he should be. People say when Miss Hamilton does not look at him, he look at her like he should not look. Miss Hamilton husbands was good, good man. Gorton Harkin is not that. That why I asks last nights the man with big boat to help move trees for you. Maybe not safe for Miss Hamilton to go upriver with Harkin alone. So you should go soon."

Apparently the people in Bilokut were not aware of Gorton Harkin's legal problems back in Georgetown, but still had sensed that he was not a good man. Terrance could feel his face flushing with anger at the thought of the beautiful missionary traveling alone upriver with a man that everyone disliked and distrusted, a man who was also a wanted criminal.

Terrance pushed his empty plate back from the edge of the table, politely thanked the mayor's wife for the fine meals and comfortable bed, and motioned to Perto that it was time for them to leave.

Before leaving, Perto exchanged further words with the chief in fluent Creole. The two men spoke rapidly and there was gesturing and pointing and questioning looks back and forth. Finally they shook hands and patted each other on the shoulder.

"What was that all about," Terrance asked after they were outside. The sun had finally made its appearance and the people of the village were beginning to stir.

"My friend warn Perto about other troubles up river. He say sickness only bad two villages. But he say some mens with army boat and guns that shoots lots of bullets go upriver before storm and not come back. Samuel say he asks army mens why they go upriver. One fat men on boat tell Samuel, mind his business only. Samuel tell Perto bad army mens sometime go upriver far and steal gold from miners."

Chapter Twenty

*T*he kindly man who had offered to use his boat to drag trees out of the way so Terrance and Perto could get upriver was waiting at the dock when they arrived. He was a tall, black man with fine features and a wide smile that was marred only by the fact that his left eye tooth was gold.

His boat was an older model, plywood hull cabin cruiser. In spite of its age, the craft was in beautiful condition with an abundance of well oiled mahogany trim and polished brass up top. Underneath was a powerful 430 cubic inch inboard motor that had once powered a luxury Lincoln Continental. The engine had been professionally rebuilt and was idling almost silently when Terrance and Perto arrived at the dock.

Terrance strode over to shake the man's hand. The man with the gold tooth introduced himself as Harold Williams, formerly of New Orleans. The man's voice was strong, his handshake firm and his eyes honest.

As soon as they had dispensed with the formalities and Williams had laid out his simple plan, they were off. The cruiser turned and sped upriver with Terrance and his guide doing their feeble best to keep up. They had not gone more than a couple of miles before it became readily apparent that the storm had hit the area farther up this watershed much harder than around Annari and Bilokut.

The further upstream the two boats traveled, the more devastation they encountered. One area, a mile or two long, looked like a tornado had touched down. Hundreds if not thousands of trees had been uprooted or snapped off halfway up their trunks, as if by a giant scythe. One particular tree of some stature stood alone on one stretch of riverbank. All the trees around it had been flattened. This giant had been stripped of all its leaves but had somehow managed to withstand the awesome onslaught of the storm. Oddly, though, lodged in its branches a good forty feet above the ground was a wooden canoe.

For some time, the going was slow as Williams' cruiser cleared tree after tree from the channel. Two shirtless, young men stood at the rear of the cruiser holding heavy ropes. One end of each rope was attached to a ring at the back of the boat and there was a grappling hook attached to the other end. Williams would back in close and the two men would throw their hooks over the top end of the fallen tree. Williams would then reverse course and drag that end back downstream and to the side so as to open the channel for passage.

In a space of about two hours, the cruiser had successfully cleared the way to the first major fork in the river. The skipper reduced his engine speed to an idle and motioned Perto to bring his little boat alongside.

"Which way do we go now?" he called out to Terrance and Perto. "I can help for another hour or so and then I am afraid you will be on your own. I would stay longer, but I have to be back at the coast today."

"One village we go to is this way," Perto said, pointing to the left toward the Arakaba village. "Other village is this way," he said, pointing to the right fork and the Napoteri village. "No one know what village Miss Hamilton go first."

"Then I will take the fork on the right," the skipper replied. "It looks a little wider and deeper. Let's see how far upstream we can get you before I have to turn back downriver."

Perto nodded and Terrance thanked the man again for his kindness.

"Think nothing of it, young man," the skipper replied. "When John Hamilton was alive, he did me a favor I can never repay. In this life or the next," he added. "I pray you find Rebekah soon and that she is well. Perto, when you get back to the village, radio me and let me know how things went. My prayers will be with the both of you."

The severe devastation of the storm continued to be evident as they navigated their way up the right fork of the river toward Napoteri. Gradually, though, the devastation lessened the farther upriver they went. The larger boat cleared the way for another two miles of winding river before the skipper finally ordered his men to stow the ropes and hooks. He turned his craft around and with a wave and a salute started to head back downriver. Perto motioned for the man to stop.

Perto pulled his boat alongside the larger craft and reached up and handed the skipper the gold coin Terrance had given him.

"Take coin to coast for me. Maybe find out how much worth. Very old. Coin belongs to friend here but some for expenses."

The skipper examined the coin for a few seconds.

"I have never seen one like this," he said. "It doesn't look like any of the old Spanish or Portuguese coins that show up from time to time. I will check it out. It might be worth a pretty penny."

With that, the skipper waved again and headed his boat off downriver leaving a large wake behind.

All the yelling back and forth between skipper and crew and the noise of the cruiser's engine, when its power was being tested, had made Terrance forget the remoteness of where they were. It was only after the larger craft had disappeared around a bend in the river and the noise of its engine had faded away did it sink in just how alone they really were. The river was a desolate place when there was just Perto and the piranhas and crocs for company.

"How far upriver to the Napoteri village, Perto? Can we get there by dark?" As he was speaking, a very large serpent slithered off the shore and into the dark water on the side of the boat nearest the shore. The snake was long and had a thick body. It was large enough to catch both their attention.

"Anaconda. Big one," was all Perto said. He had shut down the outboard while speaking with the captain of the cruiser. He turned and pulled the cord and little engine sputtered to life. "Perto always like engine running when big snakes and crocs around. Not good when they come close and look into little boats."

The look on the little shopkeeper's face suggested that he was recalling a memory of something that he was not inclined to relive. Terrance watched the large V-shape ripples where the snake had entered the water. The beast appeared to be headed somewhere downstream and not directly in their direction.

"Remember, only man alone in paddle canoe ascared of big anacondas," the shopkeeper said with a half laugh. "But we go now. Napoteri one hour now."

Perto turned the bow straight into the slow current and opened the engine wide. It appeared that the bulk of the storm's devastation was behind them now. There were a few small trees in the river here and there, but Perto was able to maneuver his boat around them. One tree was all the way across the river, but Perto was able to get a run at it, raise the motor out of the water, and then drift through the smaller branches at the top of the tree and into clear water again.

After that there were no major obstacles to slow their progress. A good ten minutes before they reached Napoteri they caught the strong scent of smoke. It was like the smell of a hundred campfires that had been doused in water. The smell increased the closer they came to the village.

Around the next bend, a bank of dense smoke hung over the water like fog. Terrance glanced back at Perto who had let off on the accelerator.

"This smoke not normal village smoke," Perto said. There was a worried look on his face. "Maybe something not good. Maybe forest catch fire near village."

From memory, Perto maneuvered his way through the thick smoke, fighting off the sting and the watering of his eyes. He slowed the engine just a little too late and the boat lurched to a stop as the bow made contact with the dock. All about them, there was an unnatural silence in the air.

Terrance quickly tied the bow to the dock and without looking back scampered up the ramp in the direction the village must be. The sight that met his eyes there was one he would never forget. There were bodies lying everywhere. Men, women, children, old people; they were all dead. Tiny holes, the kind small caliber automatic weapons make, riddled the bodies. Quickly, Terrance made his way from body to body, hoping against hope that none of them was that of the woman with the reddish brown hair and lightly freckled face.

Some of the things Terrance saw during the next moments were hard to take in. He had never been in a war and had never witnessed senseless slaughter. The man's eyes began to water and it was not entirely due to the smoke.

There was no mistaking the calloused cruelty of the thing that had befallen this peaceful fishing village. It did not appear that a single soul had been left alive. Who would do such a thing, and why? Terrance had heard of such senseless violence in the tribal wars of Africa and the killing fields of Southeast Asia, but not in a country so close to home.

The village was a small one and it didn't take long to search the bodies for signs of life. It seemed like an eternity before Terrance was certain that the woman he sought was not among the dead. He was at the far end of the village standing over the body of a pregnant woman who was clutching the body of a small child in her arms when he sensed Perto standing behind him. Unbeknownst to the American, the shopkeeper had been following him from body to body.

The little man's eyes were full of tears that he made no attempt to hide.

"Perto think army men come here. But why they kills all the peoples? Why they they kills childrens and mothers?"

"Judging from the condition of these bodies, Perto, these people have been dead for less than a day. I counted eighty-seven bodies so far. There are possibly more in the burned out huts. It may be morning before we can check on those. The spent cartridges on the ground appear to be from automatic weapons. These men were likely mercenaries, but what were they looking for? Why did they come here and why did they kill all of these villagers? Could it have been for gold? I see no sign of mining equipment."

"Miners more far up river. Not here," Perto replied.

Except in a newspaper photo, Terrance had not seen the nine hundred bodies scattered around the Pavilion back in Jonestown, so the sight of so many men, women, and children lying dead in this little village had a shocking and profound effect on his soul. He had not known these people, but he knew that every one of them had been human beings with souls. Someone had snuffed out their lives as if they were nothing. But why? It made no sense. There was no way it could, not to a rational mind.

While they were standing at the far end of the village, Terrance thought he heard something, maybe a weak cry coming from the direction of the jungle. They stopped talking and listened for a few moments of silence.

Finally, there it was again. It seemed to be close by. The sound was more of a whimper than a cry, but it sounded human. Both men turned and stared in the direction from whence the cry had come. It suddenly occurred to them that in their rush up the ramp, both men had left their weapons leaning against the coils of rope in the bow of the boat.

"Go get the rifles, Perto," Terrance whispered. "I will see where that sound came from."

Without replying, Perto turned and ran towards the river while Terrance kept his eyes trained on the jungle. There it was again. This time it sounded like a low groan.

Without waiting for Perto and the rifles, the American entered the jungle.

Chapter Twenty-One

*C*laspen Dortin was a sergeant in the Guyanan army. His parents had immigrated to Guyana in 1933 at the height of the depression. They came from the part of India that would later become the nation of Pakistan, a decade or so down the road.

Dortin was a proud man in his early fifties with a streak of cruelty that bordered on sadism. He beat his wife and routinely boasted about it to his fellows. He was even more cruel to the men who served under him, often driving them to their limits just because he could.

Before entering the Guyanan army as an enlisted man, Claspen Dortin had spent several years as a mercenary, working for any third world dictator who was willing to pay for his services. He had spent time in Africa, mostly in Uganda, and had reportedly led one of the many death squads commissioned by General and President Idi Amin. No one knew why he left Uganda.

After immigrating to Guyana in 1974, Dortin had risen quickly to his current rank. His quick advancement was primarily due to his currying favor with his superiors and by his consistent willingness to do any unsavory deed they wanted done – and then not talk about it.

Claspen's dark face sported a long ugly scar that ran from just below his left eye, down his left cheek and to the tip of his chin, an ever present reminder of a knife fight he had won, but at a price. Claspen was not a heavy man. He had one of those round, protruding stomachs that was entirely out of sorts with his slender form. In spite of his noticeably paunch, Claspen Dortin was not a man to be trifled with. He was wiry and had lightning fast reflexes. Rumor had it that he had sent eight or ten men to early graves with the long, slender blade he always carried somewhere on his person. It was said that some of those men died for the pettiest of slights.

To look at Claspen Dortin, one would presume that such a creature was incapable of love or loyalty, but that would be a mistake. Claspen cared deeply for one thing and one thing only. That was his son Carlos. Since the boy had been a toddler, Claspen had doted over him, lavishing him with favors and gifts, sparing no expense. The fruit of such misguided parenting was a son as lacking in moral character as his father, a boy who always wanted more than he had and felt fully entitled to every desirable thing he set his eyes upon.

It was a fateful day indeed when twenty-year old Carlos first set eyes on a pretty, doe-eyed girl from Napoteri. Carlena's village was far upriver from the base where Carlos's father was stationed, so the chances of the two ever meeting were slim. But meet they did.

On that fateful day, Carlena was visiting the big city with her parents. It was the first time in her fourteen years that the young beauty had been anywhere beyond Bilokut and her own river. The trip to the city was more exciting than the girl had imagined. The sights, the sounds, the crowds, it was all so much. She had never seen an automobile or a truck. She had never seen a two story building or electric lights. She was having the time of her life. It was in the midst of all this excitement that Carlena had the misfortune of crossing paths with Carlos Dortin.

Carlena and her mother were at an outdoor market, a place usually frequented by tourists from the United States and the larger cities of Venezuela and Columbia. Carlena was holding up a heavy silver bracelet and showing it to her mother, who was standing two tables away. The bracelet had little shapes like the sun, moon, and stars, all made of silver, suspended from the main band. When Carlena smiled, her face exuded youthful innocence and purity. Her thick, wavy hair was long and shiny and its darkness only accentuated her perfect face.

Carlos Dortin just happened to be passing by with a couple of young men from his father's unit when he saw the girl. Carlos was not actually in the army, but often hung with some of the younger soldiers, usually the baser sort. Carlena caught his eye when she held the bracelet up and shook it.

Carlos wanted the girl from the moment he laid eyes on her. To his weak mind, it was love he felt. Call it what you will, but he desired this young beauty above all other things and immediately determined in his dark mind that nothing would stand between him and the glorious object of his misguided affection.

Carlos immediately approached the girl and introduced himself. When Carlena's mother came around the end of the table and stood next to her daughter, Carlos did not once glance at her, though she was in her mid-thirties and lovely in her own right. His father had engrained in him from childhood that women were not important unless one wanted them to be, and at the moment there was only one female who was important to the young man.

From that moment on, Carlos had followed the girl around the market, giving her no peace. Then when the Carlena's father appeared on the scene and ordered him to leave, Carlos responded angrily, even threatening the man.

Over Carlena's protest, the family cut short their visit to the city. The girl's parents assumed that the threat Carlos posed to their daughter was over once they were safely back at their own village. A week later, however, the young man arrived at the little dock at Napoteri with presents of silk dresses and jewelry for the girl. He even brought the silver bracelet Carlena had been showing to her mother the moment he had first laid eyes on her. No one had any idea how the man had discovered where the girl lived.

Again, the family made it clear that their daughter was not to be won at quite so young an age and that the young man's suit was not welcome. Carlos persisted, however, until the chief and several men of the village intervened and sent him packing.

Carlos Dortin was not at all accustomed to being denied the things he desired and found he did not care much for the experience. He returned to the village a second time a few days later. Again he was sent away. This time, however, Carlos had brought along several friends and had left only after a fight that had left Carlos with a bruised face and one of the young men of the village near death from a knife wound to his abdomen.

That might have been enough to end the matter. It should have been. But Carlos did not stay away for long. The next time he returned, he brought four heavily armed men from the army barracks. He would have this girl and he would have the revenge he was owed for the affronts to his dignity he had suffered at this worthless little village. Everyone in Napoteri would die and he would *take* the prize they had dared deny him.

The day of the attack, Carlos and the four troops came upriver in an official military craft similar in size to Harold Williams' cruiser. They sped past the Napoteri village without so much as slowing down. They continued upstream another four miles to a place where the river was faster and shallower and large rocks dotted the surface of the water, making passage beyond that point dangerous.

After they had finished with their business there, they had headed back downstream and anchored just upriver from sleepy little Napoteri and waited. It was the afternoon before the big storm. Just as the sun was beginning to set, they pulled their boat up to the village dock, stormed up the ramp and began firing at everyone they encountered, men, women, and children alike. The only instruction Carlos gave was to not shoot at any pretty teenage girls.

Except for the sick, the people of the village were all gathered by the river for a town meeting. They had tried to flee into the jungle at the first sounds of gunfire, but they were cut down before they could escape the clearing. Those lying sick in their beds were either shot as they tried to escape when the village was torched, or died where they lay.

When the killing was over, the one person the murderous lot had not seen was the doe-eyed girl whose extraordinary beauty had proved the village's undoing. Carlos's wounded pride had been assuaged by all of the senseless bloodletting, but his desire for the young woman remained unabated.

Taking their time, the men searched the bodies of the villagers, taking souvenirs at will, mostly inexpensive rings and bracelets. One of the soldiers, a short pudgy man, found the body of one of the men lying across the body of one of the women. The side of the woman's face was covered with blood, but she wore no jewelry. The man was wearing a thin rawhide necklace with a long, curved eagle talon suspended from it. Kneeling on one knee, the pudgy one removed the necklace from the body and then placed it around his own neck, carefully tucking the sharp talon under his shirt.

Chapter Twenty-Two

*T*errance let his eyes adjust to the darkness behind the foliage before moving farther into the jungle in search of the source of the groan he had heard. Even with all of the smoke drifting about, in the air was the heavy smell of damp, rotting vegetation. The smell was at once dank and sweet.

Terrance called out. His voice was soft and non-threatening. Again he heard the low groan farther into the jungle and off to his left. As he made his way toward the sound, he became aware that Perto had joined him. The shopkeeper had obviously wasted no time getting back to the boat and retrieving the two rifles. He handed the American one of the thirty-thirties and together they pushed toward the sound.

Perto called out to the source of the groaning sound, speaking in a dialect Terrance had not heard before. The response was immediate, but weak. This time it was not a groan, but some kind of language.

"Perto know this man. He friend."

In a few moments, they had located a slender, middle-aged man lying on his back on the jungle floor. Perto knelt over the man and spoke quietly in his ear. The shopkeeper gently ran his hand back and forth over his friend's forehead brushing the man's dark hair back and away from his forehead. The two exchanged words several times before the man slipped into unconsciousness.

"We take friend back to clearing. Friend not strong now."

Terrance handed his rifle back to Perto, stooped down, and slipped his strong arms under the wounded man. He gently lifted him off the ground and with Perto leading the way carried the limp body back to the clearing. Perto hastily removed a shiny, blue shawl from the shoulders of an older woman lying face down nearby and stretched the piece of cloth out on the ground. He motioned to Terrance, who gently laid the wounded man on the shawl.

Perto knelt low and put his cheek close to his friend's nostrils. There was shallow breathing, but the man was unconscious.

The foamy blood on the man's lips indicated that he had likely taken a bullet to a lung and without immediate help would not survive.

"There is nothing we can do here for this man, Perto. He needs a hospital."

"Friend die soon. Perto know. Friend know."

Terrance nodded grimly. "What did he say to you back in the forest? Did he tell you what happened here?"

"Friend say four maybe five mens come in boat and shoot all peoples here. One men come two time before. Want young girl. Father say no. Chief say no. Men come back kill all people. Girl no here when mens come. She go away in boat with one men and missionary lady and take medicine to Arakaba village. Before that, one men buy canoe from this man, then go. Then friend say, he die now."

Perto knelt beside his friend and again gently stroked the man's forehead. In a few moments, the man stopped breathing.

"Perto must go back to Bilokut and use radio. Must tell what happen here. Must bury many peoples. Must get help. Then we look for Miss Hamilton."

For a few moments, Terrance stood staring at the body lying there at his feet and those scattered all about the smoky clearing. A thousand thoughts were running through his head. Then he turned and looked directly at the shopkeeper, a man he had learned to like and respect.

"We must get to the Arakaba village quickly, Perto. The men who did this might do the same thing there. It sounds like Miss Hamilton does not yet know what happened here. We must get to her quickly before the men who did this find her and the girl they are seeking. There is nothing we can do for these people now."

"No, Mr. Terrance. We must go to Bilokut and use radio. Tell police what happen. Too long now. Must bury bodies quick. Too hot."

Terrance shook his head. "I must get to the other village, my friend. Your friend said Miss Hamilton went to the Arakaba village and so I must go there now. Is there a way to get to the village without a boat and without going all of the way down river and back up the other fork, which may or may not be passable?"

"There is trail through forest. Hard walk. Big hill. Take most of day for strong man like you. Maybe more time. Long time by boat too, but more easy."

Terrance was not excited about trekking off into the jungle alone, but the thought of wasting precious time in what might be a race for Rebekah's life did not sit well with him. Whatever danger the young woman might be in from Gorton Harkin was probably less than she faced if the men who had perpetrated the massacre of this village found her with the girl they were seeking.

"Then, Perto, I think you must go back downriver to Bilokut and report what happened here and I will go overland to the other village and pray that I can get there before the men who did this arrive. It may be too late already."

The thought of the red haired missionary woman with the light freckles and radiant smile lying dead, her body riddled with bullets, like all these poor souls lying all around him, made the tall, handsome American wince.

"There is nothing more to say, Perto. I will take a box of ammo and a little food and get started now. Just point me to the trail."

"Take machete too," the shopkeeper replied. Trail start other side of river. Not good trail sometime. Perto take you other side of river, then go. We meet at other village next day with mens from Bilokut and guns. Perto hurry. Very bad men. Here, take pack with food and water."

Back at the boat, Perto handed his American friend a light knapsack from under the back seat. The shopkeeper's wife never let her man leave in his boat without a pack with enough food and water for at least a few days.

At the other side of the river, Terrance shook his friend's hand and said goodbye. Perto turned the boat around and was just starting back downriver when Terrance yelled out to him.

"One more thing, Perto. When you get to a radio, please send a message back to Timmy and tell him I am okay and will be back to get him as soon as I can. Tell him that I have not forgotten him. . .and never will."

Perto waved and opened the throttle on his little boat and headed off downriver with all due haste. Terrance Clark from Oakland, California stood there at the edge of the jungle and watched the little boat disappear into the thick smoke. When he could no longer hear the putter of the little engine, he turned and looked around him. Across the river were the remains of a village, still smoldering. From where he stood, he could not see the bodies, but he knew they were there. Behind him and towering far overhead was the dense foliage of an untamed tropical forest and the beginnings of a trail that for all he knew was overgrown and perhaps even indistinguishable from the surrounding jungle. He was alone in the wild again and this time the loneliness was palpable. This time, however, he had a rifle.

Terrance was confident that if he became lost or could no longer make out the trail he would still be able to find his way out. As long as he bore slightly to the left he would eventually meet the other fork of the river or come back to this one. His biggest fear was that he might miss the Arakaba village completely or arrive too late.

Gripping the thirty-thirty Winchester in his left hand and the machete in his right, the private investigator disappeared once more into the tangled growth of a Guyanan jungle.

Chapter Twenty-Three

W hen Rebekah Hamilton heard of the illness that had struck the two villages that lay one watershed north of Annari, she had wasted no time getting supplies together and seeking transportation to the villages. She had been to the Arakaba and Napoteri villages many times and loved the people there. Her husband had won several converts there. On her many visits to the two villages, Rebekah had added to the number.

As fate would have it, Gorton Harkin's little boat was the only craft available to take her to where her mission called her. In spite of her serious reservations about the man and his less than subtle advances toward her, she had set her mind to go to the villages and get there by any means possible. Unfortunately, the beautiful missionary knew nothing of the criminal accusations against Harkin back in Georgetown.

As she and Gorton were loading his boat and preparing to leave Annari, Rebekah couldn't help but notice all of the excitement at the dock. She had heard that a white man and a boy had been rescued from the top of the falls and took a minute to join the crowd gathered on the riverbank above the dock to greet them.

She had not expected the event to be of much import, but when the tall, handsome man on the dock spotted her in the crowd and smiled at her, she had smiled back and had done so with the kind of smile that had not crossed her young face in a long time. Immediately embarrassed by her behavior, the young widow had turned and hastened her way to the Gorton's boat and motioned him to push off immediately.

She and Gorton had stopped only briefly at Bilokut before heading upriver. She had enough of the antibiotic for both villages, but wanted to pick up a supply of vitamins for some of the older villagers and pregnant mothers. There was a shop in Bilokut that usually kept a fair supply on hand.

Rebekah had sat in the middle seat of Gorton's boat on the trip from Annari to Bilokut. The entire way, she never lost the sense that the man behind her was staring at her, devouring her with his eyes. Whenever she would turn to look at him, he would immediately avert his eyes upriver, so as to conceal the lust that had been building there. But Rebekah had seen it and it made her all the more uncomfortable. She knew they were headed for some pretty remote places and a woman would have little defense if such man became aggressive. Were it not for the sick villagers who desperately needed her, she would have not risked setting off alone with Gorton Harkin.

Harkin was not altogether unattractive to look at. He was well built, though there was a hint of thickness through his middle, the kind that is common to men who down too much beer with too much regularity. Gorton's hair was black and wavy and his thick mustache was almost becoming. He had remarkably white teeth, a trait the girl had always admired in a man. But there was something about Gorton's eyes that betrayed an inner darkness that to the American missionary was unmistakable. She did not trust Gorton Harkin and knew she never could.

Rebekah and Gorton left Bilokut the afternoon before the big storm hit. They arrived without mishap at the

Napoteri village. About half the people there were seriously ill, mostly women and children and a few of the older men. Rebekah quickly dispensed antibiotics to the sick ones and left an extra supply with the chief in the event the sickness spread, something she suggested was more than likely. She also left half of the vitamins she had brought along.

As soon as her business in the village was completed, she told Gorton it was time to depart for Arakaba. She hoped to make it there before darkness fell. Rebekah did not relish the idea of spending the night alone with Gorton, whether in a jungle camp or on the river in the man's small boat. That was part of the reason she had so quickly consented when fourteen-year old Carlena had asked to catch a ride with them to Arakaba to visit a family friend.

Actually, it had been Carlena's parents who had suggested the idea, thinking it might be safer for the girl to be somewhere where Carlos Dortin would not know to look for her. After his last encounter and the violent side he had exhibited, they were more than a little concerned that the man would return.

Gorton initially objected to bringing the girl along, but Rebekah had insisted. She sternly reminded Gorton who was paying for his services. Even after Rebekah's chiding, Gorton seemed determined not to bring along another passenger. When he saw the girl, however, he instantly changed his mind. Carlena may have been young, but her beauty was undeniable. In Gorton's dark mind, the only thing better than staring at Rebekah Hamilton all day would be staring at Rebekah Hamilton and this beautiful young girl at the same time.

Earlier in the afternoon, while the missionary had been busy comforting and administering antibiotics to the sick and conversing with the chief, Gorton had taken time to stroll around the tiny village. Down by the river, he spotted one of the most well crafted native canoes he had ever seen. It was light of weight with just the right curves. The moment Gorton laid eyes on it, he wanted it. The owner was easy enough to find and after a few minutes of serious haggling over price, the prize was his, though he had paid dearly for it. When his little party left the village, the light canoe coasted along behind Gorton's boat, tied securely by a ten-foot piece of yellow nylon rope.

To get to the Arakaba village required that they retrace their way back downriver and then up the left fork. Carlena decided to lie down in the bottom of the boat at Rebekah's feet and sleep. She was lying there, fast asleep, when Gorton's boat came around a bend in the river and ran almost headlong into a military cruiser moving rapidly upstream. Four of the men in the boat were dressed in army camo and brandished what appeared to be automatic weapons. The man at the wheel was dressed in civilian clothes. Rebekah took all that in as the two boats swerved to miss one another, passing quickly.

Rebekah could not help but notice how closely the men in the larger boat scrutinized her and Gorton, as their boats passed. For a moment, the larger boat slowed and then, as if dismissing the two in the smaller boat as inconsequential, continued its way upriver.

"What would a military boat be doing this far upriver," Rebekah asked.

Gorton's boat was bouncing back and forth in the wake created by the larger boat and the canoe was dancing behind them like a cork. It was clear from Gorton's face that he was as perplexed by the appearance of the other boat as Rebekah was.

"After Napoteri," he replied, "there are only a few scattered mining camps farther upriver. This must be a routine patrol run." They gave the affair no further thought and continued on downriver.

Half an hour later and well before they had made the lower fork in the river, the sky suddenly began to fill with dark, foreboding clouds and the trees on both sides of the river bank began to sway back and forth in a steadily growing wind. It was as if a serious storm had appeared out of nowhere. Five minutes later, the surface of the usually peaceful river was as rough as an ocean. Swell after swell threatened to capsize Gorton's boat, which suddenly seemed small and inadequate in the giant swells.

With no more warning than that, a savage storm released its fury upon them. Hurricane force winds and torrential rains struck with a fierceness that seemed to be born of hell. Neither of the adults had ever seen such an angry sky.

Awakened by the roughness of the water and the bouncing of the boat, Carlena got up and sat next to Rebekah in the middle seat, huddling as closely as she could.

"What is happening?" the girl asked, her voice trembling. "Are we going to die?"

"We must make for shore the first chance we get," Gorton yelled above the howling of the wind. "We will not be able to keep the boat afloat out here. The river is too rough. I have never seen a storm this bad, except on the ocean."

With dense jungle crowding the shore on both sides, places to pull ashore were few and far between. Here and there, they had seen croc wallows along the bank, and while those would normally not be a good place to tie up a boat, this was not a normal time. Running the boat ashore at the next wash they came to might be their only hope of survival. Gorton was reasonably certain the crocs would all be lying low in the deeper water about now or holed up in some muddy den, riding out the storm. Besides, crocs were the least of his concerns at the moment.

Gorton may have had a dark soul, but he was a man's man and had grown up on the river and in the jungle. In that regard, his river and jungle lore were as good as anyone around.

"There's a place," Rebekah shouted, pointing down-river a hundred feet. The rain was coming hard now and she had to cover her eyes with her hand to look out that far.

Gorton nodded and standing tall in the back of the boat, turned the bow toward the shore and revved the engine to full speed. As the craft turned sideways to the wind, a heavy gust all but capsized them. There was a snapping sound behind them and Rebekah turned to see the canoe they had been towing being swept downwind like a dry leaf in a hurricane.

Gorton heard the sound too, and turned. He swore loudly as he saw his prize disappear from sight. But there was no time for bemoaning such things. The bow of their boat hit the muddy bank with enough speed to slide well up onto the mud, leaving a little more than half of the boat still in the water.

"Get ashore, quickly," Gorton yelled. Both girls leaped out of the boat, Rebekah Hamilton still clutching tightly to the knapsack that held the medicine for the other village. As soon as her feet hit solid ground, she slipped her arms into the straps of the knapsack to leave both hands free.

Gorton followed close behind them. As soon as his feet were on the muddy riverbank, he turned and grabbed the coil of rope out of the bow, intending to tie the boat to a strong tree, lest it blow away and leave them stranded where they were. With rope in hand, he turned and dashed toward the jungle. The mud was slick and the bank sloped, but he made it a dozen feet or so before a powerful gust caught the boat and spun the back end around, dislodging the bow from the bank and driving the boat away from the shore. The end of the rope was ripped from Gorton's hands and all but flew across the ground toward the river. Gorton dived for the rope and caught the end with one hand. For half a second, it appeared that his effort would be rewarded, but the mud was slick and he had caught as much mud in his hand as rope. The boat was catching the wind full tilt now and the weight of the boat and the force of the wind easily tore the rope from the man's fingers.

Rebekah and Carlena turned just as the muddy end of the rope was slipping through Gorton's fingers. There was nothing they could do but look on in dismay as the boat disappeared into the rough waves and the pouring rain.

"Look," Carlena yelled. "Boat sink."

Gorton and Rebekah strained their eyes as they peered out into the rain. Neither of them could see the boat or tell whether it had gone under. Gorton turned and faced the two girls. The entire front of his body was covered with dark mud. At that precise moment, a bolt of lightning flashed with a blinding brightness that lit up the entire area. Gorton Harkin, standing before them covered with mud and illuminated by the brilliant flash from the lightning, was an eerie sight.

The crash of thunder did not follow after the bolt of lightning. It was simultaneous and powerful, rumbling through their bodies and rattling their bones. As one, the three turned and ran headlong into the jungle. Their every instinct told them that they had to find shelter and they had to do it quickly. Trees are hardly a safe refuge when lightning is striking, but they had to enter the forest if they were going to find shelter.

With Rebekah in the lead, the three tore through the dense underbrush. Everywhere the foliage was whipping about. The leaves cut and stung their skin where they hit. Off to their right, the top half of a large tree came crashing to the ground with a cracking sound as loud as gunfire. The wind had snapped the tree off about halfway up. All around them there were cracks and pops as branches broke off and entire trees were snapped in half like kindling or uprooted as if by a giant unseen hand.

For a moment they were in an open space and Rebekah grabbed the younger girl's hand as they ran. "Lord Jesus, protect us," she prayed out loud while on a dead run. Carlena gripped Rebekah's hand tightly as if her life depended on her hanging on. She understood the words the missionary had prayed and their meaning. Rebekah Hamilton had come to their village several times and had told the people about the one called "Jesus." Carlena had liked the stories the pretty red haired woman had told them, though she had not yet decided if she believed them. The stories seemed too good to be true, but the missionary lady had always told them with such certainty and the look in her eyes had always been sweet and honest. At this moment, Carlena hoped the missionary's stories were true and that this Jesus she spoke of would answer her prayer.

Onward the three plunged, deeper into the jungle, dodging fallen trees and flying branches. Their clothes were torn by briars and whipping vines. The bare flesh of their arms and legs were scraped and scratched. They protected their faces and especially their eyes as they ran, keeping their heads down and their free hand up. The two girls gave no thought to Gorton and never noticed when he was no longer behind them. They never heard when he cried out in search of them.

Suddenly the ground dropped off in front of Rebekah and she stopped in her tracks. In front of them was a small gully with a creek at the bottom. It was rushing with reddish brown water. A large tree had blown across the gully and formed a natural bridge.

"We cross on log," Carlena yelled over the howling wind.

Rebekah stared at the log and the way it rested securely on both sides. She turned to the younger girl and shook her head.

"No, it is no better on that side of the gully than on this side. Follow me." With that, she pulled the teenager down the muddy slope and dragged her back under the shelter of the fallen log.

Where the large root ball of the tree had torn back the earth, there was a small opening back under the bank with just enough room for the both of them to squeeze in. Rebekah hoped to God there were no snakes there as she pulled young Carlena in behind her.

The two frightened women huddled there beneath the fallen giant, feeling safer than they had felt since the fierce storm had struck. Yet all around them, lightning flashed and trees continued to crash and fall. One tree fell directly over the log under which they were hiding, but the heavier log did not budge. If anything, the thick foliage of the crashing tree provided at least some shelter from the driving rain.

By now, it was fully dark outside, though it was impossible to tell whether night had fallen or if the storm had completely blocked the sun. With great frequency, flashes of lightning would light up the jungle around them with a strange and eerie brightness.

Rebekah could see the rushing water in the stream just below them slowly inching upward toward them as the storm wore on.

Once, when the lighting flashed, Carlena yelled and pointed across the gully, saying she saw a man standing on the opposite bank looking in their direction. But when the lighting flashed again, Rebekah looked and there was no one there.

The storm lasted well into the night. The two rain drenched girls leaned into each other and tried to sleep as best they could, but it was a fitful night's rest at best. Morning found them huddled there under their log, wet and exhausted, but safe and sound. Other than super-ficial scratches and bruised knees, they had somehow come through the storm unscathed.

As soon as it was light, Rebekah and Carlena crawled out from their hole and stretched their stiff muscles. They had huddled in pretty tight quarters for several hours and were more than a little stiff. The first thing they noticed upon exiting their hole was that it was not really that early. Their hiding place back under the log had been shaded by the tree that had fallen across them. Now, as they looked about them, plainly the morning was fully broken now and there was blue sky overhead.

There was in fact much more blue than either of them had expected. The storm had literally torn the tops out of two-thirds of the trees and many of those still standing had been stripped of their leaves. The sheer devastation reminded Rebekah of pictures of a war zone. Nothing around them looked the way it had the night before.

As they had run away from the river the night before, they had taken the path of least resistance, turning this way and that with no regard for bearings. Now they had no idea where they were. They knew the river was on the same side of the creek that they were on, but as for which direction it lay they were at a total loss. The winding gully was all but useless for plotting a way back to the river.

"You look a fright, girl," Rebekah said, holding her new best friend by both shoulders and staring into her face. She hoped her light-hearted demeanor would cheer the poor girl.

Carlena laughed. "You not look too good too, Miss Hamilton."

The two women washed their faces and arms and legs in the water of the stream, which oddly enough had receded somewhat and was now running almost clear. Everywhere around them, the air was filled with the smell of rotting vegetation and bare earth. The air was fresh and clean, but the smell of a wet jungle after a storm was unmistakable.

Here and there, tropical birds with bright, colorful plumage were flying from one barren tree to another, as if searching for homes and roosting places that were no longer there – or mates that were nowhere to be found.

"The birds look as lost as we are," Rebekah remarked. "It is as if their entire world has been destroyed."

Carlena nodded, but her expression was a troubled one.

"Before night," she said, "you pray to Jesus and soon we find place to hide from storm. Do you think he find us this good place?"

"Yes, I believe He did, Carlena. When I am afraid, I always call on Him. Sometimes He makes things right and sometimes He just gives me strength to endure the painful things. When my husband died not too long ago, God did not give him back to me no matter how much I cried, but He made me strong enough to survive the pain. It was a hard time though. It is still hard."

"I remember you husband. He laugh when he talk. He good man."

"Yes, he was. The best. I still miss him, but I know he is up in heaven with the Lord now. I don't know why he had to die, but I am okay with it now. I am not mad at God. I do not understand some of the things He does, but I know that He makes no mistakes and that I will understand His plan some day. He is an awesome God and does not have to explain things to me. My job is more to trust Him than to understand his ways.

"Sometimes when bad things happen, people blame God and become bitter. Maybe you would say it more like, they become angry at God. But people who believe in Jesus must decide whether they really believe Him or are just pretending. If they *really* believe, then they must *really* trust. If they do, when something bad happens they may hurt or be sad, but they do not become angry at God because they believe in their hearts that He does not make mistakes and can be trusted when things are going well and when things are going not so well."

Rebekah was not sure how much of what she was saying was being understood, but Carlena's sober expression and the look in her eyes suggested that she was seriously pondering what she was hearing. The girl had beautiful, intelligent eyes. She was young, but she was as pretty as any girl Rebekah could remember. Even with wet hair, torn clothes, and scratches on her arms and legs, she was striking.

"Carlena think Jesus hear Miss Hamilton words. We find place to hide and we alive today. Carlena was much ascared before. Not so ascared this time."

Rebekah gave the young lady a long hug. After a few moments, she leaned back a little and looked into the girl's eyes.

"Well, let's pray again then. . .Let's do it together. Without waiting for approval, she whispered a prayer for help and deliverance. She asked her God for provision and for guidance. She asked for protection. Then she hesitated for a moment before continuing.

"And Lord, I pray for Gorton Harkin. We don't know where he is or whether he survived the storm, but I pray that you will look out for him and even save his immortal soul. In Jesus name, amen."

"Carlena think Miss Hamilton not like Mr. Gorton too much. But you pray for him the same."

The girl looked puzzled. Rebekah knew she had not said anything bad about the man, but somehow the young girl had picked up something in her attitude toward him.

"You don't have to like someone to pray for them and wish them well. There is something about Gorton that I do not trust. Even now, lost in the jungle and the two of us alone with no weapons, I am not certain whether I wish he was here to protect us or whether we are perhaps better off alone."

"Yes, it hard to know," Carlena replied. "He strong man and maybe brave too, but Carlena afraid of some strong, brave mens."

The image of a brash, young man flashed before Carlena's eyes. She remembered the anger in Carlos's eyes when her father and the men of her village had sent him away empty handed. She recalled the violence when he had returned and the knife fight that had broken out.

Mercifully, the young girl had no idea what that angry young man and his friends had done to her village the evening before. She had no idea that her entire world and the only home she had ever known were gone. If she made it out of the jungle alive, the time would come when she would have to learn the terrible, painful truth. But for the moment, she had plenty to handle just staying alive.

Rebekah was puzzled by Carlena's remark about being afraid of some strong, brave men, but before she could pursue the thought, she saw the expression in the girl's eyes change. She saw fear there, the powerful kind. Carlena was looking back over Rebekah's shoulder, staring at something behind her.

Following Carlena's gaze she turned and saw what had grabbed Carlena's attention. Standing on the bank opposite them was a large, black cat. It was a jaguar. Faint, barely discernible spots covered its dark body. The cat's eyes were fixed on the two females. As Rebekah turned to face the beast, it leaped off the bank and landed on the other side of the narrow creek, a scant twenty feet away.

The grace and strength the large cat displayed in leaping so easily to the bottom of the gully was not lost on the missionary. She knew she was looking at certain death for one or both of them. As she watched, mesmerized by the animal's fluid motions, the jaguar waded into the shallow stream. Its cruel yellow eyes never once leaving Rebekah's face.

Chapter Twenty-Four

*T*urning his back to the river and the still smoldering Napoteri village, Terrance Clark had little trouble following the trail as it led upward away from the slow moving water. Perto had given him the impression that some pretty steep and rugged terrain stood between Napoteri and Arakaba. If that was the case, there was no time to waste.

The narrow path wound through the jungle, weaving its way up the hillside. There were signs of the storm everywhere. The storm had hit with considerably less force here than the places they had seen downriver, but still there were fallen trees to scramble over or around and broken branches hanging in the underbrush everywhere. Always, Terrance was able to pick up the trail again on the other side of each obstacle.

On several occasions, he came face to face with a deer or a wild pig using the same trail he was on. At sight of a man the frightened creatures would invariably turn and run crashing or thumping off through the brush, leaving Terrance alone on the trail. At one point, while he was still fairly near the river, he came around a bend in the trail and saw a few feet in front of him what looked like the back half of a huge snake slithering across the trail and into the underbrush to his left. The serpent was jet black with faint gold-colored markings on its back. Terrance estimated by what he saw of it that the snake was at least twenty-five to thirty feet long and more than a foot in diameter. He stopped and waited a full five minutes before proceeding and then with no small amount of trepidation ran past the place on the narrow trail where the monstrous snake had disappeared into the brush.

After he and Timmy had escaped from Jonestown two weeks ago, Terrance had spent ten days in the jungle with Timmy, armed with only a machete and a home-made spear. There was no overstating the increased level of confidence imparted to him by the rifle he now carried in his right hand. A man armed with a good rifle can overcome any beast he might encounter in a South American rain forest, *provided of course that he was not ambushed at close quarters.*

Those days had left Terrance a changed man. He was stronger, not so much physically, but mentally and emotionally. The thought of being lost in the jungle or spending the night alone in the wild struck no fear to his heart now. There was, however, a new fear, a worse one – the fear that the men who had perpetrated the massacre at Napoteri would find Rebekah before he did. There was also the fear that the beautiful missionary might befall some harm at the hands of Gorton Harkin, though that fear was now at least somewhat lessened by the fact that the two of them were no longer alone.

Terrance was also troubled by the possibility that he might have to pull the trigger on a human being before this affair was over, and maybe more than one. He had never been in a situation that demanded that he kill another man, but the events of the past day had sud-denly made such an event a distinct possibility. The men he was trying to head off deserved to die for what they had done back at the Napoteri village. He knew that. Still, he did not want to be the one who had to draw down on one of them and pull the trigger. He steeled his mind against that moment and determined that he would do whatever had to be done and sort out the emotions later.

Terrance had climbed for several hours now and had come to a bench on the side of the hill. At least for the moment the ground had leveled off. It was beginning to get dark and it was becoming harder and harder to stay on the trail, Terrance had no idea how much farther he had to go, but it seemed certain that he would not be able to find the village if he lost the trail and took off aimlessly through the jungle. He had no choice but to stop for the night.

A hundred yards back, he had spotted two large boulders off to the right maybe fifty feet or so. Quickly, he backtracked. He could still see the two dark shapes rising out of the underbrush. Using his machete, he cut his way through the underbrush to the boulders. There was no overhang to provide shelter if it rained, but he would feel reasonably safe sleeping with the boulders at his back.

It had been a long and draining day. He took off the knapsack Perto had given him and laid it on the ground beside him. He sat down on the soft ground and leaned back against a flat space on the larger of the two rocks. After a quick meal and a few gulps of the lukewarm water, he laid his rifle across his lap and with his chin on his chest fell fast asleep.

Several times, Terrance was awakened to the piercing noises of the jungle night, but being somewhat accustomed to such sounds now, he was able to drift back to sleep. The only sounds that kept him awake for any period of time were the rustling sounds in the brush around him, sounds that in all likelihood were mice or small animals moving about through the wet leaves. Those sounds kept him awake, for fear of what they might be. He had not forgotten the monstrous snake he had seen on the trail or the jaguars he and Timmy had encountered. And there were always bushmasters, which hunted under the cover of night.

Though awakening several times, he was able to sleep enough to awaken in the morning reasonably refreshed. It was the sound of the birds that roused him from his slumber. It takes the conditioning of a lot of nights in the forest to sleep through the racket jungle birds make at first light. It was barely daylight when he opened his eyes, but there was light enough to see. Donning his pack, he stretched his cramped muscles and set out.

The crude path he had cut to reach the boulders the night before was still plain. His footprints were visible in the soft mud of the forest floor. Quite by chance, he looked down and saw in the middle of his boot print the pug mark of a large cat. It was going in the opposite direction he was now walking.

All senses went to full alert. Terrance turned and saw other tracks he had missed. They were leading straight back to the boulders where he had slept. Retracing his steps, he found that the jaguar's tracks stopped about ten feet from the spot where he had spent the night. Sometime during the night, a large jaguar, probably a male, had followed his trail right up to where he slept. The cat had stood and watched him sleeping, and then had simply gone away. The thought was hair raising. A jaguar that could have killed him easily had looked him over and then walked away. One of the sounds of rustling in the underbrush, a sound that he had dismissed as probably just mice, could very well have been an adult jaguar standing a scant ten feet from him.

Terrance turned around and walked quickly back to the main trail. Turning to the right he headed toward the Arakaba village and another day. The day ahead was going to be one that, if he survived it, could never be forgotten. But all Terrance Clark knew at the moment was that he had wasted time sleeping and now had to make it up.

Terrance had a canteen of potable water, three bis-
cuits, and some venison jerky in the knapsack Perto
had given him. He stopped for a moment to remove the
canteen and take a couple of swigs of water. He took
one biscuit and left the rest and the venison for later.
Slipping the pack back over his broad shoulders, he
continued on up the trail, nibbling on the biscuit as he
climbed.

Just up ahead, a single log had fallen across the
trail. The log was less than two feet in diameter and one
a tall man could easily step over. His left leg was in the
air and just starting back down when something in his
head told him not to step down. He withdrew his moc-
casin covered foot and took a step backward, standing
one step from the log.

Suddenly, over the top of the log appeared the scaly
head of a large snake, a bushmaster. The deadly viper
had been lying just on the other side of the log and
Terrance had come within inches of stepping right on
top of it. The serpent's head was heart shaped with
grotesque looking scales protruding slightly from both
sides. Behind that hideous head followed a long, sinuous body.

The snake was not coiled into a position from which
it could strike and Terrance stepped quickly backward.
The bushmaster increased its speed. As it slithered over
the log, its head extended upward off the ground and
followed Terrance's every movement. The snake just
kept coming. It was not backing down. By the time its
full length had cleared the log, a good ten feet of snake
lay stretched out in front of the American.

Deadly poisonous. I remember that. Very aggressive
when cornered or threatened. I've seen that before. Have
I ever! I miss my snake boots.

Terrance continued backing down the trail. He didn't
want to fire his rifle, but the snake kept coming. He
pulled the rifle to his shoulder and took aim even while

his right thumb was pulling back the hammer on the lever action Winchester. With an explosion that echoed through the forest, the bullet crashed into the bushmaster's body about six inches below its head.

Immediately the snake curled into a ball and writhed in what was an unmistakable death throe. The back end of the serpent seemed to be acting independent of the front end. The snake's jaws were open and it was snapping at the air. Suddenly its fangs caught hold of its own body three or four feet back and clamped down. While the grotesque scene was still playing out on the trail in front of him, Terrance took to the jungle and skirted that section of the trail and hit it again further up. His heart was still pounding. He had not wanted to fire the rifle, but the snake had taken enough of his time, time he feared he didn't have to waste.

If that was you, thank you, Lord, that I didn't step down on the other side of that log. I would be lying there in the trail dying about now and there would be nothing anyone could do about it. If you're listening, I ask that you help me to get to this village on time. And protect Rebekah Hamilton in the meanwhile. I am not there to watch over her, but maybe you are.

It was hardly a prayer of faith. It was more the words of a man who was searching, a man who had been taught the truth as a child but had walked away or neglected the things that build faith and maintain it. Just in case there was someone up there looking out for him, Terrance was not sure he wanted to thumb his nose at Him. He was beginning to hope that the things his mom and dad had told him were really true.

From the level bench on the mountainside, the trail began once again to make its way upward. It was hard to see up ahead, because of all of the brush and because the trail wound this way and that, switching back on itself again and again. The trail was steep now and the climber's hair and clothes were soaked with sweat. Still he pressed on.

Then, just when it seemed the climb would never end, it did. Just like that, the trail broke out on top. For the next half mile or so, the terrain was level and the going easy. Terrance broke into a run, covering the distance with as much speed as he could muster. Then as suddenly as the climb to the top had ended, the trail turned sharply to the left and started a steep descent down the other side.

Immediately the man recognized that he was at the top of a small mountain or perhaps a very big hill. As he started down the other side, through breaks in the foliage off to his right, he could see for some distance. There was jungle as far as the eye could behold. Occasionally he caught glimpses of a wide, winding river far below him. He had no idea what river it was, but many tributaries broke off of it, running in every direction like the veins on a giant leaf.

The path leading downward became narrow and rocky. A short distance later there ceased to be any forest at all on the right side of the trail. The path was now a narrow ledge, tracing its way along the side of a sheer cliff. Peering over the edge, the drop-off appeared to be at least four or five hundred feet. Far below were the top of trees further down the mountain. The height would not have bothered the man so much had the trail remained firm and the ground beneath him solid, but in several places tiny springs and rivulets of water flowed out of the uphill side to his left. Each one deposited mud and tiny bits of gravel on the steep trail. Time and again Terrance was forced to grab onto and entrust his life to branches and vines growing out of the cliff to his left to keep from sliding and falling over the side of the cliff.

As much as the descent was dangerous, Terrance was perturbed more by the fact that he was forced to go so slow. More than once he thought that maybe he should have just stayed in the boat with Perto. Who knows, he might have even made it to the village more quickly. But then again, the other fork of the river might have been impassable by boat. It had not yet been cleared like the fork that led to Napoteri. In any regard, this was the chance he had taken and it made no sense to rethink it.

Eventually, the trail made its way back down to the forest floor. From there, it led away from the side of the cliff and through the jungle at a gentle downward slope. Terrance was able to jog now and hopefully make up some of the time he had lost.

Carrying the rifle and the machete were slowing him down and he decided to drop the machete and carry only the thirty-thirty, which he could switch from hand to hand as he ran. The trail widened and he broke into a run. His long, even stride ate up the miles. Finally, down on the flat, the trail grew wider still and showed signs of much use. Occasionally there were forks off to the left and right, but always it seemed clear which was the main path.

Terrance was confident that he was approaching the village, the village where he hoped to find a beautiful, young missionary woman safe and sound and happily going about her work. What he would do or say when he found this woman was still uncertain, but find her he must. That much he knew.

Up ahead was a large boulder. It was a good twenty feet high and the trail appeared to circle around it. Terrance was almost at a full run when he rounded the left side of the rock. Coming in the opposite direction was a young woman. She too was running. There was no time for either to stop. The two collided heavily and the heavier body of the man swept the girl backward. Instinctively, Terrance let go of the rifle and threw his arms around the girl to keep her from falling.

The sight of the man struck fear to the heart of the young woman and she began to beat at him desperately with her hands, trying to escape his clutches. Terrance held her tightly for a moment and spoke low in her ear.

"I am going to let you go now. I am not going to hurt you. Why are you running and why are you so afraid?"

Slowly, he loosed his grip on the girl and he felt her body relax just a little.

"What are you running from," he asked quietly. "I am a friend. I want to help."

Terrance let go of the girl completely and she immediately stepped away from him. She was tall for an Amerindian and thin. Slowly, the girl looked Terrance up and down and somehow seemed satisfied with what she saw. She looked intently into his eyes for a moment or two, trying to read what she saw there. Finally, she spoke.

"Bad men at village. Army guns. Look for two peoples. Say they will kills peoples at village."

"Are they looking for two women or girls?"

"Yes, two womens. One Americans and one from Napoteri."

"Are the two women there? Are they in your village?"

"Marita not know. Maybe so. Marita not know."

"Thank you, Marita. You must hide in forest now. Don't go back to the village until it is safe. The men at your village are very bad. I will go there now."

Just then there was a single rifle shot from somewhere just ahead. Terrance picked up his rifle and with one smooth motion worked the level, feeding another cartridge into the chamber. As he did so, he turned and dashed down the trail in the direction from which the girl had come.

It was only a few hundred yards from the big boulder to the village. Terrance saw the shapes of huts through the trees and stopped a few feet from the clearing, being careful to keep his body hidden behind a sturdy tree.

From where he stood, Arakaba did not appear to be a large village. There, standing in a clearing surrounded by a ring of huts were five men with automatic weapons at ready. Four of the men wore green and beige camo and one did not. They were all standing with their weapons trained on a man who looked to be the village chief. Behind the chief was a large woman, who seemed to be in her twenties or thirties. Beside the heavy woman were three other men, all of whom appeared to be somewhat elderly.

Lying on the ground near the man who looked to be the chief was the body of a large dog. It appeared to have been shot in the side.

One of the men, the one not wearing camo, had placed the barrel of his rifle up against the chest of the man who appeared to be the chief. He was shouting.

"Where are the two women who came here from Napoteri? I know they came here. One is white with red hair and the other lives in Napoteri. Her name is Carlena. She is young and beautiful. Give them to me or we will kill everyone in your village."

The chief stood tall, as if he was not afraid. When he spoke, his voice was firm and unwavering. Terrance could not help but admire the man.

"Many sick people in village," he replied. "We send for missionary for she bring medicine to help. She not come yet. More people sick. We wait. Maybe storm stop her. Why you use guns to find two womens?"

The chief's words seemed to anger the man even more. He pushed the barrel of his weapon even harder against the chief's chest, forcing the man backward. The chief tried to stand his ground, but his resistance seemed to irritate his attacker even more and he pushed all the harder. The chief stumbled and fell backward onto his back. At that, the man raised his weapon to his shoulder to fire.

Up until that moment, Terrance Clark had not been sure what course of action he should take. The decision seemed to have been made for him. Almost without thinking, he raised the thirty-thirty to his shoulder and took aim. As the front sight of the rifle crossed the man's chest, he squeezed the trigger. The reaction was immediate and catastrophic. The bullet caught the would be shooter in the right side of his chest, spinning him around and knocking him backward. He fell to the ground and lay there limp and unmoving.

For a brief moment, the other four seemed shocked. They turned toward the place from which the rifle blast had come. As their weapons came up, Terrance ejected the spent cartridge and readied a second one. He trained his weapon on the nearest man and squeezed off a second round. The bullet caught the man high in the right arm and spun him around. Somehow he was able to stay on his feet.

Seeing a second comrade take a bullet, the other three unleashed a hail of lead into the forest in the general direction from which the bullets had come. The bullets tore through the brush all around him, but Terrance stood sideways behind the tree with only a small part of his body exposed. None of the bullets so much as grazed him.

Then the three, the cowards they were, turned and fled toward the river and their boat. The wounded man followed close behind, his right arm hanging useless at his side.

A few moments later, Terrance heard an engine roar to life and a boat speed away down the river. Only then did he leave the concealment of the jungle and step out into the clearing.

The chief was just getting up off the ground. The woman and three elderly men had not moved from the place they had been standing when the firing began. The woman turned and helped the chief to his feet.

Chapter Twenty-Four

Terrance strode toward them, his rifle pointed to the ground.

"Is everyone okay," he asked. "Did they hurt anyone?"

"Thanks to you, no one in the village was hurt," the woman responded in perfect English. "Who are you? Where did you come from? I think the chief owes you his life. Maybe we all do. But who are you?"

"My name is Terrance Clark. I am from California in the United States. I came across the mountain on foot, trying to get here before these men did. Yesterday, these same men came to the village across the mountain. Napoteri, I believe it is called. They were looking for a young girl.

"I think this one," Terrance said pointing at the body of the man he had shot, "wanted her for himself and planned to take her by force. When he found that she wasn't there, he and his men killed everyone in the village."

At that, there was a gasp and some whispering among the four men standing behind the woman. Those who understood English were apparently trying to relate Terrance's story to those who did not.

"One of the men of the village was shot but escaped into the jungle. He spoke to us before he died. He said that the young girl the men wanted had left the village with Miss Hamilton, who was coming here to bringing medicine to your village. Did they not arrive?"

"Those men killed everyone in Napoteri?" There was a fierce anger in the woman's voice. "What pigs! They would probably have done the same thing here had you not come when you did. We have many friends in Napoteri. And relatives, too. So many good people dead for nothing. Are you certain they are all dead?"

Terrance nodded and the woman walked over to the body of Carlos Dortin. She rolled him over with her foot. The man's eyes were open but blank. She kicked him roughly in the side with her foot and spat in his face. Then she turned back toward Terrance.

"Rebekah Hamilton has not arrived here. She must have been caught in the storm. I know her. She would have tried to get the medicine to us, no matter what. A moment ago, you said the dying man in the village spoke to 'us,' and yet you are here alone. Where are the others in your party? And do you know the name of the young girl this pig was looking for?"

"I came to Napoteri with one other man. He had a boat and I hired him to take me there. His name is Perto, a shopkeeper from Annari."

"I know Perto. He is the man who shot a jaguar at one pace and is still trying to sell the hide. He is a good man. But do you know the name of the girl?"

"I'm sorry, I don't. I think she was fourteen and left with Miss Hamilton to visit a friend in this village."

"Then it was Carlena and she was coming to visit me," the woman said. "She is fourteen and very beautiful. She is much too young for this pig. And much too innocent. I'm glad you killed him."

Terrance glanced over at the man he had just shot. Strangely, he felt nothing. There was no remorse. There was no guilt or uneasiness about what he had done. Maybe that would come later. He knew the deed had to be done and that at the moment that he had pulled the trigger there was really no other decision to make. Still, he had just killed a man and felt nothing. That seemed strange to him.

By now, the chief and other men had gathered around Terrance and the woman. The chief called out in the local dialect of the village and slowly heads started popping out of the entrances to the huts. Terrance noticed that the chief had picked up Carlos's weapon and was holding it close to his chest. Carlos had been carrying an AK-47, the most widely used assault rifle in the world. Even with only one clip the gun was a nice trophy for the chief, and he had earned it. And if Carlos's friends decided to return to the village any time soon, at least one man, a brave one at that, could meet them on their own terms.

Over the next several minutes, total strangers gathered around Terrance to pat him on the back and shake his hand. Small children shyly reached out and touched or patted him on the leg. Never had Terrance Clark been the center of so much affection. Even the girl he had crashed into back in the forest was somehow there to thank him.

The whole affair was cut short when someone heard the sound of a boat coming up the river. Fear quickly replaced the happiness on the villagers' faces. The chief ordered the people to move close to the jungle and to prepare to flee and hide in the forest if the men with automatic weapons were returning. Then he came and stood next to Terrance, the AK-47 firmly gripped in both hands.

It was Terrance who first recognized the man standing at the rear of the first of the three boats. It was Perto! Terrance ran toward the little dock, shouting and waving at his friend. The people of the village, seeing that the bad men were not returning, followed close on Terrance's heels.

There were three men in each boat. Each held a rifle or a shotgun, though many of the weapons looked to be quite old. Before the boats reached the little dock where Terrance was standing, Perto shouted out to his friend.

"We pass army boat on river. Boat go very fast. Four mens," Perto shouted. "Perto afraid they come to village first and kills everyone. Did mens come here?"

When the men had climbed out onto the dock, Terrance explained to them all everything that had happened. Then he led Perto and the others to the body of the man he had killed. Perto did not recognize the man, but one of the villagers from Bilokut did.

"He son of army officer," the man explained. "Father bad man. Son bad man. His name Carlos. Carlos something."

Perto explained that as soon as he had arrived at Bilokut the night before he had radioed officials at the coast who said they were sending armed investigators and would be on the lookout for the rogue men and their boat. He explained that other boats had been dispatched from Bilokut to bury the dead in Napoteri.

"On your way here, Perto, did you see any sign of Miss Hamilton or the boat they were in?" Terrance asked anxiously. "They left Napoteri before the storm hit and traveled down the river, but they never arrived here."

"No, Mr. Terrance. We watch for sign of any boat, but see nothing."

"That's what worries me, Perto. Remember the canoe we saw high up in the tree on our way upriver? Before your friend in Napoteri died, he told you that Rebekah's guide bought a canoe before he left the village. If that's the same canoe, then they could be anywhere. They may have been caught in the storm and capsized. They could have pulled ashore and escaped into the jungle, but if that's what happened, where's their boat?"

Everyone seemed puzzled that Rebekah's party had disappeared completely, but the consensus was that their boat had probably capsized and they had all drowned or been eaten by crocodiles. The locals seemed rather matter of fact about that possibility. People who live out their entire lives in the primitive forests and on these untamed rivers seem to take death and its inevitability as a matter of course.

Death at the hand of nature, however, was one thing to them, the senseless slaughter that had happened at Napoteri was quite another matter. Such an atrocity had never before intruded into their simple world. They could not comprehend it.

"We can all search for them," Perto offered.

"And we will help," the heavy woman stated matter of factly. "There are many sick people in our village and we desperately need the antibiotics Mrs. Hamilton was carrying. And if Carlena is with her and they are alive, Carlena is the last survivor from her people and we must find her. She probably doesn't even know that her family is dead."

"But where do we start?" Terrance asked, looking around for anyone to give him some kind of answer, some kind of hope. No one spoke.

Finally, the mayor from Bilokut answered. He was carrying a hunting rifle with a scope and had refused to stay behind when Perto had started back upriver with others from his village.

"We will not find them in forest," the mayor stated with a certainty that seemed beyond question. "Too big. Much too big. We go up and down river in boat. We make noise. We listen. We shoot gun in air. They come to river or we not find them."

Everyone nodded in agreement with Mayor Samuel Torsono's assessment. These men had lived their entire lives on the river and in the forest and knew that it was hopeless to find someone when you had no idea where they were. The jungle was simply much too vast and too rugged to search.

Terrance turned to the woman. "We will get more antibiotics and have them sent to the village as quickly as possible. We will dispatch one of these boats specifically for that purpose. I will pay the cost, if that is a problem. Try to hold on until then."

The woman nodded and took Terrance's right hand in both of hers and kissed it. "We already owe you our lives, Mr. Clark," she whispered.

Then she said for all to hear, "Our village will send our best hunters and trackers into the forest and search the area between the two rivers the best we can. Our people know this part of the forest well and if Miss Hamilton and her party are anywhere in that area, there is a good chance we will find them, though it may take a few days to search completely. If, on the other hand, they are somewhere on the other side of the two rivers, then the area is too big to search. They will have to come to the river for us to find them."

The woman said additional words in the native dialect and heads nodded and men started back to their homes to prepare for the search. It wasn't much, but no one had a better plan than the woman had outlined.

One boat was immediately dispatched to go for antibiotics, enough for the entire village. Perto guaranteed full payment for the antibiotics and everyone agreed that the shopkeeper's word would be sufficient to acquire what was needed. The men in the other two boats agreed that they would go up and down the river, yelling and firing off rounds to see if they could spot the lost party or some sign of their boat. The chief of Arakaba suggested that it might take time for the lost party to make it to the river once they heard the gunshots or shouts, so the boats would have to canvas the area more than once.

Heads nodded in agreement. With that, the trackers from Arakaba were given instructions to go straight to the river and flag down the next boat that passed by in the event they found the missing party.

There was no more to say. Everyone knew their assigned tasks. Two boats would search the two forks and one would cover the area below the forks all the way down to Bilokut. Given the fact that the canoe lodged high in the tree below the fork may have been the one Gorton Harkin had acquired before leaving Napoteri, there was some possibility that the missing party had made it ashore somewhere below the forks.

Terrance was torn between riding up and down the river and shouting and firing guns into the air, which seemed such a hopeless waste of time, and heading back into the forest with the trackers and scouring the jungle for the proverbial needle in a haystack. Neither plan seemed to offer much hope, but he had nothing better to suggest. Ultimately, he decided to ride with Perto in his boat, which would scour both sides of the riverbank on the Napoteri fork and then head back upriver to Arakaba.

"What about the body," Terrance said, pointing toward what was left of Carlos Dortin. His corpse was still lying in the dirt in the middle of the village.

"I will see to that," the heavy woman said. "The rest of you spend your time on the living."

After the search parties had all left, the woman recruited the assistance of three of the villagers and together they dragged Carlos's body down to the dock where she unceremoniously shoved it over the edge with her foot. It splashed heavily into the dark water, sinking slowly out of sight.

"There, the crocs can have you, you despicable piece of garbage."

Those were the only words spoken over the young man's body. That was the last anyone would ever see of Carlos Dortin, but unfortunately it was not the end of the trouble he would cause.

Chapter Twenty-Five

As the jaguar waded the shallow stream, its eyes never once averted from the face of Rebekah Hamilton. Her beauty was wasted on such a creature. To the cat, the pretty missionary was but a meal. Each step the jaguar took, its muscular body close to the ground, was a singular motion, followed by another. Its movement was at once graceful and jerky as it paused momentarily after each step.

Facing the jaguar, Rebekah Hamilton slowly moved Carlena behind her, positioning herself between the cat and the girl. As soon as the jaguar had forded the stream, it dropped to its belly. Behind its powerful body, its long sinuous tail began to twitch ever so slightly as it crept forward inch by inch, its belly touching the ground.

Every instinct in the woman told her that the animal's behavior meant it considered them prey and was going to charge. The animal was not merely curious or moving in for a better look. It was coming in for the kill. Rebekah looked deep into the cat's gleaming yellow eyes and saw something resembling a cruel hatred. Death had removed its mask and embodied itself in the form of a dark slinking beast. And it was staring her in the face.

Try as she might, the missionary could think of nothing she could do to protect herself or the girl. Their situation was hopeless. The best outcome she could envision was that one of them died and the other escaped.

Then, almost unconsciously, she ever so slowly began to remove the knapsack from her back. Her body was taking the action before her conscious mind realized what she was doing. Confident that there was no way its prey could escape, the jaguar stopped for a moment, eyeing the woman's movements. Rebekah was certain the cat could easily leap the distance between them.

As she slowly removed the pack, she spoke quietly to the girl behind her. She was surprised at how steady her voice sounded. She did not wish to die, but she was strangely unafraid of that outcome.

"When it attacks, do not run," she whispered. "Walk slowly away and don't look back. Keep going until you are safe. *Make* your way to the river and someone will find you."

There was no reply, but Rebekah could feel the girl's trembling body pressed up against her back and Carlena's fingers digging into her side.

The pack was off Rebekah's back now. She was holding it at her side. Again, without realizing that she was actually doing it, she began swinging the pack back and forth, holding it by one of the straps. She could see the cat's eyes following the rhythmic motion of the pack. After three or four swings, as smoothly as she could, she let go. The pack sailed through the air straight at the black face and yellow eyes.

As providence would have it, the cat raised up to meet the strange thing flying at it. When it did, one of the pack's straps went over the beast's head while the pouch portion of the pack dropped in front of the cat's neck. The reaction was as strange as it was unexpected. As if it had been attacked, the jaguar tore viciously at the pouch. It fought back as if it was in the battle of its life. It rolled over onto its back and into the water, snarling and tearing at the sturdy canvas bag.

Rebekah grabbed Carlena and dragged her down the creek bank and away from the snarling, growling beast. She was certain that this was but a momentary reprieve and that the jaguar would dispatch the feisty knapsack in short order and be upon them with a vengeance. But for a few seconds, it seemed preoccupied.

The two girls scurried up the muddy bank to the top and just as Rebekah looked back, the strap around the cat's neck snapped and the pack dropped harmlessly to the ground. As if to finish it off, the cat bit down on the pack with its powerful jaws and shook it vigorously. The large glass bottle of antibiotics in the bag broke and little capsules went flying everywhere, spilling into the water.

Sensing that it had thoroughly vanquished this strange, bloodless foe, the jaguar raised its head and searched for its intended prey. The two girls were just disappearing over the top of the embankment, a distance the powerful beast could cross in three or four powerful bounds.

As Rebekah and Carlena turned to run, they were stunned to see Gorton Harkin standing right in front of them, only a few yards away. There was a startled and confused look on the man's face. Much of the mud from the night before still caked his clothes and his hair was matted and dirty. Gorton looked a wild man. He started to speak as the girls dashed toward him.

"Jaguar!" Rebekah Hamilton shouted. The sound came out too hoarsely to be a shout, but Gorton heard her clearly enough. But before the man could react, the cat was over the bank and upon him.

This was hardly the prey the jaguar had anticipated. Gorton was larger and stronger than the two frail looking things the carnivore had spotted near the creek bed, but the contact between the man and the cat occurred before either knew what was happening. The die was cast – for the both of them.

Instinctively, Gorton threw up his left arm to keep the powerful jaws away from his head and throat. His right hand searched desperately for the knife that always hung from his belt. He felt the searing pain as powerful fangs closed on his left forearm and he heard the loud crack as the bone was crushed. He let out a loud groan as the cat's teeth dug into his flesh. At that same moment, the knife came loose from the scabbard at his side and with all the strength his body could muster Gorton plunged the long, thick blade deep into the cat's side. The blade entered just behind the jaguar's left shoulder.

The cat screamed out in pain as its own blood began to heavily stain its dark coat. Again Gorton plunged the knife into the cat's side. The jaguar let go of the man's limp arm and tried to close on his face. Gorton had no defense now. His left arm was worthless and his right hand was down at the cat's side. As the jaguar snapped at his face, barely missing, Gorton let go of the knife and somehow got his right hand at the beast's throat. The cat immediately twisted its head and seized Gorton's right arm just above the wrist and with the same motion forced its powerful jaws into the place where the man's neck and right shoulder met. As its jaws closed on Gorton's neck and shoulder, the jaguar arched its back, reached both of its hind feet up to the man's chest and tore downward, its long claws horribly strafing poor Gorton from his chest down to his thighs. Immediately Gorton's body went limp.

The cat, sensing that its prey was finished, released its grip on his neck and shoulder. For a moment, the jaguar stood over the man, looking down at the empty eyes that were staring upward. Blood was visibly pulsing from the cat's side and it made no effort to move. Momentarily, its legs wobbled. It struggled to stay on its feet for a few seconds and then collapsed on top of Gorton Harkin's body.

The two girls were standing less than twenty feet away. They watched as the beast's heaving sides stopped moving and it lay completely still.

Rebekah knew they should have kept running when the jaguar collided with Gorton, but they hadn't. Hearing the growls and groans of the struggle, they had turned and watched the savage ordeal unfold. Both Gorton and the jaguar were dead now, of that the girls were certain. But the wild, primitive nature of what they had just witnessed would never leave them.

Gorton had not fought the jaguar to save them. That they knew. He had really had no choice in the matter. But still, had he not been there and fought so valiantly, the women knew that at least one of them would be dead by now.

Cautiously, Rebekah stepped closer to make sure there was no life left in the cat. Its sides had continued to move for only a few moments after it had collapsed atop poor Gorton. Now it lay completely still. Carefully, the missionary reached down and with some effort withdrew the bloody blade from the jaguar's side and wiped it on its back. Gorton's lifeless eyes stared up at her. Gently, she reached down and closed them. He would lie where he died. They had nothing to bury him with and not the strength to do it anyway. Still, there was sadness in Rebekah Hamilton's eyes when she turned and looked at her young friend.

"They both dead?" Carlena asked, though she was sure she knew the answer. "You prayed for Mr. Gorton, but he killed now. Jesus not answer prayer?"

Rebekah reached down and took Carlena's hands in hers.

"I have prayed many prayers in my life," she said quietly, "and this thing I know. We pray based on what we know and God answers based on what He knows."

Carlena thought for a moment and then nodded. She was young, but even by age fourteen most humans recognize that there are limits to what any of us know or understand. It may take many more years to come to accept that reality fully, but it hits most of us in the face long before we learn to accept it and live with it. Those who don't, live bitter lives.

There was no more reason for the two women to stay where they were. Without looking back at what remained of the life and death struggle they had just witnessed, Rebekah and Carlena started off in what they thought was the direction from which they had come the night before. It wasn't.

The powerful winds of the night before had raised havoc with the jungle all about them. Nothing was the same as before the storm had struck. There were fallen trees everywhere and heavy limbs dangling from branches that had withstood the onslaught of the storm. The two girls slowly picked their way through the maze of downed trees, sometimes walking along the trunks of the larger ones and sometimes getting down on their hands and knees and crawling under. By the time they realized that they should have made it back to the river by now, they were hopelessly lost somewhere near the middle of the rugged terrain that lay between the two forks of the river. Knowing nothing else to do, they kept moving, choosing the easiest possible route through the dense brush, regardless of which way it led them. Always, the missionary carried Gorton's sturdy knife in her right hand, ever at the ready.

As evening approached, Rebekah accepted the fact they were hopelessly lost. Young Carlena on the other hand was not so willing to acknowledge that reality. She assured her older friend that if they kept moving they would eventually come to a river. As they trekked on, the terrain became increasingly muddy. To add to their plight, the heavy rain seemed to have brought out more snakes than Rebekah had ever seen before. The little red ones with black bands were everywhere. They even saw rattlesnakes, the tropical kind, but they were not aggressive and moved out of the way when they heard the girls approaching. Carlena pointed out to Rebekah the snakes that were to be feared and which were harmless. The native girl's fear of one particular snake, one they had not yet encountered, was palpable.

One time while they were down on their knees crawling under a monstrous deadfall, Carlena whispered low. "Miss Hamilton, please ask Jesus, 'No bushmaster, Jesus. Please, no bushmaster.'"

Rebekah knew of these snakes and the widespread fear the Amerindians had for them. She knew that they killed them any time they got the chance. The bushmaster's poison was deadly, especially when one was far from help when bitten. She had been told that they were sometimes very aggressive. Over the years she and John had spent in the native villages, she had seen several dead bushmasters that villagers had killed in the bush and brought back to their village. Some of snakes she had seen were in the neighborhood of ten feet long and thick.

The missionary had not thought much about bushmasters before today. She had never seen a live one in the wild. But remembering the stories she had heard about them and the frightening sight of the dead ones she had seen, she did as Carlena asked and prayed that they would not meet up with a bushmaster or any other deadly denizen of the jungle.

As darkness settled in, the two women huddled together with their backs to a giant Greenheart tree that had withstood the powerful winds. Rebekah held tightly to Gorton's knife through the night and barely slept. Carlena on the other hand slept through the night, her head resting peacefully on the older woman's shoulder.

Shortly after daybreak, the two women rose and scoured the area for anything edible. Neither of them had eaten since they had left Napoteri a day and half earlier. Carlena spotted a nest a dozen feet up in a tree. With the agility of a monkey, she shimmied her way up and then carried the whole thing back down fully intact. There were five eggs in the nest from the storm, but underneath they looked fresh.

"What do we do with those?" the missionary asked. "We don't have a fire or anything to cook them in."

"Watch," the native girl said, smiling a mischievous smile. She lightly cracked one of the eggs and sniffed its contents. Satisfied with what her nose told her, she leaned her head back and opened her mouth, emptying the contents of the shell down her open throat.

"Disgusting," the beautiful missionary said, shaking her head back and forth to reinforce the point.

"Now, you try," Carlena replied laughing out loud. "Two for me and three for Miss Hamilton."

Rebekah seemed determined not to try this delicacy, so Carlena downed another.

"Not eat. Not taste. Just swallow," she said. To her surprise, the missionary volunteered to try one. Rebekah leaned her head back and Carlena cracked an egg and dumped the contents down her friend's waiting throat. Rebekah swallowed the raw egg in one gulp and then turned and faced the girl.

The look on Rebekah's face made Carlena laugh so hard she had to sit down to keep from falling down. In a second, Rebekah was there beside her and laughing just as hard.

A couple of minutes later, though, they took to the task with earnest and Rebekah downed the last two eggs.

"My stomach feels like I really ate," she said after the last raw egg had slipped down her throat.

Just as Carlena started to reply, they heard the muffled sound of a gunshot somewhere off in the distance. Both girls jumped to their feet, looking off to the north and the apparent direction of the shot, hoping to hear it repeated.

There was no way for Rebekah or Carlena to know that Terrance Clark, a private detective from Oakland, California, had just shot a bushmaster on a jungle trail a good three miles north of where they stood.

Thinking the gunshot had come from the river or perhaps the Arakaba village, they changed directions and started moving north toward the sound. They had no way of knowing that the left fork of the river was only half a mile away in the direction they had been traveling before they had stopped to feast upon the contents of the birds' nest.

The two girls had not traveled far when the jungle floor in front of them began to slope upward sharply. They attempted to climb the hillside and continue in the direction of the shot, but the terrain grew increasingly steep and rugged. Eventually, it was impassable to continue.

Finally, discouraged and disappointed, the girls sat down on one of the many small boulders protruding from the hillside and rested. They had been sitting there for quite some time when again they heard the crack of a rifle. It was still some distance away, but this time it sounded closer.

Carlos Dortin had just shot a dog that had been barking aggressively as he stood facing the chief, a woman, and some of the village elders in Arakaba.

Moments later, there was another crack. The heavy bullet from a thirty-thirty hunting rifle had just ended the life of one Carlos Dortin, a thief and a mass murderer.

That shot was followed by another and then a volley of shots, which sounded like the firing of automatic weapons. Carlena had never heard the sound before, but the missionary knew what she was hearing.

"It sounds like a war is going on," Rebekah whispered. They stayed where they were and listened for more gunshots, but the volley of automatic fire was followed by silence.

A few moments later, off to the downhill side to their left they heard the sound of a boat engine, maybe more than one.

"Boat," Carlena cried. She turned and dashed down the hillside and back the way they came, the missionary close on her heels.

Running through the jungle with reckless disregard for snakes and whatever else might be in their way, they hastened toward the increasing sound of boat engines. As fate would have it, the underbrush was sparse where they were and they were able to make good time. But as they broke out of the jungle at the riverbank just above a muddy croc wallow, they saw in an instant that they were a few seconds too late. To their right three boats were passing out of sight around a bend upriver.

They yelled and waved their arms, but the boats were out of range and no one looked in their direction.

At the sound of their loud voices, the half dozen Caimans basking in the mud just below them dashed into the water, alarmed by the loud noises on the bank behind them.

"Well, we find river," Carlena said simply. It was plain to see the disappointment on her young face.

"Others will come," Rebekah assured her. "We can just wait here. Someone will come. At least we're not lost anymore."

For three or four minutes, they stood staring at the place where the three boats had disappeared. Suddenly, from the same spot where those three had disappeared another boat appeared. It was larger and moving rapidly. The girls waved their arms and yelled as loudly as they could. The men in the boat spotted them right away.

Chapter Twenty-Six

*T*he four men Carlos Dortin had enlisted to assist him in his ill-fated attempt to steal young Carlena were all soldiers as a matter of profession, but as a matter of practice and character, they were merely unscrupulous mercenaries, the vile, brutish sort who would do things for lucre what no honorable man would do. As such, they had no reason to stay another minute in the Arakaba village once they saw their employer lying dead in the dirt and another bullet crash into another of their band.

There was nothing in that poor fishing village worth dying for, so the four men wasted no time making a hasty retreat. Hidden in the boat was the treasure these four had come upriver for, two nice sized bags of gold flakes.

Sure, they knew there would be hell to pay with Sergeant Dortin if the man ever discovered that they had accompanied Carlos on his little quest but had left the boy lying in the dirt in some remote village. But that was a bridge they preferred to cross if and when they came to it. Besides, there was plenty of time to contrive a believable story before they got back to the base and met up with old man Dortin.

None of the four knew that it had been Claspen himself who had approved the mission and funded it. It had been Claspen who had recommended these four men by name. Had they known these things, they would have found less comfort in their ability to lie their way out of a problem they now owned.

As it was, the four raced away from the village as fast as the cruiser would carry them. They had traveled only a couple of miles downriver when rounding a bend they barely missed colliding with three smaller boats headed upriver, all carrying armed men. All things considered, there might have been gunplay on the river at that moment had there been time for either side to contemplate the situation, but as it was the boats passed each other so quickly that there was hardly time for anyone to react.

Three or four minutes later, the four mercenaries spotted two women waving at them from the left riverbank. In a moment they were close enough to see that one was a white woman with reddish brown hair and the other was a native girl, young and beautiful. They immediately recognized who the two women must be.

The driver turned toward the shoreline and maneuvered the boat in close enough to be heard.

"You look lost," he shouted. "Do you need help? We have been patrolling the river searching for two women and a man feared lost in the storm."

The driver of the boat spoke perfect English. "You must be the two women we have been searching for, but where is the man?"

"We *are* the ones you are looking for," Rebekah Hamilton replied. "Our boat was swept downriver during the storm and we have been lost in the jungle for a couple of days. Our guide was killed by a jaguar yesterday. His body is back there somewhere." Rebekah waved her arm back in the general direction from which they had come.

The driver whispered to the other four that this stroke of luck might work out well for them and they might be able to make some money off the two females. The others nodded their agreement and the driver quickly nosed the boat in closer to the muddy riverbank. Two of the men helped the girls onboard and as soon as they were safe on the deck, the driver backed the boat away from the shore and sped off downriver. Carlena noticed that the man at the helm kept turning and tossing nervous glances back upriver.

The first thing Rebekah observed when she stepped onboard was the man seated on the bench seat at the back of the boat. Unlike the others, who were black, this man looked to be perhaps half white and half Asian. He was a large, well built man with short hair and a hint of grey around the temples. Most noticeable, he was naked from the waste up and had a thin camo shirt tied around his upper arm. The shirt was soaked in blood.

"What happened to you?" Rebekah asked. "It looks like you've lost a lot of blood."

"Someone fired at us from the riverbank," the man lied. "We were patrolling up and down the river looking for you, when someone fired out of the jungle for no reason and I was hit. It just happened a little while ago. Are you a doctor?"

"No, but my husband was. I know enough to at least take a look at your wound and assess the damage."

"We fired back," the man continued his hastily contrived story, "but we couldn't see a thing. Whoever shot me was hiding in the jungle. When he started firing again, we got out of there as quickly as we could."

Rebekah knelt beside the man and carefully removed the blood soaked shirt. The wound was awful to look at, especially from the back side, where large shards of bone were mingled with shredded muscle tissue and small pieces of lead. It was obvious that the bullet had shattered the bone in the man's upper arm. Rebekah was surprised that he was still conscious and had not gone into shock.

"You are going to need hospital care right away or you could lose that arm. It is a very severe wound, the kind that could easily become infected. The bone is shattered and exposed."

The man didn't even blink. It was not the first time he had been shot.

"Is there anything you can do before we can get to a doc?" he asked coolly. "It's a long way from here to the nearest hospital. We can't even call ahead. Our radio is out." The man lied again.

"There are only two things I might be able to do, sir. I can try to stop the bleeding and if we can find something to use for antiseptic, we can at least reduce the chance of infection."

There was a first-aid kit in the tiny cabin below deck. One of the men fetched it and handed it to the missionary unopened. Rebekah searched through the contents and found one small bottle of antiseptic. She applied the whole bottle, applying most to the exit side of the wound. Then she deftly dressed the man's arm, using all of the gauze and tape in the kit.

"That is the best I can do for now," she said. "But you need a hospital soon. It's odd that someone shot at you from the riverbank as you were passing by. We heard the gunfire. Why would anyone do that?"

The man only shrugged. The less he said, the easier it would be to keep up the lie.

The boat continued on down the river, making good time. Eventually, Bilokut came into view, but the driver made no indication that he was stopping. Rebekah jumped to her feet and hailed the man at the helm.

"Where are you going?" she shouted over the roar of the engine. "We must stop here and radio for more antibiotics for the Arakaba village. I lost the ones I was going to deliver and the people there are seriously ill. This is where I want to get off and the girl too."

The men cast sly glances at one another. For a few moments no one responded. Rebekah Hamilton turned to the men beside her on the lower deck.

"What's going on?" she demanded. "Why didn't we stop? We want off at Bilokut. Turn around and take us back." Rebekah was standing with her hands on her hips in a suddenly defiant pose.

Safely out of sight of Bilokut, the man at the helm slowed the boat so he could be easily heard when he told the lie he had carefully contrived.

"I apologize, Mrs. Hamilton, but we cannot explain what we do not know. We had orders to search for you, and when we found you, we were to bring you back to the base for questioning. It seems there was some trouble upriver and you are to be questioned about what happened there."

"What kind of trouble?" the missionary demanded. "I have heard of nothing except for the illnesses I have been trying to address."

The driver continued.

"Well, two days ago you and the man you now say was killed by a jaguar visited Napoteri, a small village up the right fork of the river. You then left in a hurry later that same day. When we arrived at the Napoteri village, everyone there was dead, shot down in cold blood."

Carlena gasped. "My village? Everyone dead? This cannot be. Everyone okay there when we leave. Mother and father there."

The girl had just heard news that she could in no way grasp. Her mind and emotions were swirling.

"When we arrived," the driver continued coolly, "everyone was dead and the village burned. We have been patrolling up and down the river ever since trying to find out what happened. That's when someone fired from the shore and hit Armando there in the arm. We assume it was your friend Gorton, the man you say is dead. We will have to sort this all out when we get you back to the base."

By now Carlena was sobbing uncontrollably. Rebekah put her arms around the girl and held her close.

"Surely you don't think we had anything to do with whatever happened up there," the missionary said. "Are you sure we are talking about the same village? Are you sure it was the Napoteri village, the one up the right fork of the river?"

The driver nodded his head and then dismissively increased the boat's speed, effectively ending the conversation. By now, the boat was in the channel of the main river that led back to the coast. From then on, the driver ran the boat with the engine wide open, making it all but impossible to converse over the roar of the craft's powerful motor.

When the driver hit the accelerator and the boat shot forward, Rebekah fell back onto the seat at the back of the boat and almost landed on the man the driver had called Armando. Armando was able to use his good arm to steer the woman into the seat to his left.

Carlena immediately slid over next to Rebekah and the two of them sat silently, staring down at the floor. Nothing they had heard from these men made sense.

Carlena put her head on Rebekah's shoulder and sobbed quietly for some time. Suddenly, the older woman sat up as if she had just thought of something and just as quickly settled back in her seat. When she saw that none of the men had noticed her action, she whispered quietly in the teenager's ear.

"These men could not have been sent to your village because of some report that the people of Napoteri had been killed. We passed this same boat on the river shortly after we left your village in Gorton's boat two days ago. That was just before the storm hit. This boat was already heading upriver toward your village. You were sleeping at the time, but I recognize these men.

And there was another man with them, but he was not wearing a uniform. He was driving the boat, I think, but he is not here now. Perhaps that one got off upriver, but this is definitely the same boat I saw. There is something wrong with what they are telling us.

"Yes, I'm sure of it. These men must have arrived at the village just after we left! If the people of your village have been killed, God forbid, it would have been these men who did it."

"Was one man, one driving boat, young?" Carlena asked. There was a hard, cold look on the young girl's beautiful face.

"Yes, I think so," Rebekah replied.

Chapter Twenty-Seven

A s soon as the trackers had been dispatched into the jungle to begin the land search, Perto and Terrance patrolled slowly back down the river from the Arakaba village and then all the way back up the other fork to Napoteri. There was no sign of the two females, Gorton Harkin, or the boat they were in. At regular intervals, Perto would stop the engine and he or Terrance would call out or fire into the air. The only response was the angry shrieks of the birds and the occasional scurrying of crocs into the water.

When they finally arrived back at Napoteri, there were two boats from Bilokut tied up at the little dock. A half dozen men could be seen working away in the hot afternoon sun. They were digging holes as fast as they could and burying the bodies of the poor villagers. One man had a tablet in his hand and it appeared that he was writing on it.

"One man in Bilokut move there from Napoteri not long ago," Perto explained. "Marry wife and live in Bilokut now. He know all peoples at Napoteri. Write down names of people before they bury."

"What a sad day this must be for him," Terrance replied. "We can only pray that the men who did this will be brought to justice. At least one of them has paid."

Perto nodded grimly and turned his boat around. Slowly, they started back the way they had come. They were both painfully aware that the entire area had been covered now. Nonetheless, Terrance and his friend carefully scanned the water and the shoreline, searching in every direction for some sign of the missing party or their boat.

The image of the canoe they had spotted far up in a tree the day after the storm continued to trouble Terrance, though he never spoke of it. He knew it would be difficult to survive in a small boat in a storm with the force to do that. Slowly he felt himself being overwhelmed by the hopelessness of their search. Perto on the other hand had come to that same conclusion a couple of hours earlier, but continued the search on for his friend's sake.

Terrance and Perto had made it back to the fork again and had turned north and were traveling upriver toward Arakaba. Suddenly up ahead Perto spotted a man on the right side of the river. The man was waving his arms wildly in an attempt to get their attention. As the boat drew nearer, they recognized the man as one of the trackers from Arakaba, part of the team that had been sent to search the forested area between the two rivers.

Perto steered the boat in close to the shore, where the excited man wasted no time sharing his report.

"I track fast. No find womens. Find tracks. Find one dead mans with dead *tigre* on him. Dark one. Follow two womens track easy. Track come here and stop.

"See deep track there?" the man from Arakaba continued, pointing to the soft earth at the top of the bank.

"Womens walk hard here. Maybe walk up on boat. No more tracks. Gone now. Womens gone. No more track."

The man's English was not so good, but neither Perto nor Terrance had any doubts as to what he had just told them. Assuming that the dead man was Gorton Harkin, the two women had made it to the river and had been picked up by a boat. Whose boat was anyone's guess. But they were alive and safe. Terrance Clark's heart leaped within him. There was hope.

Perto climbed out on the shore and looked at the tracks for himself.

"One native sandal track and one shoe track," he said knowingly. "Perto sure this Miss Hamilton and girl from Napoteri," he said, pointing at the tracks in the soft mud.

Terrance wrinkled his forehead, uncertain as to the meaning of this new evidence. He suggested to Perto that he instruct the tracker to get help and retrieve Gorton's body and bring it to this same spot where it could be picked up. Gorton's brother was an important man back in Annari and he would want the body.

"You and I should head back to Bilokut and see that the two girls arrived there safely, as it now appears. We can use the town's radio and report the goings on at Arakaba and explain why I had to shoot that Carlos fellow."

Perto agreed and quickly instructed the tracker to do as Terrance had suggested. Before pushing off, Terrance congratulated the tracker for his excellent skills and thanked him for all he had done. The man beamed at Terrance's words and then turned and disappeared into the jungle.

"Man will find other men that track with him. Trackers bring body here," Perto said.

He quickly turned his little craft around and headed off downstream as quickly as the little engine would take them.

Terrance sat in the middle seat and stared ahead at the river. She was alive! In another two or three hours, he would finally meet the beautiful Rebekah Hamilton face to face. He was not entirely sure how he should feel about that. All he knew of her was that one brief smile on a crowded riverbank and that everyone who knew her loved and respected her.

This woman knows nothing of me. I can't exactly tell her what I have gone through to find her. Truth be told, for all my effort I have done her no good, not really. I guess it is enough to know that she is safe now. Still, it would be nice to see that smile one more time.

A certain nervousness was beginning to creep into the man's mind. He had been confident when he had set out on his search. He was going to find the woman and rescue her. Now, all he was going to do was meet her.

The ride down the river in the little boat seemed interminable to the American. At long last, however, Bilokut came into view. Perto edged his boat up to the dock, and as soon as they were close enough, he asked the men working near the dock if they had seen Miss Hamilton.

The men stared back at the shopkeeper blankly, as if confused by the question. Perto had been there the day before and had used the short wave to report to the authorities what had happened at the Napoteri village. He had left this very dock earlier this same morning with two other boats to go up river and rescue Miss Hamilton. Two additional boats had been loaded with the men who had been dispatched to help bury the bodies of the slain villagers. Yet, here was Perto, the shopkeeper from Annari, back at Bilokut, asking them if they had seen the woman.

The men did their best to assure the two visitors that they knew nothing more than they knew earlier. They added that the only boat that had come down from upriver this day had been a military boat and it had been moving quite rapidly and had not stopped at the village. The men at the dock did not know if it was the same boat that had gone up river two or three days earlier, but they thought so.

Chapter Twenty-Eight

*O*ne day earlier, when Perto had used the radio at Bilokut to contact the authorities at the coast, he had used the official channel, the one reserved for emergencies or government matters. Because Perto was reporting a major crime, the murder of nearly a hundred Amerindians by army personnel, the call was referred to the duty officer. On this day, that officer happened to be one Sergeant Claspen Dortin.

Dortin's superiors were away investigating the mass suicide at Jonestown, the assassination of a U.S. Congressman and members of the American media at a nearby airstrip, and the link between all of that and a murder/suicide in Georgetown involving a mother and her three daughters. The mother and three daughters were all members of the Peoples Temple and had been found slain. The murder weapon, a knife, was found lying at the mother's side.

When Sergeant Dortin heard the news of the Napoteri massacre, he immediately started thinking of plausible explanations he could offer to his superiors. Part of that analysis included naming potential scapegoats if the affair could not be covered up.

Dortin was not so much troubled by the death of so many Amerindians as the possibility that he might personally get caught up in the affair or his son might. At this point, it had not occurred to him that his son might be in danger. The boy was, after all, on a military boat accompanied by a team of trained soldiers, all carrying automatic weapons.

Dortin immediately threw together a small crew of dependable men and before daybreak the next morning started upriver in a boat identical to the one his son had left in. Claspen knew he had to follow up on the report. Too many people listen in to the official channel to ignore it. And he knew someone would have to take the fall for the death of so many natives, even if the story never made the papers. He simply had not decided yet who that *someone* was going to be.

It was a long way upriver to the Napoteri village, so the sergeant had plenty of time to think. He was well on his way when another call came over the short wave. Claspen took that call, as well, and immediately recognized the voice on the other end as American, probably a West Coast accent. As is usually the case with short-wave radios, the sergeant and Terrance Clark were not the only ones listening in.

"Good afternoon, sir," the voice began. "My name is Terrance Clark. I'm an American citizen."

"My name is Sergeant Claspen Dortin," the voice came back. "And you're no more an American than I am," Dortin said curtly. "You're just a North American. Do you grasp that?"

"Sorry, sir. You're right about that. Habit I guess. I understand that you have already received the report of the massacre at the Napoteri village. A friend of mine, a shopkeeper from Annari, filed that report. I was with him and we were the first to discover the bodies. I counted eighty-seven. When my friend left Napoteri to go downriver and file the report via the radio here at Bilokut, I hiked overland to the Arakaba village. That's where we were told the men in the military boat and army uniforms were headed next."

"Who told you that?" Dortin demanded. "I thought you said everyone in Napoteri was dead."

"Yessir, that's true. But there was one man who was not dead yet. He was sorely wounded and before he died he told us what had happened. He told us there were four men in army uniforms and one in civilian clothes and they were searching for a fourteen year old girl. Apparently one of the men wanted her and the girl's father and the chief would not turn her over."

The sergeant cut in, lest more be said than he wanted heard at this point.

"We are still investigating that report and are on our way to the scene. Are you saying that you and this shopkeeper were the first ones there?"

"Yessir," Terrance continued. "And as I was saying, I hiked over the mountain from Napoteri to Arakaba and arrived there just as this same band of men were holding the leaders of Arakaba at gunpoint and threatening to kill the chief and all of the people of the village, if they didn't turn over the girl to them. Oh, and also an American missionary woman that was supposed to be with the girl.

"Anyway, one of the men, the one not wearing a uniform, raised his rifle to shoot the chief. At that point I had no choice but to fire. I was carrying a thiry-thirty that belonged to my friend from Annari."

Terrance thought he heard the man on the other end gasp, so he stopped speaking for a moment.

"Are you alright, sir?" Terrance continued. Hearing a hushed, "Yes," on the other end, he continued.

"So, as I was saying, I fired. I had no choice. The man dropped and then the men who were with him raised their rifles to fire, so I shot one of them in the arm and then the other three opened fire at me as they turned and fled to their boat. One of the men in Arakaba recognized the one that fell as a civilian named Carlos, but he didn't know the man's last name."

The voice came back over the air, but the signal was scratchy. There was discernibly more emotion in the man's voice.

"The one you shot, how badly was he injured?"

"Well sir, I have to tell you that he was killed. I didn't. . ."

The voice on the radio exploded.

"You fired on a Guyanan civilian in the presence of four army personnel before anyone else fired a shot! Then you fired on our nation's military personnel! You come here from the United States and kill our people. You will be held accountable, Mr. Clark. I promise you that."

Images of his nineteen-year old son lying dead in some worthless village flashed through the sergeant's mind. He groaned in anguish. The thought of the four men he had sent with his son fleeing the village and leaving his beloved Carlos there bleeding in the dirt sent the sergeant into a murderous rage.

The sergeant bellowed into the microphone, "Stay right where you are and consider yourself formally detained. I will be in Bilokut by nightfall. You had better be there when I arrive!"

Terrance stepped back from the microphone. He was visibly shaken. He had done nothing wrong. The people of Arakaba were witnesses to that. But the man on the radio was arresting him. Terrance knew enough about South America to know that justice cannot be taken for granted, especially when a corrupt military is involved.

The men who had committed the atrocities were, after all, wearing military garb and had made their escape in a military craft. Whether the army knew what they were up to or just wanted to avoid any embarrassment related to the massacre, Terrance knew he could end up the scapegoat, proof or no proof.

Terrance Clark, however, was no more shaken by the sergeant's reaction than the three men transporting

Rebekah and Carlena back to the coast. Their "broken" radio worked just fine when they wanted it to and the three had just heard the American tell Dortin that they had fled and left his son dead in the Arakaba village. The four of them, all carrying automatic weapons, had fled from a single man armed with one little hunting rifle.

The sergeant would have their heads when he found them. Literally.

Chapter Twenty-Nine

The two women seated at the rear of the boat were not aware of the conversation that had just taken place on the upper deck. All they knew was that without warning the boat made a wide turn in the river and with the throttle wide open headed back upriver.

Rebekah jumped to her feet and climbed the short ladder to the elevated deck where the driver stood. She placed her hand on the man's arm.

"Why did we turn around?" she demanded. "Where are we going now?"

The driver snarled something unintelligible at the woman and with a vicious, swiping blow, sent the woman tumbling backward off the upper deck. Rebekah clutched at the rail, but could not stop her fall. She fell flat on her back on the lower deck. She gasped for a moment, as the breath was knocked out of her. The side of her head stung where the man had struck her and a bright red spot appeared on her lower lip.

Carlena leaped to her feet and knelt by her friend's side.

"You hurt, Miss Hamilton? You hurt bad?"

When her breath finally returned, Rebekah slowly made it to her feet and returned to her seat. The wounded man beside them was unconscious and had not witnessed what had happened. The three on the upper deck were whispering back and forth and casting quick glances toward the lower deck.

"We've turned around and are heading back upriver, Carlena," Rebekah whispered. "I asked the driver why we turned around and he struck me. Something is very wrong here and I don't know what. I am beginning to suspect that these are the men who killed the people in your village and are looking for someone to blame it on. Why they did it, I don't know. But we are not safe, and I'm not sure what to do."

Carefully, the missionary removed Gorton's hunting knife from beneath her shirt where she had felt inclined to hide it when the boat had first approached them on the riverbank.

"What you do with that?" the girl whispered.

"Shhh, I don't know. But if these men killed your people, they are not going to let us live. Whatever they were planning to do with us has changed. Something has happened and we are now going back upriver."

There was hot hatred in Carlena's eyes as she contemplated the likelihood that these very men had killed her mom and dad and everyone else in her little village. If these men had indeed arrived at Napoteri right after she and Rebekah and Gorton Harkin had left, then they were the last ones there. They were the killers. And Carlos Dortin had something to do with it. She was sure of that.

Just then, the pudgy man on the upper deck turned and began to descend the short ladder. The man came down the ladder backward with his face toward the back of the boat and Rebekah and Carlena. There was a sinister look in his eyes. As he leaned forward with his hands gripping the rails of the ladder behind him, a long curved eagle talon slipped from his shirt and dangled from a strip of rawhide.

Both Rebekah and Carlena saw the necklace, but only one of them knew what it meant. That one's eyes narrowed to mere slits as she stared into the man's face. The fat one's hands were still extended backward, gripping the rail behind him as he lowered one foot onto the lower deck. Before Rebekah realized what was happening, the younger girl seized the knife from where it lay concealed between the two of them. Diving forward, the girl buried the blade to its hilt into the pudgy man's chest, just above his protruding stomach. The man let out a low groan and slumped forward on his face.

Chapter Thirty

About an hour before dusk, the other two boats that had been searching the river for Gorton and the missing girls returned to Bilokut. As arranged, one boat had met up with the trackers from Arakaba and had picked up the bloody corpse of Gorton Harkin. One of the trackers had skinned the jaguar and had carried the hide to the riverbank so it could be brought down-river with the mutilated body of its victim.

Only one of the boats from the burial party had returned from Napotcri. Three single men had volunteer to stay behind and finish burying the small handful of remaining bodies.

Terrance was sitting in the town meeting hall, which also served as the town's church and the chambers of the town council. Terrance was a young man and had only partially recovered from the shock of being placed under house arrest by some sergeant in the Guyanan army. When everyone from the other boats had arrived, he relayed the details of the conversation he had with a man named Sergeant Claspen Dortin. The leaders of the village were at a loss to explain the quickness with which the sergeant was willing to blame the American for shooting at men who were undoubtedly brutes of the most villainous sort.

Suddenly, one of the men who had been upriver at Arakaba earlier in the day jumped to his feet.

"Dortin! Carlos Dortin! That name of man Mr. Terrance kill in Arakaba. Sergeant Dortin dead man's father! Son bad man. Father bad man."

Mayor Torsono thanked the excited man and motioned for him to take a seat. Then he said his piece.

"Men from army kill all the people at Napoteri. Kill our neighbors to steal one young girl for this Sergeant Dortin's son. Now Sergeant Dortin comes here and blame Mr. Terrance from America. Mr. Terrance good man. Save many people at Arakaba. We now not let army take Mr. Terrance. Not this man Dortin anyways."

Terrance stood to his feet. Before speaking he stopped and looked all of the men in the room in the eye, one by one.

"When the boat arrives for me," he said, "the men will be packing automatic weapons. If you try to protect me, many people will die. It might be better if I go with them peacefully. Or maybe I could disappear into the jungle or head back upriver before they arrive. That would buy us some time. In the meanwhile, I could try to figure out how to contact the American embassy."

"Not safe for you go with them, Mr. Terrance," Mayor Samuel Torsono continued. "We will fight for you, but if you go hide upriver, they sure not find you. Perto fix that."

There was a quick discussion, including almost universal proclamations of willingness to stand and fight, but Terrance cut the discussion short when he raised his hand for silence. He thanked them all for their loyalty, then announced in the most decisive voice he could muster that he would borrow Perto's boat and go alone upriver.

Perto vigorously objected to the plan and refused the loan of his boat unless he went along. Seeing that it would do no good to argue with the little shopkeeper, especially considering the fact that the sergeant and his men could arrive at any moment, Terrance agreed.

With rifles in hand, the American and the little shop-keeper ran for the dock as quickly as possible. The mayor and council members ran after them. One of the men yelled out to wait one minute and he would bring food. The man's shop was close to the dock and he fumbled with the lock on his door for a second or two and then rushed in to grab some quick supplies.

The man had only been inside for a few seconds when around the bend in the river came a military boat at full tilt. Time had run out.

Chapter Thirty-One

*R*ebekah Hamilton was so surprised by Carlena's actions and so shocked at the suddenness with which the girl had struck, that for a moment she sat there in disbelief staring at the body of the pudgy man lying at her feet.

When she glanced up, to her surprise the two men on the upper deck were still looking upriver. They had not heard the dying man's groan or the muffled sound of his soft body slumping to the deck.

"What have you done, Carlena?" Rebekah whispered as she knelt over the body of the man and checked his pulse. Carlena reached over and carefully removed the rawhide from around the man's neck.

"I make necklace for father when I twelve. He never take off one time. Story true. Father and mother dead. All people in Napoteri dead. This mens kill father."

For a moment, Rebekah's mind spun with the reality of what had just played out before her. An innocent fourteen-year old girl had just exacted revenge against a man that had killed or helped kill her parents and everyone in her village. It was a primal thing, a natural human reaction, but what were they to do now? When the body was discovered, revenge would be exacted against her. She felt sure of that.

Then without further thought, Rebekah glanced back up at the upper deck. Seeing that the deed was still undiscovered, she seized the body by the shoulders and whispered to Carlena to grab the feet. Then with some effort, the two of them quietly slid the body up and over the low rail at the right side of the boat. There was a quiet splash and the two girls watched as the body scooted across the surface of the river and then slowly disappeared behind them.

The heavy man had not bled much, but still there was a six inch patch of blood on the deck where he had fallen. Rebekah grabbed the camo shirt that earlier had been tied around the arm of the one they called Armando. She cleaned up the blood the best she could. When she was finished, she dropped the bloody shirt overboard and returned to her seat. As she slid past the man with the bandaged arm, she saw that his eyes were partly open and that he had begun to regain consciousness. Rebekah wasn't sure if he had witnessed what had happened or was just beginning to come to.

Realizing that their comrade had not returned from his errand to the cabin, one of the men on the upper deck leaned over the rail and called out the man's name. Apparently the pudgy one had been called *Burto*. Rebekah and Carlena sat where they were, both with blank looks on their faces as the man looking down on them waited for a response from his friend. Hearing none, he started to climb down to the lower deck. Before his foot reached the first rung, he spotted the dark red stain.

He grabbed for the weapon lying on the bench beside him. There was nothing either of the girls could do. He trained the weapon on them and yelled over the sound of the engine. "Where is Burto?"

The girls continued to stare at him blankly. Then Armando spoke. His voice was weak and barely discernible over the roar of the engine.

"I was just coming to and saw Burto coming at the girls with a knife. They struggled and one of them stabbed him. They tossed his body over the side. I don't know which one did it. I was too weak to stop them. Then I passed out again."

Rebekah leaped to her feet. "I did it. I stabbed him when he came for us. He was an evil man and it was self defense."

Rebekah didn't have much experience at lying, but she told this one with a straight face.

There was rage mixed with a little disbelief on the face on the man staring down from the upper deck. It was clear that he was unsure as to what to do.

"Where's the knife?" he asked bluntly. "The one you stabbed Burton with."

Rebekah had removed the blade from Burto's body before tossing it overboard. She removed the knife from beneath her leg and held it up.

"Toss it overboard. Now!"

Rebekah leaned over and let the blade slip out of her fingers and into the water. Then she sat back, folded her arms across her chest and awaited her fate. The pretty missionary knew there was nothing she could do under the circumstance. Her life at the moment was not in her own hands.

The man with the weapon stepped back and appeared to be explaining the situation to his comrade, the driver. The man at the helm had been partly aware that something was awry behind him, what with all the yelling and all, but he had not slowed the boat even for a moment.

The two men conversed for a couple of minutes. The one with the weapon kept his eyes trained on the two women the entire time. Finally, he turned and yelled down to them, gesturing with the barrel of his weapon.

"Get in the cabin below and close the door behind you. Armando, get up and fasten the latch behind them. You can do that, can't you? You sat there and watched a white woman kill Burto. The least you can do is lock them in the cabin."

Rebekah and Carlena raised no objection. They had expected to be shot, so being detained in the cabin was at least some reprieve, short-lived as it might be. Without hesitating they stood, stepped over the bloody patch on the floor, and climbed down into the dark interior of the cabin.

With some difficulty, Armando rose and fastened the outer latch on the door. His shoulder had stiffened and he groaned with every step.

The two men up top continued their conversation and finally settled on a plan. They knew the American who had killed Carlos was waiting at Bilokut, which was now only a short distance ahead. They knew Sergeant Dortin wanted the man dead and probably wanted the both of them and Armando dead, too. They calculated that their best chance of surviving lay in returning to Bilokut before Dortin got there and killing the American. They would kill him for killing Carlos and claim it was for "firing on uniformed military personnel."

They doubted that Dortin would care much about all those worthless natives at Napotcri. He had probably done worse in Uganda. What *would* matter to the sergeant was revenge for the death of his son. And of course he would care about the gold, the real reason the four of them had come along in the first place. Only Carlos had cared about the girl. For the rest it had always been about the gold. That had been their original mission. They had gone upriver and killed three miners in a mining camp beyond the Napoteri village and absconded with two respectable size bags of gold flakes. The stop at Napoteri had been just for fun.

It had all come about because one of the miners had been loose of lip during a trip into town a week earlier. Over a game of pool and one too many shots of Canadian whiskey, he had let it slip that his camp's last three cleanouts had been more than a little lucrative. The fool's bragging had cost him and his two companions their gold and their lives.

This was not the first time Sergeant Claspen Dortin had sent these same four men on such a mission, though it was of course the first time any of them had ended up dead.

The two men up top continued their scheming until they were in agreement. Killing the American and giving all of the gold to Dortin was the best chance they had of getting out of this pickle. But first they had to find the American. It was with that deed in mind that they turned into the side river and headed toward Bilokut.

Chapter Thirty-Two

When Terrance saw the military cruiser speeding toward the Bilokut dock, he assumed it was Sergeant Dortin and that all was lost. There was no way he could fight the Guyanan army, and if he tried, he knew innocent men would die. Good men. The decision as to which course of action to take was not going to be his to make.

At six foot three inches, Terrance Clark stood out among the locals standing there on the dock. When the man standing next to the cruiser's driver saw a tall American standing there with a rifle in hand, he raised his weapon and opened fire, planning on spraying the dock with a hail of bullets. However, just as his right index finger squeezed the trigger, the driver pulled sharply back on the throttle to slow the boat lest it crash into the dock. The boat lurched forward as its momentum slowed. That motion caused his comrade to stumble forward as he squeezed the trigger. Instead of spraying the dock with bullets, he fired harmlessly into the water in front of the dock.

The reaction from the dock was instantaneous. Terrance, Perto, and three of the members of the Bilokut council opened fire. In less than two seconds the driver and the man at his right were hit several times each. The one with the rifle was knocked backward by the impact of two thirty-thirty bullets hitting him square in the chest. He landed sideways on the lower deck and rolled up against Armando's feet.

The driver up top was caught on his left side by four or five pellets of buckshot. As the impact spun him around, his right arm caught the throttle and pushed it forward. The driver was dead, but the boat reacted all the same. Its aluminum side scooted and bounced roughly along the side of the dock, picking up speed as it went.

With the speed of a running back, Terrance raced along the dock and leaped out onto the boat just as it passed the end of the dock, still clinging to the rifle in his right hand. He leaped to the ladder and a second later was on the boat's upper deck. Freeing the dead driver's arm from the throttle, he cast the body aside.

Once he was in control of the wheel, he turned the boat in a wide circle and brought it around, pulling up a dozen feet out from the dock.

"This is not Dortin's boat," he shouted at the men on the dock. These are the men who killed the people of Napoteri. I recognize them. Sergeant Dortin and his men could be here at any moment.

"All of you will be in danger if he finds this boat at Bilokut and these bodies on board. I will take the boat upriver and hide it. Tell the sergeant I escaped into the jungle or stole a boat. But do not let down your guard!

"And thanks for everything, my friends. You are brave men. Perto, I owe you much. Go home to your family."

Perto raised his hand to protest, but before any words came out, Terrance pushed hard on the throttle. Responding instantly, the boat shot forward. In a matter of seconds Terrance Clark, a former preacher's kid from Oakland, California was out of sight upriver in a commandeered military boat.

If you weren't in trouble before, Clark, you sure are now. You're driving a stolen army boat and if you're caught, you'll be shot on sight. This baby sure moves though! God, if you're watching, help me through this mess.

For a few moments, Perto and the councilmen stood there on the dock, stunned by all that had just transpired. Eventually, they turned and were making their way back toward the council building, hotly discussing what it all meant. They had only walked a short distance when they heard the sound of a boat approaching hard. It was coming from down river.

"That will be Sergeant Dortin and maybe much trouble," the chief whispered. "Let us go to the chambers and decide about what we tell him. Hurry!"

Chapter Thirty-Three

*T*errance had no plan in mind. He had acted on sheer instinct and reflex, but even now, as he found himself alone on the river with darkness settling in all around him, he knew that he had done the right thing. Even if there had been no time to think it through in advance, his actions were the best chance there was to avoid further bloodshed and the loss of innocent life. He didn't know that he had disappeared upriver only three or four minutes before Sergeant Dortin's boat had arrived at Bilokut.

He also didn't know that there was a wounded man sitting on the back bench of the lower deck, a man he had personally shot the day before.

Fumbling around the control panel in the rapidly fading light, Terrance found and flicked a toggle switch. Instantly the river in front of the boat was flooded with bright light. Glancing down at the dash, which was now illuminated, he looked over the gauges and saw that the fuel level was touching the upper side of the empty mark. He pulled back on the throttle to run at half-speed and conserve fuel.

Terrance had no idea where he would go, except away from Bilokut. Wherever he was going, running out of gas would not be helpful. Turning and looking behind him, he saw that the running lights at the stern were lit and casting a reddish glow on the lower deck. To his great surprise, there was a man sitting on the back bench seat. The man was wearing no shirt and his upper right arm was heavily bandaged. He was staring forward with half-open eyes.

That would be the fellow I shot in the arm in Arakaba yesterday. There were four of them, so one is missing. Better check the cabin.

Just then, he heard a thumping noise coming from the lower deck. It sounded like it was coming from beneath his feet. He immediately let off on the throttle and let the boat slow down in the middle of the river. With rifle in hand, he descended to the lower deck, keeping his eye on the wounded man at the rear.

The pounding continued. "Let us out of here!"

The voice came from behind the cabin door. It was a woman.

Chapter Thirty-Four

*T*errance unlatched the cabin door and swung it back toward him. There were two dim light bulbs on opposite walls of the cabin, but the face of the woman facing him was shrouded in darkness.

"Who are you?" a woman's voice demanded. The voice was strong and perhaps a bit cross.

"I am Terrance Clark from Oakland, California. Are you Rebekah Hamilton?"

Stepping out onto the deck, the woman looked surprised.

"I am, but how did *you* get here? And how do you know my name? You were not here before. I heard gunshots a few minutes ago and then the boat took off again. We had no idea what was happening."

"Come on out, ma'am," Terrance said in the most reassuring voice he could muster. "The men who captured you cannot bother you anymore. I am a friend. We have never met, but I saw you on the dock back in Annari. Do you remember the day a boy and I were rescued from the falls? You were there on the riverbank when we arrived at the village. I have been looking for you since the day after the storm."

"Yes, I remember, but how did you know where to look for me? And why were you looking for me?"

Rebekah felt a tug on her right arm and moved out of the way so Carlena could climb up out of the cabin. Both girls glanced quickly at wounded Armando and then down at the dead soldier lying at his feet. Armando was still sitting precisely where he had been sitting when Rebekah dressed his wound earlier in the day.

"He hasn't moved since I took over the boat," Terrance reassured them.

"The bone in his arm is shattered. I dressed it the best I could and used all of the antiseptic they had onboard. His wound will become infected and he will die if he doesn't get to a hospital. But where are the other two?"

Carlena had not spoken. She had been staring at the wounded man on the back seat, her desire for revenge still unsatisfied. Killing Burto had not been enough to achieve that.

"Let dis man die," Carlena interjected. "Bad man. Help kill all people in Napoteri."

The teenager spit in the direction of Armando, who did not react. Rebekah put her hand on Carlena's shoulder and gently turned the girl's body toward Terrance.

"This is Carlena. She is from Napoteri. She left with me before her people were killed by the men on this boat. We do not know for sure that her people are dead, but these men said they were and then accused us of doing it."

Terrance hesitated for a moment, glancing at the girl and then back at Rebekah Hamilton.

"I'm sorry to say this, but they are all dead. I and a man named Perto, a shopkeeper from Annari, were the ones who first discovered what had happened at Napoteri. Perto went back to Bilokut to contact the authorities and bring back help to bury the dead, and I. . .I went over the mountain on foot to try to arrive at Arakaba before the men who attacked Napoteri killed those people, too.

"The men were looking for this girl," Terrance said, pointing at Carlena.

"I made it across the mountain and arrived in Arakaba just in time. I shot the one name Carlos, just as he was going to shoot the village chief."

"You shoots Carlos?" There was an almost frightening expression of happiness on the young girl's face when she asked the question.

"I had no choice," Terrance said slowly. "But I can't say that I regret it. I honestly believe that he and his men would have killed everyone in that village too, if they did not turn you over to them. And possibly even if they did."

Rebekah was studying the man's young face. The light was dim, but he could tell that she was watching him closely. The fact pleased him and made him remarkably uncomfortable at the same time. Finally, the beautiful missionary spoke.

"What I don't understand is why you came to Napoteri in the first place. What brought you there?"

"I came for you," Terrance replied.

There was emotion in his voice, emotion that had built steadily over the past couple of days. As soon as the words came out, Terrance was sorry he had said them. They just kind of spurted out. Embarrassed, he turned and with the grace that reminded the missionary of a cat, he scrambled up the ladder to the upper deck.

"You might not want to come up here," he yelled back. "There is not much room and there is another body. That was the shooting you heard. It was at the dock at Bilokut. That's where I commandeered this boat. We are upriver from Bilokut now, maybe a couple of miles or so. We're low on fuel and I have no idea where we are going.

"You should also know that there is another boat that could be following us. The father of the young man I shot at Arakaba, a man named Sergeant Dortin. If they do not follow us tonight, eventually they will. We need to keep moving or find a place to hide."

Rebekah stood for a moment, not sure how to respond. Carlena broke the awkward silence.

"I coming up. I know river good. I know places to hide boats."

As Carlena climbed the ladder to the upper deck, Rebekah Hamilton went down to the cabin and retrieved a wool army blanket. Returning, she draped it over the shoulders of Armando. It was obvious that the man had gone into shock hours ago.

Carlena stood next to Terrance and studied the river in front of them, looking for a landmark she recognized. The storm had changed things considerably, but the girl did not seem to be without some confidence. While Carlena was standing beside him, Terrance told her that five men had attacked her village, but that he had accounted for four. He asked her if she knew what had happened to the fifth man.

"That mans die. Carlena kills that mans. Then Miss Hamilton and Carlena throw man in river."

Terrance could not quite fathom what the girl had just told him, but he knew that the boat was one man short. Just then, out in front of them was the fork in the river.

"Go this way," Carlena said, pointing to the right toward Napoteri. "Know place."

"Before we take one of these forks," Terrance replied, "this might be a good place to dump the two bodies on board. No need to carry them around. If we drop them later, someone following us might figure out which way we went."

Without another word, he slowed the boat and grabbed the body of the driver, which was still on the upper deck. He lifted the body above his head and tossed it into the river where it hit with a loud splash. He scurried down the ladder to the lower deck and did the same thing with the other body. The entire exercise was completed in about fifteen seconds. Not knowing what to say, he did not look at Rebekah Hamilton. Instead, he hustled back up to the safety of the upper deck. Taking the wheel, he steered the boat into the right fork.

They had only traveled a short distance, maybe half a mile, when Carlena told Terrance to steer the boat towards the right shore.

"Go this way. Not fast." Carlena was pointing directly towards the dense brush that lined the bank. The moon had risen in the sky and it was almost full. The moonlight backlit a tall cedar tree that towered over the lesser foliage around it. Carlena moved her right arm in a wide curving motion as if to tell Terrance to turn the boat in a circle and go straight toward the shoreline just to the right of the big cedar.

Terrance was hesitant to follow the girl's instruction. At that moment, he felt a hand lightly resting on his right bicep.

"Do as she says, Mr. Clark. We are in her world now." It was Rebekah Hamilton and her voice was soft. Terrance noted that she kept her hand on his arm for a couple of seconds after she had finished speaking.

Terrance nosed the craft into the dense foliage, expecting at any moment to feel the thud as the hull came into contact with the river bank or the trunk of a tree. Instead, the boat glided through the branches and a moment later broke through to the other side. Beyond the foliage they had just passed through was a small body of water about a hundred feet across and maybe two or three hundred feet deep. The bright lights on the bow lit up the jungle before them. Terrance glanced back and the foliage had closed behind them, effectively hiding them from even the keenest eyes that might be scanning the river bank. The jungle had swallowed them up.

"This *is* a good place to hide," Terrance whispered. "I guess we can spend the night here." He reached over to turn off the bright lights, lest anyone using the main channel at this late hour be alerted to their hiding place.

"No stop yet," Carlena responded, pointing towards the far end of the cove. "Go more this way."

Terrance obediently edged the boat slowly forward, still remembering the soft voice that had told him to do as the girl says. He was vaguely aware that Rebekah Hamilton was still standing close behind him.

As he approached the far end of the open water, the light on the bow revealed a small stream feeding into the cove. To the right of the stream was a narrow beach of small pebbles.

"There," Carlena said, pointing toward the graveled beach.

Terrance slowly nosed the boat up onto the smooth gravel and shut off the engine. He left the lights on for the moment, but placed the ignition key in his pocket. The hull seemed to be grounded well enough to not drift, but to be sure, he took the rope coiled on the deck in front of him and leaping into the soft gravel, tied the bow securely to a stout tree trunk just beyond the little beach.

Carlena followed close behind and without so much as a word or a backward glance, walked confidently up the narrow beach to the edge of the stream, then entered what appeared to be a trail. A few seconds later, Terrance saw a dim light coming from a window somewhere back in the forest. A few moments later, Carlena reappeared, walking back down the path.

"Sleep there," Carlena said pointing toward the light.

Rebekah joined them on the beach and she and Carlena went back up the path together.

Terrance climbed back on board the boat. Somehow, Armando was standing on the lower deck, leaning against the rail. His eyes were wide open now.

"I am thirsty," he whispered weakly.

Terrance was not sure how he should feel about the man. He was a criminal and a scoundrel, to be sure. And he deserved his wound and worse. But he was, after all, a human being.

"I'm not sure what we are going to do about water," Terrance replied. "I don't know if the water in the stream is drinkable."

"There is water down there in the cabin, and rations, too."

The man sat back down, as if he had already expended all of the energy he could muster. The dim lights were still on in the cabin and Terrance stepped down into the enclosure to see for himself. Sure enough, there were tins of water and no short supply of military rations.

He returned to the deck, opened a tin of water and handed it to the man seated on the back bench. Armando drank long and deep, finishing the container before lowering it.

"Thank you," he said simply. His tone sounded truly appreciative. "What are you going to do with me, if I may ask?"

"I don't know. I thought about tossing you to the crocs when we were back on the river. That's probably what you deserve."

"I guess I could not blame you, if you did. You're the one who shot me, aren't you?"

"I am. I wasn't aiming for your arm."

"No, I don't suspect you were. I didn't shoot any of those people in the village, you know. You don't have to believe me. I came along for the gold. We were going to steal it. I didn't know we were going to kill the miners. I didn't know we were going to kill all of the people in the village. Carlos was crazy. Did he die when you shot him?"

"He did."

"I'm glad. He was like his father. I think his father made him that way. Sergeant Dortin is an evil man. There is no good in him. But he loved Carlos and he will find you and kill you if you do not kill him first. He will not stop until one of you is dead."

"I suppose you're right," Terrance replied. "Listen, I am going to tie your feet together and lock you in the cabin for the night. If you try to escape or I hear any noise at all from you. I will leave your feet tied together and throw you to the crocs. I won't hesitate."

"Fair enough," Armando said matter of fact. "I believe you would."

Terrance helped the wounded man down into the cabin and tied his feet securely together. Before leaving, he placed two of the blankets together and loaded them with tins of water and rations. Then he tied the four cor-ners together. After securing the cabin latch from the outside, he carried the rifle and the supplies ashore. He followed the path toward the light in the window. The cabin sat back from the cove less than a hundred feet. In the dark it was hard to tell what the structure was made of, but it looked sufficient to protect them from the elements.

With his arms full, Terrance tapped on the door with his foot and stood waiting. The door opened momen-tarily and before him stood Rebekah Hamilton. An oil lamp lit up the interior of the hut and framed the young woman's face in a magical way that seemed to enhance her every feature. Terrance caught himself staring and started to look away. Just as he did, the woman's face lit up with that same radiant smile he had seen that first day at the dock at Annari. That was the smile that had sent him on this quest, a journey that at this moment he knew still might not end well for either of them.

But come what may, there was that smile. In that moment, the man from Oakland, California knew that everything he had endured and every unsavory thing he had been required to do to get to this place had been worth it. If all he ever knew of Rebekah Hamilton was this one moment, he was sure it would be enough. Of course that could not possibly be true.

Chapter Thirty-Five

Sergeant Claspen Dortin marched briskly from the dock to the Bilokut council chambers. Behind him followed his little band of misfits, all brandishing AK-47s.

Dortin had never been to the town before, but a generator was humming up ahead and the windows of the meeting place were well lit. He rightly assumed that this building should be his destination.

The ride up the river had done nothing to assuage the sergeant's intense hatred for the men who had failed to protect his son and the American who had killed him. When he was finished with the American and those four, the lot of them, then and only then would he let his mind stop and grieve his great loss.

Not once did the thought enter his mind that his son was a dark product of his own misguided ways, an acorn that had not fallen far from the tree. Never did it occur to him that his son deserved a fate worse than death for his murderous rampage, which had resulted in the deaths of an entire village full of innocent people. Sergeant Claspen Dortin would blame everyone before he would blame himself or his son. That had always been his way.

Dortin's hand never touched the handle of the meeting house door. Instead he opened it with the heel of his boot, sending splinters of wood flying into the room before him.

As he burst into the room with four men at his heels, the scene that met their eyes was entirely unexpected. The leaders of the village, who had been sitting in chairs facing the door, rose to their feet as one, all with rifles or shotguns trained on the chest of the sergeant or one of his men. Dortin's revolver was still holstered and though his men were well armed, the odds were about three to one against them.

Dortin hesitated for a moment, then blustered loudly, "I am here for the American, the one who killed a Guyanan citizen and fired upon army personnel."

Samuel Torsono spoke calmly, with a low voice that showed neither fear nor hesitancy. "The man you seek is not here. He leave after you speak with him on radio. He say you blame him for shooting at men who kill everyone at Napoteri and try kill everyone at Arakaba."

"You let him leave after I gave him orders to stay put?" the sergeant demanded. His voice was loud and intimidating. It was obvious that he had grown accustomed to the native populations backing down in fear of the army.

If Samuel was intimidated, it never showed. "You speak to American on radio, not us. He not tell us you order him stay. He just say you angry at wrong peoples. Then he leave."

That last exchange was not exactly true, but there was no way the sergeant could know that others had listened in on the entire conversation between him and Terrance. And he didn't know that three of his own men had listened in on the other boat's radio and had been made fully aware that their boss was on a murderous rampage.

Dortin focused his attention on Perto. "You are the shopkeeper from Annari. I know of you. What are you doing here? Wait, aren't you the one who called in the initial report?" the sergeant demanded.

There was hatred in Perto's eyes, which had become narrow slits. He stared straight and unwavering into the eyes of the dark soul standing before him. The shopkeeper's finger gently massaged the trigger of the rifle he held on the sergeant's chest as he weighed his response. Many people would die if gunfire erupted. He knew that. The automatic weapons on the other side of the room were intimidating, but the little man who had shot a jaguar at one pace was thinking more about the bodies of all of those innocent men, women, and children he and Terrance had found scattered all over Napoteri. How dare this man seek revenge against the one man who had done the most to prevent even more senseless deaths!

Before Perto could speak, Samuel responded. "Perto my friend. He discover deaths at Napoteri. He report. He do nothing bad. You leave now."

Dortin raised his fist in anger. No small town chief or mayor was going to talk to him so dismissively.

As Perto and Dortin were talking, the ends of barrels had gradually lowered on both sides of the room. No one likes to talk with a loaded gun pointed at his chest. When the sergeant's fist went up, however, so did the barrels of every gun in the room, and at that moment the tiniest miscalculation or misinterpreted move could have resulted in lead flying in both directions with devastating consequences.

Dortin could not help but notice that more than half of the barrels on the other side were aimed directly at him. That fact, as much as anything, contributed to his next move.

"There was another army boat here today," he said, deftly changing the subject. "Where is that boat? I tried to raise them on the radio, but there was no answer."

The sergeant's tone was stern and demanding, but the volume was lower, slightly easing the tensions in the room.

"Yes, other boat come by dock but not stop," the chief replied honestly. There was no reason to volunteer a description of the incident that had led to Terrance taking command of the boat and heading upriver. "We not know where other boat go. Maybe you go look now."

"Where is the body of the civilian who was shot?" Dortin's voice was just a bit husky and more emotional than before.

"We not know this, Sergeant. No one here know." The chief spoke truthfully. The body of Dortin's son was somewhere in the river or tenderizing in some Caiman's lair by now. There was almost no chance it would ever surface again.

Dortin had more questions, but something told him there might be a better time and place to ask them. The sergeant was not used to this level of defiance and was not quite sure how far he could push these people. He stared at Torsono for a moment, glanced again at the barrels pointed in his direction, then abruptly turned on his heels and strode from the room. His men followed close behind, leaving what was left of the door behind them.

For a full minute, Perto and the others stood without moving, every barrel still trained on the open doorway. Finally, Perto broke ranks and walked over to the door and looked out into the night. Satisfied that Dortin had left, he stepped outside and the members of the council followed. Seconds later, they heard an engine roar to life down by the dock and then saw the bright lights of Dortin's boat as it turned and headed upriver.

Chapter Thirty-Six

*I*t was dark, but the moon was near full and reflecting gorgeously off the smooth surface of the river. A couple of miles upriver from Bilokut, a small boat with four passengers was making its way down the river toward the village. The man standing at the rear of the boat and controlling the outboard saw the bright lights of a larger boat coming upstream toward them.

Quickly, he motioned the others to silence and turned the boat toward the shore where he maneuvered it back under the dark foliage that overhung the water. There might be snakes in the trees and other dangers, but the chance seemed one worth taking.

Those in the small craft watched from concealment as the larger boat passed them by. The one sitting alone in the middle seat trembled noticeably as the boat passed. It was hard to tell whether the one passenger's shivering was brought on by the coolness of the night air – or whether it was something else entirely.

Chapter Thirty-Seven

*I*n the cabin at the back of the hidden cove, Rebekah Hamilton stepped aside so Terrance could enter could the room. His eyes quickly scanned their dimly lit surroundings.

There were no beds, just sleeping mats laid out on a rough plank floor. There were four makeshift chairs and a rough table that looked to have been crafted from the same planks as the floor. An oil lamp sat in the middle of the table. The glass globe had been blackened by smoke and desperately needed to be cleaned. There were two crude fishing poles leaning in one corner and on a shelf on the far wall were boxes of matches, a bottle of extra oil for the lamp, a can opener, and five cans of what looked to be tuna fish.

All in all, the abode had the appearance of a Rocky Mountain hunting cabin. All that was missing was the fifty-five gallon oil drum that elk hunters back in the States routinely converted to a makeshift camp stove.

In one corner, Carlena was lying on her face on one of the mats, sobbing quietly. The last two or three days had stretched the girl's emotions to the breaking point. She had endured a terrifying storm and a jaguar charge. She had seen a grown man ripped apart by the same cat that had threatened them. She had learned that her entire village had been murdered, including her mother and father, and then she had killed a man with a knife and helped toss his corpse over the side of a boat. It would be difficult for a fourteen-year old to survive all of that. There was probably little left in the poor child but bitterness and tears.

Terrance laid the supplies and blankets on the table and untied the knot that held the package together. He took one of the blankets and gently laid it over the young girl. Carlena never looked up. Her only response was to reach up and pull the blanket up over her head.

"I will lie down with her until she goes to sleep," Rebekah whispered. "She is exhausted, both physically and emotionally. Perhaps you and I can talk after that."

Terrance nodded and sat down at the table while Rebekah curled up next to Carlena. The missionary pulled the blanket back a bit and gently stroked the girl's hair.

It was a good twenty minutes before Carlena commenced the regular breathing of sleep. Finally, Rebekah came and sat down across from Terrance. It was the first time they had had an opportunity to talk.

"So, who are you Terrance Clark," the girl began. "Tell me why are you here in the backwoods of Guyana protecting two damsels in distress? I heard that you got lost in the jungle and were rescued from the falls above Annari. How did you come to be in the jungles above the falls? There's nothing up there for many miles. And how did you come to be in possession of a military boat with two dead soldiers on board? Oh, and where's the wounded guy? Armando, I think they called him. Is he still on the boat?"

"Well, I guess that's enough questions to start a conversation," Terrance quipped quietly. Rebekah had spoken in a low whisper and he followed suit.

He began by telling her about his escape from Jonestown with a ten-year old boy named Timmy and how they had found a cave and lived off the land for ten days.

He explained how they were hiking their way out cross country and how they had been marooned at the top of the falls and had to be rescued by Jonny and Thomas and some of the other villagers from Annari.

"After being rescued from the falls," he continued, "the boy and I spent the night in Annari at Leroy Harkin's house. Mayor or chief or whatever he is. The storm hit that night. The next day I met Perto, the shopkeeper, and learned from him that you had left with the Harkin's brother, apparently unaware that Gorton Harkin was on the run from authorities in Georgetown for allegedly raping or assaulting two women."

Rebekah's eyes betrayed her surprise. "I had no idea. I never liked the man and never trusted him, but I never suspected he was that bad. So you came to warn me about him?"

"Well, yes, I guess you could say that. The storm was an especially bad one and Perto told me the river might be blocked with fallen trees and you might not be able to get back downriver. I was worried about your safety and wanted to make sure you were okay."

I already stuck my foot in my mouth once. I am not going to be so careless with my mouth this time. I don't want this poor woman to think that she went from escaping one bad guy only to fall into the clutches of another.

With a steady gaze, Rebekah studied the man sitting across from her. His eyes were honest. He could use a shave, but he was undeniably handsome. He was tall and built like an athlete. His words were calm now and seemingly unattached, but she was certain that there had been emotion in them when first they had spoken back on the boat, when he had said to her, "I came for you."

Those were words a woman would not easily forget.

Terrance went on to tell Rebekah of his arrival at Napoteri and what they had seen there. He told her about the information they had gleaned from the dying man they had found in the forest behind the village. He told her about his trek across the mountain to Arakaba and what had happened there, the death of Sergeant Dortin's son and the wounding of Armando. He told her that they had sent a boat for antibiotics for the villagers, a detail which brought the woman noticeable relief.

Then he told her about the desperate search everyone had launched for her and her party, and about the news from the tracker who had found Gorton's body and had followed the girls to the place on the riverbank where they had been picked up by a boat, though at the time they had no idea what boat.

From time to time, the girl nodded, but mostly she just listened and stared intently into the man's eyes.

Terrance expressed to her his shock at being told over the radio that he was under arrest, even though he had done nothing wrong. Finally, he told her about the incident at the dock at Bilokut, which explained how he had come into possession of a Guyana military boat with two dead men on board.

When he was finished, he looked down at the table and said, "Well, I guess that's about it. I've had a pretty exciting past two weeks, to say the least. Does that sufficiently explain how I got here tonight?"

Rebekah laughed. It was a quiet laugh, but it was the most beautiful sound he could remember hearing.

Lord have mercy on me, even her laugh is perfect. Control yourself, Clark. This woman is a missionary. Sure, you're a preacher's kid, but in more than one way she is way out of your league and she's probably still mourning the death of her husband.

"So," he said, "It's your turn. Tell me, Rebekah Hamilton, what happened to you after you left Napoteri? The storm hit and then what happened?"

Rebekah fidgeted in her chair a bit, as if settling in for a long story. She leaned forward and placed her elbows on the table and cupped her chin in both hands.

"Well," she began, "Carlena and I were separated from Gorton in the storm and hid under a fallen log 'til morning. It was a terrible night, the worst storm I have ever seen down here. When we came out, right after daybreak, a jaguar appeared out of nowhere and started creeping towards us, clearly preparing to attack. Out of sheer desperation I tossed my knapsack at it and ran. We didn't have a chance, but we ran square into Gorton and the jaguar got him instead of us. While it was killing him, he killed it with his knife. I guess you could say that he died saving our lives, but it wasn't like he had a lot of choice. It just happened. Actually, nothing 'just happens' to those who have put their trust in God, but anyway you say it, it worked out that way without us planning any part of it.

"So, I took the knife that was sticking in the side of the jaguar, it was one of those black ones, and we took off looking for the river. We heard gunfire and then right after that four soldiers picked us up. We thought we were rescued, but it turned out that these were the men who had killed all the people in Napoteri. They accused us and Gorton of doing it and said they were taking us back to the authorities at the coast for questioning. They said they thought Gorton was probably the one who shot Armando from the jungle as they drove up the river in their boat searching for us.

"They were such liars," she exclaimed, gently pounding her little fist down on the table. "And I believed them at first.

"Later on, one of them, a chubby fellow named Burto, was coming down the ladder from the upper deck when an eagle claw necklace popped out of his shirt. Carlena recognized it as one she had made for her father. Before I realized what she was doing, she grabbed the knife from between us and stabbed the guy. No one was looking, so we tossed the body overboard. Later, the others saw the blood on the deck and locked us in the cabin, which is where we stayed until you let us out. We heard the gunshots when you took over the boat, but had no idea what was going on 'til you told us.

"I guess that brings us both up to date," she continued. "But there is one more important thing we haven't talked about. You seem like an even-keeled kind of man. What were you doing in Jonestown and why didn't you kill yourself when all the others did? Why did you escape? Did you lose your faith in Jim Jones?"

Terrance chuckled. "I was never a follower of Jones. I'm a private investigator from California. I was sent to Jonestown on an assignment to find a woman whose parents hadn't seen her for ten years. The last thing my clients knew of their daughter was that she had gone to Jonestown with the Peoples Temple group. I was looking for her in Jonestown when out of nowhere they tossed me into a locked hut after I refused to drink the Kool-Aid during one of their practice suicide runs. They called them '*White Nights.*' I was locked up for a month before I escaped."

"Who is the little blonde haired boy who was with you when you were rescued from the falls? Why did you bring him along?" Rebekah asked.

"Timmy? Timmy is just the boy who brought me my meals the entire time I was locked up. I didn't know him other than that. But he is a great kid and I just couldn't let him stay there and be forced to drink poison and be killed. So, I brought him with me."

"So, you rescued him. He would be dead, you know, if you hadn't taken him with you."

Terrance chuckled. "For a while there, I wasn't sure I was rescuing him or leading him into the jungle to die some other way."

"If you've seen the pictures that came out of Jonestown," Rebekah objected softly, "It's pretty clear that you saved his life."

Terrance was uncomfortable with the whole *hero* thing. To date, he had not told anyone about his desperate plunge into the river to save Timmy from going over the falls. Timmy might figure it out someday, but it was not something Terrance was going to talk about.

"Well," the woman continued, "they are still putting the pieces together, but only a handful of people escaped dying there. They are saying there were something like 914 suicides. But nearly three hundred of those were babies and little children who were murdered by their own parents because Jim Jones said they would all go to a better place when they died. Unrepentant murderers don't go to a better place; I can assure you of that."

There was a lot of emotion in that last sentence. Terrance had thought the same thing, but Rebekah said it plainly and with feelings that usually come more easily to women than men.

"I could hear them talking over the loudspeakers," Terrance said, "as Timmy and I were making our escape. They talked about dying with dignity like good communists and socialists. They talked about reincarnation. They said nothing about Jesus Christ or God. The people in Jonestown were barely even religious, though Jones referred to himself as a prophet."

"Yes, I know," the girl said with sadness in her voice. "I was there a little over a year ago. There was a nurse working there and sometimes when the need would arise she would give me antibiotics and other medications from their supplies. She and I talked a lot about what the whole Jonestown thing was really all about. She said Jones didn't even believe in God and openly disparaged the Bible. She said he was actually an atheist who used religion to move people into his true religion, which was socialism."

"That's consistent with what I heard in the short time I was there," Terrance replied. "I heard him say things like, 'If you're born in *capitalist* America, *racist* America, *fascist* America, then you're born in sin. But if you're born in socialism, you're not born in sin.' I'm pretty sure that's not a Bible definition of sin."

Terrance chuckled at his last remark, but not because it was funny.

"I also heard him say over the public address system," he continued, "that he was the reincarnation of Gandhi, Father Divine, Jesus of Nazareth, Buddha and Vladimir Lenin all in one. To me, that made the man certifiable. How can hundreds of people follow someone like that?"

"Yeah, my friend told me the same kind of stuff," Rebekah replied.

"Anyway," she continued, "my friend died shortly after my last visit. They said she *'took suddenly ill.'* She was a genuine Christian and not at all like the others. I was told that they buried her there in Jonestown. Her name was Sarah Stanford."

Terrance sat up in his chair. "Sarah Stanford? Are you serious? That's who your friend was? Sarah was the woman I was looking for. She's why I was in Jonestown in the first place. She's dead?"

"Yes. A year or so now. She didn't come to Guyana as a member of the Peoples Temple. She had nursing training and was hired on as medical personnel. She took the job because she needed the money.

"What I am going to tell you now, Mr. Clark, I don't know for sure because I never actually met him, but Sarah had a little boy. Blonde hair. Nine years old back then. I'm sure his name was Timmy. Sarah talked about him all the time. Your Timmy might be Sarah's little boy. And if he is, you just saved the life of your clients' grandson."

Terrance could hardly speak. By the time he had been taken prisoner, he had already concluded that Sarah

Stanford probably wasn't in Jonestown any longer, if she ever had been. It was not likely that a blonde haired woman Sarah's age could have escaped his notice for over a month in a community of less than a thousand people and most of them dark skinned.

"I can't believe I never put that together," Terrance mumbled. "My clients don't even know that their daughter had a son. But that explains a lot of things. Timmy was not like the others in Jonestown when it came to spiritual things. When we were in the jungle and things got desperate, he prayed. He prayed like he really believed someone was listening."

Terrance shot an embarrassed glance across the table. Rebekah didn't respond, so he continued.

"The little tyke prayed like someone who is used to praying and not someone who only prays as an act of desperation. He said his mom used to read him Bible stories and pray with him every night. I never thought to ask him his mother's name. I guess I should have."

Rebekah never responded and for a while the two of them sat there in silence. Finally, the missionary spoke.

"So what are we going to do now, Terrance Clark? If there are troops looking for us and one sergeant out to kill you, there may not be much sense in coming out of hiding for a while, at least 'til we can get help from authorities higher up the chain – above the sergeant's head."

Terrance spoke from his heart. "I will protect you and the girl first and above all. There's not much fuel left in the boat, so we can't go far in it. That's a problem. And I don't know how long we are going to be safe here in this cabin, though this little cove seems to be a perfect hiding place. But who knows how many people know about it."

Rebekah smiled and leaned forward, looking deeply into the man's eyes as if to relieve some of the burden he felt.

"Before you came back from the boat with the supplies, Carlena told me that men from her village built this little cabin as a stopover place for their people when they travel by paddle boat down to Bilokut. She said no one else knows of its existence. Based on that, I think we can probably stay here safely for quite a while. But, we do have a wounded man to consider. What are we going to do with him?"

"Well, he's safely locked in the boat's cabin for the moment," Terrance replied. "We will see how he is in the morning. Maybe we would be better off if we find him dead when I check on him."

The missionary frowned. "It is challenging to love your enemies sometimes, but we must. If he lives, he can stand trial for his crimes, but in the meanwhile we must treat him kindly. May the Lord give us the grace to do that."

"Before I locked him in the cabin," Terrance continued, "he told me that he had played no part in the shootings at the mining camp or at Napoteri. He seemed genuinely remorseful about it all, but still, I know enough about criminal types to know they are all 'innocent' and all very good liars."

"That's not really for us to decide, Terrance. Carlena already killed one of them out of a sense of vengeance. She will have to live with that the rest of her life. Even if he deserved killing, it will always trouble her that she did it.

"At any rate, Mr. Clark, maybe we should get some sleep now. It has been a very long day for the both of us and I hardly slept at all last night. It has been a pleasure talking with you, though. Good night, Terrance from California."

The pretty missionary with the reddish brown hair and light freckles reached over and placed a much smaller hand on the man's. She let her hand linger there for a few moments, making the private investigator from

Oakland wonderfully uncomfortable. Then she smiled, got up from the table, and went and laid back down next to the young girl.

Shortly after he had fallen asleep, Terrance was awakened to what he thought was the sound of a larger boat passing by on the river. Whoever or whatever it was, it was moving slow and was already past their location when he heard it.

Chapter Thirty-Eight

Terrance awakened early the next morning just after sunrise. Shaded as it was back in the trees, it was barely light in the cabin. He turned over and saw that Rebekah Hamilton was already up and was kneeling by one of the chairs. Her eyes were closed and her lips were moving. Terrance got up soundlessly and made his way to the front door. The planks on the floor were heavy and never gave out a single creak. He turned and looked back as he went out the door. Rebekah was watching him. He saw a hint of a smile on her face and then she bowed her head again.

The cove looked different in natural light. The water was only about ten feet deep in the middle and very clear. From the back of the cove where the creek came flowed in, the narrow pea gravel beach extended in both directions about half way around the cove. Already, the morning sun was beginning to filter in through the leaves overhead, giving the entire setting the feel of a shaded tropical paradise. The effects of the storm seemed less here.

Terrance was just about to climb aboard the boat when he felt a presence behind him. When he turned, Rebekah was at the end of the path and coming toward him. He waited until she caught up.

"It's beautiful here," she whispered. "If the water in the stream is drinkable and there are fish in this cove, we could stay here for a long time. We could let things cool down out there and maybe not have to deal with this Sergeant Dortin at all. He has to leave eventually."

"I was thinking the same thing," Terrance replied. "This is a special place. It's also possible that the authorities will catch on to Dortin's part in all this and take care of him on their own. The people of Arakaba were witnesses to enough of what happened to hopefully bring him down."

Rebekah placed her hand on the man's arm and stood beside him.

"There's still one problem with our little plan. When I fixed Armando's arm, it was really torn up and I saw several large bone fragments. Infection is all but inevitable in such cases. Either he gets to a hospital or he dies, or he loses his arm or both. It's just a matter of time.

"There's one thing I forgot to tell you when we were talking last night. When Carlena stabbed one of the soldiers, Armando lied for us and said the man was attacking us and that it was self defense. I'm not sure what is going on with that man, but we can't just let him die."

As if on cue, there was a knocking on the door of the cabin. Terrance climbed onboard and answered a little gruffly, "What do you want?"

"I really need to use the can and there is none down here."

Terrance glanced back at Rebekah. "You'd better let him out for a minute," she whispered laughing.

When Armando came out on deck, he looked surprisingly good for man with his wound. He could barely move last night, but today he seemed remarkably spry for a dying man. The rope around his feet was too well tied to loosen quickly, so Terrance cut it to allow the squirming man to get off the boat quickly and do his business. Terrance followed the prisoner a short distance into the foliage and then waited.

In a couple of minutes, Armando returned. "Maybe I could stay on deck for a spell," he suggested, his expression confirming that he knew that he was totally at their mercy. "The fresh air feels pretty good, but my arm hurts a lot and my muscles are pretty cramped. I am no threat to you, you know. There are a couple of loaded pistols down in the cabin. They're under the seat just inside the door. If I had wanted to use one, they were right there for the using."

Terrance looked more than a little skeptical at the man's story. He jumped back on board and opened the door to the cabin. He could hardly ignore what the man had said. When he came back out, he held a handgun in both hands.

"He was telling the truth. They're both loaded. He could have shot me when I opened the door if he had wanted to."

Both of them stared at the wounded man, begging an explanation.

"Look," the shirtless man began. His voice was low and even. "I know I can never make up for what happened at the girl's village. But I didn't shoot anyone there. I never tried to stop it either, so I'm guilty. I wanted to, but there was bloodlust in the air. I have seen it before. It's a craziness that you can't stop. I know now that I should have tried. I chickened out. I was a coward. Some things in life you can never undo and that was one of 'em.

"Same thing at the miners' camp upriver," he continued. "I didn't know we were going to kill them. The gold we took is in two bags under the seat next to the one where you found the guns. I don't know if any of the miners have families, but somebody should get their gold."

"Why are you acting this way?" Rebekah asked. "Are you just feeling guilty for what you did?"

"I don't know. I've done a lot of bad things in my life and I guess I'm just tired of carrying all that around and being who I am. I've hurt a lot of people. So I guess you're probably right, ma'am. I *am* feeling guilty. I *should* feel guilty."

There was pain in the wounded man's voice and on his face. Rebekah sized the big man up for a moment and then spoke with a tenderness that surprised both the prisoner and Terrance, who was standing with arms folded, still skeptical.

"I know of a man who did some really awful things, things that it's hard to believe a good man could do. He stole his neighbor's wife and got her pregnant while his neighbor was away at war. Then, to make sure that no one found out what he had done, he gave the man a sealed note to give to his commanding officer when he went back to the battlefield. The note said, 'Put Uriah in the hottest part of the battle and then tell everyone else to retreat.' Well, that's what happened, and the neighbor was killed. It looked like he had died a good soldier, but he had been murdered.

"This man thought he had gotten away with his crime, until one day a prophet from God came and laid the man's sins bare before him. The man knew he had been found out and deserved death for what he had done, but he confessed his crimes against the law of God and God forgave him and spared his life. This guy reaped some pretty bad consequences for his actions later on in his life, but his sins were forgiven and those who believe in God's Son will see that man in heaven someday."

Terrance was looking back and forth, watching Rebekah talk and then watching Armando's face as he listened.

"If God can forgive a man who did something as terrible as that, Armando, he can forgive you, if you are willing to ask Him."

Terrance wasn't sure what he felt about what was going on in front of him. Part of him was embarrassed by the bold, unabashed way Rebekah was talking about God and sin and forgiveness. Then another part of him wasn't quite sure that the man standing in front of them *could* be forgiven. He was nothing like David, the man in the story Rebekah had just told. All King David and Armando had in common was they had both done terrible things.

"I have been thinking about God a lot lately," Armando replied. His voice was soft. There was a tenderness that was incongruous with the man's rugged exterior.

"I thought about him while I was sitting down there in that cabin all night, remembering all the things I did or should have done these past few days. I thought about Him when I remembered the guns under the seat. When I thought about God, I was afraid. Somehow I knew that if I used those guns against you, all would be lost for me. I don't know how I knew that. But I did. I just don't know what to do now. What does God expect from me?"

Terrance had seen his dad talk about Jesus with total strangers he met on the streets and with men locked behind bars when he was doing prison ministry and brought his son along. If he was not mistaken, this pretty young missionary was attempting to lead a corrupt South American soldier to Jesus Christ. In a court of law, the man would likely face the death penalty for whatever role he had played in the Napoteri killings, and probably the miner affair as well. Armando may not have pulled the trigger, but he had consented to some pretty unspeakable acts.

Unaware of Terrance's inner turmoil with what was going on, the missionary continued.

"What do you know about Jesus Christ, Armando? Do you know who He is?"

"Not much. I've heard his name used in bad ways and have said it as a swear word," Armando replied. "I've seen crosses in churches and I know he's the guy hanging on them, but I don't know much else. I guess I always assumed he was some kind of make-believe person, not a real one."

"Oh, he's real alright," Rebekah replied. "And he has saved the souls of millions of people every bit as bad as you. I will tell you who He is, if you want to know."

"If he can help me and make my guilt go away after all I have done, then I want to know."

"Well, first of all, Jesus is the Son of God. He is the One who created everything there is, everything you see around you and everything in the skies above. He's the one God the Father sent to earth to die on a cross to pay for the sins of everyone who would put their faith in Him. Jesus lived a perfect life without sinning even once. Then He died on the cross to pay for our sins so we wouldn't have to pay for them when we die. After that, He defeated death by rising from the dead three days later. No one else has ever done what He did. No one else could.

"Some day, every man and woman who ever lived will stand before God, Armando. Those who have put their faith in God's Son will be allowed to enter heaven because all of their sins will have been paid for, paid for by Jesus' blood. Those who stand before God without having put their faith in His Son will be lost forever. No matter how good of a life they think they have lived down here, it won't be enough. God would not have given up his Son to die for our sins if we could make it to heaven without Him.

"That's the bottom line. You can't save yourself. You can't be good enough to get to heaven based on any good deeds you have done. No one can. No one is good enough, even the best people you know. Salvation is a free gift that we either accept or reject. The Bible says that when we put our faith in Jesus Christ, He forgives all of our sins, wipes the slate clean, and makes us a new creature and makes it as if we had never sinned."

Terrance had heard all of these words before. And for the most part, he guessed he believed them. He had forgotten them and questioned them, but when it came right down to it, what the woman was saying was right. But when it came to offering that kind of grace to a man like Armando, it seemed too easy. The man simply didn't deserve it.

Rebekah was sensing a breaking in the soldier's spirit, so she pressed on.

"Right now," she said, "the Spirit of God is speaking to your heart and urging you to put your faith in God's Son. He is telling you that God loves you more than you can imagine. Now it is up to you to obey that voice. You are free to reject it if you want. God has given you that choice. But if you reject what God is offering you, don't reject it because of how bad you have been. You are no less deserving of God's mercy than I am."

Good Lord, she just confessed that she is as bad as Armando. She's a missionary! She's probably about as good as they come. But she's saying she's as bad as he is!

There were tears in the big man's eyes. They were welling up and spilling out. Armando was big. He was tough. Standing there, muscular, shirtless, military haircut, and his arm half blown off, he was letting the tears flow and allowing his heart to be softened.

"Even after all I have done, God still loves me?" he blurted out. "That seems impossible. It seems impossible that God would love someone like me enough to let his son die for the things I have done. I don't understand how that could possibly be."

Terrance found himself speaking. He was surprised to find himself speaking. The words just came out.

"That's what the Bible calls grace, big fellow," Terrance said.

Armando turned and looked at the man who had shot him the day before. Oddly, the expression on his tear-stained face was more like that of a child asking a question than that of a hardened soldier. Terrance continued.

"Grace means God gives us what we don't deserve and haven't earned. He gives it to us because He is good, not because we are good. All He asks is that we believe Him and accept the free gift His Son offers."

"You have done this?" Armando asked, looking hard into Terrance's eyes. The soldier's expression was piercing, as if he was trying to penetrate behind the Terrance's eyes and know for sure whether he was being told the truth.

Terrance stepped closer. He could sense that this man was teetering on the edge of a decision that would have eternal consequences and somehow he felt himself being drawn into it.

"I have, Armando. And it is the most real thing in the world. Jesus Christ became my Lord and Savior sixteen years ago. I was as bad a sinner as you. I just didn't know it at the time. Your sins may be more obvious than mine, but mine were just as bad. I was just as lost."

For a moment, it was as if time stood still. Armando stood there on that little pebbled beach, weighing the most important question in the universe. Then a smile came over his face. Something had broken.

"I want to do this, too. I want my sins to be gone. I want God's Son to do this for me. How do I do it?"

Terrance glanced at Rebekah and she nodded to him to continue.

"Tell God what you just told us. Tell Him that you are a sinner but believe in Jesus Christ, his Son. Ask Him to take away all of your sins and make you a new person. Tell him that you surrender your life to Him and that from now on your life is His, not yours. Tell him He can do with you whatever He wants. Talk to God as if we are not here. This is between Him and you. There's no magic words."

The big soldier turned his face toward the sky and prayed the most simple and honest prayer one could imagine. He poured out his sorrow for the things he had done. He expressed his deep remorse, and then he asked God to make it all go away because of what Jesus did on the cross.

Tears poured in a steady stream down the man's face. He held nothing back. And when he was finished, he looked over at Terrance and saw tears in the American's eyes, too. He looked at Rebekah and she was crying and smiling at the same time.

Rebekah came over and stood next to the man.

"Armando, I will tell you a secret. There are a bunch of angels up in heaven right now, real angels standing in the presence of God, and they are rejoicing and celebrating what just happened to you.

"Now there is one more thing that you need to do. You need to be baptized. Do you want to do that? If you do, Terrance will baptize you right here in this cove."

Terrance took a step backward. He had never baptized anyone before and wasn't sure he wanted to. He recalled something his dad had said many times from the pulpit; that in the Bible people got baptized immediately when they got saved. They didn't wait a week or a month or a year or until they could take a class on baptism, they just found water and got baptized.

Terrance looked at Armando and the big man nodded. So, there in the pristine waters of that little cove, Armando Articillo, a soldier in the Guyanan army, was baptized by Terrance Clark, a former preacher's kid who happened to have shot the man the day before.

As the two men were coming up out of the water, Terrance saw young Carlena standing at the end of the trail staring at them. Her eyes were wide. From where they stood, it was impossible to read the expression on the girl's face. Following Terrance's gaze, Rebekah turned and saw the girl.

The moment their eyes met, Carlena turned and ran back to the cabin. Rebekah followed after her and found the girl face down again on her sleeping mat again. She was sobbing uncontrollably. She never looked up when Rebekah knelt beside her. The missionary put her hand lightly on Carlena's shoulder and spoke gently.

"Remember all the stories my husband and I told you about Jesus when we came to your village? Remember how He forgives really bad people who have done really bad things? Well, this soldier just met Jesus and all of his sins have been forgiven."

Carlena turned over and through tear filled eyes looked hard into the woman's face.

"This man kill mother and father and everyone in Napoteri village. Jesus not forgive that. If Jesus forgive this man, I not like Jesus. He bad, too."

"Carlena, it is not up to us to decide who God can forgive. That is up to Him. Maybe it would help you to know that this man said he did not shoot at anyone in your village. I hope he was telling the truth. Remember how he tried to protect us back on the boat when you killed the soldier who was wearing your father's necklace? Armando may have done some terrible things, but we must try to forgive. If God forgives him, so must we.

"I am still young myself," she continued, "but one thing I have learned for sure is that bitterness kills a person on the inside. You have a lot to be angry about and you have a lot of sorrow in your heart right now, but eventually you must heal. Hating this man will not help you do that. You will never get over what has happened to you and your family as long as you hate this man.

"When my husband died, I was angry at God for letting it happen. I was angry at Guyana for killing him. I was even angry at the village where he died, because in my mind those people were the reason he was where he was and why he caught the illness that killed him. Eventually though, I had to come to grips with the fact that I either trusted God with my life and John's life, or I didn't. Do you understand what I am saying?"

There was confusion and hurt in the eyes looking back at her.

"Carlena not speak English pretty good, but understand English pretty good. Miss Hamilton trust Jesus. Carlena not sure she can. Too hard."

Chapter Thirty-Nine

When Sergeant Dortin left Bilokut, he was seething with anger and lust for revenge. He directed the man up top to head the boat upriver toward Arakaba, the village where his son had died. The first thing on his agenda was to retrieve the body of his son. He told him to drive slow, that the plan was to get to the village just at daybreak.

As the boat made its way through the darkness, Dortin made himself comfortable and contemplated his next move. Too many people knew about what had happened at Napoteri and knew that army personnel had been involved. It was possible that they would even discover the connection to him, though his involvement in the entire escapade had been limited to "confiscating" gold from what he could claim was an illegal mining operation upriver from the Napoteri village.

Technically, Dortin had not actually approved killing the miners. He had made sure of that. But he *had* known that killing was a distinct possibility, given the obvious fact that the miners were not likely to meekly hand over their precious treasure to a band of strangers just because they demanded it – even if they were wearing army uniforms and arrived in a military boat.

Dortin was also pretty sure a court of law would side with the dead miners and lay the blame on him if he was connected in any way. The Napoteri massacre, well that was a different matter. There was no covering that up now. Someone would have to pay for that. The army might keep the massacre out of the media, but someone would have to pay for wiping out an entire village. Now, if it just so happened that if the men involved all ended up dead, then there would be no witnesses tying him to the crime – and justice would have been satisfied.

All things considered, it seemed apparent to the sergeant that this ought to be his first order of business, as soon as he had recovered his son's body. He would kill the cowards who had deserted poor Carlos and take the gold, which he assumed was hidden somewhere onboard their boat. To accomplish that, however, he had to find the rats.

Claspen Dortin had no idea that all the men involved, except for one, were dead already. And he had no way of knowing that the American he hated so passionately had commandeered their boat. There were other things the sergeant didn't know, things which had he known them would have concerned him more immediately. For the moment, however, he continued to believe, in his arrogance, that he was the master of his own destiny.

Claspen and the rest of his men settled in for the long ride upriver, leaving the driver to himself on the upper deck. The boat moved slowly along in the darkness. There was still the threat of large trees that may have become dislodged from the shore and drifted out into the current. There was no need to chance breaking off a propeller by running over one of them in the darkness.

Quite by chance, the man at the helm hugged so close to the right side of the riverbank that when he came to the wide place where the river split, he missed the fork completely. Instead of heading up the left fork toward Arakaba, he took the right fork and slowly continued on upriver toward Napoteri.

Sometime in the night, Dortin's boat passed the little cove where the missing boat was hidden. That was the sound that had awakened Terrance in the night. Unbeknownst to Claspen Dortin and his men, in the darkness they had also passed by another boat, a smaller boat like Perto's. The little craft stayed hidden behind the foliage at the side of the river until the Dortin's boat had passed it by. Then it made its way back into the main channel and continued downriver toward Bilokut.

As Dortin's boat neared Napoteri, the smell of burnt wood hung heavy in the air. All that was left of the once happy little village were blackened poles and boards, the charred remains of cabins and huts where families had lived and children had played. When the heavy smell made its way to the olfactory senses of the sleeping sergeant, he awakened and jumped to his feet. Hastily, he made his way to the upper deck to investigate.

"What's burning?" he demanded. "I smell smoke."

"I don't know, Sergeant," the driver replied. "There is a clearing of some sort over there on the right shore. I think it is a village or what is left of one."

"We should be at Arakaba by now," the sergeant replied. "What could have happened here? Let's tie up at the dock and wait for daylight and check it out. I am here to retrieve the body of my son and I am not leaving without him."

At first light, the sergeant roused his men and together they made their way up the ramp to the clearing. The scene that met their eyes was an eerie one. There were burned out shells of huts and cabins, some still smoking lightly. Everywhere in the clearing were little mounds of fresh dirt marking what were obviously graves.

"This is not Arakaba. This is Napoteri," the sergeant shouted angrily. The man's loud, angry voice seeming entirely out of sync with the hallowed feel of the place where they stood. He turned to the man who had been driving the boat. "Did you take the left fork of the river or the right?"

The man looked nervously at the ground and then at the sergeant's chin.

"I didn't see a fork, sir. I just followed the river. There was no fork."

"You fool," the sergeant screamed at the man. With no one to unleash it on, Dortin's anger had continued to seethe and fester. Suddenly, almost faster than anyone saw, the sergeant's knife was in his hand and the man felt its keen blade enter his chest just below his heart. The poor fellow sunk to his knees with a groan, clutched at his chest, then fell forward on his face in the dirt.

Less than a minute later, Dortin and the remainder of his men were back on board and their boat was screaming back down the river.

Chapter Forty

While Rebekah was comforting Carlena back in the cabin, Terrance and Armando were standing by the cove assessing the realities of their situation. Terrance was fully aware that there were still ramifications attached to the wounded man's actions and inactions over the last three or four days. But the fact that Armando had foregone the opportunity to use the loaded revolvers, which had been readily at his disposal, and the fact that he had told them about the gold hidden onboard the boat, spoke volumes to the American about the soldier's sincerity. Those two facts might not change everything, but they did change some things.

Terrance explained the problem with the empty fuel tank and how that limited their options. Armando, however, assured the American that their fuel situation was not as dire as he had supposed. Armando had been out on this same boat many times and was certain that the gauge would go quite a bit below empty before the tank would run out. He estimated that they could run the engine for another hour or so on what was left in the tank.

The two of them examined the AK-47s they had onboard and Armando showed his captor where the extra ammo clips were stored. They easily had enough weapons to put up a pretty good fight if push came to shove. The two of them discussed their odds, given the fact that there were after all only two of them and the girls could not reasonably be expected to take part in a gunfight against trained soldiers.

Of course there was the other option. They could simply stay in the cove and hide out. They had everything they needed to survive and appeared to be quite safe, at least for the time being. Armando was aware that the radio was fully operational, but just as he was about to explain that fact to his new friend there came the sound of a large boat approaching rapidly from upriver.

Immediately the two of them ran along the edge of the cove toward the riverbank, hoping to see who was heading downriver in such haste, though they both had a pretty good idea. Armando winced with every step, his arm throbbing with pain, but he kept pace with the younger man.

They made it to the shore just as the boat went flying past them. They could see just well enough through breaks in the foliage to tell that except for the numbers painted on the bow, the craft was identical to theirs.

"That's Dortin driving," Armando whispered. "I wonder where he's going in such a hurry?"

"Arakaba!" Terrance replied. "He's probably after the body of his son. Remember, that's where I killed him."

"If he is going to Arakaba, there is probably nothing we can do to stop him," Armando suggested. "But I am willing to try if you are."

"No, I don't think so," Terrance replied. "It's too risky and we have to think of the girls now. But this might be our chance to make a run for it back down to Bilokut. We could make a stand there or radio for help. There has to be someone in the government who would stop this maniac."

Armando thought for a moment. "There is. There is one man Sergeant Dortin fears. There are plenty of corrupt officers in the middle ranks, but the commander of our base is a straight shooter. If we could get to the radio at Bilokut, I could speak to him. There is no love lost between us, but he would listen to me and he would send enough men to stop Dortin, if there's time."

Armando's words about the radio were less than honest, but they were not without purpose.

"But you're right about the two females." The big soldier continued. "I think we should leave them here. What if Dortin is headed back to Bilokut and not Arakaba? If we ran into them, there could be a fight and the girls could be caught in the middle of it."

"Okay, agreed," Terrance replied.

"You like the missionary, don't you?" Armando said simply.

"Yeah, I guess I do."

"Then go tell them where we are going and say goodbye to her. Then let's get moving."

Terrance ran back to the cabin and rushed inside, startling both girls.

"I came to tell you that Dortin just passed by going downriver and is probably headed up to Arakaba. Armando and I are going to make a run for Bilokut and radio the military base for help. You are safe here."

He looked at Rebekah for a moment. "Just stay here until I come back for you. Okay?"

Rebekah rushed across the room and gazed up into the man's face. She gently put her hands on his chest and started to speak. Just then, they heard the roar of the boat's engine coming to life.

With a confused look on his face, Terrance reached quickly into his pocket and brought out the boat key.

"There must have been a spare key hidden on board!" He all but hissed the words.

Turning, he bolted out the door and raced down the path just in time to see the boat, their boat, bursting through the foliage and out onto the river.

"You dirty scoundrel," Terrance yelled at the top of his lungs. "And I believed you."

Rebekah and Carlena had followed Terrance as he had raced to the cove. The missionary put her hand on his arm, but said nothing.

Just then, Carlena spotted two little finely woven cloth bags lying in the gravel near where the boat had been moored. And there was an automatic weapon and two extra clips.

"Look," she said. "He leave something."

Rebekah walked over and picked up the two bags. They were heavy for their size.

"The gold," she said. "What bad man would leave us weapons and two bags of gold?"

Chapter Forty-One

*T*he boat Armando was driving was faster than Dortin's. Plus, with only one man on board, his was a little lighter in the water. The big man was not able to catch up with the other boat by the time he had reached the fork, so he went with Terrance's hunch and turned to the right and headed up the left fork with the throttle wide open. As Armando maneuvered the boat into the middle of the channel, he made his second request to his God.

God, help me stop this man. He is an evil man. Help me catch him and stop him. I don't care what happens to me, okay?

Armando was new to this praying thing, but he said what he had on his mind and he believed God was listening. He knew that he was not likely to survive what he planned to do when he caught up with the other boat, but he was at peace with that. He was truly at peace for the first time in his adult life.

Holding the steering wheel with his stomach, he reached for the microphone and flipped the switch to turn on the boat's radio. It was still set for the official channel. A man at the base answered his call and Armando quickly indentified himself and the boat he was on. Then, while the fellow on the other end jotted down notes, Armando explained everything that had happened since they had left the base days earlier. He told about murdering the miners and stealing their gold. He explained that the mission had been undertaken at the instigation of Sergeant Claspen Dortin. He told of the massacre at Napoteri, which he explained had occurred under the leadership of the sergeant's son, Carlos Dortin. Finally, he told the man on the other end to contact Bilokut and tell them that the American was in hiding with the two missing women and was innocent of any wrongdoing.

"The American shot me yesterday and today he and a missionary lady saved me," he stated simply.

"Yes, but. . ." came the response from the other end, but Armando had already clicked off the radio. He had just rounded a sharp turn in the river and spotted the other boat less than two hundred yards ahead on a long straight stretch. Grabbing one of the rifles resting on the bench to his left, he clicked off the safety and readied himself. In a minute more, he was close enough to get Dortin's attention.

Again holding the steering wheel steady with his stomach, he lifted the heavy weapon with his good arm. He aimed the weapon's short barrel at the boat just ahead and squeezed the trigger.

Out of nowhere, hot lead came crashing through the windshield of Dortin's boat, peppering the entire boat and killing the man standing next to the sergeant on the upper deck. Wheeling about, Dortin saw the other boat closing in on him from behind. Without a moment's hesitation, the sergeant turned his boat in a wide arch, screaming at his men below to open fire on the other boat. The order was hardly necessary. Both men had turned and opened fire.

The two boats passed each other with Dortin's boat on Armando's left. Hundreds of bullets flew back and forth. Two caught Armando high in his left thigh and one grazed his stomach, barely breaking skin. He returned fire but the men on the other boat were crouching below the rail and firing from concealment. He peppered the other boat, but none of the bullets struck home.

Hampered by the loss of his good arm, the big man laid his weapon on the bench to his left and turned the boat for another pass.

The two boats circled again and came hard at one another a second time. The angle of approach was the same. Armando knew he had little chance of out-shooting the men on Dortin's boat, but he had devised another plan. As the boats approached each other for another pass, he dropped his weapon onto the bench and grabbed the wheel with his left hand. When the boats were close enough, he steered sharply to the left in an attempt to ram the other boat head on. Set for a collision course, he grabbed the rifle and lifted it halfway to his shoulder.

Dortin reacted to Armando's maneuver. He swerved hard to his right in an attempt to avoid the collision. The sudden turn threw both of his men below from their cover. They raised their weapons and fired just as Armando cut loose on them. Both men took several bullets to the stomach and chest and sank limply to the floor of the lower deck. Two of their parting volleys, however, caught Armando full in the chest. With his last ounce of waning strength he drove the accelerator all the way forward and turned his bow into the other boat.

Dortin's last-second maneuver had been soon enough to prevent a head-on collision, but not soon enough to stop Armando's boat from plowing headlong into his rear quarter with a thunderous crash.

Instantly, both boats were dead in the water. Dortin's engine was ripped from its mounts on impact and was rotated sideways to the boat's body. The inertia of Armando's engine had driven it forward enough to bury the propeller in the boat's frame.

One moment there was the roar of engines and the loud cracking of gunfire and a moment later there was only silence. Only one man was left standing, the one man Armando had hoped to stop.

Fuel from Dortin's boat was spilling into the water, leaving a light blue skin on the surface of the river. Both boats were beginning to take on water.

The left side of Armando's boat was pressed hard against the left side of Dortin's crippled craft. The sergeant, spewing out curses, crawled over the rail to the rear of other boat. Claspen was limping badly, but other than a bruised knee, which he had suffered on impact, he appeared to be unharmed.

The collision had thrown Armando forward and Dortin found him there, slumped over the front rail.

There was blood coming from Armando's mouth but he was still breathing when the sergeant reached him. Dortin hissed in the man's ear.

"You fool! You thought you could steal my gold and get away with it."

Armando's eyes were open but he offered no response.

"You thought you could leave my son to die in some worthless village and not have to face me some day. You were wrong!"

Armando whispered something, but it was hard to understand. Dortin leaned in closer.

"Your son was evil, sir, and so are you. And I tossed the gold overboard. It was blood money and I wanted no part of it."

The dying man, his voice barely audible, spoke the truth.

"I don't believe you," the sergeant screamed. "Where's the gold? Where's the man you allowed to kill my son, you coward?"

"I am not that man anymore, sir. I stopped being a coward this morning."

Armando coughed two weak coughs, then closed his eyes and breathed no more. Dortin turned Armando's face toward him. There was just a hint of a smile on the man's face, but it was enough to throw Dortin into a fit of rage. How dare the man die before he could exact his last ounce of revenge.

Angrily, Dortin pounded Armando's back with both fists. He screamed at him. He cursed him. But the man he cursed was no longer there. Armando Articillo had gone home.

When Sergeant Claspen Dortin had finally vented his last measure of fury upon the dead man's body, through bloodshot eyes he looked around him and surveyed his surroundings. As his sanity slowly returned, he recognized that he was very much alone in the middle of the river. His men were dead and his boat was hopelessly incapacitated. There was nothing for him to do but swim for it or drift with the current. He tried both radios, but there was no power to either.

For the first time in his wicked life, Claspen Dortin had no idea what to do. He climbed down into the cabin of Armando's boat and tore it apart looking for bags of gold. He found nothing. Perhaps, he thought, the fool had told the truth.

Water was entering through a gaping hole in the boat's side and the cabin was filling with water, so he gave up his search and climbed back to the upper deck. He sat there for a good fifteen minutes, wracking his brain for answers.

Slowly, the current was moving the two helpless boats down river toward the fork and then beyond. If the boats stayed afloat, eventually he would drift pass Bilokut. He was not entirely sure he wanted to go there. His last visit had not been a friendly one and this time he would be alone.

From the upper deck of his own craft, Claspen studied the shoreline some fifty feet away on the closest side. Off to the left was a muddy bank with a half dozen Caimans lounging in the sun. Two of the beasts looked to be a good sixteen feet long. Looking across at the other boat, he could see where Armando's upper torso still hung over the rail. Blood was slowly dripping into the river below him. Flashing back and forth in the water was a school of maybe thirty piranhas. Their razor sharp teeth protruded from their mouths as they bit and snapped at the bloody water. The water fairly boiled with the little monsters.

Swimming for shore was obviously not going to be an option at the moment. It finally sunk in that all he could do was drift along with the slow current and hope the boats stayed afloat.

Chapter Forty-Two

A little later that afternoon, a small fishing boat broke through the foliage at the side of the river and motored its way to the back of the hidden cove. Terrance, Rebekah, and Carlena heard the low hum of the engine and threw nervous glances at one another. Terrance grabbed for the automatic weapon he had left leaning against the wall by the front door and stepped outside. Rebekah Hamilton followed close on his heels.

They had no knowledge of the fight Armando had taken to Dortin and the price the man had paid to ensure that they would be safe. All they knew for sure was that he had *stolen* their boat and left them stranded and now someone knew where they were.

Through the branches they could see a small boat running ashore at the end of the cove. From where they were, he could not make out who was in the boat. He ran down the path, his weapon at the ready. The little man he saw standing at the back of the boat was a welcome sight indeed.

"Perto!" Terrance shouted his friend's name. "How did you ever find this place?"

"She say she know where you hide," Perto said, pointing at the woman sitting in the middle seat. The woman wore a white bandage on one side of her face, but sat strong and straight in the little craft.

"But I thought only people from Napoteri knew of this place," Terrance replied. "That's what Carlena told us."

Just then, Carlena flew past the American on a dead run.

"Mother!" she screamed. "Mother! You alive."

Carlena jumped into the boat and threw her arms around her mother. There were sobs and tears of joy and neither was willing to let go for some time.

When finally the woman was able to speak, she told them what had happened at Napoteri when Carlos and his men had showed up. People were running everywhere, she explained, and the men from the boat were shooting everyone. Her husband grabbed her by the arm and tried to make it to the jungle. Just then, a bullet grazed her head and she fell to the ground. Her husband knelt to pick her up but at that instant several bullets struck him, killing him instantly.

She told how she lay there on the ground staring up at the sky, her head spinning. The last thing she remembered was a big man with gray temples looking down at her and telling her to be quiet.

"Big man lay husband body on me, say 'be quiet,' then go away. Head hurt. I sleep. I not wake up 'til men come to bury me."

"That big man was named Armando," Rebekah said simply. "I guess he saved your life."

Chapter Forty-Three

*P*erto's little boat returned to Bilokut with Terrance, Rebekah, Carlena, and the girl's mother all crowded in. Carlena had to ride up front on the pile of rope to make room for them all.

Back in Bilokut, Terrance turned the two bags of gold over to the town council. The men promised to do their best to locate its rightful owners. Oddly enough, no one in the village had seen or heard of Sergeant Dortin or Armando and no one had seen either boat.

On the trip downriver, Perto had related the story of how the council had faced down Dortin and his men at the council chambers and had sent them packing at gunpoint. Though the story hardly needed embellishment, it lost nothing in the telling.

Shortly after they arrived at Bilokut, Terrance was able to get on the radio and get a message to Timmy in Annari, telling his friend that he would be back for him the next day. He told the person on the other end to tell the boy that Terrance had a big surprise for him.

That evening after dinner, Terrance excused himself and asked Rebekah Hamilton if she would like to take a little stroll with him around the village. Together, the two set off into the night.

The moon was full now and casting its cool light across the village landscape. Across the clearing, four or five children were chasing giant fireflies that were dancing about clumps of shrubs growing near the edge of the clearing.

The man from Oakland led the pretty missionary lady toward a little bench nestled in the shadows of a huge red cedar tree that stood in the center of the clearing. Terrance had eyed the place earlier and thought it perhaps a perfect spot to revisit later on – when he was not alone.

"Would you like to sit for a bit," he asked.

"No thank you, I would prefer to stand," Rebekah said. The woman's voice was pleasant, but Terrance was thrown a little off balance by her reply.

"Okay. Well, I don't know exactly how to say this, but the first time I saw you on the riverbank back in Annari, you smiled at me. I'm sure it was nothing to you, but my heart was yours from that moment on. I knew nothing about you, but I knew I loved you.

"I followed you up these rivers to rescue you from Gorton Harkin, but as much as that, I just wanted to see your face again. I know it sounds silly, but I believed I would be happy if I could only see you smile at me one more time. I was wrong about that. When I saw you last night at the cabin door, I knew right then that once more was not enough. I want to see your face every day for the rest of my life. I love you, Rebekah Hamilton. I don't want to let another day pass without you knowing that."

The woman stood there gazing up at him and for what seemed like an eternity, saying nothing. Finally, she began.

"My husband has been gone now for two years. During that time, I have not looked at another man. I have grieved and hurt and missed him. I loved John. I guess I would have to say that I still do.

"I don't know why I smiled at you the way I did the day you were rescued from the falls. I know I did, though. That's why I walked away so quickly. I realized I had just smiled very warmly at a handsome man, a total stranger no less, and I felt guilty that I had. I suppose it's time to stop feeling that way, but I felt like I was somehow being unfaithful to John's memory.

"I know you so little, Terrance. I have really only known you for one day and that is not enough time to get to know anyone. You seem to be a very brave and honorable man. And the way you helped lead poor Armando to the Lord told me that you are also a man of faith.

"And I will confess that when I look at you, I feel things that I have not felt for a long time. I don't think I have been able to hide that from you.

"However. . .

However! Here goes the part where she turns me down or lets me down easy.

"However. . . I cannot tell a man that I love him when I have known him for as long as I have known you. That's Hollywood love. It is not based on commitment or friendship or trust, just a feeling. And feelings come and go.

"So, I am not turning you down. And I don't want you to disappear from my life. I just want to know you better than I do now. I want to know if our goals are the same. I have committed my life to doing the will of God. When you make Jesus Christ the Lord of your life that includes making Him Lord over your heart. Can you understand that?"

This was not the way Terrance had wanted the evening to go. He had hoped the woman would throw her arms around him and tell him she loved him and then seal the whole thing with a long, sweet kiss. He knew now that the prize he sought would be harder to win than that.

"Yes, I have thought about that," he said softly. There was some disappointment in his voice. He didn't try to hide it.

"My dad was a preacher and he spoke of such things. I can't say that I always followed the things he said, but I understand the principles. I have thought about the fact that you're a missionary and what it might involve for you to leave that life and come back to California with me. And I have thought about what it would be like for me to stay here and work with you.

"To be honest," he continued, "I don't know the answers to those things. I just know I don't want to lose you."

Now that she was ready, Rebekah took a seat on the bench. As she did, she took Terrance by the hand and with the slightest tug pulled him down beside her. Their faces were close together and her voice was just above a whisper.

"There's one more thing I want to say to you. It may sound like I am being very analytical about all this, but that doesn't mean my heart doesn't want to just leap in and see what happens. It does. The effect you have on me would make that an easy thing to do. But let's be cautious for a while, okay? You saved my life. You saved the lives of a village full of people that I love. You were a hero, and what woman doesn't want her very own hero? That can be a powerful thing.

"My husband was a hero in his own way. He made a million sacrifices to serve the people living in these jungles. He was offered a full-ride basketball scholarship at a major university, but he turned it down because he believed this is where the Lord wanted him to be. Instead of sports, he poured himself into medicine. He died much too young, but he saved people's lives and he saved souls in the short time he was here. Even though he died young, he did not die in vain.

"I just need time to. . ."

Just then, they heard Perto's voice calling out to them from the council building.

"Mr. Terrance, Timmy is on radio. Do you want to talk to him?"

"Yes," Terrance shouted back. "Tell him I will be right there."

Terrance looked long into the face of the woman sitting close to him. The moonlight had found its way to the bench where they sat. Her face was the most beautiful sight his eyes had ever beheld. Putting his fingers to his lips, he kissed them and then touched the girl's lips gently.

"I should go talk to Timmy," he whispered as he rose to his feet.

Together they started walking toward the lights of the council chamber. "Where are you going from here, Missionary Hamilton?" he asked. "Where do you actually live, anyway? And how will I see you again?"

"I stay at different places while I am in the field. But I have an apartment in Vreed en Hoop. I spend most of my time in the villages up these rivers. If you don't mind, I will return with you to Annari tomorrow. I would like to meet this Timmy. Sarah told me so much about him and I know he means a lot to you. So it's probably time for me to meet him for myself."

"Good!" Terrance exclaimed. "He will be excited to meet someone who knew his mother. Maybe we can tell him together about his new grandparents. I'm not sure how he will take that news, but I'm pretty sure it will be a big surprise."

By now they were at the council chambers. When Terrance sat down in front of the microphone, there was a very excited little boy waiting on the other end of the radio.

Chapter Forty-Four

*T*he goodbyes at Bilokut were hard. Carlena miraculously had her mother back. The poor child still had a lot of pain to process, but at least she would not have to do it alone. Carlena had spent three or four of the most gut-wrenching days of her life with Rebekah Hamilton and letting go so abruptly wasn't easy.

Down at the dock, Rebekah said goodbye to her young friend with sadness. She knew that, for a fourteen-year old, Carlena had gone through a lot and it would take some time for her to process it all. Only time would tell whether the girl would heal or be destroyed by the bitterness. Knowing that all of the men who had attacked her village were gone now and having her mother back should help her find some kind of closure. But still it would not be easy.

One of the Bilokut council members had heard Armando's confession over the shortwave and his indictment of Claspen Dortin and his son Carlos. The councilman related the entire account to Terrance and Rebekah. Armando's confession seemed to indicate that whatever his reasons for taking the boat and leaving it in the cove had been, he was not trying to escape responsibility for his actions.

Other pieces of the story came together when one of the fishing boats from the village returned from upriver.

As soon as the men had tied up their boat, they ran to the place where Perto's boat was just preparing to leave the dock.

The two fishermen described to Perto's party a strange sight they had seen on the river just below the fork. They said it looked like two military boats had crashed into each other and were either drifting slowly or were maybe snagged on something. The two villagers described a big man with no shirt slumped over the front of one of the boats. They thought the man looked like he was probably dead.

They said there was another man sitting up on top of the other boat. When he saw them, he motioned for them to approach, but the men said they were not sure what to do so they rushed back downriver to report what they had seen.

For the first time it became clear to Terrance and Rebekah what Armando had done when he had left the little cove in *their* boat. He had gone after Dortin by himself and had died trying to stop him.

"I guess Armando wasn't the coward he thought he was. In his own way, he was trying to make sure that Dortin was stopped and at the same time make sure that no one else got hurt in the process."

As Terrance spoke of Armando, Carlena stood off to the side listening carefully. Rebekah shot a glance at the girl to see how all this talk about Armando was affecting her. Carlena's brow was furrowed in deep thought. When she spoke, her voice was soft.

"Armando bad man one day. Good man next day. He die good man."

Rebekah nodded and with moisture in her eyes, she put her arm around the girl and hugged her one last time.

Before they pushed away from the dock, Rebekah assured her new friend that as soon as she could she would return to Bilokut, or wherever it was Carlena and her mother settled. Carlena's mother hugged the missionary and thanked her for keeping her daughter alive. The night before, Carlena had told her mother how the missionary had kept herself between Carlena and the jaguar. The story had deeply moved Carlena's mother. The bravery and selflessness of that deed would be told over and over throughout the villages of the region. Even Gorton Harkin's fight to the death with the rogue cat would become the stuff of legend.

With the goodbyes all said, the four of them started off, puttering up the river like a car full of elderly folks out for a Sunday drive.

Chapter Forty-Five

*L*ater that same morning, a detachment from the military base at Anna Regina found Sergeant Dortin about half a mile below the fork in the river. The two incapacitated boats were sitting very low in the water, snagged on a submerged log. Dortin was sitting on the upper deck of his little cruiser smoking a cigar as if he didn't have a care in the world. To everyone's surprise, the bow of one of their own cruisers was buried deep in the rear quarter panel of Dortin's boat.

The troops found the bodies of three soldiers in the cabin of Dortin's boat. There was one shirtless body draped across the front railing of the other.

Dortin greeted the detachment as rescuers. He had carefully crafted a perfect script, explaining away everything that had happened. He was confident that there were no witnesses to his wrongdoing. Dead men would take the blame for all that had transpired and no one would be the wiser. He had done this before.

Claspen Dortin had no way of knowing about the report Armando had filed over the radio minutes before he had overtaken and fired on Dortin's boat. The self-incriminating testimony of a dying man would not be quickly dismissed.

To his surprise, the sergeant was immediately taken into custody and handcuffed. He was to be taken downriver to face military justice. The detachment never even slowed as it sped past Bilokut. For its own purposes and to protect Dortin's immediate superiors, all of whom claimed total ignorance of the rogue sergeant's misdeeds, the army would put a tight lid on the affair at Napoteri. Stopping and talking to the good people at Bilokut did not fit well with that strategy.

As for Sergeant Claspen Dortin, they were sure he would never walk free among men again. Or so everyone thought.

Chapter Forty-Six

When Perto's little boat finally pulled up to the dock at Annari, Timmy was standing there waiting. Except for Perto's family, Terrance Clark was the only person in the whole world the ten-year old knew. Perto's family had treated him well and he had learned a fair amount of Creole over the past several days, but still, he had missed Terrance terribly. Their ten days together had been a nonstop, life and death struggle with nature and the experience had created a bond that would last for many years to come.

The mutilated body of Gorton Harkin had arrived at Annari the day before Terrance and Perto returned. The story behind Gorton's death was the talk of the village. Reports of the body's condition and the details of Gorton's demise had not done much to lessen Timmy's concern for the safety of his friend.

In addition, the people of Annari had heard the chatter on the official shortwave channel and knew all about the massacre at Napoteri. They knew that a certain army sergeant of ill repute had been hunting for the American and planned on arresting him, or worse. Then the next day, they had heard Armando's detailed description of what had really happened and who had been behind it all. Those events, coupled with the goings on at Jonestown, had made November and December of

1978 the two most exciting and terrible months anyone in Annari and the region round about could remember.

When Terrance and Timmy met at the dock, Terrance was surprised at the emotion he felt when he embraced the boy. When Timmy finally let go, Terrance turned to help Rebekah from the boat.

"Rebekah Hamilton," he said, "this is Timmy Stanford, Sarah's son."

Timmy looked at Rebekah and then he looked at Terrance. There was puzzlement in his eyes.

"Nice to meet you, Miss. Hamilton. But Terrance, how did you know my mother's name? I don't think I ever told you that. I know I didn't tell you our *last* name."

"You didn't tell me. Miss Hamilton here was friends with your mother. She used to visit her in Jonestown. She says your mom used to talk about you all the time. She has been very excited to meet you in person."

The pretty missionary flashed Timmy Stanford one of those smiles that somehow made the whole world a brighter place.

"It is a pleasure to meet you, Timmy Stanford. You are a handsome young man, and brave too. Your mother would be very proud of you. Terrance told me much about your adventures together. I'm so glad you went with him when he made his escape. That's what your mother would have wanted, you know. I'm sure of that."

"Yes, ma'am. I know you're right. I wouldn't be alive, if I wasn't here."

Timmy realized what he had just said and stumbled to say it differently. "I mean. . ." he stuttered.

"I know what you mean, Timmy," Rebekah said laughing. Then she gave the boy a big hug. The embrace was a long one for two people who had never met. But neither was quick to let go.

Chapter Forty-Seven

*T*hat night, Terrance Clark, Rebekah Hamilton, and Timmy Stanford dined at Perto's house. Mayor Harkin was nowhere to be seen. He had not met them at the dock and hadn't called on them afterward. Harkin was reportedly in town, but for some reason had made himself scarce.

They all had stories to tell, some of which none of the others had heard yet. And of course Perto's wife and sons had heard none of the stories firsthand. The stage was set for a long evening. Even Terrance was surprised by the emotions around the room when he and Rebekah shared the story of Armando and his last minute conversion and the way he had died trying to protect them. The man's story was one of redemption and a powerful one at that.

Perto tried to play down the confrontation with Sergeant Dortin at the council chambers in Bilokut, but the image of a room full of men with weapons pointing at one another was just too compelling and inspiring for the shopkeeper's sons, who all gathered around their father and hugged him and patted him on the shoulders. He was a hero in their eyes, and their sentiments were not misplaced. When the situation had called for a man to be a man, their dad had not wavered.

When it came time to tell Timmy about his grand-parents, there was complete silence in the room. Ter-rance told the boy why he had come to Jonestown in the first place. He told him a little about his clients back in San Francisco, and then he told Timmy that he had just learned from Rebekah that those same clients were Timmy's grandparents, his mother's mom and dad.

Timmy's eyes were big, but his reaction was impos-sible to read. The expressions on his face seemed to change from second to second as he processed what he had just been told.

"Well?" Terrance finally said, "What do you say?"

Timmy hesitated for a while, looking down at the floor. When he finally looked up, he looked deep into Terrance's eyes and said, "That's good to know, but I want to stay with you."

Terrance smiled and nodded. The nod was barely per-ceptible, but Timmy caught it. Clearly there was much for them to think about. Nothing more was said about the matter for the rest of the evening. Other exciting stories were yet to be told and questions asked, but the question of Timmy's future was still hanging there and was not going to go away.

Later that night after Timmy was asleep, Terrance and Rebekah sat on the front porch of Perto's home and talked for several hours. They spoke of growing up in California and growing up in Indiana. They talked about their parents and the way they each had been raised. Rebekah seemed most interested in hearing what it was like growing up a preacher's kid.

Terrance was a smitten man. He was happy just sit-ting and listening to this amazing woman talk. He was happy just looking at her. Sometimes her laughter would bubble up in this magical way that sounded almost like the laughter of a child. A second later she would turn a steady gaze on him and ask him some piercing question that betrayed the depths of her thinking. As the evening progressed, Terrance became aware that it would take quite some time for him to understand this remarkable woman.

The next day, word came from Harold Williams, the kindly man who had used his cruiser to help clear the river after the storm. He had taken the gold coin Perto had given him to an expert in antique coins in Georgetown. That man had in turn consulted with professors at two major universities back in the States and another in Mexico City. Their consensus, based on the verbal description given to them by the coin dealer in Georgetown, was that the coin was not actually a coin. More likely it was what was known historically as a Tepuzque gold piece. The Tepuzque were gold discs that were produced at Mexico City around the year 1525 or so because the official silver coinage was inadequate for larger business and real estate transactions. The discs were stamped with the weight and the fineness of the gold they contained, and then used like gold coins.

The "coin" Terrance had given to Perto had been countermarked with the royal seal after it was minted, as was reportedly common practice in that era. "Tepuzque" was an Aztec word for copper, though the discs that bore that name were actually made of gold and called at the time *peso de oro*. The professors and the coin dealer in Georgetown were certain that no samples of these coins were known to exist today. In fact, they had ceased to circulate around 1591. The professor from Mexico City agreed with the assessment of the others and was anxious to see the piece firsthand.

"If this 'coin' is what it appears to be," the dealer had concluded, "Its value is difficult to measure, but would be at least $20,000 and perhaps much more." The dealer said he knew of private buyers who would be interested, but felt morally obligated to give first right of refusal to the Mexican government. He said the government would likely purchase the piece for display in one of Mexico's national museums.

Terrance fumbled in his pocket, and without pulling them out, counted six more of the coins.

"Perto, the coin I gave you is yours. It is your decision what to do with it."

"No, Mr. Terrance. Too much money for Perto. Just work four or five days."

Terrance laughed. He found it funny that Perto would characterize what the two of them had gone through as if it were all in a day's work.

"The coin is yours," Terrance insisted. "I owe you far more than that, my friend. Besides, I am just proud to know you."

"If you give so expensive gift, Perto give you gift," the shopkeeper said matter of fact. He whispered something to his oldest son, who returned momentarily with a gorgeous, finely tanned jaguar hide, the one he had displayed earlier at his shop.

"This for you," the son said. "Father give."

Terrance smiled. He knew that it would not be polite to refuse such a magnanimous gesture. He accepted the skin graciously and laid it across his lap and nodded his appreciation to Perto. He couldn't help but notice that Rebekah, who was sitting next to him, shuddered when the hide was brought into the room. Her experience with the cat that had killed Gorton was one she would not soon forget. Even though *her* jaguar had been black, the effect was the same.

Later that same evening, when Timmy was sitting alone with him and Rebekah, Terrance removed the six Tepuzque coins from his pocket and counted three of them out and handed them to Timmy.

"These are for you, partner. I found them in the cave and they are as much yours as mine."

The boy's eyes lit up when Terrance handed him the coins, but all he said was, "Neat! Real gold."

Timmy stood staring at the coins for a minute, then he laid them on the table and ran into the room where he had been sleeping. When he came out, he was carrying his rabbit skin pouch. He carefully poured out the contents on the table. Among the normal odds and ends that a young boy might collect were dozens of little green stones and one larger one. Timmy divided the stones into two equal piles and slid one of the piles over to Terrance's side of the table.

"Like Perto said, 'You give gift, I give gift.' These are the rocks I took out of the pool of water by our cave. You can keep them to remember that we were there. And this big one here is for saving my life two times. You got me out of Jonestown, else I woulda died, and you saved my life at the top of the falls. It's just a green rock, but if you put it in one of those polishing thingies, it could look really pretty."

Terrance thanked his young friend and put the stones in his pocket.

The Californian knew he had a lot to think about. First there was the question of Rebekah. She was quickly becoming the center of his universe, but a center over which he had no control. Then there was the question of Timmy. Terrance felt a fiduciary responsibility to his clients to report to them the news about their daughter. They would be greatly saddened to learn of her death. Terrance was reasonably certain that under California law, Sarah's parents would automatically become the legal guardians of her son, unless of course there was a competing claim by the boy's father or the father's parents, though that seemed unlikely.

To complicate matters, Timmy had made it clear that he wanted to stay with Terrance. That, however, was not the kind of question a ten-year old boy usually gets to decide for himself.

The next morning he asked Timmy if he knew who his father was. Timmy said his mother had always told him that she wasn't sure about that.

When Timmy was out of the room, Rebekah was able to add somewhat to the story. During one of her visits to Jonestown, Sarah Stanford had told Rebekah that she had given birth to her son outside of wedlock, back during her "free-love" hippie days. Sarah had said that she was not sure who the father was, but as the boy had grown she thought he looked more and more like a certain college professor from Berkeley who at times would party with the students and dabble in LSD. Sarah said she had never attempted to contact the man after their one night together, but she was pretty sure the professor was Timmy's father.

Sarah had explained that her parents were a prominent San Francisco couple and would have been embarrassed to learn that their wayward daughter had gotten herself pregnant with some stranger while high on an acid trip. So she never told them about Timmy and never asked for their help.

Terrance kept all this to himself, undecided as to whether he should even share these details with his clients. He decided that he would cross that bridge when he came to it. For the moment, however, the most important thing in his life was a beautiful missionary woman.

Terrance and Rebekah spent the next couple of days at Annari just getting better acquainted. As usually happens, reality came crashing in one morning at breakfast when Rebekah announced that the next day she would return to her apartment in the city. She explained to a clearly anxious Terrance that she had business to attend to, supplies to pick up, and probably a ton of mail to answer. She explained to him how her ministry to the locals survived by means of support that came in from churches and families back in the States and how the funds they provided allowed her to purchase the medical supplies and Bibles she distributed to the villages.

As soon as they were alone, Terrance asked her if she would be willing to go for a boat ride with him up to the falls, just to get away and talk. Rebekah agreed and a couple of hours later, they were on their way upriver in Perto's boat, just the two of them, a rifle, and a lunch that Perto's wife had packed for them.

Both were lost in their thoughts and hardly spoke as they rode along. The waterfowl were plentiful and noisy. Here and there, Black Caiman, which Terrance preferred to call crocs, slid quietly into the dark water as their little boat approached. They even saw a ten-foot Arapaima rise to the surface near the right side of the boat. The fish rolled before disappearing back into the dark depths. Its white underbelly and red tail were a magnificent sight to see so close up.

It was as if seeing the giant fish rise from the depths brought the woman's deepest thoughts to the surface.

"I love this wild country, Terrance," she said. "I am willing to go wherever God would have me go, but I fell in love with the people here and I fell in love with this land. It is hard for me to imagine going back to the States on any kind of permanent basis."

"I know," Terrance replied softly. "I've been thinking about that a lot. I love you, Rebekah. I am sure about that. And I want to be where you are. Right now, though, I have to take Timmy back to my clients in San Francisco. It is not up to me to decide where he lives. I'm not sure, but they may want him.

"I don't think they are quite the kind of people Sarah described to you. She was a rebellious, young hippie, you know. Back then, lots of kids thought their parents were squarer than they actually were. It's likely that Sarah's parents will fall in love with Timmy and offer him a good home. They are very wealthy and if he lived with them he would be able to get the best education money could buy. At any rate, I need to take him back to them and see what happens. Don't you agree?"

They had reached the mooring place downstream from the falls, which was as far as the little boat could go. Terrance cut the engine and raised it as the bow of the boat slid up onto the soft shore. He leaped onto the bank with rope in hand and secured the craft to the closest tree.

"I don't see that there is any other option," the girl replied seamlessly, as if there had been no disruption in their conversation. The sun was shining bright overhead and the red in her hair came alive as the sunlight danced through it. Her soft curls and the little freckles sprinkled across her cheeks and nose only added to her beauty. Rebekah had proven that she could be a tough woman when she had to be, but there was at the same time a feminine sweetness about her that was so undeniably appealing. None of this was lost on the man who stood before her. Terrance was certain that he had already memorized every freckle on the woman's face.

"If for some reason Sarah's parents don't want to raise their grandson, you may have a tough decision to make. Timmy may have no place else to go. You have already gone far beyond the call of duty in your quest to find your clients' daughter for them and they will owe you a large sum of money. When you collect that, you will be pretty well fixed for a while. But you may have to make a hard decision about Timmy – one way or the other.

"Plus, if you sell your coins, you should end up with a tidy sum in hand from those. That should give you even more options."

They had been talking while walking leisurely along the trail to the falls and had made it to the edge of the large pool of deep, green water. Terrance didn't reply to the things Rebekah had pointed out. Instead, he stopped and pointed to a place at the top and near the center of the falls, a good two hundred feet above where they stood.

"That's the place where we were stranded," he said. "By rotating my body just a little I could see down into this pool. It is only the grace of God that we did not slip over the edge. Every little movement I made caused us to slip a little closer. At the time, I had little doubt that we were both going to die. It was pretty hopeless."

"Well, the Lord protected you, maybe so you could rescue me and Carlena and help me lead Armando to Him and maybe because He has a plan for the rest of your life. Whatever his reasons, I'm glad He did."

There was a look in Rebekah's eyes when she added that last part. It was a look Terrance had been longing to see. At that moment, he longed to take this beautiful woman in his arms and kiss her, but he held back.

"I was thinking," he said gently, "that maybe we could use the money I can get from selling the coins to purchase a specially outfitted boat, one large enough to serve as a portable medical facility. We could make the rounds to these villages on some kind of regular basis."

"Are you saying that you would be willing to stay here with me," she asked, her eyes boring holes right into his soul. "Is that what you mean, Terrance Clark? Or are you just saying you would be willing to donate the money?"

"Well, I don't know if I am ready yet to be a full blown missionary," he said laughing. "But I am saying I am willing to come back here after I take Timmy to California and be with you from then on. And I would be honored to use the money for such a purpose. There are good people here and they love you and need you."

"Well," the red haired missionary lady replied, "I will be here waiting for you when you return, Mr. Clark."

Now was the time. The preacher's kid from Oakland pulled the woman close to him and kissed her full upon the lips. She clung to him as if she too had waited a long time for this moment. Finally, she leaned her head back and looked up at him.

"I like you a lot, you know," she said softly. Her voice was barely discernible over the roar of the falls.

Rebekah Hamilton rested her head against the man's chest and left it there.

Chapter Forty-Eight

When Terrance and Rebekah returned to Annari from the falls, there was a tall, slender man standing on the end of the dock, apparently waiting for them. The man's skin was very white, too white for the tropics, and he was wearing new blue jeans that needed to be washed a few more times before they were worn and a thin, navy blue windbreaker. There was a government-issue sidearm on his hip and the letters ATF embroidered above the bill of his baseball cap.

"Are you Terrance Clark?" the man asked before the boat had even reached the dock.

"I am. Who are you? Is there a problem?"

The man waited for Terrance to tie the boat to the dock before answering.

"I'm special agent Jeff Messner with the ATF. We're still following up on the mess at Jonestown and tying up loose ends – you know, matching names to bodies and all that. Anyway, we found your passport in one of the residences there, but no body to match it. Obviously, that created questions. There were reports that some people were buried there in unmarked graves."

"Well, I'm obviously not dead, sir. Do you have my passport?" Terrance asked. He had forgotten about that small technicality.

"I do," the agent replied. "We caught wind through unofficial channels that an American matching your description was caught up with some military related mess in this region and decided to check it out. So, Mr. Clark, what is your connection to Jonestown and how did you end up way over here?"

Terrance introduced Rebekah to the man as they walked up the ramp to the village. After they found a place to sit, Terrance filled the agent in on his reasons for coming to Jonestown, his escape, and all the goings on that had occurred after his arrival at Annari.

The man took copious notes on a long, skinny pad. He only interrupted when Terrance described the shooting at Arakaba and the later run-in with the military boat at the dock at Bilokut. Terrance was surprised by how few questions the man asked. Apparently there were some things he preferred not to know.

The agent's primary concern seemed to be learning where Terrance got the gun he used in his fights with Sergeant Dortin's men and whether he had seen any guns while he was in Jonestown. Once the man was satisfied with the answers to those two questions, he seemed interested in little clsc.

An hour after they had met, the agent handed Terrance his passport, wished him well, and headed back to the coast on his chartered boat.

Chapter Forty-Nine

Terrance Clark and Timmy Stanford left George-town, Guyana the first week of December, 1978 on a direct flight to San Francisco. Terrance had called ahead and informed his clients of Sarah's death. The Stanfords were deeply saddened by the news, but said they would welcome Timmy into their home with open arms and asked Terrance to bring the boy to them with all due haste.

The Stanfords' home was a palatial estate. Terrance had not been there before and even before he entered the residence proper he found himself a bit overwhelmed by the wealth it represented. A butler led the two of them to the sitting room where the Stanfords were waiting to meet their grandson for the first time.

As soon as introductions were made, Mrs. Stanford reached for the checkbook sitting on the ornate over-sized coffee table that occupied the middle of the room.

Ever mindful of the business end of things, the woman immediately wrote out a check and paid Terrance the same bonus for returning little Timmy as they would have had he returned with their daughter Sarah. She handed Terrance the $100,000 check, plus a separate payment for his per diem allowance as well as the itemized list of expenses Terrance had prepared in advance.

With that out of the way, Mrs. Stanford politely offered the man a chair. With Terrance and Timmy seated across from her and her husband, Mrs. Stanford started on a long list of questions.

"Mr. Clark, if you wouldn't mind, we would like to know what it was like for the both of you in Jonestown and how you and Timmy escaped and what happened after that. It seems you were lost in the jungle for a long time. How did you have to survive before you were rescued?"

"Well," Terrance began, "if you don't mind, why don't we let Timmy answer those questions. He can speak for himself."

Mrs. Stanford seemed surprised by Terrance's suggestion, but her husband liked the idea and encouraged the boy to go ahead and tell them what had happened.

Timmy sat back on the padded leather chair and asked politely how much time they had. The Stanfords cast quick smiles at one another, pleased by the ten-year old's easy but straightforward manner. Mr. Stanford replied that they wanted to hear all about everything and had as much time as Timmy needed.

So, starting at the beginning, Timmy told them how he had grown up in a small apartment on the edge of the city, not more than ten miles from where the Stanford's massive estate was located. He told how his mother struggled to survive as a single mom, how she somehow put herself through nursing school while holding down a full time job, and how she eventually became a Christian while shopping for a used mattress and a nightstand at a Teen Challenge center in Oakland.

"Mom said she was led to the Lord by a man working behind the counter. I would like to go to that place someday."

The Stanfords nodded. They were somewhat stoic people, or at least tried to be, but the story of their daughter struggling as a single mom and barely getting by just a few miles from their home seemed to touch them deeply. Every few moments, Mrs. Stanford dabbed her wet eyes with a tissue. Her husband responded outwardly merely by leaning forward in his chair.

Some of the things Timmy described he learned from his mom, some he remembered. Some of what he shared he had learned from Rebekah Hamilton. Rebekah had told Timmy *almost* everything she had learned from Sarah during her visits to the compound. The two young women had spent many hours together sharing intimate details of the ups and downs of their lives.

Timmy told the Stanfords how he and Terrance had escaped from Jonestown and all about their lives in the jungle and the cave and their near death experience at the falls. The boy went on and on, and the usually reserved Stanfords were literally on the edge of their seats. Timmy went on to share the story of Terrance's fight with the Dortins and the massacre at Napoteri. He even threw in the part about Rebekah and Carlena and the black jaguar that had killed Gorton Harkin.

It was as if the boy had this untapped mass of emotions welling up inside of him and it all needed to come out. He just kept on talking and no one interrupted him. Terrance couldn't help but smile. The boy had it all down. Every detail was right. Terrance found himself glancing over from time to time at the Stanfords to see how they were taking Timmy's long story. About half way through, he noticed that moisture was beginning to collect in Mr. Stanford's eyes too.

When Timmy was finally done, he placed his hands on his lap and just stopped talking. Everyone just stared for a few moments.

"Well, I guess that explains how I got here in this big, fancy house alive," he said, to break the silence.

As soon as Timmy said that, Mrs. Stanford did what she had been holding off doing for the past hour. She rushed across the room and got down on her knees in front of Timmy's chair and gave her grandson a long, warm hug.

Mr. Stanford sat back and let his wife do the hugging. It wasn't that he wasn't touched. He would express his feelings later, when he understood them better. In the meanwhile, he turned to Terrance and asked pointedly, "Son, are you satisfied with the hundred thousand we just paid you?"

"Yes sir, that's what we agreed on. More than enough actually. That's a lot of money."

"Well, I'm glad to hear that. It makes it a little more pleasurable to do what I am going to do now."

He leaned over and picked up a little silver bell off the stand next to his chair and rung it. As if by magic, a second finely dressed butler appeared and asked what the man of the house wished.

"Bring me my checkbook, Samuel. The brown one on the desk in my study."

The man disappeared and reappeared a few moments later with a leather folder, which he handed to Mr. Stanford.

"Mr. Clark, we sent you to Guyana to find our daughter and you brought us back the worst possible news. But that's not your fault. You did what we asked you to. And I guess the news about Sarah wasn't the worse possible news. At least she didn't commit suicide with the rest of those poor souls. I never liked Jones even when he was here in the Bay area, though a lot of the liberal politicians sure did.

"But, as sad as the news about our Sarah is, the treasure you brought to us this afternoon is of immeasurable worth. We sent you there as a private investigator and you returned to us a hero. I feel inclined to give you another bonus."

Terrance stood to his feet and began to resist the payment of any further sum. But Charles Stanford stopped him before he got started.

"Son, let's both agree that no amount of money would rightly compensate for what you have gone through and the selflessness you exhibited down there in that God forsaken country we sent you to. And let's agree that you did not do what you did for the money. I can see that in your eyes and I like what I see. You don't get to where I am in life by being a bad judge of character, though my wife would argue about that, I suppose.

"But we have all the money anyone could ever need and more. Forgive my presumption, Mr. Clark, but I simply can't let you walk out of here without expressing our gratitude in a tangible way. Take this check and put it in your pocket. Use the money however you wish. If you think you don't deserve it, go start an orphanage or something. But my heart is moved by what you have done.

"You know, we watched the news coverage of the whole Guyana affair. I can't tell you the anguish we suffered knowing that our daughter was there and thinking that she in all likelihood had been taken in by Jones's lies and had followed him over the cliff like a lemming. You brought us peace about that. And you brought us her son, our grandson.

"So, I plead with you as one man to another, don't deny us this opportunity to thank you; not just pay you, but thank you."

There was no way for Terrance to gracefully say "no." From the start, money had never been the issue. He hadn't gone to Guyana just for the money, though to be sure, he had got a lot more "adventure" out of the deal than he had bargained for.

Terrance accepted the folded check and put it in his pocket. Then he asked for a moment alone with Timmy. The Stanfords obliged by leaving the room, leaving Timmy and Terrance to themselves. There was a splendid fire crackling in the fireplace. Dark mahogany paneling covered all the walls and finely milled trim from the same wood encased all the doors and windows. The chairs and couches were a soft burgundy leather and on the floor was the largest oriental rug Terrance Clark had ever seen. Terrance was surrounded by opulence such as the son of humble preacher might never see.

"Well, Timmy my man, how do you like your mom's folks? Pretty great, aren't they?"

"Yeah, they're alright. And I know what you are going to say. I don't know them, Terrance, and I want to go with you. They're nice, but I still don't know them."

The boy spoke his mind plainly and simply. Already a tear was beginning to well up in each eye. Terrance knelt down on one knee to look the boy in the eye.

"Timmy, I am going to go back to Guyana in the morning. I am going to spend as much time there as it takes to see how things go with Miss Hamilton. I love her and want to marry her. You need to stay here for now and see how things go with your grandma and grandpa. We both need to give something new a chance to happen and see how it all works out.

"The law says this is where you belong right now. That's a fact. And it's plain to see that your grandparents love you and will do everything they can to make you happy. I will not forget you. I promise. You will always be my friend. I will call you in a week or two and see how you are doing. If things are not working out here, we can talk about that. Okay? Can you handle that?"

Terrance expected a bigger push back than he got. He expected Timmy to fight harder, but to his surprise Timmy accepted the terms Terrance had offered.

"I guess so. I will try it here. They're both real nice and stuff. But if I hate it here, can I come live with you?"

"Well," Terrance replied, "let's cross that bridge when we come to it. Give this place and your grandparents a chance, okay? If I say yes now, you might not try so hard or give them a fair chance. Do you understand?"

Timmy nodded, then threw his arms around Terrance and hugged him as hard as he could, for a moment holding on for dear life. Though one of them was a man and the other boy, the bond between them had become a powerful force.

They couldn't know it at the time, but the two of them would one day return to the jungle together, and not just in Guyana. But that is a story for another time. Timmy's fascination with the big cats they had encountered in Guyana never left him and down the road that fixation would lead the both of them into places and situations they could never have dreamed of at the time.

Terrance said his polite goodbyes to the Stanfords and headed back to his apartment. He had not been home for nearly three months and even now he was only going to have time to stop over for one night. There were bills to pay and personal business to attend to before heading back to Guyana and Rebekah. His hundred thousand dollar paycheck should cover his personal overhead for a while, plus there was another check for more than $12,000 for travel reimbursement related to the trip.

It was the next morning before Terrance glanced at the other check, the "thank-you" check. He had placed that one in his pocket without unfolding it. He had been watching Timmy while Mr. Stanford was talking about the other bonus. At the time, he had been anxious to know how the boy was handling all of the affection that was being lavished on him by a woman he didn't know. Consequently, Terrance had missed much of the praise Mr. Stanford had heaped on him.

To Terrance's surprise, he saw the words *One Million Dollars* written on the dollar line of a personal check made out to him.

One million dollars! I think my banker will be a little surprised when I deposit this one. . .

The very next day he was on a plane bound for South America. The three thousand mile trip back to Guyana seemed to take forever. Visions of a beautiful woman with dark reddish brown hair and a light case of the freckles were on the forefront of his mind. The memory of their brief time together beneath the falls played over and over in his mind the entire way. Within hours he would see her again.

When he was finally back in the terminal at the airport in Georgetown, he found the nearest payphone and called Rebekah's apartment. The phone rang and rang. Finally, an answering machine picked up.

"This is Rebekah Hamilton. I'm out, so please leave a message. Terrance, if this is you, I'm sorry I wasn't here when you returned. I had no way to reach you, but a very dear friend of mine is in serious trouble in Uganda. She runs a Christian orphanage there and some insane dictator is doing terrible things to Christians. The children in her orphanage are in mortal danger. I am going there to help. I have to. I will come back to you as soon as I can. I promise."

Rebekah's voice was followed by a loud beep, but Terrance Clark barely heard it.

For several moments, the private detective from Oakland stood there in the airport terminal, staring at the phone and gripping the receiver tightly in his hand. There was a man-sized lump in his throat. All of his hopes had just been dashed to the ground. The tone in Rebekah's voice said she loved him. But he knew about Uganda. Where she had gone was the pit of hell, the most dangerous place on earth right now, especially for Christians. Churches were being burned, sometimes with the people still in them. Christians were disappearing, never to be heard from again. And *she* had gone there. His Rebekah had gone to Idi Amin's Uganda.

Amin's *reign of terror* had been hidden from the news media for several years, but of late things had become to come to light. Unspeakable things were happening in Uganda. Tens of thousands of people had been murdered or had simply disappeared. The man was either certifiably insane or the very manifestation of evil.

The haze had only begun to lift from Terrance's eyes when he walked up to the ticket counter and asked the agent for a ticket to Entebbe, Uganda.

The End

CPSIA information can be obtained at www.ICGtesting.com
Printed in the USA
BVOW010406091112

305068BV00001B/14/P